BETTER Day

KAREN DEEN

Published by Karen Deen

Edited by Contagious Edits

Formatted by Lee Reyden

Cover Design by The Book Cover Boutique

About the Author

Karen Deen has been a lover of romance novels and happily-ever-after stories for as long as she can remember. Reaching a point in her life where she wanted to explore her own dreams, Karen decided now was the time to finally write some of her own stories. For years, all of her characters have been forming story lines in her head, just waiting for the right time to bust free.

In 2016, Karen put pen to paper for the first time, with Zach and Emily being the first characters fighting to have their story written. From that first word, she hasn't been able to stop. Publishing Love's Wall (her first novel in the Time to Love Series) in 2017 has ignited her passion to continue writing and bring more of her characters to life.

Karen is married to her loving husband and high school sweetheart. Together, they live the crazy life of parents to three children. She is balancing her life between a career as an accountant by day and writer of romance novels by night. Living in the beautiful coastal town of Kiama, Australia, Karen loves to enjoy time with her family and friends in her beautiful surroundings.

Contact

For all the news on upcoming books,
visit Karen at:
www.karendeen.com.au
Admin@karendeen.com.au
Facebook: Karen Deen Author
Instagram: karendeen_author
TikTok: karendeenauthor

Dedication

To the ones I love, who are my strength.

BETTER DAY

KAREN DEEN

Chapter One

GHOST

After staring at the screens in my office for the last five days straight, my eyes are as dry as the desert. I feel like I haven't slept in days, but I've had no choice. There was no way I was leaving Bull and his girl without making sure they were safe. He's my best friend, and being on the run with his girlfriend Asha, the stress levels were high. It was my job to help keep them alive and get them through the danger, until it's over and we can all breathe easy again. I needed to know every move being made by all the players, good or bad, before it even happened in this shitshow.

It's not very often I get caught off guard in this job, which is something I take great pride in. I could never live with myself if anything went wrong. Of all the jobs I've controlled in my life, this has been one of the most important.

It ranks second to only one other job.

That job has become my life!

What started out as a job of inconvenience turned into the fight

1

that I'll never give up on. Not until the day I can finally say it's over, and the reality is, that day may never come. That's something I accepted a long time ago, with no regrets.

Even before the security system alerts me to movement outside the door, I know. No matter where I am, I can always sense her and how near she is. When you have been so close to someone for seven years and their safety is more important to you than your own life, you're in tune with them to the point that it's second nature.

The door slides open quietly as Cassie softly steps in, checking if I'm on a call, not wanting to disturb me if I'm in the middle of any major operation. Even though I messaged her earlier to let her know Bull and his girlfriend were safe and it was all over, she knows sometimes things change at the drop of a hat and I'm on to the next case.

As she gets closer, I pull off my headset and flick the override switch to send all communications through my phone for the rest of the night.

My computer system is technical enough that it's almost like a person. It has the power to think on its own, monitoring all the targets and locations I have programmed in at any current time. It knows if someone sneezes or goes to the toilet and determines if I need to know that piece of data or to log it in the database. It took me years to get to this point with my operations, but when a sense of fear for your family drives you, it's worth it. The lengths you will go to keep them safe is above and beyond.

"Hey there, handsome, I think you need a break. And more importantly, some sleep." She slides her hands from my shoulders down around onto my chest, her sweet lips kissing the top of my head and then continuing down to my cheek.

Her scent wafting around me has my heart slowing down. She is my calm when the world seems crazy. And the last few days have certainly been that.

But the last words she whispers in my ear have me finally understanding what she is saying.

"The kids are in bed asleep, and I miss my husband. Care to join me for a shower before bed?" The softness of her voice is no indication of what she is really like under that sweet exterior.

Even if I was struggling to keep my eyes open from exhaustion, there is no way I'm passing up that offer.

My cock is already stiffening at the chance to finally get reacquainted after a few days of being apart.

"You know I can't say no to you, nor do I want to." I raise my hands and clasp them around her arms that are still lying on my chest, lifting them and using them to pull her body around in front of me. The glint in her eye tells me she knows exactly where I want her. Reaching around her back, I pull her sideways onto my lap, a place she fits like she was made for me and only me.

"Hmmm, what have we here." I run my hand up the inside of her exposed leg. "Did you think I'd need some tempting?" My eyes rove over her body and the blue button-up shirt of mine she has on, that has parted slightly as she sat in my lap. Only a few buttons in the middle hold it closed, barely covering much of her.

"Possibly." I lean forward and kiss slowly up her neck as she tilts her head to the side, her beautiful soft brown hair falling to give me plenty of skin to devour. "Not that I think I needed it." The words coming out are more of a moan than before.

"Not at all, but I must say it's a nice surprise." Trailing down her neck with my tongue, I continue down her chest to where her cleavage of beautiful soft olive skin is hiding, just under the first button of the shirt. A button won't stop me, though.

"Fuck, I've missed you!" I can hear my own voice getting deeper in tone and with that edge it gets whenever I'm starting to lose my control around my wife. From the day I met her, she has had this effect on me.

Using my teeth, I pull the shirt hard enough that the button slips out and the shirt falls to the side, letting her dark pebbled nipple appear, all ready for me. Taking her into my mouth and letting my hand wander up the smooth inside of her leg, I can feel Cassie giving over her body to me.

She knows exactly what I need.

I need her.

"Noah." My name slips from her mouth. It's the only time she uses my given name, and it's like she treasures this connection on a

3

level no one else will ever get to feel. My whole body shudders at the word, and I know we need to move. As much as I want to lay her out on my desk, this is not the place where I need a constant reminder of my wife, naked and screaming my name as I ravish her. This room is where I need to be able to zone out the world, which at times means even zoning out Cassie too.

My mouth makes a popping sound as I release her nipple, and I pull back and see her already slipping into her happy place.

"Shower, now. Get the soap ready so I can clean you after I make you filthy dirty for the first time tonight, but rest assured, it won't be the last time." Helping her to her feet, she smiles with a twinkle in her eyes.

Walking toward the door, the back of the shirt just covers her ass cheeks as she turns, looking at me over her shoulder. "Promises, promises." She then slips the shirt off her shoulders and slides it down her body, leaving it in a pool on the floor as she sways her sensual naked ass and disappears out of my control room.

"Fuucckkk." I push my palm into my cock that is trapped behind my jeans, trying to stop from exploding before I even get to move.

That woman is going to kill me, but oh, what a way to die!

I shut down the room with the security codes as quickly as I can and close the door behind me, the picture of Cassie walking out of here still burned into my brain. I flick the button on the top of my jeans and pull my shirt over my head while I'm moving down the hallway toward the end of the house where our bedroom is, preparing to be on my knees in seconds, worshiping her pussy while the warm water runs over our bodies. My name will be echoing off the tiles as she screams the orgasmic release I'm about to give her.

Suddenly, my feet stop as I hear the faint sound of tiny footsteps on the floor and my daughter's sniffling before I make it to her door.

No, no, no, not now, my little princess. Daddy needs to take care of Mommy first.

But like every parent knows, your child's tears trump everything.

"Daddy?" Bessy, the mini version of Cassie, is standing there peering up at me through her water-filled eyes, the long eyelashes moist and her little brown ringlets falling softly down each side of her face. Her big brown eyes ask me for the one thing that always makes it feel better. Crouching down before her and opening my arms, she launches herself into my body like I'm her lifeline.

"What's wrong, princess?" Her little tears fall on my naked chest, slaying me more than a sharp knife could.

"I don't know, I just woke up crying." She looks up at me with confusion.

"That's okay. Sometimes that happens. How about we just go and tell Mommy that I am going to read you another story." She nods her head up and down and the tears are drying up.

"Where's Mommy?" she asks as we head toward the master bedroom.

"In the shower that I have a feeling will now be cut shorter than she was hoping." Bessy, having no idea what I'm talking about, just continues to burrow her head into my neck, and already I can feel her body relaxing in my arms.

"What took you so long? I was going to start—"

"Mommy, we have a visitor." My words stop Cassie before she said something that we would be spending the next ten minutes trying to explain our way out of. Bessy may only be five years old—or nearly six as she would say—but growing up with only adults around her, she is wise beyond her years, which does make me sad in a way, that she doesn't have a normal childhood, as hard as we try to make it happen.

"Ohhh." She sticks her head out of the steamed-up glass shower door. "What's wrong, Bessy?" Straight away, she switches to Mom mode and her own desires get pushed to the side.

"I missed my daddy," Bessy says, the little sniffle still present in her voice.

I wrap my arms just that little bit tighter around her.

"Me too, Bessy, me too." The sexual longing in Cassie's eyes is burning. Okay, so maybe not all the desire has been pushed aside just yet.

"I'll take her and get her settled again, read another story, and then I'll be back." I wink at Cassie, letting her know we are far from over. "I think you should finish your shower and get ready for bedtime too. We have some serious issues to be resolved."

"And that's a promise I expect you to keep," Cassie replies as she closes the door, and I start heading back to Bessy's room.

Oh, you better believe it, bright eyes. I never leave a job unfinished—or my wife unsatisfied.

That's more than a promise, it's a fact!

Walking back through the house to Bessy's room, taking in my surroundings, my mind drifts to how lucky I am. Not many would consider the life we live fortunate, but I'm not like them. It was never how I imagined it, but I wouldn't change a thing. Thinking back over the seven years and how we got to this point, part of me wonders if I will ever be able to free my family, or if this is what our life will always be like.

No matter what happens, I will always love them and keep them safe. They are the air I breathe.

Without them, I cease to exist.

---

7 YEARS AGO - WHERE IT ALL BEGAN

GHOST

"Seriously, is that the best you can do?"

I lean my back against the wall, watching Bull take his shot to try and sink the 3 ball in the corner pocket of the pool table. I speak out loud at just the right moment, as his stick is about to collide with the ball.

"You are the worst. Asshole." He stands up and glares at me after I succeeded in exactly what I was planning, distracting him just at the right moment, and instead of the ball sinking straight into the hole he was aiming for, it bounced off the side of the pocket entrance. And, as an added bonus, the cue ball instead dropped straight into the hole.

"You do know that the cue ball is not what you are trying to sink, right? Not that I mind you giving me the extra shot, but it's not helping your shit game that you're playing. Not that you ever stood a chance against me. I'm the king of the pool table." Lining up the 14 ball perfectly, I push all outside noise out of my head. It's a skill I use every day in my job, and it's coming in handy now.

"For fuck's sake," Bull mutters when I look up smirking at him as my ball drops perfectly into the pocket straight across from me.

"Watch and learn, buddy, watch and learn." I love pushing his buttons. It's what makes us as close as we are. We can give each other absolute crap, all day long, but when shit gets real, I know without a shadow of a doubt that he has my back, just like I have his.

"The only thing I'd learn from you is how to cheat. Do you hear me trying to distract you as you shoot?" he says, running his hand through his hair in frustration. "No, I didn't think so, because I'm not so pathetic that I need to resort to those tactics."

"You can try, but we both know it won't work. Just face it. I'm a far superior pool shark than you."

"Bullshit." He coughs into his hand.

As the 9 ball drops into the next pocket, a groan now coming from him has me laughing harder than I should.

"Eight ball, corner pocket." Leaning down nice and low, I focus with my laser point of concentration.

"I'll just get the next round of beers, shall I?" Bull racks his pool cue, draining the last of the beer out of the glass he had sitting on the shelf to the side.

"What, you don't even want to stay and watch me win game number three for the night? I mean, there is such a thing as a sore loser, you know." There's the crack of my pool cue hitting the cue ball with force, shooting it to hit the eight ball with precision. "Boom! And that's another victory to the reigning champion." Looking up from the table as I'm standing up again, all I see is Bull's back as he disappears to the bar, flipping me the bird over his shoulder so there is no mistake what he's thinking.

"Make it a Jack instead," I yell as I start putting the balls back onto the table and racking them up for the next people who want to play.

I think three games of torture are enough for my buddy for tonight.

Downing the rest of my beer, I place the empty glass on the bar next to Bull, waiting for our drinks.

"Remind me again why I bother playing against you?" he grumbles before placing a handful of nuts out of the bowl on the bar into his mouth.

"Can't help you there. You're a glutton for punishment, I guess." We both look at each other and burst out laughing.

The bar attendant slides our glasses of whiskey in front of us, both of us picking them up.

"Bottom's up," Bull says as we clink our glasses together. I don't even get to take a sip before I feel one of my phones vibrating in my pocket.

"Fuck." I know what that means.

Placing my glass back on the bar, I pull my work phone from the pocket inside my jacket.

When your work phone rings, you don't ignore it. Not in the job we do.

"Seriously, we are supposed to be on leave!" Bull glares at me, knowing by the look on my face who it is. He also pulls out his phone to check for messages, but it looks blank.

"Boss," I answer, not really wanting to hear what he has to say.

Bull and I have just come off a six-month job of protecting a guy who, if I had a choice, I would have let the wolves at him. He was the lead witness in a case for human trafficking, but from what we knew, he was involved in the whole scheme too. He just decided to roll over and be the rat in the group. Some parts of my job are harder than others. When our job is to protect a scumbag, it leaves me questioning why I do it.

I've been working as a WITSEC officer for the last sixteen years, and together with Bull for the last twelve years. We met when he was put into my team, and I had to train him. Not that he needed much training. His basic instinct was on point from day one. He took to the job straight away and was more in tune with his senses than half the agents I had worked with for a few years. That can be the most important part of the job. But the reason we work so well together is not only that he's in tune with his own senses, but with mine too. When we are pushed with our back to the wall, no words are needed. We just know what the other is thinking and get on with doing it. That keeps our target safe and both of us alive, which is just as important.

"Ghost. Where are you?" Never any idle conversation with our boss, code name Rocket. Straight to the point.

"At a bar with Bull, just relaxing. Remember that thing people do when they're on leave?" My sarcasm ignored, he just continues.

"How many drinks have you had?" Fuck, I don't like the sound of this.

"Two beers, and I'm just about to get reacquainted with my friend Jack here. Again, remember the words. On. Leave." I look at my full glass that I already know I'm not going to be able to finish. I push it toward Bull, who may as well enjoy what he paid for.

"Not anymore. Sorry, Ghost, you need to report to the office at five am tomorrow. We've had an urgent job just come up, and the witness is in transit. You will be briefed in the morning. Tell Bull he isn't needed. Now go home and get some sleep. See you tomorrow."

"Roger that." The phone call now over, my mood has changed in the few seconds since I answered it.

I want to kick the bar, but I don't. It will only injure my foot, and the boss won't give a crap.

"What the fuck, man! We were supposed to be off the job for a week. My mom is going to be pissed as hell when I call her to say I'm not coming home again." Bull slams his whiskey glass down on the bar.

"You're still on leave, it's only this lucky idiot who has been called in," I say, pushing my phone back into my pocket.

"Wait, what? Why has he only called you in? Who are you working with?" Bull looks like he is about to explode with questions.

"Buddy, how long have you been working this job? You know I

don't have any clue until I show up in the morning." I roll my eyes at him.

Normally we would both be jumping all over this shit, and both be wanting to get on the job now. Bull would be annoyed that he didn't get called in, and I would normally be feeling sorry for him being left out. But after the last job, which was a big one, we could have both done with a break. Even a few days would have been nice. We only clocked off last night. So, part of me is at least happy for Bull to get that break.

"I know, I'm just frustrated that they haven't even given you time to take a breath from last night. I get it, they must be short if they're calling you in, but still, we can't work at our peak if they don't give us a break." I can see Bull's shoulders are tense and fists clenched.

"Thanks for looking out for me, buddy, but I'll be fine. You know how it goes. No rest for the wicked, and I have been called wicked more times than I can count." We look at each other and start to laugh, my comment having the desired effect of breaking the tense moment.

"I'm not even going to ask who has called you that, because that may open the door on way too many stories that I don't want to hear." Bull slaps me on my back, picking up his glass and downing it in one mouthful.

"Oh, shit, that must have burned." I watch him, waiting for his reaction.

A flick of his head tells me I'm right.

"Well, that will help me sleep if nothing else. This one's for you," he says to the bartender, pushing my glass back across the bar to him and slapping cash down on the bar to settle our tab. The guy probably isn't allowed to drink on the job, but it made Bull feel like it wasn't wasted.

Walking out the front door together, we both look for a taxi. Bull flags one down that was up the road, parked.

"You call me if you need me and I'll be there, no questions asked."

"One of us may as well get the break. Just let me know when you're back from your parents' place."

As the taxi pulls up in front of us, Bull moves with purpose and speed until we're toe to toe and his face is close enough to mine that he is almost kissing me, and that's not something I ever want to contemplate.

"I don't give a flying fuck where I am. If you need me, you better call me. That's what we do, and I know you would expect the same from me. So don't give me that bullshit." The emotion in his eyes is one of anger mixed with friendship and even as close as brotherhood.

"Understood," is all I reply, nodding my head.

As much as I want him to rest, I know if I need help, his is the first number I'll call.

"Now, can I go home? Because apparently according to the boss, I need to get my beauty sleep for tomorrow. Which in my mind means they are needing my technical skills, as well as my pure muscle," I say, flexing my arm as I push him into the backseat of the taxi.

"Well, then they are out of luck if that's what they're looking for in you."

Laughing out loud, I jump into the front of the taxi. "Take this loser home first. He must be drunker than I thought, he's become delusional." Rattling off Bull's address then mine, we are on our way, and all the talk about work has stopped until we pull up out front of his apartment.

None of us have anything very big or very permanent. No pets or plants, because we never know how long we will be home for— tonight being the perfect example.

His hand lands on my shoulder from the back seat as he gets ready to open the door. "Remember what I said. Call me, no matter how big or small." With that, he is out the door, and it's slamming shut. He taps on the roof, letting the driver know he is good to pull away from the curb again.

Bull's a good friend. I lay my head back on the headrest. It's not far to my place, but my thoughts are already drifting to what I'm going to be walking into tomorrow.

I've never felt frustrated and anxious about a job, but for some reason, tonight I feel on edge. Maybe I've been in the game too long, I'm losing my touch.

Or it's as simple as I'm exhausted.

I guess tomorrow we'll see, won't we.

Cassie

Stand your ground, stay strong. Don't let them see that you are petrified on the inside.

He can't get you here. You must do this, otherwise no one else will stand up to stop him.

"I won't say a word until you put it on the record that you will protect me."

"Okay, we will protect you," the female detective across from me just blurts out without any meaning behind it.

"Do you think I'm stupid? You need to agree to put me under witness protection until he has been charged and the court case puts him away for a very long time. I want the whole package deal, otherwise nothing I know is leaving my lips." *Please, can you just help me? I need to get out of here. Once he finds out I have gone to the FBI then there is no turning back. He will arrange for me to be hurt, disappear, or even worse, killed.*

"Until we find out what you know, how can we promise that? You might have nothing we need," the bitch in the chair opposite me replies.

"Fine, then I'll just take it straight to the media. I'm sure they will want to know all the information that I have on my partner, Senator Jason Condell. Especially the part where I tell them that the FBI didn't want to help me and had no interest in what I have for them."

What the hell is going on here? I thought this agency was supposed to be here to help keep this country safe. Instead, they are interrogating the innocent woman who is trying to bring what is going on to their attention.

"If I had a dollar for every scorned woman who turns up here after breaking up with a high-profile person with some supposedly useful information, then I wouldn't still be working in this over-worked, underpaid job."

Oh my God, what is this woman's problem?

I think I've made a huge mistake. I need to get out of here. I just need to run on my own. Take what I have in cash, which is all my life savings, and disappear. Surely, I can find somewhere far away to start over. It's not like I have anyone here waiting for me.

My mind is racing and my stomach churning so much I feel like I'm on the verge of throwing up.

I jump as the door bursts open and a very serious-looking man storms in, slapping a folder down on the desk in front of the agent who has been the devil in disguise. I have no idea what it is, but it looks thick.

"Dismissed, Agent Cole."

The shocked look on her face says it all. This guy is some big deal. "Sorry, sir, I don't understand," she says, standing up to look at him face to face.

"That's the problem, isn't it. I will speak to you in my office later. You can leave now." The way his eyes are, there is no way you would want to argue with him.

"Yes, sir." Picking up her phone and leather portfolio folder, she doesn't even give me another look as she exits the room.

I'm so confused, but I must say, I'm not disappointed she's gone.

Although something tells me this just got very real. The blinds on the room are drawn, and the man proceeds to turn off the recording device and the microphone that allowed what is being said in this room to be heard from outside. I'm not sure that's a good thing, but I suppose it will remain to be seen.

The other agent, who had been in the room all along but spent most of his time messaging on his phone, finally steps forward.

"I'm terribly sorry about that, Miss Templeton. This here is Senior Special Agent Lester. He would like to talk to you and discuss the information you have."

It's like the whole tone of the room has changed, and I can't gauge what is happening.

"Okay," is all I manage to get out as I try to watch the body language of Agent Lester. He is looking me up and down, and it feels intimidating to say the least.

"Leah, my name is Tom. Is it okay if I call you Leah?" His tone is totally changed from the first time he spoke after bursting into the room.

"Um, okay, yeah." My brain is spinning with so many thoughts and the constant change of what is happening.

"Thank you, and as Paul just said, we are sorry about Agent Cole. She didn't realize who you were. So, let's start again. You have some information that you feel may be of interest to us, and in return, you would like to be protected because you feel your life will be in danger. Is that correct?"

"There is no feeling about it. The moment I stepped into this building I signed a death warrant. So, I need to know I'm going to be protected. I can assure you, this is more than some woman trying to get social media fame. Otherwise, I would have done that straight up. I packed a bag with my essentials, closed my bank accounts, and threw away my phone. Took a bus, then a train, and a taxi, all paid for with cash to get here. So, I would say that gives you some sort of indication of what information I have to share, wouldn't you agree?" Finally finding my strength again, the anger that I've been feeling for days, knowing I'm about to give up my life because of him, is resurfacing now.

"Yes, I would. I can't say much, but all I can tell you is I have already started the process of getting you placed into emergency protection tonight, and you will be transported to a safe house under our WITSEC program. We believe you may be of great help in an ongoing investigation that has already begun." These guys are good at not giving away a single emotion on their faces.

"Shit. Then you know." My voice trembles a bit from sheer relief that finally someone is going to believe me, and maybe, just maybe I'm going to make it out of all this alive, and Jason will pay for the terrible things he has done.

"Oh, I know plenty, but I need you to start from the beginning and tell me what you know. Don't rush, take your time, and don't leave any parts out. We are here to help you, Leah."

My heart skips a beat.

The next words I say are going to change my life forever, but I didn't come this far only to stop now.

"Thank you." My lips are quivering, tears about to break the dam wall.

"It all began a few months ago…"

Chapter Two

CASSIE

It feels like I have been in this room forever. I've lost track of the time, and although I'm exhausted, I feel like I should be scared. Instead, it's a feeling of intense relief to finally tell someone everything I suspected about Jason for months, and finally, found out the truth this week.

I thought I loved him once, but now all that's left is disgust, and I won't lie, but there's also a lot of fear.

They explained everything that going into witness protection would mean. Change of name, identity, and appearance. I knew I would have to agree to all of it, but I don't think they knew what hit them when I stood my ground about cutting off my hair and changing its color. Not a fucking chance that was happening. I just couldn't do it. It was my one stipulation I stood my ground on. I look like my mom. Our hair is the same, and I don't have much left but my memories of her, so I wasn't letting them take that. Looking in the mirror on the tough days when I miss her, I can feel her looking back at me. No one gets to take that from me. I'd rather die than give it up, and I think with my screaming, they worked that out pretty quickly and accepted defeat.

After that, things settled down, and we got on with it. I gave them everything I had, including copies of all the information I found. Nobody knows that I also kept a copy for myself, that is my insurance policy.

Thankfully, we are finally at the point where it's time for me to go into the unknown.

"Once we put you in this car, Leah, your life here ceases to exist. You will be given a new identity when you reach your safe house in the morning, and they will keep you safe. If you need to be in contact with us, just inform your agent who is with you. We will keep in contact with you as things progress, but don't panic if there is time in between where you don't hear anything from us. These things take time, and everything needs to be in perfect place before we can progress the way we need to." We're standing in the underground parking area of the building, and a black SUV with tinted windows pulls up beside us.

I can never understand why the secret agent cars are always big, black, and with tinted windows. To me it gives us away, but I have to trust them. Because right now, I have no other choice.

Placing his hand on my arm, Tom looks at me with the first sign of compassion I have seen today. "Do you understand?"

"Yes, I do. Let's get on with it."

He nods his head and opens the door for me, lifting my bag into the back seat and waiting for me to get in and get settled.

"Good luck, Leah. I will see you when the time comes." With that, the door is closing before my eyes, on both the car and my current life.

As we drive down the road, I realize how late it must be. The darkness of night I expected, but there's not much traffic as we head west out of Washington D.C.

Silent tears are slowly streaming down my face. I have no idea where I'm headed or who I will be when I get there.

To say I don't care would be a lie, but I can't live that life anymore. That I know for sure.

"We have a long trip ahead of us, ma'am, feel free to close your eyes and get some sleep." My driver, whose name I don't even know, smiles at me through the rear-view mirror, and his partner in the passenger seat just keeps looking straight ahead and in his side mirror.

I'm not sure I could sleep even if I tried. My body is on high alert. I feel so anxious. My palms are sweating, and my right foot is bouncing up and down. I find myself also looking at every car that passes us or comes alongside.

What if Jason already knows?

Did he have someone follow me?

Has he got people on the inside at the FBI?

Stop it! You need to stop overthinking this. He's away on a business trip and would have no idea yet that you have left. The only thing he'll be furious about is that I'm not answering my phone so he can know what I'm doing. As far as his team know, I'm still tucked up at home where my phone is in the garbage can. I left before sunrise out the back door and set the television to turn on at my usual breakfast time, where I watch the morning news. Not that I ever enjoyed it, but that is what Jason expected. I needed to keep up with current affairs for when we were at functions together. I'd be happy to just turn off the world some days. The news sadly can be so depressing, and it just seems to be full of everything bad that is happening, which certainly is not a great way to start the day.

Thinking back on it, that's all I really was to him. Someone to have on his arm at every important campaign dinner, fundraisers, and events he was expected to attend. I owned more ballgowns than I did pairs of jeans and runners, which is not really me. I got swept up in the dream of living a better life. The promises that Jason made, when he told me how much he loved me and that I was all he needed in his life to come home to after a long day.

Complete bullshit!

I was just a front for him. The sweet innocent girl from a poor background, someone people felt a little sorry for. Someone who had worked hard to get where I was in my life. No baggage to hide behind, my history was so clean I had nothing to tarnish his image.

Now I understand he was doing enough himself to not only tarnish his image but to paint it black, as black as can be.

I'll be damned if he is going to take me down with him.

The rest of the night became a blur. I'm not sure if I actually slept at all or just closed my eyes and zoned out. The sun's rising, and we are about to stop for a driver change and to pick up breakfast. I have held off using a restroom, but there is no way I can drink coffee now if I don't pee. I was too scared to leave the car in the dark while we've been traveling, but at least now I can see my surroundings.

It's a little chilly as I open the car door and slide my feet to the ground. It takes me a moment to actually get them to move. I have been sitting so rigid since we started driving that my muscles are tense.

We are at a small gas station just outside of a small town. I heard them say before that they never stop in big cities if they can avoid it. Too many surveillance cameras and traffic monitors. Better to stop in the little places in the middle of nowhere. And this is exactly as they described. A few gas pumps, one attendant in the shop that sells the basics, and the toilet is out back in the smallest little single room. At least it's clean.

One of my drivers positions himself outside the door which makes me feel better but also self-conscious. You know how hard it is to pee quietly when you've been holding it in for hours? In the end, I just let it all go. It's not like he can see me, and who knows if he is even listening anyway. Probably listening to some radio scanner in his ear, I wouldn't have a clue. All I know is that both of them have earpieces in.

Washing up and settling back in the car, I get handed a couple of donuts and a coffee.

"Sorry, it's not much, but they will have food for you once we reach the safe house."

I'm probably the only human in America who doesn't love a good donut, but it's surprising what you will eat if you have no other choice.

"Thank you, I appreciate you getting me something."

I try to stomach the donut before my coffee so I can wash the taste away.

I shouldn't have bothered. The coffee tastes like what I imagine thick motor oil would taste like.

Trying not to think is hard, yet somehow, I manage to numb myself for the next few hours. It's not as good as sleep would feel right now, but it's all I've got. Until we are close to our destination and the voice of one of the agents pulls me from my daze to let me know we are getting close. I haven't even paid attention to any towns we have driven through, but looking now, I wonder exactly where we are.

It looks suburban, with rows of average houses, one after another. People moving about their everyday tasks, oblivious to what is happening around them. I don't know why that stands out to me because that is why I'm here, isn't it? To blend in, so no one knows who I am or where I've come from.

Finally, we turn into a road where the houses start to spread out a bit more. The land around them is bigger, and as we slow down at the end of the street, we turn into a driveway that is longer than the rest, with no house to be seen. The car is now heading through a row of trees, and my heart wakes from its frozen state and my panic is back.

"Where… where are we?" My nerves make speech difficult. I don't even know if I'm allowed to ask that.

"Your current safe house." It's all the reply I get, for now. When he says current, does that mean I'm going to move again? I guess I'll just have to wait to find out.

The trees open out to a small cottage with a porch along the front. It's not anything to get excited about. White clapboard with green trim. The paint is faded, and the place looks weathered, like it hasn't seen any tender love and care in a long time. But I suppose no one lives here long enough to worry about it.

All that surrounds the house is trees, no gardens or anything to make it distinctive. On the porch there is one lone thing, a chair, looking out of place there all by itself. A lot like me, completely out of place and already feeling so alone.

Something I will need to accept and get used to.

Pulling around the back of the house, there is another black SUV, much the same as the one we're in. Seriously, like that doesn't look weird, two luxury cars at a rundown cottage in the middle of a very middle-class suburb. And then I see finally a more normal vehicle for what I would expect here. A blue Toyota that looks like it has seen better days.

The car pulls to a stop at the back of the house.

The donuts and disgusting coffee are threatening to come back up from my stomach before I even manage to get out of here. I'm not sure I can move, it's like I'm frozen with fear. As much as my mind is telling my hand to reach out and open the door, I don't know if I can even do that simple task.

"Wait here," the agent in the passenger seat tells me as he leaves us here.

Watching him walk into the house, I hold my breath that it's only the good guys in there. I know I need them, and they are doing their job, but I would be devastated if something were to happen to any of them because of me.

Finally, after what feels like an eternity, the agent walks back out the door and straight to my side of the car.

Opening up my car door and looking to the driver, he says, "All clear." It's enough for the driver to finally turn off the motor and undo his seatbelt. I guess he was here if we needed to make a quick getaway.

"Time to get out now, ma'am." He's looking at me, waiting for a response.

If it was just that easy, I would be moving by now.

Come on, Leah, you can do this. You already made the hardest step yesterday. From now on, it is just one foot in front of the other foot until it's over.

Because I have to believe there will be an end date.

One day I will walk away from all of this and never have to look over my shoulder again. When that day will be, that is the big question, but it will be a better day than today.

GHOST

Walking into headquarters at the start of a new job always brings mixed feelings. There is the adrenaline surge of not knowing what your assignment will be, but then part of me always has the thought that I'm only here because someone is in trouble and needs my help to stay alive.

That fear that my new client must be feeling right now, I will never understand it because it's never been me. When we are on the run and keeping them hidden, I always know what's happening in front of me. That's the handler's job, to make sure I have the information I need to navigate me through the worst of it.

"Morning, Boss," I say, placing my coffee on the desk as he slides a file across to me.

"Ghost. Sorry to do this, but I needed you. Bravo has a family issue, and he needed to leave urgently." That's one thing about this job, you never get told more information than you need to know at the time. It's obviously something personal for Bravo, so it's none of my business.

"No problems, Rocket." I drop the word Boss now that we're sliding into the case; it's more appropriate to call him by his agent code name. Although I was complaining last night to Bull, this morning I'm back in work mode and ready to go.

"Good to hear, now let's get on with it. Your client is Leah Templeton. She's been placed into protection due to providing information to FBI agents about her partner, or shall we say ex-partner, Senator Jason Condell."

"Oh, just what we love, men in high places with resources at the tips of their fingers."

This job just got a little more interesting.

"Exactly. Nothing new, Ghost. We've been here before. Same shit, just different politician this time." He sits back in his chair and rolls his eyes at me.

"So that's why you needed me. This is an intelligence job, as well as protection." My head is already running through the list of things I want to be looking at in the background about our senator.

We aren't given much information on the actual case, just the basics we need. Our job is to keep the witness safe, not investigate the case. But to do the best job I can, I need to know what I can about this guy and what resources he has at his disposal to find my client. That's where my computer skills come in handy. The boss won't tell me to go and drag up all the intel, but he knows I will. Sometimes you just need to assume things, but to keep your nose clean, you don't say the words out loud. To get the information I need, I'll be hacking into places I shouldn't be. All I can say is, they should be grateful I'm working for the good side of the law with what I'm able to get access to.

"Glad you understand." He looks down at his phone to read a message that has come in. "Now the FBI already had an investigation underway on the senator, but Leah coming forward has given them the information they need to put the wheels in motion. They expect to bring charges within the week and will be pushing for an early court date to try to nail him before he gets a chance to manipulate the system."

"The power of money and having politicians in his back pockets. And who said the justice system in this country isn't full of corruption." I take another sip of my coffee as I open the file to flick through and get the details I need on Leah.

The first thing I see is an A4-size headshot photo.

My senses are on overload, and the protective nature I get just hit overdrive.

Staring back at me are the biggest brown eyes, and they already tell me her story. She's scared. Which is not unusual and something I see in almost every client, but these eyes pull at something in me that I've never felt this strongly before. Lust, and it's racing through me like a freight train. Fuck, this isn't a good sign for a job where I need my full concentration.

I try to push it down to wherever it came from while I take in her whole face. This is the face I need to have imprinted on me for however long this job lasts.

Her skin is a beautiful, flawless olive complexion, with not a single blemish on it. Straight, brown, shoulder-length hair.

I can see why the senator would date someone like her. She would look very attractive on his arm in his line of work.

Now I just need to make sure he never gets to see or touch her again.

Realizing I have been staring a little too long at her picture, I quickly turn it over to read through her personal details.

Leah Templeton, twenty-six years old. Height five-foot-three, brown hair, brown eyes, and olive complexion. Born in Cleveland to Frank and Beatrice Templeton who are both deceased. Was living in New York before moving to Washington. Occupation, accountant for Roblowen Financial, a large firm in the Big Apple with offices around the country.

Okay, so I have her basics.

Next is her new identity.

"All you need is there. The usuals—driver's license, birth certificate, social security number, passport, and medical ID." I hear my boss's voice, but I'm still taking in all I'm viewing in front of me.

Time to meet my new client.

Miss Cassandra Matheson.

The drive out to the safe house takes me a few hours, giving me time to try to work out what that deep feeling of lust and sexual energy in my gut was, as soon as I saw her picture.

What is it about those eyes that speaks to me on a level I have never felt before? This is not an appropriate way to act on a job. I try to convince myself that the only reason it happened is that I'm tired, coming off the back of the previous job. My instincts need sharpening, and I only have an hour and a half left to do that.

Instead of thinking about Cassandra, I turn my mind to thinking about what I need to find out about the senator, the more intel the better. That is a more productive use of my time and simpler to rationalize in my head. I want to know what he has done to this poor woman to make her take the drastic step of going to the FBI and going into hiding. Nobody gives up everything in their life unless they are petrified of the situation they have found themself in.

So, what has you running scared, Cassandra?

My phone ringing brings me out of my thoughts. Glancing at the screen, I can't help but laugh.

"What the hell are you doing calling me? At least one of us should be on leave, lazing on the beach and eating some of your mom's famous food you're always craving. By the way, that is a hint to bring some home for me."

"Well, hello to you too, grumpy. Thought I would just check in before I go totally offline for a few days. Think you can handle this job all by your lonesome or do you need big tough Bull to come and protect your ass?" Both of us chuckle at that comment.

"There is never any reason why you need to be anywhere near my ass. We might be close but not that close. I think I have my ass under control, thanks anyway." Looking at my GPS screen, I calculate I still have about forty-five minutes until I reach the house, so I settle in for a chat to pass the time and keep me from overthinking things.

"I see you still have your sense of humor, so the job can't be looking too bad. When do you start?" Bull knows he can't ask me much more than that because he isn't on the case.

"In forty minutes and counting. On route now. Let's just say it might be an interesting one. I can't get a feel on it yet, but once I meet the client maybe I might get the vibe I need. Let's just say it's one where we are up against a lot of money and power, which we all know means connections in dangerous places." I lean my arm on top of the center console, trying to stay relaxed. My body feels restless, which is never a good sign.

"You need me." The tone from Bull is all work and no emotion.

"No, I told you I'll call if I do. Now fuck off and go have a holiday good enough for both of us. Eat, drink, and get some action if you're lucky enough to find someone who has no taste." I smile to myself, knowing he is frowning on the other end of the phone, as I haven't even acknowledged his concern for me.

"All I can say is at least I tried. I'll remember this conversation when you call me begging for my skills to help you. Now, thanks to you making me drink all that whiskey last night, I have the pleasure of turning up at my mother's place with a hangover." Finally, Bull has got the message that I don't want to talk about work.

"Bullshit, that's not my fault. If you were stupid enough to drink it, then that's on you, buddy."

Bull starts laughing at his own problem. "I forgot it's been a while since I've had any alcohol, and I'm a bit of a lightweight these days. Lucky you hadn't started on your drink."

"Wouldn't have mattered if I had. I could drink you under the table any day of the week, just like I can beat you at pool. Let's face it, you aren't much competition against the master," I say, knowing I have just poked the bear with my comment.

"Fuck, you are an arrogant asshole sometimes," Bull complains.

"Just sometimes? I must be slipping."

I hear him groan again. "I'm not sure I can put up with you for much longer, I don't have a spare vomit bucket in the truck with me."

"That's okay, I need to go anyway. I'm getting closer, and I need to call in and give them notification I'm almost there. Time to go to work," I say, taking a deep breath.

"Okay, keep that ass that you're so fond of safe." Laughing out loud, I don't even give him time to say anything else.

"Roger that, dickhead. See you on the other side." Hanging up on him, I know I will have pissed him off. There are two versions of our relationship. Exactly like this, where we are constantly trying to one-up each other. The other is the "completely submerged into work mode" version, where there is no room for humor or error.

Slipping into that mode, I place the call to the agents in the safe house and immerse myself in the new case.

Arriving thirty minutes before the estimated ETA is perfect because it gives me time to walk the perimeter and get my bearings. I have used this house once before, but it was years ago. We tend to use a house then leave it dormant for a while, just to take any heat and suspicion off it.

There are trees along the back boundary that are useful, in that they keep the house private but also makes it harder to see who is lurking around you. Just means I need to be vigilant on surveillance. Hopefully the security system is up to the grade it should be. If there is one thing that pisses me off in my job, it's the lack of funding for the technology we need in the field to do our job effectively. I get sick of hearing all the bullshit that head office spouts about budget cutbacks. One day the lack of quality equipment is going to cause the death of a client that we should have kept safe. I'll guarantee it won't be happening on my watch, that's for sure.

"I'm happy with the setup so far, although the security system is shit, like I expected. I assume you've tested all the monitors and triggers?" I'm signing off on the paperwork for my staff who were sent here before me to get the house livable and stocked with food, clothes, and necessities.

"When was the last time you found one that was good enough to do the job?" Zero smiles at me as I hand back his pen.

"Can't say I ever have, if I'm being honest." They all know what I'm like. I didn't get this far in my job without demanding perfection from myself and anyone I work with. That's why I run the jobs now and they take their instructions from me. I've been offered a desk job plenty of times and refused. Working in the field is what I want to do and where my strengths lie.

The sound of a car pulling up around the back of the house already has me frustrated and the hairs on the back of my neck standing up.

"Why the fuck didn't the front gate sensor alert me they entered the property?" I growl, storming across to my laptop to pull up the camera vision of the driveway. "Get that fixed now!" Of all the parts of the security system that needs to be working, it's the first line of defense.

"I'll put up with second-rate systems, but when the fucking gate alarm doesn't even signal me, how the hell am I supposed to get any warning? I knew before I even got here this job was going to be in fucking shambles. I just signed off on you checking everything. Did you even leave the goddamn house? Imbeciles!"

Hearing talking behind me, Hammer's giving the all-clear to the team arriving.

Linking my computer into the system here, I find there are several cameras that are blurry or not pointing in the right direction to give me the best vantage point.

"Get your fucking asses out there and sort out this clusterfuck. I want every camera clear, operational, and at least pointing at something useful! And expect a report to the boss when I get my client settled in on what a half-assed job you both did. This might have been a last-minute job, but that doesn't mean I expect any less than our usual. I have been pulled off my leave to sort this shit out, and I don't want to be here any more than you all do, so you better get it damn well sorted so at least I'm not stuck here trying to protect some woman with nothing more than my bare hands. Understood?" This is what lack of time away from the job does. It has me losing my patience when I should have been calmly telling them I want it fixed.

"I'm sorry." A timid female voice behind me stops me in my tracks.

Shit!

Turning around, standing before me is the beautiful face with those mesmerizing eyes.

I'm screwed. I thought her photo made me stop and take note, but here in the flesh, I can't take my eyes off her.

Fuck, how am I supposed to protect someone who distracts me the moment she walks into a room, so much that I can't concentrate on what I was doing?

This is a major problem.

"Ghost, sir. This is your client. I believe you have her new identity and documents." Hammer's now glaring at me, telling me to calm the fuck down.

Looking at her standing there, I can see the fear radiating off her. Not only at her situation but the whole fucked-up location she just walked into.

"Yes, sorry. Ma'am, I'm so sorry you had to hear that. And let me say you have nothing to be sorry about. I apologize for that. Welcome, please come in and take a seat."

She's clutching her single bag to her chest for comfort. I've seen this before from other people as they arrive into our care. Everything that they own, that they haven't had to leave behind in their old life, is in that bag, and they hang onto it like it's their only lifeline allowing them to breathe.

I extend my hand out to her. "My code name is Ghost, and I will be your lead agent for the whole time you are in our care. Nice to meet you, Cassandra." Finally, her hand touches mine with a very gentle shake.

"Cassandra…" she whispers, as if trying her name out on her own lips for the first time. "That's my new name, Cassandra?"

Guiding her to the seat at the table where my files are, I say, "That's right, Cassandra Matheson, and a very nice name it is too. It will take a little time, but you will become used to it soon enough. You'll hear me call you that as often as I can so you'll get used to hearing it." She just nods her head at me. I have to say, the name doesn't suit her, but who am I to judge? It's too longwinded and sophisticated for the woman standing in front of me.

"We have a lot to discuss and get through. I'll show you the bathroom, and you can freshen up while I make you a coffee and something to eat. Does that sound like a plan?"

"Yes, thank you, that sounds amazing." I'm not sure how long it's been since she left her home, but she looks exhausted and like she has been put through the wringer before she arrived here.

"Meanwhile, all these men have work to do." Glaring at them, they all turn to move out of the house to start checking surveillance cameras and sensors, except for the agents who delivered her here. "Thank you, gentlemen. I will report in that the target has arrived safely, mission complete." With that, they give me a chin lift and turn to leave the house.

We have found that it's very daunting to overcrowd the client when they first arrive at the safe house. They have spent twenty-four, sometimes forty-eight hours with a sea of unknown faces. The sooner we get it down to just a few of us with them, the sooner we can let them start to settle a little and hopefully let us talk to them without wanting them to run as soon as they get the chance.

Now just the two of us in the room, I stand and hold out my hand for her bag.

"Let me carry that for you and show you the bathroom."

Standing up, reluctantly she lets it go.

Our fingers brush each other, and her eyes open a little wider at the sensation.

"Don't worry, Cassandra, you're safe with me. I'll protect you. I promise."

Chapter Three

CASSIE

As I get out of the car, the thought of putting one foot in front of the other is made a little harder with the yelling I can hear from inside.

I have to admit, it's not what I was expecting after the whole trip here; the men in the car have hardly spoken to me.

Stepping through the door, his words sting a little.

The guy in the center of the room is yelling at the men standing in front of him, making it plain that he doesn't want to be here, just as much as I don't.

I knew making my choice it would turn my life upside down, but I didn't mean to upset other people's lives too.

"I'm sorry." It slips out as barely more than a whisper before I can stop it.

Standing in an open kitchen, dining, and living room, it looks more like an operations room. There are laptops, tablets, and phones all over the table, with a few files. But what I wasn't even thinking about is front and center—the guns that are strapped to the men's waists and on their bodies that would normally be hidden under a jacket, I assume. Part of me is happy to see them, but it makes me feel sick to my stomach, worse than I already did. That means I really am in danger.

I knew I was, but seeing guns makes it hit home with a thud.

The man who was so busy yelling is just staring at me.

He's intimidating.

Tall, broad-shouldered, with arms that look like solid muscle. They're hard to miss in the black t-shirt that is tight-fitting on his body. His eyes are still fixated on me, and I continue to look at him, with his chiseled jaw and unshaven facial hair. Not a full beard or mustache but just a small amount of hair to give him a rugged look. His head is covered in buzzed brown hair that is so short it's almost not there, making him look fierce. It's the look of a soldier. He may as well be bald. The thing that throws me off with his appearance is the look in his eyes.

I'd built the initial image coming into the room of a strong, daunting, and in a way threatening man, but his eyes aren't telling me that, though. There is something there that shows the smallest amount of softness behind the façade he is holding up in front of his men.

The words now coming from his mouth are far softer than a few moments ago. My brain is overstimulated with everything, and absorbing anything is getting harder the longer I go without sleep.

He stretches his hand out to shake mine. My hand just automatically starts to reach out in politeness to shake with his.

"My code name is Ghost, and I will be your agent for the whole time you are in our care. Nice to meet you, Cassandra." His voice is calm as the name rolls from his lips.

"Cassandra." He was looking at me so intently as he said it. "That's my new name, Cassandra?" I thought I was just thinking the words, but they tumbled out of my mouth on the breath of a whisper.

He continues talking, and I hear the words "freshen up" and "coffee." I continue to nod my head, mumbling responses, aware of the men leaving, until it's just Ghost sitting before me. He stands, holding out his hand to me.

My brain kicks in; he said something about carrying my bag. I start to feel my muscles relax slightly and move to hand it over to him. Our fingers brush over each other, and instead of feeling frightened, it is the first feeling of calm that I have felt in weeks. It's gone as quickly as it came, and the shock of the sensation has me pulling back a little. Looking at him, I try to work out who this man is that I'm going to be stuck with for God knows how long.

I have no choice but to trust him with my life, but it actually seems a little easier than I was imagining it to be, and that alone scares me.

I trusted Jason and look where that got me.

Stepping back from him, I know I need to be cautious. Not everyone in life is who they appear to be. That lesson I've learned the hard way, and it's what has led me here.

Following him down the hallway, I feel like I'm in another world. Seven days ago, I was sitting on my bed trying to work out what I should do with the information that had consumed me since I'd come across it the night before. Now, fast forward a week, and I am in a house in the middle of nowhere, with a complete stranger who is walking around with a gun strapped to his chest. Yet for some reason, I feel safer here than I did that day in my bedroom. Shaking, I was so petrified, trying to work out what I should do.

"Here you go. Take your time. Lock the door so you can relax." Placing my bag on the floor, Ghost leaves the room, pulling the door closed behind him. Again, I am surrounded by silence, and I don't like it.

"Cassandra, lock the door." His deep voice comes through the door between us.

Oh yeah, that's me he's talking to. Fumbling with the slide bolt on the door, it clicks into place, and I hear his footsteps echoing on the floor as he heads back down the hallway.

Leaning with my back against the door, I take in my surroundings. It's not like a five-star hotel, but it's clean and functional which is all I need. All white tiles with a strip of green around the top. The shower is over the bathtub, with a shower curtain with green leaves on it. An old white pedestal sink that could have been here as long as the house, even though the décor looks a little newer. The toilet is tucked in the corner of the room. It's basic but right now looks like heaven, to be able to shower and wash away the last twenty-four hours.

Flashes of everything start replaying in my mind, and I can feel my chest tightening. Tears are building, and the panic is racing, knowing that I finally might break down like I have been trying not to do since I walked into the FBI office. Grabbing my bag, I rummage through for the small toiletries bag I packed. Nothing flashy, just soap, shampoo and conditioner, my toothbrush, toothpaste, and my sanitary products. The rest I can survive without, I'm sure.

I look around to make sure there is a towel hanging somewhere. My breathing is getting faster, and the tears escape my eyes and roll down my cheeks.

Stripping off my clothes and starting the shower, the warm water invites me to step into the bath, and I pull the curtain closed. It's like my own hideaway from the world, and I've given my body permission to finally let go. Hot water now pelting onto my back, the first sob comes out, and I wrap my arms around myself, lowering myself onto my knees in the bath and letting my body release everything I have been holding in.

My body jerks with every sob, and the only thing that helps to soothe me is the massaging water that is falling onto my skin. Mixing with my tears, it washes them down the drain, like they aren't needed here anymore.

I don't know how long I'm in here, curled up in my little ball, but finally, I have run out of tears. I have no energy left to shed them.

Time to get on with it.

Ghost must be wondering why I'm taking so long. Pulling myself up, I feel a little shaky on my legs as I start the process of washing off my old life and moving forward.

Walking down the hallway, I don't expect the reaction of my stomach to the smell of brewed coffee and bacon cooking. I didn't think I could eat, yet my stomach growls at the thought of some decent food and caffeine.

"Does that feel a little better?" Ghost looks up from the counter where he is plating just one serving of breakfast, which could almost be called lunch with the morning slipping away.

"Aren't you eating?" I ask, confused by the single plate.

"I had breakfast quite early this morning, this is just for you. To get something in your stomach. I know you will have struggled with all the upheaval yesterday, so we need to fuel your body back up. Eat." He places the plate on the table, now clear of all the computers and files from before. I see them sitting to the side on the kitchen counter. Ghost signals for me to sit and do as he's telling me to. I have a feeling he is used to people following his orders.

The place is quiet now, and I can't hear anything from outside. I think everyone has left us.

"How long was I in there?" Slowly sitting down, I look up at Ghost.

"A while, but that doesn't matter. It's what you needed to do." Oh, please don't tell me he heard me crying in there. I thought the sound of the shower would hide my breakdown, but now, I'm not so sure.

"Yes," is all I can reply.

I look at him leaning against the kitchen counter just watching me, in a way that neither of us want to look away first, but his words break the moment.

"Eat, Cassandra." The firmness in his voice has me moving without realizing I am. Like my body doesn't know how to ignore his commanding voice.

Putting the first forkful of bacon and a little egg into my mouth, it feels like the best thing I have eaten in years. It's not, but that's what it feels like. It replaces the revolting taste of the donut that I'm sure had been sitting in that gas station for at least a week before we bought it.

"Good girl," he says, and then turning around, he starts to clean up everything he used to cook my breakfast.

The first few mouthfuls have kicked my appetite into gear, and

I'm now shoveling everything on my plate into my mouth like a mad woman, likes it's my last meal. Words I don't even want to contemplate.

I have so many questions I want to ask.

"Are you going to be my cook?" And of all the ones I wanted to ask, that was not one of them, and it's a ridiculous thing to start with.

"If you need me to be, Cassandra. I'm here to protect you and make this as easy for you as I can." His back is still to me at the sink, pots and pans clanging as he continues cleaning.

"Wow, maybe this is a little five-star after all." Seriously, woman, just shut your mouth if you can't say anything intelligent. Start asking the hard questions.

Before I can, though, I hear a laugh from Ghost I wasn't expecting. It's deep and sexy, and that thought shocks me. I shouldn't even be thinking about him like that, but I'm only human. This guy is off the charts in pure sex appeal.

"Oh, there is nothing five-star about this house, I can assure you of that. But I will make it the best not-five-star stay for you as I can."

Now it's me that is finally having a little laugh which is the first time in days that I have even felt the need to, let alone the sound of laughter actually leaving my lips.

"Great, so I will wait for my chocolates on my pillow every night," I tease, smiling at him as he turns around from cleaning.

"Is that the lifestyle you are used to, Cassandra, being waited on constantly and staying in the best accommodation around?" I can't tell if he's judging me or it's just a question that he is genuinely interested to know. This guy is so hard to read. I bet he's great at poker.

Even though I don't know if I should be taking offence or not, I can hear in my voice the need to defend myself.

"I'm not going to lie, I have lived like that for a while, but if I could change the past now, I would in a heartbeat." I think back on the last eighteen months and how my life has been. "It wasn't worth it, because it led me here," I whisper to myself.

Silence follows as I wrap both hands around my coffee cup and look into it like it holds the answers to all my problems.

The chair opposite me moves, breaking me back out of my stare. Ghost sits himself down across from me. This man is big, it's the only way to describe him. His hands now resting on the table are clasped together. They look like he could wrestle a bear and win. Well, that might be exaggerating a little, but they are large and strong-looking. Not soft and manicured like Jason's were. These are the hands of a man who works. Doing what, I don't know, but they are a little rugged and dry-looking. In a way, sort of weathered.

"Are you feeling up to going through the things we need to talk about?" Ghost asks, trying to gain my attention from looking at his hands, I'm sure.

"No point in putting it off. I guess I need to know where I stand... and who I am." Saying the words out loud brings sadness to my core. I haven't done anything wrong, yet I'm the one who is giving up my life. While fucking Jason is still sitting up on Capitol Hill living the high life.

"I'm sorry, I know it's hard. And you are probably hopeful that one day you can go back to your previous home and life when it's all over, but I'm sure they explained it all to you, that it's just not possible."

"Really, like that would ever happen anyway. This is it for me, and it makes me just want to curl up in a ball in the corner and die." The anger is starting to build low in my stomach. I didn't know it was so close to the surface, but now it's taking over, bringing back the tears from earlier.

"I'm sick of being led along by bullshit in my life, so why not just walk away from it? Things I was told, I know now were just smoke and mirrors or straight-out lies."

"Cassandra." He's trying to calm me, but instead, his voice is just pissing me off more.

"Don't you Cassandra me. What if I don't even want to be called that name? I might hate it and think it's an ugly name. Who even gets to pick these names? Does someone just sit in some office with a baby name book and play with a Magic 8 Ball, asking the question of a name? Oh yeah, that sounds good for today. Who cares if it even suits them?"

I can't stop. My rant is just pouring out to a guy I don't even know, and yet he wants me to place all my trust in him.

"I know I don't want to be back in my home, but it doesn't mean I want to be here either. I mean, you said it yourself, you didn't ask to be here, so at least we have that in common, I suppose." By now I feel my heart rate peaking, palms sweaty, and my head is about to explode. I sound like a crazy woman.

All the poor guy did was ask if I was ready to talk. I doubt he was expecting me to blurt all that out.

Slamming my mouth shut, I try to stop myself from sounding like a raving bitch, but it's harder than I thought. I didn't realize how much I wanted to get off my chest. Or more to the point, how much I needed to.

"I know the point is for us to be hidden with a new name in some place that no one would expect to find us, but surely, I could at least be told where I am. I mean, what if something happens, the bad guys turn up, and they hurt you and I'm left to fend for myself…"

"Stop! Right there! You can fucking stop that thought immediately!" Gone is the calm man that made me the breakfast, kindly showed me the shower. And back is the fierce voice from when I arrived. He pushes up and leans on the table with both hands fisted, his eyes burrowing into my soul.

"You will never be on your own. Not while I walk this earth. Do you understand me!" I might be worked up, but Ghost looks like he is ready to kill someone.

"My job is to keep you alive. And I'm fucking good at my job."

His chest is rising up and down with force, and I'm not able to move. I don't know how many seconds have passed between us as he lets out a huff and slowly sits back into his seat, although not looking completely settled.

Sitting upright now and shoulders back, I can tell he is used to being in complete control and is not impressed when anyone pushes past those boundaries. I didn't mean to insult him, but clearly, I have.

"I'm sorry," I mumble, although I don't know if I really mean it this time.

"Enough. That's twice. I don't want to hear those two words again unless it's something you have done, like stomp on my toe or drink the last cup of coffee and we are clean out of it."

Knowing how much I love coffee, that scenario starts me thinking how much I would be pissed off at that.

"I don't function without a coffee in the morning, so never, I repeat never let the coffee run out here." My brain automatically makes a switch in the conversation that brings my rage down from peak irrational to just normal crazy.

We're both looking at each other, now a little lost after my outburst, and I can't help but laugh a little. It's not a full-on laugh, but I can feel a small amount of the tension in my body finally release.

Ghost has relaxed back into his chair and has this half-smile on his face. He achieved his objective and broke the strain between us.

"Now let's start again," he says, crossing his arms over his chest like he is not prepared for any answer except yes.

I just nod my head, since I don't really have a choice.

"I know you have been dealt a bad hand, otherwise you wouldn't be here. It's not easy; in fact, this is probably going to be the hardest thing you have ever done. But the one thing that isn't going to change right now is the reason you are here. You are in danger. There's no sugar-coating it. And acting like a raving bitch isn't going to help either of us. Do you understand how serious this is?" He's trying to talk less domineering to me, yet it's not working, and I still feel like I'm in the principal's office at school.

"Of course, I understand. I put myself in this position. I chose this," I say, not wanting to back down and appear weak again.

"No, Cassandra, you didn't choose this. That's the problem, isn't it. The people around you left you no choice but to do this. Nobody understands the luxury of choice in their life until it is taken away from them. So, let's take that thought off the table straight away.

Because if you don't accept that, you are going to crash later when you finally realize it. And I can't afford for that to happen at a time when we need you to be strong. If you need to cry, scream, or punch the shit out of something, let's get that over with right now."

The only thing I want to punch is him. What an arrogant prick!

When I walked in before and looked at him, I felt something. I don't know what it was, but there was something.

Now all I feel is annoyance.

"You're very blunt, aren't you. Guess you aren't here for the compassionate companion role then, are you." I cross my arms over my chest, my body language giving off the same energy as his, putting up that barrier between us.

"My job is to keep you safe so you can testify. That's it, plain and simple. Not to be your best buddy." Getting up and walking to the kitchen again, he looks back at me, then down at his computer, tapping away on the keyboard for a few minutes.

I've got no idea what he's doing, but I dare not ask and get told for the hundredth time since yesterday that it doesn't concern me.

"Now, we can do this the easy way or the hard way. You can choose, because to me it doesn't matter. The outcome is still the same." The look on his face doesn't give me much to work with.

"What does that mean?" I watch him relax his stance, leaning against the sink behind him and his hands now hanging onto the counter on either side of him. He crosses one leg over the other. It's like he is relieved he has control of the room again.

"It means that we can butt heads over every little thing we need to discuss here and end up not talking unless necessary the whole time you're here. Or we can be civil and rational in our discussions, friendly even, and perhaps I can keep you company while you have to stay in this house. Otherwise, it might get awfully lonely."

He's so smug I want to snap back at him that he's just as arrogant as I was irrational, but I'm not about to give him the satisfaction of me admitting anything.

"What did you mean, the outcome will be the same?" I'm not even sure I want to know the answer.

"You are stuck with me. I am your person." As he walks back

toward me, the words are ringing in my head. Why do I keep hearing *'I am your person'* and feel like it means something? If I thought he looked smug before, it's nothing compared to now, where he looks like he's carrying a secret.

"Well, I vote for the easy way, but it takes two people to make that happen, so don't look at me like I'm the problem." He might like to control the situation, and I get that it's his job, but I'm used to running my own career and life, and I'm not bowing down to commands like I'm some insecure girl. I've fought to get where I am in this world, and I'm not about to just lie down and let people walk all over me yet.

"Okay, easy way it is then. Now, let's get this paperwork sorted out and get you up to speed with what you need to know about your new identity. Also, we need to talk about how this will all work, including your interactions with me." Again, his eyes change with the way he is looking at me, becoming more intense, and that makes me shiver.

What is it with this guy? One minute he looks like he wants to kill me for being painful to deal with and the next it's like he is trying to break through to my soul? Great, a guy who is moody. Just what I need on top of everything else.

This could be a long stint in this place. I can't even guess a time frame, because like everything else in my life right now, who freaking knows what that is.

After trying to settle down and just listen, we get through all the logistics. To be honest, my head is now spinning, and I didn't realize how tired I am. The words are all starting to run into each other.

"I'm sorry, I'm not trying to be rude. I just… it's been a long few days, and I haven't really slept. Is it okay if we…" I'm struggling to get the words out, and I can feel my body dropping fast.

"Of course. Sleep, you need to rest. I'll show you to your room." He stands next to me, his hand outstretched to help me get up. Normally I would ignore that, but the fatigue I'm feeling is getting stronger by the minute.

"Thank you. I don't know what happened. It just hit me."

Pushing up on to my feet, my balance isn't working that well, and I'm falling sideways.

Ghost's arm comes around my waist before I even sway very far.

"I've got you. This is totally normal; I should have seen it coming." His deep voice so close to my ear makes me feel better, instead of wanting to push him away. I mean, when would you normally let a man you just met put his arm around you and lead to the bedroom.

"This here is your bed. It's not fancy, but it's better than the couch." As he sits me on the side of the bed, I wonder in my mind how many other people who are running scared have slept in this bed. Alone and frightened.

"I'll grab your bag from the bathroom for you." Quickly moving out of the room, he is back soon, with the bathroom just next door.

"Thank you. I'll just take a quick power nap and then I should be good to go again." I lie down on the dark green velvet cover. It seems to be a theme through the house, the color green.

"Sleep as long as you need, it's your body's way of coping with the stress." I want to keep my eyes open, but it's getting more difficult. Ghost steps toward the corner of the room where there is a brown leather reading chair, grabbing a blanket, and lays it over me.

The bed is lumpy and not at all comfortable, but right now, I couldn't care less.

"Just give me twenty minutes," I mumble as he walks to the door.

"Cassandra. Sleep." The powerful words are all I remember before I slip into the dark, and my mind finally goes blank.

"Hi, Jason," I say, answering my phone as I jump out of the taxi outside our apartment building in Washington.

"Leah, it's Camilla, his PA." I try not to groan down the phone. I know who the little upstart bitch is. I've only been dating Jason for eighteen months, so it's not like we haven't met or spoken a million times on the phone. I've given up even trying to explain it to her anymore.

"*Yes, Camilla. What do you want?*" It's a struggle to be civil to her most days.

"*Jason can't make dinner. He has a meeting, and he said to tell you he will be leaving tonight to head out of town for a few days for several appointments. He has his bag with him.*"

"*Tell him a call from him would have been more appropriate. Good evening.*" Hanging up before she can even say another word, I stomp up the steps and through the security doors.

"*Asshole,*" I mumble under my breath.

He promised we would spend tonight having dinner at home, just the two of us. I have hardly seen him for weeks, and even when I do, it's normally out at some charity event or political dinner.

We haven't even had sex in three months.

Like, what the hell is that all about?

Aren't men supposed to be the horny ones? But instead, it's me at home wishing I could satisfy myself when being brushed off again gets to be too much. My insecure self that I keep buried down deep is starting to think—no, actually, I'm certain he's having an affair with Camilla and she just keeps covering for him.

Broken promises are constant, and yet it just seems to be like water off a duck's back to him.

If I hear the words one more time, "*You know I need to do this for my career,*" I think I'll scream.

Storming into his office, I do the one thing I promised myself for the last week I wouldn't do. I start going through his records and searching the computer for files. I'm not sure what I expected to find, but of course, there is nothing out of the ordinary.

I know there is something not right, I just don't know what it is. Too many things are starting to piece together that his life is not what he makes me see. Standing in the middle of the room, I just take it all in. Everything looks like the typical senator's office.

Big desk, big leather chair, both to make him look important. The expensive paintings on the wall and the cabinet that has the crystal liquor decanters and glasses. And of course, the bookshelves, with all his books that are expensive first editions or priceless books, so he keeps telling me. Ones I'm never allowed to touch. They don't interest me anyway, but he is constantly making sure I never touch them.

"Well, fuck you, Senator, here's to your precious books." I'm so angry and hurt that once again I have been stood up that I can't contain myself. I've never been a person to take out my aggression on anything before, but this has been coming for a long while.

I grab the first few books, and pulling them off the shelf, I let them fall to the floor. The sound of them smacking down on the hardwood floor is somehow gratifying. Pulling more and more, it's like a waterfall of paper cascading down from the shelves where they have not moved from since he moved in here, he tells me.

Reaching up on to the tips of my toes, I start on the most precious ones. More important to him than I am, he tells me. What a complete dick!

As they start falling, loose paper starts fluttering down too, and one of the books lands on its spine, opening out flat.

My heart is racing as I scoop the pieces of paper together and stand there staring at his precious book that is hollow in the middle and contains a flash drive I've never seen.

Nervously, I pick it up in my hand, moving to his computer and signing on. I have memorized his password without him knowing. The stupid man forgets I'm good with numbers, that's what I do. Because it has linked into his log in, it doesn't ask for a password to open the hard drive.

As the documents start to open, I can't breathe.

No, this can't be. I can't be with a monster and not know it.

The more I read the more horrified I become. Reading the words in front of me is something I'll never be able to unsee, but instinct is telling me I need to copy every single file and tell someone. Not just anyone, this needs to go to the highest level. I know what I need to do now.

Sitting here, I see pictures that make me gag with disgust and fear.

No, fuck no.

I need to get out of here.

No one can know I've seen this. All of a sudden, my body hits panic mode.

"I can't breathe, need air… can't… breathe."

Chapter Four

GHOST

"Cassandra. Sleep." Almost commanding her to sleep seems to do the trick.

I hear her first deep breath as she finally starts to fall into a slumber that I hope is peaceful for her. Standing longer than I should, just watching her, I see the sadness on her face is weighing heavily. I'd love to see what she looks like when she smiles and hear the sound of her laughter when she is overwhelmed with something funny. I've seen the fire in her when she needs her strength and now her vulnerability in her unhappiness. Every part of me wants to wipe away the bad parts of her world so she only gets to live in the parts where she feels happy.

But instead, I know this woman is going to drive me absolutely crazy. She's stubborn as all hell. Right now, I'm glad she's sleeping because I was close to losing it with her, and that won't help anyone right now.

Normally my clients are so terrified I'm lucky to get two words out of them on the first couple of days. Sure, there are lots of tears usually, but the anger she is throwing at me right now shows she's got guts. She's stronger than most of the men I see in protection.

In all my sixteen years of doing this, I've never had anyone abuse me over the name that was picked for their new identity.

Seriously, why does it even matter? It's a cover for when she's in public. She needs to let go of her old name now, it makes it easier in the long run. That name is gone forever.

I want to tell her that I think Cassie suits her better, but that'd be like waving a red flag at a bull right now.

I can't believe she thought I would ever leave her alone. I mean, seriously, what the fuck! That didn't wash with me at all, and I couldn't stop from telling her straight up what I thought about her outburst.

I ended up growling at her as she was yelling at me. What am I even doing here? This isn't how it's supposed to be. This woman winds me up and has the hair on the back of my neck standing on end. I pride myself on being able to block out distractions and stay calm, even in the heat of the moment. Yet here I was standing up and leaning over the table toward her. Wanting to get right in her face to make sure she understands who I am and what I do. I hate doing it, but I've shot and killed before to keep my client safe. That's what is expected. It's all just instinct.

But this woman! She's confusing me, with an intense possessive pull that's drawing me to her like I've never felt before. The need to protect her is far stronger than I've ever known. I wouldn't just shoot any bastard who thinks they can get near her, but I can feel it in my bones, I know I'd throw my body in front of her if needed.

All agents understand when we join the program the danger that's involved. Yet, as stupid as it sounds, you tend to take that in your stride the longer you work here. Today, that adrenaline rush I felt all those years ago on my first jobs early in my career, it's back with a vengeance.

I don't need it.

I've got to shut this down and get everything back at a distance.

You can't feel this unsettled about a client. When you sign that contract that says you will not become involved in any way with any client in your care, then it's the rule you must abide by. It's what's been drilled into us since day one.

But more importantly, it's there for a reason. The minute you let it become personal, then your judgment is compromised, and that's the most dangerous place to be.

You need to be acting on instinct every second of every day. No clouded judgment.

Because the moment your brain doesn't react purely on listening to your surroundings and judgments is when things turn to shit, and you're dead along with your client. You can't spend time worrying about how someone else is coping or trying to make them feel safe.

The only way they will be safe is through your actions.

Actions speak louder than words, and I'm a man of action.

Take control of the situation, man. Get this back on track.

When I started calming myself down and got back in the zone, I could see her bringing her anger down a notch or two. It was still there, but she, like me, was trying to keep it on the inside.

Finally, I got all the initial protocol out of the way with her, explaining her new identity and what my role in her life is now.

The more I was talking, I could see in her body language that the adrenaline spike she had been riding for the last few days was dwindling. With the glazed look in her eyes, I knew she wasn't taking much in, or if she was, it was just washing over her. But the stubbornness that I've already seen was making her push on. Until she just couldn't any longer.

She finally gave in because her body can't keep going, and she mentioned needing sleep. Thank goodness, because we both needed a break from each other.

When I rose from my chair to help her up, she took my hand which actually surprised me. I expected her to brush me off. Instead, her delicate fingers reached out and wrapped around my hand. That simple gesture of trust resonated through me.

I didn't understand how tired she was until she was falling sideways, trying to gain her balance.

Wrapping my arm around her so she didn't fall was instinct, but just not the one I was thinking about in my head moments before.

That would have been to reach out and place my hand on her shoulder to steady her, not pull her close where it felt natural for her to lean on me.

I just needed to get her to bed so she could sleep, and I needed to pull myself together. Get completely in the frame of mind I need to be in to do my job.

This woman is infuriating. There will be no power-napping here. Once her eyes closed, her body went into recovery mode. She was still mumbling to me as I walked her to the door. She needed to just shut up and give in.

Taking one last look at her and shaking my head, I close the door and beat myself up once again at letting my mind wander to places it can't go.

Work, that's what I need to do. While Cassandra sleeps, I need to find out what this is all about.

Checking all the camera feeds and logging into the work system to document my reports so far, I get lost in all the T-crossing and I-dotting I need to do. I talk to Rocket and get the update from the FBI of what they expect to go down in the next few days. It lets me know when I need to be on alert for any backlash that will be immediate, upon the senator's arrest. It then usually quietens down for a period before the trial commences. If we're lucky, it'll stay quiet, and everything will progress as planned—trial, conviction, and then into hiding for a while until the threat is gone. Usually at that stage, we place them in a whole new life far away from where they originally came from and get them established. Our work as agents is then done, and they only call if something happens. By then it will be a new set of agents assigned if it gets to that point, which is very rare.

Her nap gives me time to set up my bedroom as an operations room. Cassie doesn't need to see all of this in front of her face all day. It's pointless to say you want them to feel at home, because no safe house will ever feel like home, but at least you need them to be comfortable in their surroundings and not completely stressed out. There will be enough of that when it comes time for court cases and speaking with the lawyers.

I check in on her later, though I'm not sure it's a restful sleep, as the strain on her face is still showing, but at least she is still asleep. It's been over an hour now, and I expect it will be a few more yet.

So, it's time for me to do some digging in a place the agency would never agree to, using methods they would never condone. The boss put me on this job because he knew I wouldn't be able to help myself. The players in this are not street criminals. They have money, status, and power. They don't do any of the dirty work; instead, they control the movements and continue to cover their tracks. Yet for someone who knows what they are doing, you would be surprised what pieces of information you can find. You may not have all the pieces but give it long enough and it will all make sense.

Firing up my personal computer that is untraceable and not linked to the agency at all, I start trolling the dark web.

"Okay, Senator Condell, let's see what you've been up to behind your perfect walls." My fingers tap away on the keyboard, and I fall down the rabbit hole of corruption, greed, and criminal activity most people wouldn't even dream of.

My initial search is slow, finding tiny pieces of things and nothing making any connections yet.

Screenshotting my latest find, I can hear movement in Cassie's room which makes me alert. I don't have a camera in her room for privacy, obviously, but there is one in the hallway, and I check to make sure there has been no movement that I've missed. Silence falls on the house again, and I continue searching.

Her voice starting to cry out, I jump out of my seat, slamming down the lid of the laptop to make sure my search is cut off and logged out.

"I can't breathe, need air... can't... breathe," Cassie cries out as I come crashing through her bedroom door. Hand on my gun, I'm ready until I see her thrashing on the bed, and the blanket I laid over her is now screwed up in a ball. Pushing my gun back in its holster, I slowly approach her. I've seen this before, where people in trauma are dreaming, and they're back in the middle of where they came from. Waking them up too quickly is harsh and can cause an even worse feeling than in the nightmare they're in.

"Cassandra, it's okay." Keeping my voice calm, I approach her from the side. "Cassandra, it's Ghost. I'm here. Just open your eyes."

Her breathing is getting more rapid instead of calming.

"Can't breathe… he'll kill…" She's still thrashing backwards and forwards.

"Cassandra!" My voice gets louder to try to break through to her. But it's still not working because she isn't used to her name yet. So, I resort to the only thing left. Sitting down on the bed next to her, I pull her into my arms to stop her from moving, which will hopefully wake her or at least still her.

"I've got you, beautiful." The words slip out as I cradle her against my chest, wrapping her arms up nice and tight.

Fuck, I should never have said that. I just spent the last few hours grilling myself about not getting involved, obviously with no success. Hopefully she didn't hear a word of it.

My words might not have worked, but holding her is making her fight stronger, to wake at the shock of feeling someone touching her.

Cassandra's eyes spring open, looking like a startled child. I can feel her fighting against me to get away which will make things worse.

"It's just me, Ghost. I'm here to protect you. Just relax. You were having a nightmare."

"Where am I?" Her voice is still unstable and raspy.

"The safe house, with me. Remember the less-than-five-star accommodation that I'm providing?" Slowly her eyes soften, and her body is becoming limp in my arms. "Just take your time, whatever was in the nightmare is gone." I rub my hand up and down her back, trying to soothe her.

Eventually all the struggle is gone, and her forehead falls forward onto my chest. Not saying a word, she starts to breathe a little slower, and reluctantly I loosen my grip on her. I slide my arms back so my hands are holding her up by the top of her arms.

Her head is still hanging low.

"Cassandra, look at me." She hesitates but slowly her head is rising, and I see her face that looks like the weight of the world is on her. "Are you back with me?" I don't want to, but I start to let go, hovering next to her, making sure she can sit up on her own.

"Yeah." Finally, she's acknowledging me.

"Want to talk about it?" Not a question I should be asking her.

"No," is all I get. I don't believe her, but she would have been told not to talk to anyone unless she has the permission from the FBI. I let it go for now.

"Okay, I understand. I'll let you wake up properly, and when you're ready, come out and we'll see if there's something we can find for an afternoon snack.

"Afternoon? How long did I sleep?" She runs her hands up and down her arms. Not sure if it's because she's cold or it's just a nervous reaction.

"A few hours, and before you say a word, you needed it. I'll be in the kitchen if you want me." I walk away before I say or do something stupider than I already have.

I check through the pantry for the food that the house was stocked with before we got here. A few options jump out at me. I grab the crackers, nuts, and I know I saw some cheese and dip in the fridge. I might not be great with presentation, but the food looks okay. I can't drink on the job, and it doesn't look like they have stocked any wine here either at first glance. Iced tea will have to do for the time being.

The quiet shuffle of her feet coming down the hallway has me looking up to see her. She's got her arms wrapped tightly around herself again, a sign of how uneasy she's still feeling.

"Why don't we go outside on the back porch and sit in the sunlight? They say it's good for the soul." I hold up my plate of food and the iced tea as a peace offering.

"Sounds nice." I wish I could get back to the yelling now that she's so timid.

"Let's go then." Walking to the back door, I hold it open and scan all around me as I'm doing it.

"There aren't any chairs to sit on, but I thought we could just take a spot here on the steps if that's okay with you?" I ask, placing the food down and waiting for her to take a seat on the top step next to it.

"I was joking about you being the chef." Cassandra gives me a half-smile as I sit myself down on the step below her. Being that bit taller at six feet, it still puts us almost at eye level.

"I wasn't joking when I said I will if you need me to be," I reply, putting a piece of cheese on a cracker and handing it to her. For the first time since she walked in the door this morning, I see her cheeks blush slightly. Interesting.

"Do all your clients get the full not-five-star treatment?" She looks out at the trees so she doesn't have to look me in the face.

"Only the lucky ones." I laugh at her, trying to break the embarrassment she must still be feeling from the nightmare.

"Really, and how many lucky ones have there been before me?" A slight sense of humor is peeking out now, which I'd like to see much more of.

"Hmmm, let me see." I hold my finger up to my chin, pondering the question.

"Ugghhh, so I'm not special if you need to count them." She turns her head back to look at me.

"Zero, the answer would be zero. Which means you are special." I can feel the electricity starting to crackle around us as we both just try to push down the weirdness that we're feeling between us.

This time it's me breaking the connection and looking out into the yard, trying to change the topic.

"So, tell me a bit about your life before all this. I mean, way before the senator. What did your life look like?"

"I thought you would know all my history. Don't they tell you everything, including the color of underwear I have on?"

Now that's a visual I really do not need at all.

"That's not what I want to know. I can read all that shit until I'm blue in the face. I want to know the real you. The person inside you, regardless of the name on the outside." I hold back also saying how much I'd like to know about the color of her underwear but only if she is modelling it.

"I'm not that exciting to know. Just an average woman living in a world that I don't belong in, by the looks of things," she says, swirling her iced tea in the glass in front of her.

"I call bullshit on the part about not being exciting. But that world is definitely not one we want you nearby. Let me be the judge of the rest. Start talking, woman, where did you grow up?"

CASSIE

Should I really be sharing all this with him?

I don't know what the rules are, but for some reason, I just want to. I need to talk to someone and try to get my mind off what is happening, and Ghost is the only person I'll have for a long time. Not that it will be a burden. He's easy on the eyes, and when he isn't trying to be all macho on me, I think he has this soft caring side of him that I'm not sure he means to show me.

"I grew up in Philadelphia for the first eighteen years of my life with my parents. I had a twin brother who died at birth, and my mom had to have emergency surgery to try to save me. It meant that she couldn't have any more children after that. They loved me, but we all felt like there was a hole in my family that we could never fill."

"I'm sorry about your brother, did he have a name?"

My mouth drops at the question. "No person has ever asked me that. In all the years I have shared my story, no one ever cared to ask." My heart twinges for my twin I never knew.

Ghost's reaction to that shows anger at the lack of people's empathy in life. "I care. Please tell me his name." Looking at him I can tell he truly does.

"Eli. His name was Eli." A single tear runs down my face for the brother I wish were here with me.

Lifting his glass toward me, he says, "Cheers to Eli, wherever he may be." For the first time in what feels like forever I'm smiling, like truly smiling. I raise my glass to clink with his, the warmth of the afternoon sun soaking into my bones and the kindheartedness of Ghost settling in my heart.

"Cheers to Eli, together with Mom and Dad again." The thought makes me happy that none of them are on their own.

"Tell me about your parents' deaths?" His interested look on his face surprises me.

"Didn't you get around to reading that part?"

"Don't be smart. Keep talking." He is now sitting up straight and intent on every word that I'm about to tell him.

"My parents were both killed in a boating accident. There was an engine explosion, and they were both thrown overboard but didn't have a life vest on. The autopsy showed Mom died instantly, from a blow to the head. Probably hit it on the side of the boat as she was thrown. And Dad's body was never found—well, technically. There were pieces of him in the water. They think he was probably killed instantly and bore the brunt of the explosion. I can't even think about what happened to his body. It's an image I will never get out of my head of what happened in that awful few seconds." It's been a long time since I've thought about any of this, and it's tough to be dragging it all up now when I'm emotionally exhausted already.

"Where were you at the time?" There was an image that made me like Ghost just another little bit more. He didn't have pity written all over his face but instead is just genuinely curious as to how my life pieces together.

"I was getting ready to head to college. It was their first holiday trip without me. At the time I was angry with the world that I wasn't with them. Why did I have to get left behind? First Eli, then my parents. But after a few years of pushing through the grief and pain, I took the mindset that there is something better out there for me. A reason I'm still here. I have no idea what it is yet, but eventually I'll find it."

"I knew you were one tough chick just looking at you this morning and the way you weren't backing down with me. But now, knowing where you've come from, I know you are probably stronger than others give you credit for. Including the mysterious senator who is about to regret not seeing the warrior beside him, I'm sure." It feels nice to have someone on my team. I'm not sure Jason ever was.

"Not really, I'm just living my life the best I can. And now I'm just trying to get through one day at a time." That's all I can do.

We both just sit in the stillness for a few minutes, which is what I need to settle all the feelings that always resurface when I talk about the difficult times in my life.

"You've told me all the hard parts of your life, now let's start on some of the good things. Like, what did you study at college?" Ghost now stretches his legs out down the steps, looking a little more relaxed. He knows all the answers to his questions, but it feels nice that he wants to know them from me, instead of reading them off my file.

"I studied financial accounting. There is something about numbers that I was always good at. I wouldn't say I loved it, but it came naturally. My careers advisor at school said that accounting was the way to go, and my grades got me into college, and that's the program I took."

I remember my years at college living on campus in a tiny dorm room with my friend Penny because that was all I could afford. I inherited all of Mom and Dad's assets, but it wasn't much. They had a house, but it came with debt. They had used all their life savings to have Eli and me through IVF. Then it took years for Mom to manage to go back to work. We did all right, lived a normal suburban life. There just wasn't much left for me and no life insurance policies. However, I was grateful for what I had, and it kept me from living on the streets. I learned to budget and be frugal with my money, and by the time I got through college, the inheritance was just about all gone. Since then, I have worked hard and lived a good life.

Yesterday, that changed.

The sad part now is that all my life savings are in the bag in my room, under the lining at the bottom. Twenty thousand dollars sounds like a lot but isn't much when you have no home, clothes, car, or belongings.

"Where did you just go? Your mind wandered off." Ghost is waiting to hear more.

"Just some memories of college, nothing important. Anyway,

that's enough about me for the time being. Tell me about you. What made you become an agent? I mean, it's not a very common job."

Something I learned early on with Jason is how when you're out at dinners with people you don't know, to deflect a conversation and get them talking so you can just listen. Those people could talk for hours about nothing and think they are the most important person in the world.

"Don't think I missed what you did there, but I'll ignore it for the moment." Standing, he starts to wander in the yard in front of me. Is it because talking about himself makes him nervous? I don't know, but watching him, his body language is different from before. The confidence has gone and the bravado not as strong.

"My family aren't quite like yours from what you've told me. I'm what you would call a loner. I haven't seen them in a long time." I can see his hesitation to continue weighing on him.

"One of the reasons I chose this job was to get out of town and disappear, to some extent. I like to do my own thing and live my own life. No responsibility and no ties to anyone. I don't need a family." There is hurt written all over his face.

"That's a big statement, sad too. What, you don't want any family in the future?" I can't stop myself from asking. From someone who has lost all hers, this hurts deeply.

"Nope." The anger in his voice makes me want to push for more from him, but I bite my tongue. His arrogance is on full display, but it's not fooling me. He's pacing the back yard now. This topic is extremely sensitive to him. I'm glad I haven't asked more. I need to break the tension.

"Oh well, regardless of the history, I bet they are extremely proud of you. You save hundreds of lives, I'm sure. Look at me. Right now, you're making me feel like I'm safe here for the time being. So don't worry about your family, the only one you need to impress here is me. Show me that you are big and tough and will scare the bad men and women away." I was trying to joke it off, but his stride is determined as he heads straight back to me.

"I'd like to show you more than how tough I am," he mumbles under his breath, and the look in his eyes is far different than the heat I saw earlier from annoyance. The way his eyes see right into me, it sets off a current of tingles rushing through me that I don't know what to do with except feel them.

Shaking his head and then taking the steps two at a time, he moves past me and heads through the door, calling out to me, "I'm gonna grab more iced tea to cool off. Sun's hot." His voice is now yelling out from the kitchen.

The heat out here has nothing to do with the sun.

What the hell was that? I don't know if my brain can handle any more emotional whiplash today.

There is banging and crashing of the fridge opening and closing and then silence. I don't know what he's doing in there, but I doubt it takes that long to grab the container with the tea in it. It's not like he's making it from scratch.

Finally, he emerges out the door and looks like he is a different man. The mask is back on, and he is my agent again, all serious. His silence is hanging between us.

As he pours my drink, then his own, I try to get more out of him.

"So, you found your calling as a WITSEC agent…" I don't even get to finish my sentence before he interrupts.

"Yes," he snaps, draining his glass quickly. "Would you like a newspaper to read or a book from the shelf? I have work to do."

"What, you're going to leave me here on my own?" I'm half serious but half joking, trying to bait him for a reaction.

"You'll be fine out here. Enjoy the sun while it lasts. I'll monitor you." There is no budging him from the work mode he has now resorted back to.

"Go then, I'll just sit here and rest, while you watch me from behind some screen. Because that's not creepy at all."

"Cassandra, don't push it on the first day. You know what's going on here. Don't lose your shit at me again over something neither of us can control." As he runs his hand around the back of his neck, I know I'm stressing him out. I just don't know if I feel sorry about it or want to keep pushing him more.

Sitting now on my own with just the sound of the slight breeze through the trees and some birds close by, I'm wondering what all that last statement meant.

Do I know what's going on here? Is he talking about the situation I'm in or the intense chemistry that is starting to circle us in the first day?

He's right either way, about both things; neither of us has control.

I've just walked out on a toxic relationship, and surely this attraction is just some savior complex I have.

Besides, this guy is way too intense for me. I just want a simple life when this is all over.

It will be over one day, right?

I must try to believe that.

Chapter Five

CASSIE

The next few hours I spent sitting in the sun for a while, then taking a wander around the outside of the house. I didn't venture far, though. I have no idea where I am or what is really going on outside this place, so I stay where I feel secure for the time being.

The house is wood-slatted on the outside, with a porch that runs the full length along the front of the house, and out back the porch is only half the size, just a small area that allows you some space on either side of the back door to sit. The gardens are bare of any flowers but just a few shrubs that look after themselves. No shape to them, just growing wild however they please. I envy them in a way, to be free like that. Then across the back of the property there are trees that provide privacy, but peeking through them, I can see there is a big open field behind them for as far as I can see.

There is a shed in the back yard that looks empty through the window. When I try the door, it's locked, which makes no sense when there's nothing inside, but I suppose security is the main objective in this place.

After looking at what feels like every single blade of grass in this yard at least twice, I can't be out here any longer. I need something else to do.

The house isn't big enough to explore for longer than five minutes. Looking around as I walk down the hallway, the first room on the right is the bathroom, and next to it is my room. Across from me the door is shut to the room that I'm guessing Ghost is using. Hearing the tapping of the keyboard, I figure he must be working like he said he would. Part of me just expected that was an excuse so he could get away from me.

Alongside Ghost's room is another room that has a bed in it and one bedside drawer set next to it. They really went all out with the furniture here. It's like they set this house up in the eighties, and it hasn't been touched since. Nothing matches, and each room is a blank canvas.

Oh, how I'd love to do a bit of interior designing in here. With a little bit of paint to clean it up and new furnishings, it would look like someone loved it. Not that I know anything about decorating, but I've always had an interest in it. I love to look through magazines at nice houses and apartments that have had makeovers on a budget or a full renovation where the place is stripped bare and becomes a whole new home. I might not know what I'm doing, but if I were given a chance, anything would look better than the floral cover on the bed in the unused room, that is all orange, yellow, and brown. With my room in green and Lord knows what color Ghost's room is.

I need to find something to do, otherwise I'm going to go stir-crazy, locked up here day in day out. And who knows what Mr. Split Personality in there is going to be like to live with.

Turning on the television, I'm glad at least it looks new. As the screen lights up, I can see all the streaming services are here, which at least is one saving grace. Surely, I can find some series to binge and take my mind off why I'm here.

Nothing too serious, just some light comedy.

Friends.

Perfect. I've seen random episodes over the years, but I don't even know where it all began. Guess I'm about to find out.

This couch might be old but at least it's comfortable. I'm three episodes in and am now lying down with my head on the end of it and my legs sprawled out. My whole body is a little achy. It's no wonder why, with everything that's happened today.

The light through the windows is dimming as dusk gradually turns into night. I know I had a few hours' sleep earlier, but I still feel exhausted now.

I haven't seen Ghost for hours, and although that is making me feel anxious, I understand that he has work to do. I need to learn to be on my own. I can't expect him to babysit me all the time. I didn't know what to expect in the WITSEC program, but this is not quite what I had pictured. I thought they would put me in a house and leave me there, giving me a new identity and letting me know how to get in touch with someone if I was worried. I wasn't expecting an agent to be living in the house with me. It kind of makes me worry a little more that he's here. Does it mean I'm in more danger than most people? Or is there more to this whole thing that I don't know? Taking a deep breath, I tell myself not to overthink this. Just listen to what they tell me and let them worry about the rest. Raising my arms above my head, I stretch my body completely out which feels nice.

"Okay, Cassandra, time to get up and get on with it," I tell myself, still trying out my new name and how it rolls off the tongue. It's going to take a while to get used to it, but there is no other choice. It's a bit too much for me, but I just have to accept it, I guess.

I stand up and make my way to the kitchen. I'm not very hungry, but I feel like I should at least make something for Ghost after he looked after me today, feeding me and comforting me when I needed it. I have a feeling there is a lot more to that man than he shows the rest of the world.

But to be honest, isn't that the same for all of us?

As embarrassing as it was, having someone care about me while they are sitting beside me in the same room was a nice change today as I woke from the nightmare. Rather than on the other end of a FaceTime call where the compassion lasts a few minutes and then he moves on to telling me about his day. Or better still, telling me what event I need to be prepared for and to make sure I have an outfit ready. I learned not to bother telling him anything about my day after a while. It's funny how you don't even notice those things when you are in the middle of it, but the moment you step away from a situation, it becomes as clear as day.

Shaking my head, I need to stop thinking about Jason. He's a dick, and if I'm lucky, I will never have to be in the same room with him again.

I come back to my thoughts about feeding Ghost. In the few brief moments I've seen him today, he is more than double the man my ex will ever be.

"Let's see what's in the cupboards." Opening the pantry, I'm shocked with how much food is in here. Stupidly it makes me happy and sad at the same time. They must be expecting me to be here for a long time. Either that or they think Ghost has a mighty appetite.

I decide to pull together an easy pasta for tonight, which will give plenty for Ghost to eat, and I can just have a small plate and put aside the leftovers for later. It will take me a little while to find everything in this kitchen, but at least it seems to be well stocked with all the basic cooking equipment I need.

I didn't realize how much I needed to be doing something so normal. I do love to cook, but it was wasted living with Jason. He was never home, and when he was, he would want to go out for dinner, which I'm convinced was so that people would see him in certain popular restaurants or so he could coincidentally run into another diner in the room. If on the rare occasion we got to stay home, he would insist we order in a takeout meal. The only time I really cooked was for myself. Part of the enjoyment of cooking, though, is preparing it for someone else to enjoy and then sitting down and appreciating it with a small glass of wine. Not sure if the wine will be an option here, but at least Ghost might appreciate my cooking.

The aroma of the bacon and onion frying must have been enough to lure him out of his cave, as I can hear the door opening and the footsteps of his boots coming behind me.

"Smells good, but I thought I was supposed to be the chef."

I look over my shoulder at him placing himself down on the other side of the kitchen counter.

"I like to cook. Plus, it gives me something to do to push away the thoughts," I say, turning back to check the pasta boiling in the pot and stirring the frying pan contents that are sizzling away.

"Fair enough."

A silence descends on the room for a few minutes as I continue with what I'm doing. Then his deep voice breaks the awkward pause.

"Can I help with anything? I'm not used to sitting idle either."

Smiling to myself, with my back still to him, I say, "I can imagine that about you."

His laughter breaks out behind me. "What's that supposed to mean?" I hear the scraping of the stool as he stands and now approaches me. My heart rate kicks up a little. Coming to a stop and leaning his ass against the counter next to where I'm working, he crosses his feet and his arms while he casually makes himself comfortable.

"It just means that you look like you have a lot going on in that head, and I'm sure you are used to constantly moving, with a job like yours, and making sure everything is perfect. You strike me as a perfectionist."

The pasta chooses this moment to boil over slightly, and I adjust the lid so it settles again.

"You don't even know me." Ghost's reply is not harsh or accusing, just merely stating a fact.

"True, I'm just stating what I see, which could be totally wrong."

"I could say you're wrong... but I'd be lying." His arms drop down, hands loosely resting on either side of him, hanging onto the countertop.

I'm almost scared to ask, but I'm going to anyway. "So, what about me? How do you sum me up?" I look up from what I'm doing after adding the tomato sauce to the pan, now sizzling away as dinner starts to take shape. "Wait, you probably already have that many notes on me, you have an unfair advantage."

The smile that edges the corners of his mouth up on either side does something funny to my stomach.

"Not those sorts of notes. We don't just download your whole personality onto paper. What I have is rather boring, really. Like you, I must work out the rest in the good old-fashioned way."

"And how's that, exactly?" Stepping away from the stovetop for a moment, I grab some plates out of the cupboard, needing to keep myself busy.

"Talking."

"What?" I say a little louder than I meant to.

"I know, it's shocking, isn't it."

"No, not that, silly. There's wine."

My heart is singing at the sight of several bottles of both red and white in the bottom of the cupboard I just pulled open to look for a strainer for the pasta.

"Why is that such a surprise?" There's confusion on his face, like he didn't know it was their either, though.

"I didn't think they'd allow alcohol in this place." I pull out a bottle of red, and I can't express how much I could really use a glass now.

"It's not jail here, Cassandra."

Raising my eyebrows at him, I can't help myself. "Close to it, though."

Tilting his head to the side, he finally agrees. "Okay, I'll give you that. But it's for your benefit." Compassion is written all over his face. At least it's better than pity, I suppose.

"Can I open that for you?" Ghost reaches out his hand toward me and the bottle.

"Thanks, I think I need it tonight."

We both go about getting organized to eat, Ghost setting the table while I'm dishing the pasta out onto the plates. I didn't think I was that hungry, but the smell of it has my stomach now sitting up and taking notice.

Walking to the table, I notice there is only one glass of wine.

Ghost pulls out the chair in front of that glass, gesturing for me to take my seat there.

Lowering myself into the chair after placing the plates on the table, my nerves kick in. This feels a little too intimate. And when I'm nervous, I end up blurting out things I wished I'd kept inside.

"Why am I drinking alone? What, is the wine too girly for you?"

The slightly serious look he had when he sat down is now lost, with him bursting out with a deep throaty laugh.

"Didn't realize I made a joke." I'm offended he's laughing at me.

"You know how you asked me a moment ago how I see you? Well, do you still want to know?" He's trying to hold back his laughter.

"Not sure I want to know now." I'm almost sulking as I raise my wine glass. "Cheers to me being a loner." His face totally changes at my words.

"Cassandra, you're not alone." He picks up his glass of water and reaches across the table to clink it with mine. "I love a good red, but I'm not allowed to drink on the job. Besides, it's not a good idea. My job is to be alert and ready at any moment to protect you. I can't do that to the best of my ability if I'm drinking," he says, staring at me with his intensity. "And I will not let anything get in the way of me keeping you safe. Do you understand!" The gruffness in his voice leaves no mistake on how seriously he takes his job.

"Okay," is all I can say. Taking the first sip of my wine, it tastes amazing, even if it's a cheap bottle. It's still the alcohol I need to combat the control freak in front of me and this whole fucked-up situation.

His intensity is still sitting between us. Even if I wanted to look away, I'm not sure I can. His mouth opens to finish what he just started.

"I see a strong woman who is not afraid to speak her mind but who is also kind and likes to care for others." His eyes scan over the meal before us. "Someone who's been dealt a shitty situation yet is still trying to make the best of it." Well, he's got that one right.

"But above all, I see another woman hiding behind all those attributes who isn't sure of who she really is. That's the woman I want to get to know."

Well, I'll be damned if he didn't hit the nail on the head with everything he just said, not that I'm admitting any of that.

"What you see is what you get," I say, which couldn't be any further from the truth. Taking my first mouthful of my pasta, I try to shut down the conversation topic. I don't need anyone digging under my skin, especially someone I don't know but who already has me on edge for a reason I can't put my finger on yet. And that alone makes me nervous.

Thank goodness Ghost takes the hint and starts to eat his meal too.

"This is awesome, thank you." He looks up at me as he's taking his next mouthful.

Just smiling, acknowledging his compliment, we both spend the next ten minutes or so concentrating on eating. I wasn't hungry, and even when I started, I didn't think I'd get through much of my plate, but needing the distraction of not having to talk means I've nearly finished everything I served myself.

"I'm glad you're eating. Sometimes the stress makes it hard to stomach anything."

I want to reply that I'm only eating because I'm stressed and right this moment the main nerves are coming from sitting at this table across from him. Those intense gazes he keeps giving me when he thinks I'm not looking. It's like he is trying to figure me out but can't yet.

Yeah, well, welcome to the party, Ghost. I can't seem to get a handle on how to take you either. One minute you are soft and gentle, then the next you're full badass agent mode and don't want to be near me.

After finishing everything on his plate and leaning back into his chair, his glass of water in his hand, he isn't looking at anything except me. I can feel his stare even when I look away.

I'm starting to understand the nervous feeling I have in my stomach around him.

He's intimidating!

I don't know if he means to be, but it's just oozing from him. I doubt many people mess with him. It's all getting to be too much now. Without another word, I stand, grabbing my plate and glass, and head to the kitchen.

"I'll do that," I hear from behind me.

"No, it's okay, I'm sure you have work to do." I gulp down the last mouthful of my wine and want more than anything to pick up the bottle and start guzzling that down too.

"I said I'll do it." The voice getting closer behind me makes my breath speed up. "You go and relax." Stepping up beside me, he takes the plate from me, and without even touching me, makes me feel like I need to move sideways from standing in front of the sink. He has this power with his eyes. It's hard to describe, but it's like he can control you with just the way he looks at you and directs what he wants.

Strange but intriguing.

"Relaxing. Pfft, what even is that?" I blurt out what I meant to think in my head, not say out loud. I remember that my mom used to tell me, *"That's an inside thought."* I wasn't very good at it when I was younger, and apparently tonight I'm not either.

"I understand, but we need to find something that will work for you," he says, looking sideways at me as he starts rinsing the plates and pots I was using.

"I need something to keep my hands busy."

His choking on air makes me rethink what I said. "You know, like washing the dishes. I'm not some damsel in distress, you know." I can feel the anger, that is lying dangerously close to the surface, now peeking its head out.

"Not even close," is all he says before stepping backwards away from the sink, hands in the air. "Sorry, all yours. But don't say I didn't offer. I'll dry." Great, now he's standing close to me, just staring at me while waiting for the first dish I'm now cleaning.

We both get to work on getting the cleaning from dinner sorted. I want to apologize for snapping at him, but instead, I'm just standing here almost scrubbing the blue pattern off the china plate.

"What would you normally do to help combat stress in your life, Cassandra?" I jump slightly as his voice breaks the unnerving silence.

"Exercise, run, do classes, anything to take the nervous energy down a peg or two. Instead, I'm stuck here in this old house that needs painting and being brought up to the modern decade. I mean, does anyone even care what it looks like when they just dump people here? Just because we're in hiding, it doesn't mean we have to live in something that looks like it hasn't been touched in fifty years." Throwing the sponge down in the sink and pulling the plug out, I know I need to walk away. Otherwise, Ghost is about to see a part of me that I don't particularly want to share.

My crazy-ass, bitchy side that I keep only for special occasions. Not sure this is one of those occasions, but the restraint to hold myself back is getting thinner.

Maybe I'm the one with the split personality.

"I'm tired. I'm going to bed. Good night." Not even looking at him, I turn my back and walk away. No idea what I'm going to do once I get into my room. There is no way I'm going to be able to sleep tonight.

My mother would have whooped my ass for being as rude as I just was, walking away and not even acknowledging Ghost. I don't know what came over me, but what I do know is that I need to be on my own to try to calm my brain and stop from letting it all out. Everything that I've been holding in for days now. To be honest, it's probably been months that this frustration and mental anguish has been building. So many promises, talks of dreams ahead of us. Then nothing. Just lonely nights, days on my own, and the schedules of appearances to keep.

I can't even remember the last time Jason and I just curled up on the couch to watch a movie or talked. Why was I so stupid!

I didn't see it. I let myself be treated like crap, and it took something like this for me to see the real life I was living. No one would believe me if I told them that I'm angrier about the life I let myself live than I am about being trapped here and losing my identity.

Maybe it was an identity that needed to be lost.

Who was I then anyway? Just a doormat for some rich asshole.

I know one thing, and that's when I get out of this clusterfuck, things are changing. No one will keep me hidden or tell me what to do. I will be making my own decisions and never depend on a man again! That's my promise to myself.

After slipping back out of my room to the bathroom and getting sorted, I'm now lying in bed staring at the ceiling, trying to take my mind to a happier time in my life. There were some with Jason in the beginning but nothing that I want to think about now. I drift off into my memories of when I first started my job at Roblowen Financial. I applied for plenty of jobs my last year of college, praying that something would open up for me. I couldn't afford to spend much time without a regular paycheck coming in.

I remember the elation that rushed through my body once Mr. Aleckson called me to tell me I had the job at Roblowen Financial. It was an entry-level accountant's position, but it was full-time and permanent, with all the health benefits, which was important to me as a woman who was completely on my own.

Those first six months I felt like I was drowning, just trying to gain my confidence in my work. What they taught me in college was nothing like the real world. Sure, the basics never changed, but the practicality of what happens in business is nothing like the textbook cases they give you.

I made a few friends in my section, Kylie, Elton, and Bruce. They helped me to fit in, and before long, I felt like I had been there for years and was part of the team. We had some fun nights out at the bars close to work and quick lunches in the café downstairs from our office. There was the occasional work function that we were all required to attend, where the bigger clients were wined and dined to keep them paying the big bucks.

It was at one of those schmoozing nights that I met who I thought was the man that would give me a great life. He swept me off my feet with all the right words, flirting with me until I took the bait. I ended up in his limousine at the end of the night and back to his penthouse suite. I was all lust and starry eyes that I look back on now and wish I had made better choices. He bought me gifts, sent me flowers, and turned on all the charm every time we were together.

Even my coworkers kept saying we made the perfect couple and how lucky I was. Oh yeah, so lucky, to be used as a pawn in his big masterful game. Never once did Jason miss a date or let me down in the early days. Life was good, and when my lease on my apartment was due, he convinced me that I should move in with him. I was ecstatic. His penthouse was beautiful and about a hundred times bigger than my place. Kylie came and helped me pack up my things into boxes. I didn't have much, but it was all precious to me because they were things from my parents or that I had worked hard to save the money and pay for. Jason then paid for the movers to come and transport my boxes and the pieces of furniture I wanted to keep.

But that day should have been the first red flag, when he insisted that all my things would be stored in the storage room in the basement until we got time to decide where we would put them. They are still sitting in that storage room. They weren't good enough for his home. Yes, and those are the important words.

His home.

It never became *our* home.

Not long after moving in, things began to change, or more accurately, Jason changed. No more sweet words and flowers, date nights, or quiet time for just the two of us. I became one of his staff, with my schedule and the way I got more messages from his secretary than I did from him. I excused his behavior, saying that he was busy and once he got his career where it needed to be then things would go back to normal. But instead, that became the new normal. I saw him less and less, and the sex almost became nonexistent. And on the rare occasions we did get naked together, it was what I would call a quickie that he needed to get himself off and find relief. It was never about me.

Rolling onto my side, I kick myself that I've let me mind wander back to him. Curling my body up into a ball, hugging the other pillow on the bed, I bury my head into the one I'm lying on. The tears slide down my cheeks, but I don't want to make a noise. I've already made a fool of myself today. Tonight, I'll just let it all drain out, and hopefully, when the exhaustion from crying kicks in, I'll close my eyes and sleep.

I'm swearing off all men forever. I don't need them or the crap that goes with relationships. I'm sure they aren't all like that, but I can't let my heart get walked over like that again. I've known enough loss in my life, the kind of loss that makes your heart feel like that pain alone will kill you and you aren't sure you'll ever get through it. I'm not setting myself up to get smacked down again, having to pick up the pieces, like I'm trying to do now. I might act all tough in front of Ghost, but the truth is, I'm not. Not in the slightest.

I'm weak and vulnerable, but most of all, confused. Why does everything bad keep happening to me? Why do some people get to go through life blessed with love and happiness? Yet I get to live through hurt, loneliness, and betrayal.

I give up on trying to find the pot of gold at the end of the rainbow.

Mine would just be filled with coal.

Hearing movement outside my door, I hold my breath so as not to make any noise to give away my tears.

Thank goodness my back is to the door, as it opens very slowly, and the light from the hallway creeps in. I can feel Ghost behind me, and without understanding why, the tears that have been streaming down my face slow, and a feeling of warmth falls upon me.

Assuming I'm already asleep, the light starts to dim again as he begins closing the door. The whisper from his lips is so quiet I almost don't hear it, but the still of the night around us gives me just enough to catch the words.

"Good night, bright eyes, you're safe with me."

His words and the name send shivers down my spine.

As much as I've sworn off men forever, for some reason deep down, I believe him.

To be honest, I don't really have a choice.

I just hope he won't be the next one in line to let me down and leave me a mess all over again.

As the door clicks shut and the footsteps walk away, I whisper the one word that I was holding in.

"Promise?"

Chapter Six

GHOST

I 've spent the last few hours pacing the grounds outside, checking all the cameras and for any traces of movement. I know I'm going overboard, but I can't sit in that house while I know Cassie is in there crying. Hopefully now she is finally sleeping and resting her weary head. I know I shouldn't call her that, but to me, that's who she is.

The emotions that are pouring out of Cassie are pissing me off.

It's not her fault, but just watching the anguish, anxiety, and pure rage that is lying under the surface within her makes me want to find that asshole and kill him myself with my bare hands.

I have never felt so invested in a case as I am right now. In all the years I have been doing this job, sure, I've felt sorry for my clients and even gotten attached to them as friends in a way. But nothing like this. Not to the point that I want to hurt someone because of what they have done to my client.

Yes, client! You need to remember that, you idiot. This needs to stop, and I've got to put a lid on it.

Work, that's what I need to do. Distraction is the best way to handle this.

I wish there were a way that I only had to stay here with her for a few days until she is settled in, and we'll see how the senator reacts to her being missing. To distance myself from the hole I'm digging myself with being attracted to her. But deep down, no matter what I try to tell myself, I know I could never leave her here on her own. I can't. There is something pulling me to her that is not going to stop, no matter what I try to do.

I've seen this type of thing go bad on the job, and I don't want to be the one left a shell of a man like *he* was a few years ago. I need to remind myself of what happened to him.

Focus.

Do the job.

Keep her safe.

Then leave.

That's how it's supposed to be.

Yet already I'm calling bullshit on myself.

Back inside my room, I wake up my computer so I can check the cameras, then dial on my personal phone the one man who will smack me around the back of the head and tell me to get the fuck out of this situation.

"Ghost, you good?" Always the same, his instant reaction is that there is trouble.

"Badger. Alive is the answer you need."

I can hear his sigh through my earpiece. "I'm sensing a but coming, though." In a way he has been like a father figure to me in this job. He has seen so much in his time in the military and then WITSEC that it's almost like he has a sixth sense.

"Because you are like a fucking voodoo man. I'm sure you have some weird-ass powers to read minds or some shit like that. We should have called you Wizard instead of Badger." His laughter, deep and gruff, helps to put me at ease somewhat.

"Yeah, right, you bastards thought it was hilarious to call this old man Badger, with my gray streaks in my hair. But I'll take that.

Better than going bald…" He gives a fake cough into the phone, hinting at my thinning hair.

"Such a funny prick, aren't you?"

"Someone has to be. You're too busy being the serious one."

"Yeah, right, you have met Bull, haven't you? He thinks he's funnier than all of us." Both of us are now laughing which is what I needed.

"You on the job tonight?" There's importance back in his voice. That's one thing about Badger; he is very cut and dry. He thinks I'm the serious one, but we all know it's a strong part of his personality. It's what made him good at his job. Up until recently, he was my handler but is now retired. A blow-up with the hierarchy had him telling them to fuck off, and he walked away. We all saw it coming. He struggled to follow the rules after everything he has been through. No one can blame him for it, although I miss him. Best there was in my squad, alongside Bull.

"Yeah, but it's turning out to be a curly one, with lots of hidden secrets." Leaning back into the desk chair, I prop my hands behind my head and look up at the ceiling.

"What, the job or the client? Or is it just another WITSEC clusterfuck they've dumped in your lap?" The bitterness in his voice is still as strong as ever.

"Hmmm, not sure how to answer that one." And I'm really not. The more I look into the senator, the more I don't like what I see. But that's not the biggest problem with the job.

"Start at the beginning." There is that fatherly tone that makes me take a deep breath and lay it all out there. The words are flowing freely as I tell him what I know and about Cassie.

"Fuck, Ghost! You know what I'm going to say." If I could see his face right now, his mouth would be a straight line, his jaw locked, and the eyebrow would be twitching.

"What if I don't want to hear it?"

"Then you wouldn't have called me!" And he's right. Wasn't that what I wanted? For him to tell me to walk away from this job. Call in for a swap-out with another agent.

"I hate when you're right."

"You're saying it like it's something that doesn't happen often. Now listen up, buddy, and listen hard."

"Do I have a choice?" I ask, knowing full well I don't.

"This is fucking dangerous for both her and for you. And I'm not talking about any of this fluffy shit like your heart getting broken. I couldn't give a shit about that. But what I do care about is you keeping her alive and in the process keeping your sorry ass safe too. We both know I'm talking from experience. You can't think straight when you are blinded by thinking with your dick. Your decisions aren't quick enough, and that split second where you stop to think of her is a second you don't have. It will end in the worst possible way."

"It wasn't your fault." I feel bad that I have dragged this back up for him, but I needed it to push me back from where I was heading.

"So they say. I fucking knew better." The low grumble in my ear tells me not to reply, I don't want to get into an argument over it.

"I hear you, but I'm not sure I can trust anyone else. My head is telling me to get the hell out of here before this goes anywhere, but my body is ignoring every single word I've got going around my brain." I take a breath while Badger sits silent on the other end of the phone. "There's just something about her... She's already under my skin and making me twitch, and it's been less than twenty-four hours."

"Then nothing I say is going to matter, is it?" Already the tone in his voice lets me know he doesn't see the point in pushing me on this.

"I was hoping it would. But..." My mind wanders to the look of fear in her eyes that I desperately want to take away.

"But nothing. What do you need from me? Because Lord knows you're going to need help to get through this alive, with your job still secure and your dick still in one piece."

"I'm not a rookie at this!" I snap, sitting up, his words pissing me off.

"Really, says the guy that has just laid claim to his client and made the most fateful mistake we can make in this job. Tie a knot in that dick before you make this any worse than you already have."

"Fuck, I'm not that stupid," I say, defending myself when I don't need to, but I can't help it.

"Famous last words." His laugh rumbles deep in his chest.

"Whatever!" Trying to tamper down my annoyance, I change the subject.

"So, what's your lazy ass doing these days in retirement?" I know full well there is no way Badger could sit still, even if he tried.

"You did not say the R word to me, did you? I'll be kicking your ass next time I see you." He's old enough he could have taken his military pension combined with the payout from WITSEC and taken life easy. Obviously, it's not an option for him.

"Who, me? Not a chance I said that." My mood settles a little the more we keep talking.

"Good." Pausing a second, he then continues, "A bit of private security work. There's a company that gives some of the military guys, who are either home on leave or just got out, work to keep them occupied. With brains like ours and what we've seen, we can't sit idle. Beauty is, I can take jobs when I feel like it or walk away at any time." Although Badger never talks about it, I know the visions haunt him. His eyes tell you that. The way he keeps a blank demeanor and never shows any emotion. He has learned to block it all out, which can't be healthy, but it's not my life to live.

"Money is probably better too." Not that it would be hard. What we get paid for putting our lives on the line for people we don't even know is a pittance. After all, we are just government public servants.

"You know it, but like it matters to you, Richie Rich." Asshole, he was always going to throw that back at me.

"Should never have told you, smartass."

"What did you call me before, the Wizard? I would have known even if you didn't tell me. I hear and see all." I hear movement in the background of his voice, a woman's whisper.

"Fuck, why didn't you tell me you had company?" I ask, hoping like hell she didn't hear any of the conversation we'd been having.

"Because you needed me, and that always trumps a wet pussy.

And before you panic, I was far enough away, but now, you're boring me. I have a better option standing in front of me."

"Well, far be it from me to stop you from getting your dick some action."

"As long as it's only mine and not yours having all the fun."

"Way to make it shrivel up, knowing you are thinking about my dick. Now go, don't keep your lady waiting." My mind is already drifting off, picturing Cassie asleep across the hall.

"Ghost… think about what I said. Okay?" The concern in his voice comes from years of friendship.

"I will. Thanks, buddy. Talk soon."

"I'm here if you need me, just not for the next hour."

"Like you need more than five minutes. I'm out." Without even giving him time to reply, all I hear as the call disconnects is him laughing.

I sit watching the cameras on my screen, where there is no movement except for a few branches on the trees. My thoughts go back to what he said. I need to try to pull away. I should schedule different agents to come in and out so I'm only here sometimes. I scroll through the database to see who's not on a case currently, and for some reason, I find a problem with each and every one of them.

The only one I trust is Bull, and there is no way I'm pulling him off his leave to cover me. I'm just going to have to keep my head on straight and enough distance that I can still do my job but that's all.

Thoughts are coming to me of how I can fix this and help Cassie at the same time. It's time to get a few things in motion so by tomorrow things can start to change.

I get started searching for everything I'm after. Ordering online for a curbside pickup that I'll send one of my agents to collect in the morning gives me some satisfaction that I have achieved something tonight.

Looking at the time on the screen, I know I should be hitting the pillow for at least a few hours, anyway. I don't need much sleep, which is lucky because in this job you never know what is around the corner. I never allow myself to fall into that deep state where you aren't aware of your surroundings either. I set my phone to alert me if any of the sensors go off.

I strip down out of my clothes and into my gray sweatpants that are comfortable enough to sleep in but also easy enough to move quickly if I need to. My gun under my pillow for quick access, finally my muscles slowly relax into the mattress. Tomorrow is a new day, and I need to go back to being just an agent on the job. Nobody's friend, just the hired protection.

Slowing my breathing is a technique I learned early in my career. When you have limited time to recharge, you need to fall asleep quickly, no time for counting sheep.

The last thing I remember is checking the time and calculating that if it's one am, I only have four hours to sleep, and my alarm will wake me again at five am.

Four hours were gone before I knew it, and the obnoxious chiming on my phone has me sitting up instantly and waking my senses. My alarm is not very loud but one my brain is tuned into. Listening for any noises in the house or across in Cassie's room, silence is all that greets me, which is a good way to start the day.

Light on my feet, I make my way to the bathroom so I can get cleaned up and ready for my morning ritual. I'm used to walking around in the dark, so I don't need lights. I sleep with my curtains partly open, the glow of the moon still peeking through, and the first hint of light from the sunrise is enough for me to get my bearings. Plus, there is the glow of the computers that are always running in my room. They may be password locked, but they're always on and ready to go if I need them.

Opening my door as quietly as I can, there is a small squeak in the hinges. I hope it doesn't wake Cassie, but I don't want to fix that. Having my door with the slightest noise, it's enough to alert me to someone entering during the night.

I step out into the hallway and hold my ear to her door. There's no sound, and I slowly open it just the slightest amount. This time I see her facing the door, curled up in a ball, clinging to the pillow. Her dark hair is sprawled out over the pillow, the green comforter pulled up and covering as far as her waist. I wish I could say she looks at peace while she's sleeping, but her face is far from it. There's a frown on her forehead and tension in her hands that are gripping the pillow so tightly that I can see the whites of her knuckles.

What must it be like to know fear? Where it never leaves you, even in your sleep. I have thought about it over the years as I've worked with different clients, but I never got close enough to my clients for their fear to be felt in my body. Yet standing here, looking at the fear that is consuming Cassie, for the first time I feel it in my soul. It's not fear that I feel but the pain of seeing it in Cassie.

When I closed my eyes last night, I was determined that today things would be all business, yet within ten minutes of being awake, I'm already battling with my inner thoughts.

I can hear Badger in my head telling me I'm already fucked.

I think he could be right, not that I'd admit that to him.

My morning walk around the property and house is complete, coffee drunk, and reports prepared. Now it's time for me to do a bit more digging on our senator in places where WITSEC would tell me not to go. The dark web is the keeper of secrets. It's not for the fainthearted and not somewhere you want to go poking around in unless you know what you're doing and have your anonymity set to the highest level.

I know from the files I was given access to that Cassie discovered a money trail of some sort that is helping the FBI compile evidence of his illegal activities. What those activities are, they won't tell me, because it's my job to protect her and not to investigate. My argument is, how are we supposed to do our job if we don't have the full story of what—or more importantly, *who*—we are up against?

First place for me to start is to work out who is funding the senator's rise to the top. Usually, the financial backers have ulterior motives and are making sure they have a yes-man in the right place for when it comes to votes that will affect their life or business. Or worst case, they use it to bribe the good senator to keep his mouth shut about something, when push comes to shove.

I can guarantee not all his bank accounts will be in the US, either. There will be offshore accounts where he drops his dirty money or keeps the cash for a rainy day that may or may not come. Compiling a list of names of the depositors into his normal accounts doesn't seem to be raising any immediate red flags, but it's early days. Just as importantly, I start to scan the payments he makes to people he has on his books. There seems to be a regular large amount to a charity.

Just as I'm about to start my search into them, I hear the shuffle of Cassie's feet as she gets out of bed. I quickly log out of where I am and store the data I've found; I don't want her to know what I'm doing. She has enough to worry about. Knowing that I'm looking into her life will just make her feel worse than she already does. Although technically, I'm not checking on her, but I will need to search her accounts too, just to make sure she hasn't been used as a pawn in whatever his activities are.

The bathroom door closing gives me the opportunity to get out to the kitchen and start breakfast. I didn't want to just open the door and startle her when she is just waking for the morning. She has already told me she's a coffee person, so I get that started as I pull out the frying pan, ready to make some pancakes and hoping that she'll be happy with that. If not, there is always cereal in the cupboard, and it just means more for me. Whipping up the batter, the noise of the shower going lets me know she is getting herself sorted for the day before she faces me. I don't care if she takes ten showers a day. If that is what she needs to help her relax a little, then I'm all for it. I just don't know how good the hot water is in this old house, so at least seven of those showers might be cold, I would say.

Pouring the third batch into the pan, I watch the batter bubble up and sizzle as it hits the hot melted butter. I can feel her presence at the same time I hear her footsteps.

"Morning." Her morning voice is soft and timid yet still sets off that same sensation in my chest.

"Morning, Cassandra, how did you sleep?" I ask, looking over my shoulder at her taking a seat on one of the kitchen stools.

A small giggle comes from her when I wasn't expecting it.

"Sleep, what is that word you speak of?" Her attempt at smiling even when she has no reason to makes me want to try my hardest to turn it into something she does more often, without so much effort.

"Sorry to hear that," I tell her, flipping the pancake in the pan. "Hopefully it gets better. Now I'm sure you're hungry. I'll feed you and get the coffee."

Her eyes widen at me, I'm not sure why.

Walking over with the plate full of pancakes, I push her cutlery and the maple syrup toward her, and her mouth drops open to say something but then closes, like she thinks better of it.

I'm not sure whether to ask or not but decide to leave it. I just get on with making the coffees.

Watching her play with her food frustrates me. "Eat, Cassandra." I put another piece of pancake into my mouth and watch those eyes zero in on me again.

"Bossy much?" But she starts to cut the first piece on her plate. I might be annoying her, but without realizing it, she is doing as I said anyway.

"You have no idea," I mumble under my breath.

"What?" she quickly snaps at me, glaring as she tries to show she isn't going to take any crap from me.

Good girl, that's what I want, to bring out the fight in you. Stand up and push back, Cassie. You are going to need more than that when it comes to the end of this. I'll make sure no one walks over you again.

"I said you need your strength today. We have work to do." I place my knife and fork on my plate, with not a scrap of food left on it, then lift my mug to my mouth and inhale the beautiful smell of coffee.

"That's not what you said, but okay." She sighs at me. "How can I only be awake ten minutes and you're already pissing me off."

"It's more like twenty minutes." Standing with my plate and

81

taking it to the kitchen, I can see the fire in her building.

Good, it's working.

If I can get her mind off what is happening out in the world and too busy getting annoyed with me, then we are making progress.

Besides, if she wants to kill me, then I'm less likely to be stepping over lines I shouldn't cross.

"I'll meet you out in the yard when you're finished, and we can get started." Without giving her time to ask me anything, I just walk straight out the back door. I can hear her talking or closer to yelling at me as I'm walking away but can't understand the words. I'm pretty sure I don't want too, either.

I laugh under my breath when fifteen minutes later she storms out the door, heading straight for me. Oh, not only did my pushy demands light a match in there but the whole fire is well alight now.

"I'm not here to work or be your slave!" She's still stomping her feet, before finally stopping in front of me where I'm standing at the shed door that I have opened.

Behind me are multiple boxes that should keep us entertained for a few hours.

"Noted. Now let's get these boxes open." Turning my back to her, I take my pocketknife out of the holster on my belt, cutting open the first bit of strapping on the biggest box.

"Did you hear me!" I can't see her, but I can imagine her hands on her hips and the look of death on her face.

"Yep, I'm just ignoring it. You going to help me put together this gym equipment or not?" I ask, smirking to myself as I continue to go from box to box, cutting the strapping.

"Wait, what did you say?" Cassie's voice is a little softer now, and she moves beside me before I can even reply.

"Gym equipment."

Standing up to my full height and flicking the knife closed and back in its holster, I wait for it to really sink in.

"Where did it come from? Like, when… how… this was empty yesterday. I can't…" Having trouble putting it all together, I take pity on her.

"Breathe, Cassandra." I don't want any injuries of her falling before we even start.

Her chest is rising as she takes in what I said.

"I organized it last night after you went to bed, to be delivered by some of my agents first thing this morning." I don't tell her that I purchased it all and didn't even bother to get authorization from the agency. I knew how much it would help her, and that was all I could think about when I was adding everything to the cart online.

"Why?"

"You said to relieve stress you work out. We can't go to the gym, so I brought the gym to you. Simple." Not wanting to let my guard down with her, I start dragging some of the boxes to the side and open the biggest one, which is the treadmill. I pull out the instruction manual that looks as thick as an encyclopedia.

"Ugghhh. You any good at reading instructions?" I push the book into her hands, trying to jolt her out of the stunned state, as she is still standing there. I don't want her to ask too many questions, just accept it and move on.

"Cassandra, what's step one?" I ask, a little louder and rougher than needed. She blinks, and then she quickly flips through the first few pages.

"Shit, where are the ones in English?" Fumbling and turning the book over, I watch as her frown lines on her forehead get bigger and she starts playing with the piece of hair that has fallen out of her ponytail, twirling it around and around her finger. Like a nervous habit.

It's hot as hell watching her trying to concentrate, not wanting to disappoint me with getting it wrong.

"Should we worry when the first line says to get a cold drink and sit down, this could take a while?"

For all the tension I'm trying to keep in, I can't help but burst out laughing at her comment. "Oh, for fuck's sake, this doesn't sound like it's going to be fun."

"Chicken, I'm the flat-pack queen from my college days. How much harder can this be? Let's get moving. You need parts A, B, and the two bolts marked number one," she instructs, looking up at me from the novel in her hands. "Chop, chop, you're wasting time."

Hang on a hot minute. How did the boss role flip so quickly to me being the boy and her the boss and cracking the whip?

Stop, rewind, that is not an image I want to be thinking about. It would never float with me. Come to think of it, whips aren't my thing either. Role play, sure, but not pain. I can't even imagine hurting one hair on her beautiful brown head.

Reaching into the box and pulling out the first few pieces, I try not to smile at the way she is now focused so hard on the words in front of her. Exactly as I was hoping. Distraction 101 has begun.

———————

"How the hell can they make something so simple, so fucking complicated!" I'm trying to pull the wire through the arm of the machine to stretch that extra inch needed to connect to the control panel as it should. "This thing is ridiculous! Three hours. Three goddamn hours, and we get to this where they make the part too short! Probably to save money or some bullshit like that. Ughhh." I want to kick something but instead bury my frustration as low as I can.

"Oh, don't tell me the perfect Ghost who can't be rattled has been beaten by a mere treadmill. The shock of it all," she says with a gasp, putting her hand over her mouth to fake her disbelief.

"Not funny, Cassandra," I grumble as I succumb to the fact that I'm going to have to pull this apart to fix it.

Her laugh, not just a shallow one, but that deep-in-your-gut laugh, tells me that she thinks this is more than a little funny. For all the frustration, that sound coming from her makes it worthwhile.

"I beg to differ, I think it's hilarious, that look on your face." As she bends forward and really lets go, I can't help but join her.

My laughter escaping, and the annoyance slips away for a moment.

It feels good to really laugh. I can't remember the last time I chuckled at something so stupid. I mean, it was probably something Bull did, but this feels different, to let my guard down for just a moment with Cassie.

Here I am trying to be the asshole so she doesn't like me, and yet her beautiful nature has me showing her part of myself I don't share often.

"Okay, enough of laughing at my expense," I say, pulling myself together again. "Let's get this bastard of a thing finished so we can eat. I'm going to need food before I attempt the next equipment. Let me assure you, you don't want to see this man hangry as well as frustrated."

My attention back on the machine, I hear her voice barely above a whisper. "There is another type of frustration that might be nice."

I know I can't look up and let her see my face now that I'm thinking the same thing. Little does she know my sexual frustration has already arrived, and I'm trying my hardest to make sure it's not seen. Please don't make it harder than it already is, Cassie— literally!

Concentrate on the task at hand, Ghost. Don't even let your mind go there.

Before I could get much further with trying to sort out this night-mare, my phone buzzing in my pocket is a welcome distraction.

Control: *Client's partner has discovered her missing. Stay vigilant. He has not been taken into custody yet but will happen today as soon as they get the warrant signed off.*

Ghost: *Roger that.*

Things are happening quicker than expected. Now the real fun and games begin.

Bring it, Senator, time to pay for your crimes.

Looking up at Cassie who is now staring at me and wondering what is going on, I know that this job is becoming harder than any other before it. All because of those eyes that suck me in every time I look into them.

Even in times of uncertainty, she is still my bright eyes.

I'm done for!

Chapter Seven

CASSIE

How is it this man can make me feel rage and then have me laughing deeper than I have in a long time?

He confuses me but not in a bad way, I'm just intrigued. There are layers there that need to be peeled back, and for some reason, I want to start scratching that first one off and dig below the surface. There is more to Ghost than he lets people see, that I'm sure of.

I wanted to ask what the text message he received earlier was, but I'm not game. I'm not sure he would even tell me if I did, but whatever it was, it changed the expression on his face instantly. I'm guessing it wasn't a favorable message. Not that he gave anything away, as he just went straight back to the job at hand.

The day has been taken up with creating a mini gym. Finally, after many hours of cursing, skinning of knuckles, trying to either undo or do up screws in ridiculously small spaces, the darkness of night is creeping in.

I tried to get Ghost talking, but he was more interested in trying to know more about me and my life. Thankfully, he wasn't asking about my last couple of years, but instead, he wanted to know childhood memories and what I got up to in college. I'm sure he was thinking those stories would be more exciting than they are. Not having much money, I tended to stay home and study or just watch TV. It was enough for me. I just wanted to get to the end of my degree and not have wasted my time or money. I was just trying to set up a career by getting the best grades I could, so I would make a good impression when the time came.

Finally standing in the shower trying to wash off the dirt and grime of the day, it occurred to me that I hadn't really thought about my current situation all day. My muscles now aching from all the holding of things and lifting equipment into place, I'm ready to get started tomorrow and get the adrenaline pumping for a good reason.

The showerhead sucks in this old house, but at least the water is hot and there seems to be plenty of it.

After we grilled some steaks, served with salad, and cleaned up after dinner, Ghost headed back into his office, offering me the first shower. I still can't get a read on him, but at least by the end of today, I'm starting to think I might be able to manage to co-exist in this house with him, for however long I need to.

Who knows, we may even manage to become friends. Well, until the next time he pisses me off, that is.

I underestimated the energy I used today and how a hot shower has finally taken some of the tension out of my shoulders. Ever since I was in high school, any stress I was carrying always landed in my neck and shoulders. Every muscle locked tight, which ends up in relentless headaches. It hasn't come to that, but I was probably borderline with all that has happened in the last few weeks. Today's hard work and the heat of the water has certainly helped. So much better than the tiredness I would feel from having to attend the events with Jason. Trying to be switched on all the time and with my smile plastered to my face is so draining. I don't want to think of those nights anymore. I'll never be back there again.

Sleep hasn't been my best friend lately, but lying my head down on this pillow tonight doesn't seem to scare me as much. Hearing the clicking of the keyboard in the other room is becoming like a lullaby and the security I feel having Ghost close by all the time. I have no idea what he's doing, but I know whatever it is, it's to help me, and for that I'm grateful.

My eyelids are heavy, and the pull of sleep is taking me under. As I feel my breathing slowing down, it's a relief that tonight I get to rest…

I wish I felt more comfortable in this green dress, it's just not my color. Not that I ever get a choice in what I want to wear to these functions. I don't even get the courtesy of the phone call. It's usually an email or text message telling me what to wear, where we're going, and what time the town car will be picking me up. On the rare occasion I actually get asked if it fits with my schedule, but I'm guessing it's when the secretary isn't actually the one writing it. Someone else, maybe an office junior who is doing her work for her and has manners, but to Camilla, I'm just someone she has to tolerate in the grand scheme of things.

"You look lovely tonight," Jason comments as I slide into the back seat of the car. He isn't even looking at me as he says it. I have a feeling it's more like something he feels he's expected to say in front of the driver.

"Thank you." I smooth the satin of the skirt down so I don't end up with wrinkles in it before we even make it the function.

"Who will be there tonight?" I ask, trying to get Jason to pull his head out of his tablet that he is reading, which is nothing unusual. I get that he needs to work, but it didn't used to be like this. When we first met, these nights out were exciting, and I had his full attention from the time he would pick me up at the door. The flirting in the car was light but enough to let me feel a little racy and that later that night, things would get heated. He wasn't ever very adventurous, but it was pleasant. Since I hadn't been with many men before him, I just assumed this is what it was all about. The movies and books just made it sound better than it actually was, just to sell the story. Life was good, and I was happy.

These days it feels more like a chore, and my head is telling me I need to start thinking about if this is what I really want. It's a safe choice, comfortable, and I don't need to struggle. Living in his home and being provided for was not what I wanted, but he insisted that it's what a man does, he takes care of his girlfriend. I thought that was sweet and was something that I longed for. After losing my parents, I felt alone, with no one in this world looking out for me. So, to hear that he wanted to take care of me was a big relief. The mistake I made was that he wasn't taking care of me, this was more ownership. I pay for you, so you owe me, or in other words, you work for me without you knowing you do.

"The usual people, plus a few more," Jason mumbles at me. "I need you to do the normal routine, stay close, smile, and don't interrupt."

Seeing the eyes of the driver in the mirror, I can tell he's thinking the same as I am. What an asshole.

"Mhmm," is all I can be bothered to reply. I turn and look out the window of the car as all the city lights are racing past because I don't want the driver to see the sadness in my eyes. While my mind is screaming, "What the actual fuck did you just say to me! When did I let you become such a rude prick to me?"

I wanted to tell him to stick it up his pompous ass, but it's not even worth it. When I spoke to my friend Michelle at work, she told me I was foolish to put up with that. I know it in my head, but taking that leap of telling Jason I want out of the relationship, I need to work up the courage for that. He has the power to be able to destroy my career in this town. Not that I would have done anything wrong, but he is the man they all love and trust. More fool them.

Pulling up to the entrance, the valet opens the door for me, and I know there is no point waiting for Jason's hand to help me out.

I stand, making sure everything looks perfect as expected, but something in my gut is twitching tonight. I don't know what it is that has me feeling out of sorts. Maybe it's just knowing that my time here is ending. I'll start looking for a new place to rent. I only need something small, which hopefully won't be too expensive.

It's been at least an hour since we arrived, and it's been the same old, same old conversation.

"Oh, you are doing an amazing job, Senator, thank you for the money, Senator," or the main one, "Can I donate to your campaign, Senator?" closely followed with, "By the way, I could use your help with this situation, blah, blah, blah."

I excuse myself, needing some breathing space. I can feel my neck and shoulders tensing up, and the usual headache that follows is simmering just under the surface. After visiting the ladies' room, I slip out a side door. The spring weather is perfect tonight. Not too cold or too warm, so standing here in a quiet secluded garden in a strapless dress is actually quite comfortable. Looking up, the moon is full, and although I'm sure the stars are there, being in Washington you can't quite see them as clearly as you would expect. The smog of the city and its bright lights ruin any chance of that. I walk farther down into the garden to see what is behind the hedge, and as I walk around the back of it, a cute wooden seat is sitting in the secret section.

I'll deal with the complaining later that I disappeared for too long. Sitting down on the edge of the bench so as not to risk dirtying my dress, I take a deep breath and feel like I'm finally breathing for the first time tonight.

Not sure how long I've been sitting here, my silence is broken as I hear the noise from inside filtering out through the door opening again. Not wanting to make myself known, I sit as quiet as I can. Hopefully it's just someone outside for a smoke and they will leave as quick as they came.

"Did you get Loretti on board? Not that he had much choice. The boss has enough on him to make him do what we need anyway." Ugghh, I'd know that voice anywhere. Even if she isn't talking loudly, I can still pick it out. Camilla has this distinct pitch to her voice that grates on my nerves, or maybe it's just because I can't stand her that she irritates me more than most people.

"Of course. He knew that he had backed himself into a corner. He will produce the goods by Monday." I don't know who the male voice is, but he sounds a little gruff for my liking.

"Excellent, that will make the boss happy." Camilla has a bit of relief in her voice about something.

"Let me worry about the boss in the boardroom, and you continue to keep him happy in your room."

Her laugh breaks out as I hold my breath, contemplating what was said. Surely, he didn't mean what it sounded like. I mean, I have my suspicions, but I don't want to believe it. It'd just be too cliché, the senator having an affair with his assistant. Jason might be a lot of things, but he isn't stupid, is he? That could hurt his career if it ever got out.

"I look after him exceptionally well, don't you worry. We just need to get the job done. The more dollars we can get in it, the more it feeds the other side of things that he is gaining traction in." Why do they seem to be talking in riddles about whatever this is. It's obvious they are talking about Jason, but I just can't help but think that not everything is as it seems.

"Oh, got to go, he's messaging me now. The dumb bimbo that he keeps

hanging off his arm is missing. Not that I understand why he keeps her around. I satisfy that man in my bedroom as well as the office, so she is just a waste of space. But of course, now I need to find her. Like I'm her fucking babysitter. I couldn't care less if she fell off a cliff."

"Duty calls. Better run along now." Both of them laugh as I hear the party noise wafting back outside as they must be opening the door again.

My silence returns, and I'm left sitting here wondering what the hell that was all about, and as much as I hate to admit it, I feel stupid. I've been suspecting it for a while, that Jason is sleeping with Camilla, and as stupid as that would be, it sounds awfully like it's happening and has been for a while now. Trying not to get upset, it explains a lot. Well, I guess I know why he is never interested in sex with me when he is getting his fill somewhere else. Or should I say, he is filling someone else. I guess one thing is certain, it's time for me to move on. If he doesn't want me, then I'll find a man who does. One who treats me like I deserve.

Standing and trying to plaster that fake smile back on, my mind is replaying the other words they were saying as I head back inside. The part about me was obvious, but the rest didn't sound great to me, although I have no idea what it was, it just had a dirty tinge to it. There have been a few things that haven't made sense lately. Like the step up in security around me and the house. Phone calls and hushed voices in the middle of the night. Last-minute trips that have been happening more frequently. I was just putting it all down to part of the campaign and things I didn't need to worry about. But looking back, maybe I should've been paying more attention.

Knowing I can't stand out here any longer, I take a deep breath and enter the building again and make my way to the room.

Casually walking toward Jason on the other side of the room, I see Camilla making a straight line for me with haste.

"Where have you been, Leah?" Ignoring her, I just keep walking. "You know you can't just disappear for half the night." Who is she kidding? I was gone for thirty minutes at the most.

"Fuck off, Camilla," I hiss at her, and it has her stopping dead in her tracks. Her mouth opens and no words come out. It's the first time I've ever spoken to her like that, and I guarantee it won't be the last. I'm not going to sit back and take all this shit. As angry as I am, my mind is still trying to work out what she was

talking about back in the garden. One thing I do know, though, it didn't sound great.

"I'm leaving, I don't feel well," I spit at Jason before he even has time to open his mouth.

"Leah." The tone in his voice tells me he is pissed, like I give a fuck.

Walking toward the door, I hear my name being called again in Camilla's high-pitched voice, but I just keep walking. I can hear her heels clattering on the floor as she tries to keep up. Of course, he has sent his lap dog to follow me.

Reaching the doorman, I'm sure he can tell by the look on my face and the way I'm walking that I need his help.

"Taxi, madam?"

"Please and quickly." Nodding, he opens the door and raises his hand. Before I even have time to think, a taxi is pulling up in front of me and he is opening the car door for me. Sliding into the back seat as Camilla bursts through the outside doors, I just smile at her and wave as the door slams, and we pull away from the building.

I can feel my bag vibrating against my thigh. My phone is blowing up, and it's either Jason or Camilla or both. Ignoring them feels like a win in an argument they don't even know we're having. I don't even care and can't be bothered to give them any clue.

Just staring aimlessly out the window, my mind is racing, and when I made up the excuse to Jason of being sick, I think I just preempted what was about to happen. My stomach is rolling, and the closer we get to the apartment, the more I feel like I'm about to vomit.

Quickly tapping my card to pay, I'm out the door and up the front steps. Pushing my key into the lock and trying to get the door open. Tears are building at the same time, and my body is about to break down.

What a sight I must be. On the bathroom floor in my satin gown, right next to the toilet bowl, I lose anything I ate today into it.

I'm just shattered.

My life is unraveling around me.

I can't see him, not tonight. Sliding my phone out of my bag that's lying on the floor beside me, I unlock it, making sure I'm not looking at any of the words. I do a voice-to-text message to Jason that he should stay away tonight. I could be contagious, and he doesn't want to catch this.

Then I shut down my phone, not waiting for any reply.

I'm not sure how long I've been sitting here, but my ass is now numb and telling me to move. Pulling myself up on the vanity, the picture of the woman in the mirror is not appealing. There are black streaks down my cheeks and my lipstick is missing. The tears have been falling for a while, and the makeup is now all over my face, making me look like a horror show character.

Fuck you, Jason. Fuck you!

Waking slowly, I hope I'm not back living in the nightmare and that everything from the last two days that has happened is instead the dream. But the stale musty smell that awakens my senses tells me that's not the case. I'm in the house with Ghost, and that is a bigger sense of relief than what I was expecting it to be.

Time to get on with it. No going back now. Forwards is the only option, one day at a time.

Pushing aside all the anxiety that constantly sits with me, I've managed to survive the first few weeks of living in the house with Ghost. I hadn't realized how much I needed to keep using up physical energy every day to keep my sanity. But I know deep down that Ghost saw it that first night we spoke and made sure he made it possible for me to be able to train as hard as I needed on the equipment he arranged. I spend most days working out at least twice a day. Sometimes with Ghost and other times on my own. With music playing in the background, I can manage to lose myself in the repetitive nature of the exercises or running on the treadmill and forget about my life outside of this house. Not sure I needed to drop any weight, but it's happening naturally, between the stress and the extra exercise.

I keep expecting Ghost to tell me to back off, but it hasn't happened yet. Training becomes a bit of an obsession. And when I'm not working out, then I spend my time cooking for us because I can't be idle. I have even gone so far as begging Ghost to get some paint delivered and let me start painting this dreary house. His laughter told me I was crazy and it's not happening, that it's someone else's problem.

We have fallen into a good rhythm where I could almost say we're friends. If I'm honest with myself, what I'm feeling for him is more than what a friend should be feeling. I've just come out of a toxic relationship, yet I'm developing tenderness for a man that I have no right to be even looking at in that way. Although, every time I get a little close to him, he backs away and the distance is back with a wall between us. After getting him to admit in one of our late-night chats that he's single, I can totally see why that is. He is so hard to read. His mixed signals confuse me most days, but there is still that dominant part of his character that I can't seem to turn my hormones off to. I just wish he would use that voice on me to tell me to do more than eat or getting me to stop overthinking something.

Last night when Ghost was telling me that they have arrested Jason and he's been in custody for over a week awaiting his initial hearing, I felt numb for a small moment. Every word he spoke was bittersweet. I was feeling like all this was worth it, but then the realization hit me that my life just got so much more dangerous. Now he will be piecing things together, that me disappearing has something to do with his arrest. It's too coincidental not to be connected. I have put a target on myself, which I knew would happen, but once Ghost delivered the news, reality sank in that he will already be using his connections to try to find me.

My bravado didn't last long. We had just sat down to eat, and I couldn't even stomach a mouthful until that voice across the table ordered me to eat. The panic that was building inside me had me snapping at him, telling him what I thought of his orders and how high-handed he is, standing and screaming at him like a possessed woman.

Before I knew it, he was up out of his seat and wrapping me in his arms. I was bashing at his chest with my fists, taking out every fear that was racing through my body on him.

Taking it all, he just held me tight until all the fight left my body, and tears followed straight behind the aggression. Collapsing into him and sobbing, my body shook with the outpouring of all that I've been holding inside me on a daily basis. I tried to stay strong, but last night, I failed miserably.

Walking me to the couch, we sat there in silence for a long time. The feeling of having his strong arm around my shoulders, my head resting on his chest was the safest I have felt in a very long time. Even before my life started to unravel, I don't think Jason ever made me feel as secure as Ghost did in that moment last night. But the more I relaxed into his body, suddenly the stiffer he became. The change in him was so noticeable that I pulled away. I looked at him, trying to get some reaction, but instead, his non-reaction was even worse. I don't want to be that stupid woman who starts falling for someone who is just being kind because it's his job. And the way he is so hot and cold with me, I know that's all I can be to him.

Another client, another job.

Needing to keep me calm, he just used his body to stop me from losing my mind, but that's all it was to him. A means to an end, a way to calm me down.

Lying in bed last night, I couldn't get the feeling of being in his arms out of my head. For that small moment, I know I felt something more from him. He might not want to feel it and thought he hid it well enough as he shut it down, but it was there, I'm sure of it. I'll let him pretend all he likes, and I'll try to make sure it's not just my imagination, but I'm not letting that fleeting moment go in a hurry.

This morning, his mood tells me that something is bothering him. Or he didn't get much sleep either. One way or the other, his single-word grunts are pissing me off. Since I walked out of my room in my workout gear that he bought online and had shipped to the house for me, he hasn't looked me in the eyes once. Instead, he's just ordering me out to start our circuit, like he needs the release from exercise more than I did.

Standing in the shed this morning, staring across at him pulling himself up and down on the chin-up bar, I can see the strain on his face. I've watched him do this every day, yet today, the strain looks like it is more than just from hauling his masculine body up in the air.

Dropping to the ground, his eyes zero in on me.

"What are you staring at?" The grumpy attitude is back in his voice this morning.

"You." I'm not ashamed to let him know.

"Don't go there," he growls at me as he grabs his towel and storms past me out of the shed.

Watching him retreat to the house, I can't help it. I shout after him, "No point in telling me, since you won't." I smile like I got one up on him.

All I can hear is grumbling under his breath as he storms up the back stairs of the house and disappears inside.

"Yeah, go and cool off under the shower. Wash the grumpy Ghost off while you're at it."

I don't know if the testy mood is because of me or something he knows about my case that I don't. Standing here for a few minutes, my temper just keeps building. I'm sick of being kept in the dark about things, so I'm not prepared to let it go.

I storm off after him into the house, but just as I'm about to tackle him on his shortness with me, I hear the bathroom door slam a little louder than normal and the water start running. Damn it, I was too slow.

Getting my back up, I decide he isn't getting out of this. I'll just sit here and wait him out.

Sitting down with my back against the wall opposite the door to the shower, my mind keeps running over the tenderness he shared last night. Why can't he just let me see that side of him? Why is he so scared to let the shield down that he constantly keeps putting back up between us every time it falls even slightly? I remember he told me on day one that we could do this the easy way or the hard way. I chose easy, but he forgot to tell me he chose hard.

With the minutes ticking away, the urge to pick a fight with him dissipates as fast as my temper flared. With the pent-up emotions leaving my body, I start to panic and push off the wall to get away from here before he discovers me stupidly outside the door like some crazy woman. Noises from behind the door catch my attention before I turn to leave.

Hearing his voice over top of the shower, I know he has no idea I'm here, thinking I'm still outside working out.

My body is reacting to every sound I'm hearing of his breathing getting louder and slightly more rapid.

"Oh fuck." The low rumble gives my imagination all it needs to start running wild. Closing my eyes and my head falling back against the wall, I can picture his hand around his cock. Squeezing just hard enough to bring relief as it starts sliding up and down toward the head that I'm sure is leaking by this stage. Those breaths becoming raspier by the second and the word fuck coming quicker and louder each time he lets it out, until the final one.

"Fuc...ccc...kkk..." growls out from Ghost, and I can feel my body shuddering at the thought of him coming behind the door in the very same shower I stand in every day, dreaming about him joining me in it. Then a voice not so deep and more like a plea for help confirms my thoughts from last night.

"Fuck, Cassie. Shit." Then what sounds like the palm of his hand hitting the tiled wall in frustration, and I know I need to move. He can't know I heard any of what just happened.

Moving my feet as quietly but quickly as I can, I'm out the back door and back into the shed. Pushing the speed on the treadmill up high, I run like I'm nearing the finish line of a marathon, for more reasons than one. I need to look like I've been sweating out here since he left, and the other reason is I'm chasing that high of the orgasm I wanted to feel when I listened to Ghost take the relief I need right now.

Hearing my name on his lips like that makes me want more.

Cassie. He's never called me that, but I want it.

I want to be his Cassie.

How the hell do I get him to stop denying what he wants when it is right in front of him?

Me!

Chapter Eight

GHOST

With my forehead leaning against the shower wall, I'm trying to get my breathing under control.

That woman out there is going to kill me in a slow painful death. Truly!

I can't believe I just stood here and jerked off to her, harder than I have ever come by my own hand in my life.

She has some pull over me, and I don't know how to keep pushing her away, except to act like an asshole to her, which hurts me just as much as I see the hurt I put in her eyes.

Badger's words play in my head like a broken record all day and night, but it's not helping. I think I need to get out of here for a few hours and get some perspective. I wish that was possible, but I'm too much of a control freak to trust anyone to watch Cassie while I'm away.

Shutting off the water, I slam my hand against the tiles again in pure frustration. I wish the training would do for me what is does for Cassie, taking my mind off things. Instead, it just fuels my adrenaline, and seeing her in those skimpy fitted outfits, my cock is screaming at me that he wants to work out too. I can't be near her today, I know that for sure. Once again, I'll be needing to make an excuse that I need to work on the computer and shut myself away inside my office while she fills her time. Watching her on the cameras like a creeper, justifying that it's my job, when really, it's my feelings for her that have my protective control issues making me act irrationally at times.

Last night, watching her break down at the thought of what her life is about to become almost had me giving into her body language. I'd have to be blind not to know what she's feeling. Because it's like looking into a mirror. The difference is she's coming closer, and all I'm trying to do is back away. For her safety more than my sanity.

Knowing how much my news last night rattled her, I don't want to tell her everything I've discovered, on top of what she told the FBI, which is only scratching the surface of darkness in relation to her monster of an ex-boyfriend. There is no guarantee that when I finally come face to face with him that I won't kill him.

Cassie thinks that Jason is just selling government secrets to the highest bidder and doing something bad involving women, based on the photos she saw, but it goes so much deeper than that. He has been undermining the national security of our country for a few years. And some of the payments for these vitally important pieces of information, he received cash as well as women. Yes, the bastard is not only making money from putting his own soldiers at risk in foreign countries but is involved in the disgusting act of inflicting atrocities on innocent women and young girls. I know it's not my role to solve this case, and people far better at it than me are onto this, but I can't help but want to make sure he pays for all he has done and is continuing to orchestrate from behind bars, I'm sure, all while proclaiming his innocence to every person and media outlet that will listen.

What makes my body radiate with all the emotions possible is not just the anger at Jason, but instead, knowing how much danger Cassie is really in. This guy has money and people in very high places on his payroll. To be honest, the more I find, the more I'm starting to wonder who I can even trust in WITSEC. I wouldn't put it past him to have someone on the inside here, which means we are vulnerable.

And that fucking pisses me off!

Dressed and opening the back door, I yell out to Cassie that I'll be in my office, when I see her running on the treadmill like she's being chased. The shirt she's wearing is wet from sweat. God, I wish I could take away her stress, instead of her having to run it out of her system every day.

Her hand reaches in the air to acknowledge she heard me, but she doesn't even turn to look at me. Great, I did my job this morning and pissed her off enough that she has her fight right at the surface.

She's ready to take on the world with her anger.

The world… or maybe just me!

Working most of the day, I heard Cassie taking a shower, and I kept an eye on her as she went about her normal routine, cooking, watching *Friends*, a bit of drawing which has become a secret hobby. She doesn't show me any of her sketches, but I see her spending time engrossed in her work and then hiding it as I enter the room. I don't want to push her, and there isn't much of her life that is just hers anymore, so I want her to at least have her dreams.

I hear Cassie's voice through the door calling me to dinner. It smells amazing, and after the day I've had reading and seeing absolutely vile things, I need to see her.

My bright eyes.

No matter what the world throws at her, it can't seem to dampen the fire in her soul. Her anger might make it burn brighter, but nothing seems to be able to extinguish those flames.

One day I hope I can be her fuel for her fire.

Because I'm just about at the end of my restraint for doing what sounds like the right thing.

The burn of her eyes that ignites inside me, it can't be so wrong!

I just know it can't.

CASSIE

All day I have been trying to think of the perfect plan to get Ghost to talk to me. Not just polite dinner conversation but really talk to me. Open up and let me discover the real him.

He confuses me and intrigues me at the same time, but one thing never wavers. The intense sexual chemistry he exudes. He can try to hide it all he likes, but I see it in his face, the pain of pushing it aside every time I get that little bit closer to him.

My world has been turned upside down, and I don't know who I am or where I might be tomorrow. But the one thing I know for certain is that if I don't do something about the intense feelings that have building inside me, then I may regret it for the rest of my life, however long that may be.

"Smells good out here, as usual." His voice echoes in the quiet of the room as he walks up behind me in the kitchen where I am about to pick up our plates to carry them to the table. "Can I help carry those?" I feel him entering my personal space, my body vibrating uncontrollably as I spin around to face him.

Our bodies are mere inches apart, and I know it's now or never. I press up onto my toes so my face is almost level with his.

His lips are so close I can almost taste them, my eyes fluttering as I lean into him, but all of a sudden, he's pulling back. Stepping a few feet away, his face looks tortured as his fists are clenched by his sides.

His movement shocks me and my words just slip out. "Why won't you kiss me?" I feel like every bit of air is being sucked out of the room from the tension between us.

He groans and grabs the back of his neck, and I can see that he's on the edge of his restraint.

"Cassie." The roughness of his voice tells me he needs me to stop, but I'm done stopping. I know what I want and so does he. But the man standing in front of me is wrestling with himself. The agent in him is trying to do the right thing and not get involved with me in a way that goes against everything he originally took an oath for. I can see the man that I'm falling for clawing at the edge of the cliff, trying not to let go and take that jump.

"Why do you call me that… Cassie?" I whisper.

"Because that's who you are to me!" His growl comes out like he has no control in replying.

"Tell me who you are to me," I ask, pleading that he knows what I mean.

"Noah, my name is Noah." I can see the emotion behind his answer.

"Then tell me why you won't kiss me." I need him to say it.

"Cassie!" The frustration he feels at me pushing him is in every letter of my name.

It's time to push him over the neat line he's trying to keep his feet firmly planted on the safe side of.

"That's not an answer. Noah…" Tentatively stepping the last few feet to him, his real name slipping off my tongue, I see the moment the restraint cracks.

"Because once I do… I know I'll never be able to stop!" The creases on his forehead deepen, straining with control as he tries to stop from snapping.

His words are music to my ears. Because I know, once he touches me, I'll be lost in him, and I'm not sure I will ever want to find my way out.

"Noah, please…" I'm almost begging him.

"Fuck it. You're mine!" he grits out, finally cracking, losing all his restraint.

The hand that was gripping his neck so tightly reaches out now and takes me by the back of my neck. No tenderness, there is too much heat between us for that.

His lips crash into mine with a force that I feel like I'm being claimed in the only way he knows how, with every single emotion that has been swimming around us for days.

It's exactly like I've been dreaming, his lips rough and smooth at the same time, his tongue looking for more from me. His fingers slide up into my hair, and I can't help the whimper that has my mouth opening just like he wants. It's like he is playing my body to dance to his tune, and I'm happily following every note.

Our tongues are tangling, and it's like the electricity that we have been trying to turn off is now running directly between us. I wrap my arms around his bare back, and it finally feels like my hands are touching the forbidden land, running up and over the mountains and valleys of his muscles.

The harder he kisses me, the tighter I grip his body. My nails are now digging into his skin. I feel my back hit the wall behind me.

His lips breaking from mine, I gasp for that first breath of fresh air.

But before I have time to tame my breathing, I feel his tongue tracing down my neck, taking the softest kiss on my skin at the base. He uses his knee to push my legs apart, not asking but taking possession of me. Straddling his thick thigh, the pressure is on my sex, and there is no way I can contain the moan that slips from me.

I'm dripping from the kiss alone, but as he starts to rub his leg up and down, I can't contain it anymore.

"Tell me to stop, Cassie. Tell me to goddamn stop!"

It's like he needs me to be the one to do the right thing, but I'm done with that. For once, I want to do what I want, no matter how bad it is. Sometimes you just want to be the bad girl.

"No. Fucking. Way!" I drop a hand to his ass and squeeze what feels like pure muscle. Tense, firm, and all sorts of perfect.

"I want this. I want you," I whisper breathlessly in his ear as he's devouring my neck. "All of you."

"Then you're going to get every single inch of me," he says, his voice raspy and almost like he is struggling for air as much as I am.

Everything is moving at speed. He has my ass in his hands, and I'm up with my legs around his waist. Moving us through the room toward the hallway, he doesn't stop consuming the skin on my neck for even one moment. He walks straight into my bedroom, stopping at the end of my bed. I slowly let my legs fall toward the ground as he lowers me back down.

Noah takes my cheek in his hand, slowly stroking it with his thumb.

He's trying to slow this down, but we both know he's fighting a losing battle.

"You need to be sure, bright eyes." The strain in his words is like he's in pain waiting for my answer. That name makes my heart, that is already racing, flutter at the endearment.

"Noah," I say, which earns me a tortured growl. "I've never been surer of anything in my entire life."

Standing onto my toes this time, it's me who takes his mouth like my life depends on it. I'm desperate for this man and have been since that first day. I've never felt like this about anyone before. Not this strong yearning need that I haven't known what to do with until this moment. Where I know there is no going back.

I don't want to stop.

"Make me yours." My words aren't much more than a whisper, and I lower back down off my toes on to my feet.

My fingers fumble with the buttons on my shirt, trying to undo the first one.

"Stop." I freeze at his stern word. "I get to unwrap you." His strong hands brush mine away. "I've been waiting to see what is hidden under these clothes for so long." The ferocity of the kisses has slowed into a sensual dance between our eyes. Noah doesn't look anywhere except directly into my soul while he slowly opens my shirt and lets it slide from my shoulders.

His gaze burns my skin as it trails down to see my body for the first time. His hand follows closely, down the sides of my chest. He then trails his finger with softness up the middle of my stomach and between my breasts. Goosebumps follow his trail, and I'm already trying not to shiver at every touch. He leans down to plant his lips on my chest just above my cleavage. The intimate touch almost takes my legs out from under me.

As he continues to kiss almost every inch of skin across my bare chest so softly, I want more. More of everything I think he is holding back on.

Slipping my hands behind me, flicking the clasp on my bra, the straps start to fall down my arms. The fabric loosens from over my breasts immediately.

Hearing the raspy growl, I know I have woken the desperate beast again. His hands move from my waist and pull my bra swiftly off, dropping it at his feet. He steps back one step and just stares. The intensity of it sends a shiver through my whole body.

"Perfect." The word falls from his lips, like he's in his own world. We're both standing here shirtless, transfixed on what we see. But seeing is only half of what I want. Touching is what I've longed for.

Like he can read my mind, he leans forward, and his mouth comes down, taking my aroused hard nipple into his mouth while he wraps his hands around both breasts and squeezes with just the right amount of pressure. I can't help the gasp that comes from my mouth as he finally starts to devour me. He now reaches his strong arm behind me and pulls me toward him.

My head falls back as I'm gasping for air. The sensations that are rushing through me as Noah devours me. My brain is on overload, and I can't even imagine how I'm going to cope as he touches me lower.

Fumbling with my hands on his waist, I want to get his pants off quickly. The dominating feeling on my body that I've longed for for so long is sending me soaring already. With his button on his cargo pants open, and as I'm pulling the zipper down, I feel the vibration on my chest as he moans from my hand brushing over his cock. Dragging back up over the rock-hard cock with my fingers, Noah pulls back, and the look in his eyes is one of absolute sexual frustration.

"Bed. Now!" Which has me scrambling backwards over the bed, while I feel like his stare could make me combust if he doesn't look away.

Crawling over top of me, he's on the prowl, seeking out his next meal, and that's obviously me.

"Were you trying to get me naked?" Gently, his fingers sweep my stray hair behind my ear.

All I can do is be honest. "Yes."

"Well, two can play at this game. Pants off now." He takes another panty-melting kiss before he crawls back down the bed, laying more kisses on my body as he goes. His hands make quick work of my pants. Feeling the fresh air around my sex, I should be embarrassed, but I'm too aroused to even worry. I just want him to start exploring me, make my body sing.

"Arms above your head and hold on." The stern instruction excites me, but not as much as the total exhilaration at the sight of Noah completely naked standing in front of me.

I mean, I have been dreaming about what he would look like. Dirty, wicked dreams, but nothing compares to the man who is taking my breath away.

His cock is standing up and jutting out. Already I can see the precum leaking from the engorged tip. Long and thick, with his veins running along his cock, I know he's ready. We have both been fighting this attraction from the beginning, which is now leading us into a desperate frenzy.

"Do you trust me?" he asks, slowly running his fist down his cock as I whimper. My legs fall open wide onto the mattress in anticipation.

"Always." And that is God's honest truth.

"I'm clean, Cassie, and I know you're on the pill. I don't have any protection with me. Because you, my beautiful bright eyes, were not expected." I look up from watching his hand to see the question he's asking of me.

I'm too far gone to stop but my brain is still in the place where I know his honesty means the world to me. When we first started to open up, I told him that I can't do secrets and lies anymore. It broke me finding out my life was a lie.

"Noah… fuck me." My voice is shaky with how turned on my body is, watching the Adonis in front of me.

"Oh, I'm about to, and it won't be soft and sensual like you deserve. There's time for that later. Tonight, it'll be hard, dirty, and fast. I'm only a man, and you have me barely hanging on." He runs his hands up the insides of my legs as he starts coming toward me again. Watching his face and the passion written all over it, I know I'm about to get totally owned.

At the last minute, as his face is level with my sex, he leans down and swipes his tongue up between my folds. My hips jump up off the bed into his mouth.

"Oh, fuck!" is all I can say. I wasn't expecting it, but God, I want more, so much more.

"Mmmm, so sweet, bright eyes. I'm going to enjoy this." Before I can take time to say a word, my breath is gone, and his tongue is attacking my clit, and it's so intense I know I'm about to come. He promised hard and fast, and that's what I'm getting.

Without any conscious thought, my hands are now reaching down to grab his head, pushing down for more pressure.

His head pops up and his stare pins me.

"Hands up, otherwise I stop." His sex voice is my new favorite sound. It has me melting into a puddle.

Doing as I'm told, his mouth is back on me, and I'm screaming uncontrollably.

"Noah, oh God, Noah…" The moment he takes my clit between his teeth, I explode with absolutely no control of my body, riding his face. The sinful noises he's making as he laps up every drop of my orgasm.

My body slides down the other side of the orgasm peak, but the slowing of the sensation doesn't last long. Noah moves to kiss me and shares my taste that is all over his lips. Like he's proud of what he made me do. I'm scared of how he is about to stretch me open with that monster that is pushing into my stomach.

"You're mine, beautiful. All mine!" He growls with the rawness of an animal calling into the night sky. His body lifting and the feeling of the head of his cock sliding up and down my sex sends my nerves into a frenzy again.

"Take me." As the words leave my mouth, his cock fills me, pushing into me with such passion, we both cry out.

On his elbows, his hands now cupping my face, it's almost like he's scared to let me go.

He pounds into to me over and over again, while the heat is burning through my body. I can't hang on much longer.

The sensations have me almost at the summit again, and he knows it by the ravenous look on his face.

"Noah, I can't last… oh God, I can't…" I don't want to stop, but my body is surging on overload.

"Then let go. Fucking let go for me!" Loving his dominance, my body responds to his commands.

"Ohhhhhh, fuck, Nooaahhh!" Screaming into the night's silence, there is no stopping the pulsing of my body. My eyes close as white stars are shooting across my vision and sweat breaks out all over my body.

"Open your eyes, Cassie. Need to see you." The strain in his voice tells me he's also close to coming, as he pounds twice more into me and finally lets go too.

"Fucckkk!" His curses bounce off the walls in the sparse room as a declaration of the release we've both been longing for.

Joined in the best possible way, I can still feel his cock twitching inside of me. I'm filled with his passion.

The hard and fast is now being replaced by the sensual way his lips are touching mine. The kiss tells me everything he can't say in words. He rolls my body mid-kiss so he's on his back, and I'm draped across his body. Both of us are sweaty and still trying to take in air in between the kisses.

"Mmmm, you taste just like I imagined."

I pull back to look at him again, laughing. "And how is that?"

"Like sin." Taking another nip at my bottom lip between his teeth, I know one thing for sure.

"You might think I'm sin, but you are trouble, there's no disputing that."

A deep laugh barrels from Ghost as I slide to the side of him and rest my head on his chest.

Lying together in silence for what seems like a long time but is just minutes, I can hear his heart beating away under me, slowly returning to a normal rhythm, although I'm not sure mine is back there yet. I've been desperate for Ghost, but the truth is, I don't know what the hell this means. When this is all over, he won't be able to be with me and could be shipped somewhere else for work. I don't even know where I'm going to end up. I may never be able to return to any sort of normal life.

"Stop thinking so hard. Just stay in the moment with me." Feeling his hand stroking down my back and bringing me comfort, I look up into his eyes.

"I'm just scared. How many moments are we actually going to get?" I can't help it, with my heart open so wide and vulnerable, the tears are slowly running down my cheeks.

"No, don't do that. You need to understand." Rolling to his side so we're facing each other, he pulls me close and makes sure I'm not going anywhere. Anchoring me to him.

"I told you. You needed to be sure, because you are mine, and I'm not letting you go. Not now, not ever." He kisses my forehead, with his lips lingering there for longer than normal. Like he's marking me as his.

"But how will that even work? There are so many things we don't know. What will happen, and where will you be when this is over?" I try to sit up, but his arm just locks me tighter to him.

"With you. That is where I'll be. That's the simple answer."

"Noah."

"Cassie. Believe me. I'm not letting you go, not now, not ever."

I want to believe him, but it's hard to think. It's just a post-orgasmic bubble we are both lying in. Nothing is that easy.

Life is hard, and I've just managed to make it ten times harder for both of us.

GHOST

I can see the uncertainty written all over her face. Nothing I say will reassure her that I mean it. The moment I saw her walking in through the back door that first day, her head down and apologizing to me for ruining my day, I knew there was something special hiding behind those scared and sad eyes. I knew that if I could see the real woman behind the wall then she would be something to behold, and I was right.

When she finally let the barrier down to trust me, the change was like the birth of a new spirit. Cassie's eyes tell me who the real person is that she's been hiding for fear of getting hurt.

The sparkle and bright life that bounces around in her beautiful big brown eyes hypnotizes me.

"I wish I could believe you." Her voice is barely a whisper, and I don't push the point. I need to show her rather than trying to tell her. Too many times her concerns were ignored and dismissed. This time she just needs to work through the doubts until her eyes open and she sees the truth.

I'm her protector, body and soul.

I change the subject, trying to derail her thoughts. We need to talk about something else. "So, can we talk about you breaking the rules just now?"

I can't help but laugh at the look of surprise on her face.

"I wasn't the only one." She gives me a bit of a shove in the chest. Nice try, baby, but I'm not letting you go yet. "I can confirm I've never orgasmed that hard from my own doing."

If the thought of watching her touch herself doesn't have my dick perking up again.

"I'd like to witness that."

The soft glow on her cheeks is something I would love to try to put there more often. For someone who was so confident a moment ago, it's totally wiped off her face now.

"Don't joke about that." Wait, what?

"I'm not joking, Cassie. Watching you get yourself off in a show just for me would be hot as fuck."

"Jason told me that it was dirty and only sluts do that."

"What the actual fuck. Coming from a man who is sleeping with any woman who looks sideways at him?" I can feel my body tensing at the thought of this asshole making Cassie feel anything but beautiful. "I swear to God, if I ever meet him, that is just one of the many reasons I will punch the ever-living shit out of him. There is nothing more beautiful than a woman who allows herself to feel sexual and isn't afraid to show it. You can put that one on the top of my wish list for ways I plan on hearing you scream my name while you come." I don't give her time to blush or feel embarrassed in any way, taking her lips and showing her how turned on she makes me.

"You take my breath away every time you kiss me. You are going to be dangerous to my health." A small giggle comes from Cassie as she settles her head back onto the pillow beside me.

"On the contrary. My fucking you senseless every day will make you feel like you are on such a high. I'll make sure your body is in excellent shape."

"What, you can only cope with once a day? Must be the age thing." The cute smirk on her face, that has her little dimple coming out, shows how funny she thinks she is being.

"You didn't just call me old, did you, young lady? Because I might just have to show you what age and experience can give you."

Climbing over top of her and pinning her to the mattress, all bad thoughts of her ex are long gone, and all I see in her eyes is her longing for me. It's a vision I plan to keep on her face for the rest of our lives. I know it's too early to tell her, but I will marry this woman one day. She is it for me, and nothing will stand in the way between us.

It's been a long time since I've slept the night with a woman tucked in bed with me—although sleeping is a word I should use loosely. After showing her that my age will never slow me down when it comes to her, we spent hours talking, touching, and completely devouring each other to the point that Cassie couldn't keep her eyes open any longer.

I should have slowed down and given her a break, but now that we have opened the flood gates of our emotions, nothing is stopping either of us.

I'm used to surviving days without sleep, or a few hours just to top up. Lying here watching Cassie sleep is far more relaxing for me than choosing to close my eyes. I sat and watched her through the cameras around the house in the early days of her being here and tried to tell myself it was for her safety, which it was. I never want her to think of me as a creep who watched her just for the sake of it. There is a huge difference in what I was doing in keeping her safe, but what I saw in those cameras is nothing compared to her beauty in the flesh. Her shoulder-length brown hair, that she stood her ground and refused to cut or change the color of on that first day in the FBI office, is flowing down her back. It's like her skin is flawless.

I remember growing up, my mom used to tell me that no one was perfect, on the days I would let everything get me down and there would be words between us about getting her shit together. She would scream back at me that my expectations were too high and unrealistic. Although her words about being perfect are true, Cassie is pretty damn close.

I try to keep the thoughts in the back of my head that are screaming at me and have been since the moment I slammed my lips into hers and claimed Cassie. I've just made my role of protecting her so much riskier. How am I supposed to keep her safe when we are lying here naked and vulnerable? I tried to stop myself, but I just couldn't do it any longer. The pull toward her has been getting stronger every day we spend together, and I can't fight it any longer. I don't want to.

Now I've just got to figure out how I can protect her and fuck her at the same time.

Things just got a whole lot more interesting in this house.

Chapter Nine

CASSIE

Waking up alone is not what I was expecting. I can't remember what time it was when I finally drifted off, in what I can only describe as an orgasmic slumber. I haven't slept that well in a long time, but now, feeling the other side of my bed and the sheets are cold, I've got this unnerving feeling.

Does Ghost regret it?

It's not like he can take off and leave me here, but this will make it so awkward if he has changed his mind. Were all those words just what he thought I wanted to hear last night?

Fuck this! I'm not lying here and letting my mind send me spiraling again.

Sitting up, throwing the covers off me and standing quickly, my head is spinning a little. I'm not sure if it's from fear or just getting up too fast. My feet hit the cold floor, and as much as I'm having my own little freakout, I can feel aching muscles in places I haven't felt in a very long time. I want to enjoy this moment, but the need to see Ghost is more pressing. I need to remember that out of this bed, that is who he is to me.

Ghost, not Noah.

Looking down, I see his shirt from last night still on the floor, and sliding it on feels like a quicker option to cover myself in a hurry. That smell of his manly sweat and everything that is Ghost envelops me. It's not settling me like I thought it would, and I don't even bother looking in the mirror or using the bathroom because I just need to see him.

Through the wall I can hear the clicking of computer keys. Not even bothering to knock, I walk from my bedroom and open the door straight into his room. It looks more like a war room than somewhere he uses to sleep and relax in. I'm sure he knew I was coming, with his ninja-like senses, and he didn't jump an inch as I walked straight in behind him. His computer screens go black instantly, and anything that he's hiding from me is completely gone. That pisses me off, but I'll deal with that later.

Before I reach him, he spins around in his chair, and his smile disarms me. All the heat from my panic cools instantly, with just one simple word and action. Working out why his shirt was still on the floor, I'm left staring at his bare chest, and that starts up a whole different type of fire inside me.

"Morning." He raises his arms and opens them to me, inviting me to curl up in his lap. My worst thoughts are swept away, but I know I still need to voice them, otherwise they will continue to simmer inside of me, and I have enough demons I'm battling at the moment.

I don't hesitate to go to him, knowing it's where I belong, but I have questions.

"Why did you leave me, do you regret it? Was I that bad?" I blurt out before I even get settled, and Ghost's lips which were just touching my forehead, now jerk back, and he looks at me, stunned.

"No!" His voice is direct, and he doesn't wait for an answer. His lips are on mine and taking everything he can from me, and in return, he pours all his emotions into my body just through one touch, his powerful kiss.

Pulling back from me, I'm gasping for air. It's like he sucks every bit of it from my lungs every time he touches me like this.

"Does that feel like regret to you, bright eyes?"

Struggling even to put words together, instead I shake my head back and forth. The tension in his face eases slightly.

"I told you last night, if you gave yourself to me, there would be no turning back. We are one now, and nothing will change that." The confidence in his voice drops a little with the next sentence. "Unless you regret it… Do you?"

I don't know what it is with him, but my words always just tumble out. "No! Never. I can't… I just, oh shit, I don't know how to say it."

"Take a breath and then slowly sort out your words. I've got all the time in the world."

While trying to put my thoughts in order, he wraps his arms tighter around me, and the warmth of his body on mine brings me his calmness.

"I can't shake the fear that things in front of me are all a lie. That I'm so blinded by my want for the perfect life that I don't see the red flags. You know, like with Jason. I was so stupid…" I feel his body tense up at the mention of Jason's name.

"Don't say that." His happy voice is gone, replaced by the anger that he has building.

"But I was. And then when I woke up and you were gone, I panicked that I had made another mistake… No, shit, that didn't come out right. I didn't mean you were the mistake but that I had read more into this thing between you and me. That you just feel sorry for me, or that it's just been a while and you are trapped here with a woman who can scratch an itch."

His breathing is heavy, and the arms around me tighten to the point where I'm not sure I will be able to breathe soon.

"I will never lie to you, Cassie. Not about us. Everything I said to you, I meant. And if it takes the rest of my life to convince you, then that's a challenge I'll take on." Placing his hand on my chin, he directs my face so I'm looking straight into his eyes and can't turn away or hide from him.

"Are we clear?" His voice reminds me of the first day I arrived, and he was yelling at his men. It's the kind of voice that means business. I'm just lucky he is restraining the yelling part.

"Yes." The word slips from my lips, although I'm not completely sure I'm doing the right thing. I know only time will tell. My life has so much uncertainty, so what's one more thing to add to my worry list?

"Good. I'm glad we got that settled. Now, am I cooking you breakfast or am I having you for breakfast? Your choice." The sternness in his face is gone, and the smile on his rugged face has me melting into his lap, a little more relaxed. I rub my palm at the roughness on his chin from the few days' growth.

"The look in your eyes tells me you want to feel my bristles all over your thighs," he says.

I'm conscious that I have no panties on, and I can feel the moisture that he's already creating just with his words. I don't want to leave a wet patch on his leg. Jason's words *"cheap slut"* echo in my head.

"Surely you need food after last night, to recharge and all that?" Standing, my legs are a bit wobbly just thinking about what he did to me.

"Oh, bright eyes, I don't need any boost of energy when it comes to you. But you obviously do, so food first, then I get to eat you." He slips his hands up the back of my legs under his shirt I have on, the roughness of his hands sliding over my butt cheeks. Grabbing them tightly, he pulls me close between his legs. Before I even have time to react, his nose is buried in the shirt right above my sex. Taking a deep breath in, his manly grunt makes me shiver.

"Mmmm, smells just like I remember, and it's making me hungry." My legs almost give way at his sexy words.

His chuckle breaks me out of my almost orgasmic stupor. He releases his hands and gently pushes me backwards as he stands before me.

"But you need food first. Let's go." Turning me in his arms, he swats me on the butt, making me jump and squeal a little, while pushing me gently out of the room.

"I knew you would be trouble," he says, walking down the hallway toward the kitchen.

I can't help but smile to myself. I never had this playfulness with Jason. Life was all about image and making sure you were seen in the right place by the right people.

To be honest, I don't think I ever wore one of his shirts to breakfast, completely bare underneath. What if one of his men came into the apartment? Oh, the horror if they didn't see me in my satin nightgown with the matching satin robe. That is what was deemed appropriate for a senator's girlfriend to wear to bed.

Why do I feel at home just like this, naked and in Ghost's shirt? While he's shirtless, with black sweatpants hanging low on his hips, moving around the kitchen making me breakfast.

I could definitely get used to this, although I know I shouldn't. The rug could get pulled out from under me at any stage, and I will again be lost in a sea of nothingness.

Pull it back, Cassie, and slow down. I need to protect myself.

My lust-fueled body is looking for all the hot-and-heavy time it can grab with Ghost, but my heart is telling me that I need to protect it.

Just remember to treat this as a bit of fun. I'm sure Ghost will grow bored of me as soon as things get settled with my case. Well, let's hope my case will be over one way or another. A boring life sounds pretty perfect right about now.

The sound of the plate being placed down on the kitchen counter in front of me and the smell of raisin toast is enough to draw me out of my miserable thoughts.

Live in the moment, because I don't know how many of these I'll get.

"Eat, you'll need your strength." Ghost looks at me, all sex personified.

Okay, I give in. Feed me, then fuck me, and I'll worry about everything in my head later!

The morning went just like that. I can feel every muscle in my body telling me what fun the last twenty-four hours have been.

Now I'm lying outside on the blanket, enjoying the sun on my skin. I wasn't expecting to feel this relaxed. Ghost is working inside, and I'm sure both of us just need some time apart to sort out our emotions too. He may be big and tough on the outside, making people fear him, but I can see past that.

He can turn my body into a lust-filled mess with just a look or touch. It makes all coherent thoughts that are in my head disappear —the ones that I know I need answers to. We need to talk, but I can't do it naked. It just doesn't work.

I close my eyes just to breathe and try to stay in this relaxed state. I run my right hand over the grass and enjoy the simple sensation. Listening to the leaves in the trees behind me brush up against each other as the breeze blows them in different directions. The birds in the distance calling out to each other as they go about their day. As much as I want to get on with my life, part of me wishes I could just stay in this simple moment forever.

Just me, nature, and Ghost keeping me safe… oh, and hot and horny!

I can't believe it's been over a month since that first night Ghost took me to heaven and back… multiple times. He promised me that day he would keep me safe, and there is no safer place than to be in bed with him every night.

To be honest, it's not just been nights. Being in WITSEC is supposed to be a terrible time, but the last four weeks have been the most blissful of my life.

I have only seen a handful of agents who deliver us food and other things Ghost needs. They talk away from me like I don't know what's going on. But that first day after we finally gave into our desires, Ghost promised me he would never lie to me and told me as much as he thought I needed to know. It wasn't everything, but he asked me to trust him, that if he wasn't telling me something it was for my safety and benefit. I'm guessing he means my mental health. There would be so much that would freak me out.

I don't know why I trust him so easily, but I do. Sometimes you just have to go with your gut instinct.

The back lawn behind the house has become my favorite spot to lie while Ghost needs to work. The sun on my face and the fresh air gives me some peace. I haven't been feeling that great the last few mornings. I've been struggling to eat my breakfast, but I just think the anxiety of the whole thing is getting to me. At least that's what I hope it is. Just like I'm going with the assumption that my period hasn't arrived like it should have because of the stress I'm under. I haven't missed a birth control pill, so that's all it can be.

Being shut up in the house makes me go a bit stir crazy some days, so I find being at one with nature helps. My feet on the grass, my toes being tickled with the blades running between them. Trying to make pictures of the clouds and start a story of where that shape has come from or where it's off to. There is only so much television you can watch. My sketching keeps me sane, but this week I can't seem to settle. Closing my eyes, I take a few deep breaths and enjoy the quiet. I dream of the last time I was out here with Ghost, naked under the stars as he made sweet passionate love to me.

My silence is broken when the back screen door bursts open and hits the wall hard.

"Cassie, up! Inside now! Someone is here!" Ghost's voice tells me there is no time to think, just do.

Scurrying to my feet, I leave the blanket where it is.

I almost trip up the steps as I try to move as quick as I can. The look on his face tells me not to stop and ask questions.

"Bedroom! Lock the door until I tell you it's safe," I hear him yell at me as I hurry down the hallway. My heart is almost beating out of my chest. The gun holster on his body with two pistols in it is just second nature to me now. I don't see it most days anymore, but today, I'm glad it's glaringly obvious as I race past him.

The noise of tires on the gravel outside makes my pulse race faster. I don't know where Ghost is or what's happening. Sweat runs down my back, and I pace the bedroom until it occurs to me that I should be quiet.

I stand still, putting myself flush against the wall next to the door. Maybe I can hide behind it if someone gets in, giving myself time to get away.

The gravel-crunching noise stops and one car door slams, and then a few seconds later, another door.

Shit!

Ghost will be outnumbered. I don't know if he can handle that. I mean, that's his job, right, but what if they hurt him trying to get to me? I couldn't live with that. Not now after the last month.

Maybe I should go and help him.

I don't have a gun or anything. There has to be one in his room. I'd have no idea what I was doing. I'd probably shoot my own foot off, but still, I might be able to bluff them.

You know, the element of surprise and all that.

I feel faint from jumping up too quickly, and I realize I'm not actually breathing properly. My fear has taken over my body. Breathe, you idiot. You won't be any help to Ghost if you are passed out on the floor.

Filling my lungs with much-needed oxygen, I can now hear voices in the house.

Fuck!

Who is it? Surely Ghost wouldn't let anyone into the house he didn't trust.

What are they saying? I can't hear, it's just a mumble through the walls. But the voices all sound deep, like there are other men out there. Or maybe it's just one other voice, I can't tell.

If this weren't as serious as it is, I'd be laughing at myself for the serious FOMO I'm feeling right now. It comes from all the secrets that have been around me.

I *must* know.

Doing something that is totally stupid, I start to slowly unlock the door. He told me to stay here until he gave me the all-clear, yet here I am, trying to open the door without a sound, which is difficult considering how much I'm shaking.

Telling myself that I just want to hear the voices doesn't help my guilty conscience.

"You still could've given me the heads-up that you were coming. You're lucky I didn't put a bullet through your fucking head." Ghost is angry. Probably even worse than the first day I arrived here, and I didn't think that was possible.

"Shut the fuck up and listen. You might think you are in charge of this job, but I'm still your superior. Just remember that, Ghost!" It's a voice I haven't heard before, and by the sounds of the conversation, he isn't happy either.

"Don't push it. You know I don't respond well to the bullshit hierarchy." The feeling of fear slowly leaves me since they are both on the same side, but I can't help but wonder what is going on between them. I would have thought Ghost is the sort of man who's loyal to the job, therefore respects his boss and his opinion. But something is off in this conversation. And why didn't he know his boss was coming, like when all the other agents arrive here, without a fuss?

"I don't give a fuck what you think about me, but you need to listen and listen hard. I'm here giving you the spiel that I was told to deliver to you that we both know is bullshit. For fuck's sake, Ghost, I thought you knew me better than this, that you would know that I don't believe a word of it either. Now I'm going to tell you what you really need to know."

"It better make more sense than the load of political crap you just gave me." The edge of aggression finally slips from Ghost's voice.

I know I'm probably going to regret this, but I need to know what is going on too.

This is my life they're talking about. I deserve to be told what is happening. Because obviously something is going down, and it's not what they were expecting. Not that I'm sure anything ever goes as it's supposed to in these situations.

Not wanting to burst out there in the middle of an argument between two or maybe three men who will all be carrying guns, I tentatively walk down the hallway as quietly as I can. I decide to call out before stepping out into the room, to alert them I'm there.

"Ghost, I'm coming out." Nervousness is still evident in my voice, no matter how brave I try to tell myself I am.

The footsteps are moving toward me, and I don't want him to push me back into the bedroom, so I step out before he can reach me.

"Cassandra." His deep growl and the use of my official name tells me he is not impressed. "What did I say?"

"I'm not a child. This is about me, so I should be here!" Pulling my shoulders back and chin up, I stare him down as much as I can.

In all the tension in the room, I see the slightest smirk on his face and twitch in his eye.

Yeah, that's right, Ghost, I'm not just some meek and mild woman.

"Oh, you've got your hands full with this one, don't you," his boss comments while we're still staring each other down.

"Mmmm. You could say that," Ghost replies, turning back to his boss and walking away from me. This is his way of reminding me that I can't touch him or show that there is anything going on between us. That could spell disaster and cause them to separate us —something I'm not sure I could cope with at this stage.

"Cassandra, meet my boss, Rocket. Apparently, he's the man who holds all the answers here."

"Ghost, don't be a dick." He holds his hand out toward me to shake. "Nice to meet you, Cassandra, and I'm sorry you have to put up with him," he says, rolling his eyes toward Ghost who is now standing to the side of us but not more than an arm's distance away.

"I can't say the same about meeting you. Well, not you personally but the reason I'm meeting you, more to the point. And why were there two doors closing when you arrived?" I'm making sure we aren't about to be ambushed. I pull back my hand, not feeling all that comfortable around a man that for some reason Ghost is frustrated with.

"Well, unfortunately, none of us had a hand in the reason you're here. And don't worry, that was just me getting out the peace offering I brought for you. Donuts. Now, how are you coping?" Donuts, yuck. Why does everyone think they're the best treat? He just lost points with me. I knew I wasn't going to like this man. Before I even have a chance to reply to Rocket, Ghost is talking.

"We aren't here for chitchat, Rocket. What the hell is going on?" He moves closer to my side, yet not so much that I can feel his touch. Not that it matters, because having Ghost this close tells me I'm safe, regardless of what Rocket is about to say.

"I love how I'm Rocket today and not Boss." He smirks at me, trying to get me to relax and be on board with him. Then he turns back to Ghost who just rolls his eyes.

"Fuck off, *Rocket*." Ghost emphasizes his name.

"I suggest you go and turn off the cameras and delete the reel since I got here. No one can know I've been here. The message I had was supposed to be given over a phone call, but I knew I needed to tell you in person, because what I'm about to say, we don't want anyone else to hear." Rocket's no longer trying to look friendly. The stern eyes and straight mouth tell me this isn't going to be something I want to hear.

"Cassandra, with me, now." Ghost grasps my arm tighter than I expected and pulls me back toward his room. Not expecting it, I'm stumbling over my feet trying to stay upright. The fact he hasn't left me in the room with his boss tells me he no longer trusts him like Rocket thinks he does.

He lets go of me, only to quickly lean over his computer keyboard. His fingers move at speed and all the screens come to life at once.

Holy. Fucking. Shit!

I knew he had a lot going on with these computers, but the number of camera angles in front of me shows me how much I'm being watched. My body shudders in shock. I didn't realize. Seriously, how many other people are watching my every move? My skin starts to crawl at how much others have seen.

The agility of his fingers on the keyboard has me mesmerized before he looks up at me with compassion.

"I never let anyone see what they shouldn't. I delete and manipulate the video all the time, for your safety and our privacy." Ghost's voice is barely above a whisper, so there is no way Rocket can hear him.

The ability to talk has left me momentarily, but I'm grateful in so many ways to Ghost. I just nod at him to show I heard him. He blacks out his screens again, and standing in front of me, he quickly leans toward me, kissing me on the forehead.

"We'll talk later." With that, he turns my body and pushes me back toward the hallway. It's like my brain isn't talking to my legs to make them move.

Before I make it out of the room, I get the feeling in my stomach that I'm about to be sick, and I can't get to the toilet quick enough.

"I need the bathroom." I run across the hallway and close the door of the bathroom behind me. Leaning forward, I lose what little breakfast I managed to eat into the toilet bowl.

He knocks on the door behind me. "Cassandra, are you okay?" Worry is evident in his voice.

I don't want him to see me like this. It's one thing to see and taste parts of me that are sacred, but watching me throwing up is totally off limits on the relationship scale.

"Yes. Don't come in," I shout back before he can open the door, which I'm surprised he hasn't done already. Ghost yells a reply that everything is fine to Rocket, who must have heard him yelling at me.

I dry-retch into the toilet bowl again because there is nothing left to bring up. My head hurts.

"Cassandra, please, I'm coming in." Damn, I hate that name, it just reminds me of how much I'm in danger. I know there is no stopping him, so I need to move. Grabbing toilet paper and wiping my mouth, I push myself to my feet as he cautiously opens the door. It surprises me, I was expecting the door to come flying open and him bursting in like his ass is on fire.

"I'm okay, just anxiety getting the better of me." Turning to the sink, I run the water and cup my hands under it. Scooping water into my mouth, I rinse and have a drink to get rid of the taste.

"Are you sure? It might be food poisoning?" He places his hand on the arch of my back. Not that he should be touching me, but the comfort it brings me is helping.

"I feel fine now. Let's get this over with," I say, lowering my voice to a mere whisper. "I don't like him being here." I'm used to it just being us two, and I don't have to worry about anything. I have managed to shut the outside world out. It's not like there is anyone out there that will be missing me or wondering what happened to me. It's strange to take comfort in knowing I haven't panicked anyone by disappearing. The only person that will care is the person I ran from. But he is looking for Leah his girlfriend, and she doesn't exist anymore. And to be honest, he is only after Leah for what she knows. No matter what happens in this whole debacle, I'm not sure I would ever want to go back to that sort of life anyway.

In this life, I am Cassie, Ghost's girl.

That's all the matters to me now. To be cared for, really cared for, and to be safe.

Looking at the man behind me in the mirror, I know I have all that here, so that's where I want to be from now on.

"Okay, if you say so. But you tell me if you feel sick again. I'm not convinced you're okay, but I agree we need to get this over and done with."

I want to fall into his body for a reassuring hug, but I know I can't. So, I step sideways away from him, knowing it will be safer for both of us if I don't touch him.

I hate this, and I want it over.

But deep down, I know that may never happen.

Chapter Ten

CASSIE

As he leads the way into the dining room where we left Rocket, I can see his concern.

"Just my constant nerves upsetting me and getting the better of me," I explain.

Without giving Rocket time to ask me anything, Ghost is already talking. "Done." Ghost leads me to a chair, but I can't sit. I shake my head and stand firm next to him. There is too much nervous energy racing through my body, fingers tingling and wiggling back and forth.

"Now start talking," Ghost demands. I love his deep voice but not like this.

"With her here?" Rocket asks, glaring at him.

"No point hiding anything now. Your arrival already has her freaking out, if you haven't noticed." My gratitude toward Ghost just grew that little bit more.

"Thank you." I tell him with my eyes just how much I mean it. "This is my life. I deserve to know what the hell is going on, don't you think?" My voice comes back to me with a bit more strength. I can feel the skepticism oozing from Rocket. He doesn't know what to do or how to take me.

"It's not normal practice," he grunts at Ghost, trying to let him know how pissed off he is.

"Like that matters now. None of what you are doing is 'normal practice,' now is it." Digging his heels in, Ghost is not giving in to his boss. He wants me here, and for that I want to kiss him so hard right now.

"Fine, it's your funeral when shit goes south with this. I'm trying to protect you both. And I'm not convinced her knowing all this is going to help."

Ghost just glares at him to let him know it's time to talk.

"The official memo I was sent was to tell you it's time to bring Cassandra to Washington for the court case briefing. That she would be safe, as Jason is being watched by the FBI. But we both know that a senator is not going to get blood on his hands. He'll pay someone to do that."

A cold shudder runs over me at what Rocket means. Jason will hire someone to kill me!

Deep down I knew that, but knowing it and hearing someone say it are two different things.

Rocket continues, "Actually putting it in writing that Cassandra will be safe to come to Washington smells off to me. Besides, when do we normally take a witness for briefings? They don't even go for the court case half the time. This guy has money and power, and I think there's a mole in the camp."

"Which camp?" Ghost bluntly asks.

"I don't know. I would hope it's in the FBI, but I wasn't taking any risks by telling anyone I was coming here to talk to you. I'm in a car I rented under a fake name, and I left my work phone at home. Which you know, Ghost, how big a risk that is. I'm not only putting my own life in danger but the operatives that I look after who won't be able to contact me. Here you are dragging the client out of the room because you don't trust me all of a sudden, after sixteen years of working together. Instead, how about you use your fucking head and realize I'm here to protect your ass and hers, dickhead."

Walking closer to Ghost, the two of them are sizing each other up. I can see the anger radiating off them both.

Rocket's pissed that Ghost doesn't trust him, and Ghost is furious that he doesn't know what is going on, which makes him feel vulnerable in keeping me safe.

If there were a visible color for the amount of testosterone in this room, then it would be like a black-colored pea-soup fog, and I wouldn't be able to see two inches in front of me. If I weren't here, I can't guarantee there wouldn't be fists being thrown right now.

"Well, tell me something that reassures me of that trust."

"I'm here, aren't I?" Rocket glares at Ghost, trying to get him to see that just him being here should be enough.

Seriously, these two need to get on with this.

"Enough!" I startle myself with the loud word coming out of my mouth. "Get over yourselves. Tell me what the fuck is going on with my life!"

Both faces turn to me with shock.

"Yes, remember me, the one over here who someone or maybe several people want to kill at the moment while you two are trying to fight over who is the bigger badass or who is in control?"

Pushing myself between the two men, I look Rocket straight in the eye.

"Start talking, Rocket, in plain English. No code words or bull-shit. Lay it all out there," I demand, poking him in the chest with my index finger to emphasize I mean business.

The fear from earlier is gone and instead anger is brewing inside my body. Nothing makes me more fired up than secrets, and especially when they relate to me!

"Damn, I guessed you would be a handful, but you have fire inside you. I like it. It's going to help keep you alive. And give him grief, and I think I like that even more."

Ghost wraps his arm around my waist and pulls me back toward him, and the tingles I shouldn't be feeling right now are running through my limbs. I can't help it.

"Settle, Cassandra. Let's all sit and calm down." His voice is calmer than it has been since Rocket got here. Rocket's eyes zero in on Ghost's arm for a second and then move on.

Ghost pulls out a chair for me, and I glare at both of them before finally sitting, with them following suit.

"Start talking, both of you, but you first," I say, pointing at Rocket.

I mean business, and it's time to take charge of my own life. Well, as much as I can when I'm trapped in WITSEC in a safe house God knows where, with absolutely no resources at my disposal.

But hey, you'd be surprised what a woman can do when she's backed against a wall.

Fuck you, Jason. Fuck you!

That's my new mantra.

You don't get to win.

GHOST

I can play this game, Rocket.

If you want to show up here telling me some load of bullshit and then expect me to fully trust you, then you are stupider than I thought. I'll pretend to be on the same team for now, until I get a handle on what the hell is going on behind the scenes. For Cassie's purpose, she needs to think that the people who put her in this house have this all under control, but in the last fifteen minutes, I've just learned that nothing is under control, and the only person on my team is me. I know I could call Bull and he would be here in a flash, but I don't want to involve him in this. I have a feeling it's bigger than we expect, and it's about to blow up in our faces.

"You both know that the senator is out on bail and using any media outlet he can to claim his innocence in any wrongdoing that he has been charged with. What you wouldn't know is that his legal team has just presented to the prosecution a bundle of documents that implicate his assistant Camilla and that this was all her doing. She is the person who has been breaking the laws, using his access to sensitive documents, and then framing him. She is being arrested as we speak.

"Bullshit!" Cassie bursts out. "He was fucking her behind my back, and the stupid woman actually loved him, I could tell in the way she talked about him. He's using her as the pawn. Surely, they can see that." She's already getting worked up, and we have only just started.

"That's not for us to worry about. We aren't the FBI. Our job is to keep you safe, not to solve the case," Rocket says, trying to cool Cassie down.

"But if he gets off and is out free, then it is your problem. Because I will never be safe and never able to leave this suffocating situation."

My gut drops a little, and even though my rational brain tells me she isn't talking about me, it still jars me.

"Maybe so, but we will deal with that in due course. Now, more importantly, we need to talk about the message that I was to relay. The prosecution wanting to bring you to Washington is not normal. So, who wants you there and why?"

"I think we know why," she mumbles under her breath. Cassie looks at me, and I can see the reality of where we're at dawning on her.

"The other thing I have managed to find out is that they are expediting the trial so they can show that the senator is innocent, and he can get on with his job. Camilla can be locked up, and life will be all rosy again. A perfect world, apparently." Sarcasm is practically dripping off his tongue.

"So, what do we do?" Cassie's voice is weaker now, and I can tell she is losing the fighting spirit she had a little while ago.

"Keep you out of Washington, that's for sure." Rocket is looking at me for guidance now. I may have misjudged him a little, but I'm sticking to my instincts and not trusting a soul.

"When are they expecting us to move her?" My mind is on overdrive, making plans but not giving anything away.

"Five days from now. That gives them time to get Camilla in custody, her charges to hit the media, and for us to believe that it's a mere formality to bring Cassie back and ask her questions on what she knows about Camilla."

"I don't know anything about her except that she's a whore, who willingly cheated with my boyfriend while keeping me doing as I was told, to look perfect in public. I mean, what if she was involved too, that they were doing it together? Or maybe he's hanging her out to dry, framing an innocent person?" When she drops her head into her hands, I want to console her, but it's too risky to give anything away. "I don't want to be involved in this…" she whispers. I can see her mind trying to process all she is learning.

She looks up at me with pleading eyes. "Ghost… What if he tries to implicate me too? If he can do it to her, he could do it to me too."

Before I can answer, Rocket is already talking. "You're right, he could. But we will try to keep you safe from that."

"There is no fucking trying!" my voice booms into the room.

"Cassandra, you are safe with me. I won't let that poor excuse for a human anywhere near you. Or anyone else, for that matter." I glare at Rocket so he gets the message too.

I'd already had the same thought as Cassie, and I now know what I need to do. From the moment I knew the details for this case, I had a possible outcome in mind, and now my fears are coming to fruition. Money and status mean power, and power means they play dirty. Well, I can play this game too. But the one advantage I've got is that I have what they want, and they aren't getting her.

If they can't find her, then they can't have her. I can stay one step ahead of them. Rocket thinks I didn't know about Camilla, but he forgets who I am and what I'm capable of. I've seen the documents that have been presented to the prosecuting team. To be honest, it didn't surprise me. I didn't expect Jason to take this lying down. With the kinds of people he deals with, they won't want any of their names to be exposed. So, either they help get him off or they kill him. It's that simple. You play on the dirty side of the world, and you are only a breath away from taking a bullet at any moment. That's the choice you make when you step over the line. Everyone is disposable.

I need to get rid of Rocket so I can think, to plan what my next move is. I need to get on the computer and dig deeper. Find out where the mole in the system is.

"I understand what's going on now. Thank you for coming, but I know you need to get back. If you're offline for too long, then people will get suspicious, and that's the last thing we need."

I can see Rocket is torn between wanting to stay and work through a plan but knowing I'm right and he needs to leave. He has been here long enough.

"We will work this out, Cassandra." He puts his hand on her shoulder as he stands. She shivers from the touch. He hasn't won her over yet, and that's a good thing. The only person she needs to trust is me.

"Thank you," she quietly replies as she stands too. "I'm going to head to my room for a while, Ghost."

I nod to her. I don't know if she's doing it on purpose to give me time to talk to Rocket or if she is just overwhelmed again.

I hold my arm to the side, signaling to Rocket that he should start walking toward the back door, and I follow after.

We walk in silence until we reach the car.

"Thanks for the intel. I'll see what I can find out." I keep my tone of voice flat, not giving anything away.

"Don't do anything stupid, Ghost," Rocket bluntly says to me.

"I'm not going to."

"Bullshit. You might think you're fooling her—and me, for that matter—but I can tell you, we are both on to you. I've known you for too long. I can read you, even when you think I can't."

"Whatever," I say. One-word answers are harder to get anything from.

"How long you been fucking her?"

Before he can even take his next breath, I have his shirt screwed up in my fist and his body pinned against the car. "Don't you dare speak about Cassandra like that." I grit my teeth, trying not to punch the living shit out of a man I considered a close friend until today.

"You don't need to answer me, Ghost. Your reaction tells me

what I already guessed. Now back the fuck off or I'll have you pulled from this case quicker than you can blink."

Dropping my fists and restraining my anger takes every bit of will power I have. "Don't even think about it."

As I turn to walk away from him, he continues talking, his words echoing all around me.

"How could you be so stupid, Ghost. What were you thinking?"

Continuing to walk away, in a voice low enough he can't hear me, all I can answer to myself is the truth. "That my life will no longer exist without her in it. She's mine."

Stomping up the back steps toward the door, I hear his car door open and close. Standing with my hand on the doorknob, I don't open it until I hear his car start moving on the gravel, turning around and heading out the driveway.

Taking a deep breath, I drop my head to lean on the door.

Fuck!

I've just put both Cassie and myself in danger by letting him know we're involved. Today has just become one big clusterfuck.

Trying to get my head around everything before I go back inside, I reach for my phone. My finger hovers over Bull's number. I want to press the call button. I need someone to talk to and to help me. As I'm about to push the button, I hear her voice.

"Ghost?" The fragility in her tone tells me what I need to do.

I push my phone back in my pocket. Sorry, Bull, I need to do this one my own. It's safer that way.

Opening the screen door and stepping inside, I see Cassie standing in the kitchen with her arms wrapped around her body, looking as petrified as she did the first day I met her.

"I'm here, baby. He's gone." Stepping to her, her body falls into mine, the tears start flowing, and I feel my girl breaking in my arms.

"I've got you. You're safe with me."

Now I just need to work out how to guarantee what I'm promising.

Time is of the essence for me to get my plan into motion, but I can't leave Cassie until she feels comfortable with what's happening. We need to talk, but standing in the kitchen is not the place.

"Let me turn the cameras back on and get the loops playing so nothing looks out of the ordinary. Then we'll talk." I place my fingers under her chin and lift it up so she's looking at me.

"They want me dead," she whispers. It's not a question from her but a fact. One I'm not going to downplay to her.

"Yes, they do, I won't lie to you. But they aren't going to get what they want, are they. We aren't going to give them an opportunity to get anywhere near you," I tell her with all the confidence I can give her.

"But how do we stop them?"

The only way I know how.

"We disappear," I mouth to her with no voice at all.

"What?" Confusion is all I see in her eyes.

I don't want to talk here. I can't trust the house isn't bugged in some way after Rocket's revelations just now. I'm ninety-nine percent sure there are no bugs, but suddenly, I have that one percent of doubt in my gut.

I put my finger on her lips, silencing her. I need Cassie to understand what I'm saying. "Just give me a few minutes. Then we need to go for a walk. Understand?"

She nods her head, and I know Cassie has caught on to what I mean.

I've been telling the department that they need to get better at cyber security, but it falls on deaf ears. Now it's going to come back and bite them. They have no idea that for the last four weeks I've been manipulating all the security feeds they see from here. Which proves to me that every job I'm on, it is up to the agents to keep our clients safe, because the people monitoring our security feeds are useless.

Taking Cassie with me into my room, I leave her sitting on my bed while I go to work. The good thing about us being here for a while and Cassie not having much with her is that we have a limited number of outfits. Repeating the feeds is easy to do with the outfit that she has on today. A plain white t-shirt that fits nicely over her breasts and shows the curves of her body. She has gotten used to living in her gym leggings because they're comfortable. Plain black is what she has on today. I'm not complaining. Her legs look awesome in them, and it's hard to keep my hands off her. For me, I'm generally the same. Black t-shirt, tight so that it doesn't restrict my movements, and my cargo pants. The number of pockets in them makes it easy to carry a few weapons that are concealed but readily accessible. The most adventurous I get is to change the color. Black, navy, or on a bold day, I might even wear the dark gray pair. There is method to my boring behavior. If I need to slide into the shadows, then the dark clothes make it easier.

I have a bad feeling that I might be sliding into the darkness shortly, and I'm not sure when I will resurface. For me, it won't be hard. I've done it before, and no one thinks anything about it when I disappear for an extended period. You need to be detached from friends and family to do this job. You can't be worrying about anyone else's safety except the client you're protecting. That is what Bull struggles with the most. He loves his family and is extremely close to them. He finds it hard to know they worry when he's gone. Although he's doing the job he loves, his family miss him and just want him home safe with them. When I met them, I understood why he finds it difficult to leave them.

Growing up, I didn't have what he did. My mom and dad should have split up before I was even born. But stupidly they thought bringing a child into the circus of their life drama would make their marriage better. All the arguments would stop, and of course, they would have the perfect family. They were slow learners. Two more sisters after me and still things were the same. Truth be told, they were probably even worse. By the time I was old enough to leave home, I took the first job I could to get me out of there.

It sounds cliché, but I worked in the mail room for a gun supply company. I used to see them being made on the assembly line and started to memorize how the parts went together. I wanted to be able to hold one and fire it, so I went to night school to get my security license. They taught me how to use a firearm safely and all the legalities around the security industry. But the most important thing it did was introduce me to computers, the internet, and the use of surveillance cameras.

I saved my next few paychecks, living off ramen noodles, so I could buy my first laptop. I moved around between a few hostels, but there was one that happened to be next to the local library. It was the first password I ever hacked so I could use their internet at night to learn and start refining my hacking skills. I never used it for bad things, but I soon found out that others did. The things I was starting to see on the dark web had me fearing for where this world was heading.

Before long, I had taken a security job at the gun supply company and could afford a one-bedroom dump to live in. It wasn't much but it was mine, and it was better than living at home in the middle of the yelling and screaming. My two sisters had grown up in that environment, so now just joined in the constant shit fight that was happening. Jodelle, the youngest, asked me a few times if she could live with me, and I thought about it for a while, thinking that maybe if I could get her out of there too, then maybe I could break the toxicity.

Then the day I went over to talk to my parents about it, I found her in the house on her own, snorting coke. It turns out the only reason she wanted to live with me was so she could do her drugs whenever she wanted, and later, I learned she was selling her body to the boys in her class to pay for the drugs. My parents were too busy hating each other and blaming one another for their daughter being a drug addict that nobody stopped to try to help her. My other sister, Lucy, blamed me and said if I didn't move out then it wouldn't have happened.

That day when I walked away from the house, I knew I needed to get out and never look back. A month later, there was a transfer to the headquarters of the company I worked for as the head of security, so I took that. Even though I was young, they saw potential in me. One day, I heard one of the guys at work talking about applying to become a WITSEC agent, and I jumped straight onto researching it. There was a lot of training involved, and it took a long time to get to the end goal, but it meant I could disappear into another world. It held so much appeal. I applied that night, making my resume look better than it was and tweaking a few databases to make sure they matched up with what I listed in my application. I applied under a different name so there was no trace to my family history and just used one I had made up and planted all the data in the web I needed to exist. It was a risk because the background checks are intense, but my already skillful computer talents got me through, and I'm thankful every day for whoever wasn't doing their job properly when checking.

Sure, I went about things the wrong way, but I didn't hurt anyone in the process. I've never looked back and have given my life to the agency, saving many lives and serving my country with dedication and passion. I don't regret a thing. Everything I have taught myself I've always used to keep people safe and make sure that certain information ends up in the right people's hands to rid the world of the vile creatures who lurk in the darkness.

Setting the video feeds to run now for the next forty-eight hours without needing to be touched, I feel a bit more settled. This will give me time to get us out of here and far enough away that the trail will be cold by the time they discover we aren't here. The whole time I have been programing the computer, I can feel Cassie's presence behind me on my bed. Although I probably shouldn't call it my bed. I haven't slept in it for the past month.

Finishing putting the secure coding into the system, I turn to see her sitting there with her knees up against her chest and her arms wrapped around them. Pulling herself into a secure ball. It's a common defense mechanism in a time of stress. Make our body as small as we can and protect our most vulnerable thing, our heart.

"Come with me," I command, holding out my hand and pulling her up off the bed. If I had time, I'd take her to our room and fuck the fear right out of her, but we need to get out of here. Sooner rather than later.

Heading out the back door and off into the tree line, I take her behind the biggest tree, just in case there are any cameras I don't know about that have been planted to trick me up. I wouldn't put it past Rocket to have had a second agent with him that was outside planting things. I want to trust he is on my side, but I just can't seem to gauge it right now.

"Ghost, what's happening? I'm scared." I know she is, but I need her to be strong right now.

"To be honest, I'm not sure what is going on behind the scenes. Rocket arriving here the way he did has me second-guessing everything."

"Everything?" Her tentative voice is a barely above a whisper.

"Don't misunderstand what I mean. I'm just talking about the intel from the department. All my information is secure, and I don't doubt any of what I have found. What I'm worried about is the move to bring you into the light again."

What I really wanted to say was, there has definitely been a hit put out on Cassie, that I can guarantee. That's why they are trying to flush her out into the open.

Not on my watch.

It's more than that. This is no longer a job.

It's my life.

"What will we do?"

It's time to tell her the plan.

"We're running, Cassie. Can you trust me to keep you safe on my own?" I ask, hoping I know the answer.

"Always and forever." Although I see her fear, I also see the love behind it. We haven't said it, but it's there.

And that's all I need to know.

"Then we start packing, we need to leave now." I hope I haven't freaked her out too much that she starts panicking.

She doesn't even hesitate. "I'll do our clothes, bathroom, and food. You do all your computers and guns."

Before I can even reply, she is off toward the house.

Damn, I love this brave, strong woman. Until this moment I didn't know how much. I didn't know how long I would get to be with her, if she would understand this life.

I should never have doubted her, and now I know my answer of how long our love will last.

There is no limit to forever.

Chapter Eleven

GHOST

G rabbing my go-bag from the back of the car on the way inside the house gives me what I need. It's a bag I hoped I would never have to use, but it was something Badger taught me years ago about being prepared. Hearing Cassie moving around collecting everything we require without any complaining is a huge relief.

Firing up my personal laptop, my fingers race to get things I'm looking for quickly. Fake identities for now, printing the paperwork I require and creating a basic online profile for both of us until I have time to get something more substantial sorted tonight.

Bull and I set up a secure line of communication between us early on and sending the email to him now is the hardest thing to do. He is going to be furious at me for not reaching out for his help. He will understand in time, but he also knows I'm a lone wolf. It's why I got the code name Ghost. I disappear into the night. He'll know I'm around, he just can't see me. I will find a way to get in touch when the time is right.

With my earpiece in, I call the only person I can who will understand and not judge me. Well, not initially anyway, it will just come later.

"Talk to me." Badger knows. It's those stupid voodoo powers he has.

"I'm taking a holiday." It's a code he told both Bull and me when he left the program. That if we ever needed to get out and go dark, to tell him we're taking a holiday.

"Choosing a new destination, one above the boring predictable one?" I can hear his keyboard clicking in the background.

"Yeah, that same old holiday was getting predictable, and there was something about it that wasn't right anymore. A change of scenery is what I need right now," I reply, trying to let him know that we have been compromised.

"Understood. Go traveling, you never know what paradise you might find. Call me later and we can compare notes on the best holiday spots to visit." Badger is already working on safe places for me to stop and get some sleep tonight. Since he left WITSEC, the work he's been doing has given him contacts in places I might need now. Between that work and his ex-military buddies, there is a network outside the usual channels that I will be tapping into.

"Thanks, buddy. I really appreciate it, you know." No time to get feelings, but a lump in my throat tells me no matter how tough I think I am, I'm worried.

"Shut up and get moving. Talk soon." Badger disconnects the call, and I know he has my back.

I don't have time to sit and think. I send all the identity documents to my burner phone and a spare cell I have that will now be Cassie's, so it looks normal. I mean, who doesn't have a phone now. Hell, even damn ten-year-olds have them now. What the fuck for, I'll never know, but not my problem.

I make sure the WITSEC computers are set to play the loop and post the check-in reports I had set up just in case on a timer. All the preparation I did while trying to avoid Cassie in those early days is now paying off. Score one point for all that sexual frustration, for once.

It never takes me long to have my computers and guns packed.

The last thing I do is trigger the secret cameras I have in the house that will feed to my records. It will show me when they arrive here. Who it is and what is said. It may or may not let me know who the mole is, but that isn't important right this moment. I'll work it out, and when I do, they'll be dealt with in the appropriate way.

"Do I put our bags in the SUV or wait for you?" Cassie mouths to me as I walk toward her. She's in the kitchen, grabbing the last of the food she thinks we need. Smart woman to even think of that. The fewer number of stops we make in the next twenty-four hours the better. Less chance of being picked up on cameras.

Dumping my bags at the back door with hers, I walk closer, and leaning into her ear, I whisper, "We aren't taking the SUV, it's tracked; we are going in the Toyota. I mean, what else would you expect in the less-than-five-star accommodation we offer," I joke, trying to break the tension a little. Pulling back, I see the half-smile on her face as she pushes me away.

"You idiot." It's all she gets out, and then she throws the last of the food into the bag at her feet.

With everything in the trunk of the car, Cassie securely in the front seat, I give the car one last check for bugs, trackers, or anything that the agency has planted on it. Not that we will be in it for long.

Getting to the end of the driveway, I pull the car to a stop just on the edge of the road. Jumping out, I reach into the bush and pull the thin clear piece of fishing line across the drive and attach it to the trip mechanism I had installed. It will ping on my phone the moment they arrive at the house looking for us.

Slamming the door, I plant my foot on the accelerator, and we take off down the road.

"What was that?" Cassie quietly whispers.

"An insurance policy." I watch every parked car to see if one pulls away from the curb or for any random people sitting in them. I wouldn't put it past Rocket to already have agents here, knowing I would run. The main roads have agents that have been there all along in case I needed them, but I purposely take a little side track between two properties that brings me onto the next street over. They won't see me leave, which again, is another poor placement by the agency. The agents should have been closer, but I didn't change it once I arrived, knowing I wanted to be able to leave undetected if needed. I just had a feeling from the beginning this wasn't going to end well. That's why I had a plan in place.

The quicker I can change cars and directions the better. I don't know if it's from fear or if Cassie just knows I need to concentrate, but she's stays quiet, and her head is swiveling around looking at everything too. Although I don't want her stressed or to have to take any of this on her shoulders, the more eyes the better right now.

It's been about thirty minutes since we left the safe house, so I figure it's time to change cars. We are in an old rundown country town where I'm guessing money will talk. I spot the biker bar on the outskirts of town that I researched when I first arrived at the safe house. It pays to know what's around you, and looking at this building, I know we have found the perfect place.

"What are we doing?" The quavering in her voice tells me she's apprehensive.

"Time to swap our wheels." Grabbing her phone out of my pocket, I dial my number, and the call cuts into my earpiece.

"Keep this call open, doors locked, don't talk to anyone, and you tell me the moment you think something is wrong. There is a gun in the glove compartment. Don't be afraid to use it." The way her face pales instantly at the word gun has my heart thumping. I need to make this quick.

"I'll be fast." I can't hesitate, we need to keep moving. Putting my jacket on to conceal my guns, a cap on my head, and I'm out the door, locking it behind me.

Knowing she can hear everything I'm saying, Cassie is about to learn what our life is going to become. She hates secrets and lies with a passion, but it's what's going to keep us alive.

Opening the door to the bar, the stench of stale beer hits me like a brick wall, almost knocking me backwards, while I take my first breath of the smoky haze that fills the room. The predictable bar is in front of me. The regulars are taking up stools at the bar, one guy's head so low I can't tell if he is about to fall asleep or pass out. Pool tables to the side of the room, and on the opposite side, a few dartboards on the wall. At the back are the tables where the heavies of this bar are holding court, and all eyes are on me. The stranger in the room. Not wanting to waste time, I know these are the guys I need to talk to. I'm used to dealing with all sorts of people in my job, so they don't scare me. But what does is Cassie outside on her own.

"You okay?" I talk in the lowest voice I can that she will still hear me.

"Yes." She doesn't sound it, but I don't have time to worry.

"Good girl."

Taking steps with all the confidence I can muster, I stride to the back of the room.

The biggest guy at the table stands up as I get closer. Arms crossed over his chest, shoulders back, and the toughest look he can manage on his face.

"Got a problem?" His voice is deep, raspy from all his smoking and drinking, I'm guessing.

"Yep. Need help, and I'm willing to pay for it." Looking around the table, I pick out the boss straight away. Nodding to the muscle to stand down, he looks at me.

"What kind of help we talkin' about. We don't break the law."

Bullshit screams through my head, but I'm playing the game.

"Not expecting you to. I need a reliable car, not flagged in the system for anything, and I need the Toyota outside to disappear."

"Why?" This guy leans forward and engages me with his body language, his forearms on the table and hands clasped together. He looks me up and down. Everyone at this table is wearing their leather vest with patches all over it.

"Need to keep my old lady safe from some trouble. Government-type trouble." I don't want to give too much away, but I'm banking on the fact that they will hate all things authority.

"How much you willing to pay?" the man next to him asks, must be the second-in-command, and the side scowl from the boss tells me he's not impressed that he asked before he did.

I keep my eyes firmly on the boss, showing him respect, since he's expecting that I'm dealing with him.

"Twenty K cash, unmarked." I reach into my pants pocket where I stashed it earlier. There's more cash in one of the other pockets if I need, but never show your full hand straight-up.

"What makes you think we won't just take that cash and put you on your ass out that door right now, with nothing to show for it except bruised ribs?" The boss's look is intense, trying to scare me.

"Because you are a man of honor. I haven't threatened you in any way, I just need help," I say, keeping my voice calm, hoping it will pull him in.

"Crusher, give him your car." It isn't a question, and I get the impression whichever one is Crusher would know better than to argue.

"Thank you." I place the cash on the table in front of me, and his hands slide out and take it, passing it to his second to count it. He nods at him that it's all there.

Before I have time to say anything, the guy next to me, the muscle that has been trying to intimidate me the whole time, holds out keys.

"Green Dodge out front." His words are blunt and straight forward.

"I see it, it's fine," Cassie's voice whispers in my ear. I had forgotten for a moment she was listening in. I try not to react at how smart my girl is.

"Blue Toyota, and I need it gone as soon as we leave. I'll leave the keys in the ignition."

"Deal." The boss nods at me to let me know we're finished.

Taking no time, I turn on my heel and I'm straight out the door. The moment I break into the bright sunshine, I start sucking in the clean air again and breathing better. Seeing Cassie safe and sound, my stomach relaxes a little, but to be honest, I won't relax until we are long gone from here.

Jumping into the Dodge and starting it up, the motor purrs like a kitten. Thank fuck. I drive it straight to where Cassie is parked and place it between the Toyota and the bar, so they won't get a clear look of Cassie or the gear we have. I hear the phone call disconnect in my ear as she moves to open the door and get out. I leave the Dodge motor running just in case we need to leave halfway through moving bags.

"Grab my bag on the backseat and get in the truck. I'll get the rest." She understands by the tone in my voice that this isn't to be questioned. That bag is the most important one we have. It's got my technology, cash, and enough weapons to keep us safe and get us out of any situation we get stuck in. We haven't used any of Cassie's cash that she took out of her bank account when she ran from Jason. This is the emergency money I keep hidden in my go-bag. Cash can get you out of many situations in life. I have plenty of it to spare, and I will take care of her with it. The rest of the bags I'm loading are handy but not vital to staying alive like my go- bag is.

Not answering me, Cassie just does as I ask. She pulls the seat-belt over her shoulder as I jump back into the driver's seat. I floor it out of the parking lot, gravel spraying, and thank God it doesn't hit any of the precious bikes all lined up. That would have been like signing a death warrant.

As soon as we reach the edge of town, I pull over to the side of the road.

"What's wrong?" Cassie asks, grabbing my arm.

"We're fine. Just swapping license plates." Her eyes almost pop out of her head as she watches me pull new plates out of my go-bag.

Not waiting to explain, I'm out with the screwdriver, replacing them and throwing the old ones off into the long grass along the edge of the road. Truth be told, they were probably stolen anyway. I'm not taking any risks.

As I get back in the car and pull out again, she starts to giggle a nervous laugh.

"What else have you got in that Mary Poppins bag of yours?" Looking over at her, we start to laugh. Not because her joke was that funny, but it's a release of the tension that we're both carrying.

"Oh, you'd be surprised what tricks I have up my sleeve, young

145

lady," I say, trying to keep the moment a little lighter than the last few hours have been.

"If they're anything like the magic you have in your pants, then I'm all for it." Tears are rolling down her cheeks, and I know they are partly from laughing but the rest are scared tears.

Placing my hand on her thigh, I squeeze it firmly. "Remember, you can trust me. I'll keep you safe."

She takes a big deep breath, her tears slowing. "I do," she says, placing her hand over mine and giving me a timid smile.

Driving now in silence, we're both deep in our thoughts. I know what I'm doing and making plans in my head. While I don't know what she's thinking, I'm positive she's just trying to keep herself calm and convincing herself to trust me. She says she does, and in her head, she thinks she does. But I need her to feel it so deeply in her bones, so without any doubt, it's an instinct her body feels, just like it understands how to breathe without being told.

After we've been driving for a while, it gives her time to settle. I'm thankful that Crusher at least had a full tank of fuel for me. My mind has put all the action plan together, and it's time to focus on Cassie again. I had to push her out of my thoughts which sounds crazy when she is sitting right next to me, but there are times for both of our safety when my pinpoint focus will be what keeps us alive.

"You need to eat." In my head I said that a lot softer than the gruffness I just heard come out.

"So do you!" she spits back at me, and if I'm honest, I deserve it.

There must be something fucked up in my make-up, because her standing up to me and not taking my shit is such a turn-on. Now isn't even the time to be thinking about sex but someone should have told my dick that.

"Touché." My remark takes the edge off her scowl, but only slightly.

I can see her hesitating to say something, it's like she is throwing it around her head, and every time she almost says it, she changes her mind.

"Spit it out, what's wrong?" I'm getting ready for the onslaught of abuse or concern about the last few hours or the way I just spoke to her, but I couldn't be any further from the truth.

"I'm sorry to ask, but I need you to stop. I need to pee really, really, really badly." Oh shit, I didn't even think about that. I'm used to holding on for a long time when we're on a job.

"Cassie, baby, I'm so sorry. You need to tell me these things." I look for a clear spot ahead to pull off the road that will be safe. By the sound of her voice, I don't think she can last much longer, and I don't know how long it'll be until we find the next service station that will be safe enough to stop at.

"I just did!" she yells back at me. Oh yeah, her bladder is about to burst. "Why are you stopping here?" She's now crossing her legs.

"So, you can pee, woman." Getting out, I slam the door behind me, and I can still hear her screaming at me as I round the front of the truck and open her door.

She looks at me with the eyes of someone in an old-fashioned gun fight, waiting to see who draws first.

"Get out, Cassie." I glare at her because I think to myself, *It's not a request, lady*.

"I'm not going to the toilet in those trees, that's disgusting."

I lean across her and undo her seatbelt, taking her hand and pulling her out of the car.

"What's worse, sitting in your own piss for another few hours or squatting behind those trees and getting relief? I know what I'd choose." I look at her with a face that tells her I'm not taking no for an answer.

"Oh yeah, just squat behind those trees, like it's that easy. It's easy for you guys that can just flop it out, aim, and spray the ground, give it a shake, lock it up again, then walk away. I have to drop my pants and not get them dirty, then try to hold them off the ground enough so they don't get wet. Squat and balance so the piss is going straight down and not running down the inside of my leg. Holding myself long enough in that squat for all the drips to fall off, because it's not like I have any toilet paper to wipe myself. Then I look down and hope I'm not standing in a pool of piss all over my shoes. You men have no fucking idea what it's like to be a woman. Arggghhhh!" She screams at me like she is about to explode.

Before I can hold it in, the laughter is just pouring out of me. Not just a little but that full deep-down laugh-out-loud type.

"Asshole!" Cassie screams at me as she races toward the trees. If there is one thing that is difficult to do when you are busting to pee, it's laugh hard.

Pulling the laughter back to a very quiet chuckle, I walk toward where she ran off to. I don't want to embarrass her any further, but I'm not letting her get very far from me at any moment.

I can hear her going to the toilet, cursing to herself the whole time. Note to self: I need to check a little more often for her. Hearing the water stop running, I can't help myself.

"Do you want me to find you some leaves to wipe with?" I try to hold in the laughter that is wanting to escape again.

"Not funny, dickwad!" I can hear her shuffling her feet, standing up again. I give her a bit of space so she doesn't realize I could hear every little sound.

Appearing from behind the trees, the look on her face hasn't changed. She is still ready to tear strips off me.

Not game to poke an angry woman, treading lightly, I move toward her.

"Feel better now?" Putting my arm around her shoulder, the glare tells me she's not even close.

"You need to feed me now." Shrugging off my arm, she continues to the car.

"Roger that." The death stare over her shoulder tells me those weren't the right words to use either. She might think being a man is easy. Try being around a woman some days. I take back when I said I love when she's feisty.

"I can't win," I mumble under my breath, following her.

"That's right, and don't you forget it."

"See what I mean!" I roll my eyes at the back of her, and lucky she didn't turn around, otherwise I'm just opening myself up for more pain.

I pull the bag with the food out of the back of the Dodge. I don't even know what she packed, so there's no point in me even offering her choices.

I dump the bag in her lap, not saying a word. I figure it's just easier to start driving, and once she has eaten, then maybe my calm Cassie will return.

"Do you want something?" Her voice already sounds a little better.

"You eat first, then we can worry about me." And I mean it. I'm not sure my stomach is ready for anything yet. The adrenaline pumping through my body is not going to ease off anytime soon, and the truth is, I need that. It keeps my focus sharp.

"Ghost?" And there she is, I can see it in her eyes. My Cassie. "You need to keep up your strength, otherwise you won't be able to be my badass ninja." Then she throws the pleading puppy-dog eyes at me and who can refuse them.

"Alright, alright. What have ya got?" I don't really feel like anything, but the small smile that just crept up her face, that she could do something little to look after me, is totally worth the suffering.

We've been driving now for around six hours, with a couple of minor stops along the way for gas and restroom breaks. I think if I make Cassie stop on the side of the road ever again, she may just kill me.

I messaged Badger the last time we stopped, getting the coordinates for our safe place for tonight. It has nothing to do with the agency and is off-grid, as we call it. Whereas I have the ability to find so much through my computer to help, Badger is the one with the contacts. I don't want to know who they are or where they came from. I trust him with Cassie's life, and that's saying a lot. He is one of the only people in this world who now knows where we're headed for our final destination.

It's something I have kept to myself for years, knowing one day I would need it. I truly thought it would be for me after a job went south and I needed to decompress. But this is more intense. It's the only place I can hide until this all clears where I know I have a chance of keeping Cassie alive. We are a few days away from my property, and I need the time tonight to cover our tracks and start planting decoy information on the web. If anyone starts digging into either of us, it will send them in the opposite direction to where we're headed, and in circles a few times too.

There's an email reply from Bull, and I'm not opening it until we're settled in for the night and I have finished everything I need to do. Cassie has offered to drive to give me a break today, but I don't think it's a good idea. She has had a huge shock and upheaval, and there is no way her concentration level is where it needs to be if we start being followed.

There is so much I'm going to need to teach her as soon as we can. First port of call is how to shoot a gun, reload it, and in an emergency, to fix it if it jams. I never want her to feel vulnerable. She may not want to do it, but I know her independence will appreciate that I'm giving her some control in keeping herself safe. I fucking hope she never needs to use it.

Then will come the skill of driving at high speeds safely. I'll be thankful when we pick up the car that Badger has sitting at the house tonight. My car of choice for safety is a Range Rover SUV. Not the old style that were made for use by the Army in the war. These modern-day ones are just what I need. Of course, it's black, with dark-tinted windows and all the modern satellite navigation and Bluetooth systems I need. Lower to the ground for aerodynamics and handling on the road at high speed, but sturdy as hell. How Badger got it so fast I'll never know, but that's like I said. I don't need to know how, I'm just thankful that he managed to arrange it. Then when we leave in the morning, he will arrange for this Dodge to disappear.

I know Bull would have been perfect at helping me on the run, but he doesn't have the same sort of connections Badger does. Besides, I knew the moment I made the decision we were going into hiding that I couldn't expect Bull to do the same. He doesn't deserve to be taken away from his family with no end date on this one.

"Are we close to the place? I need to sleep, and you do too." I've seen how hard Cassie has been fighting it for the last thirty minutes, wanting to stay awake because she is too scared to close her eyes while we're out in the open. I didn't realize how much today has taken out of her. Her face is a little pale for my liking. I live this type of life every day in my job, but for her, it has wiped her out.

"About another hour. Just sleep, beautiful. I've got this." Taking her hand in mine and pulling it to my lips, I kiss it to remind her that no matter what, we still have us.

"I'll stay awake to keep you company." Her words are half mumbled the harder she is fighting sleep. Placing her hand back in her lap, it took at the most sixty seconds and the first soft snore came from the passenger side of the car.

Although her brain is strong, her body took over and won.

Sleep, my bright eyes. A few more days and we'll be home.

It's after dark by the time we arrive at the shack that looks like it's about to fall down, out in the middle of nowhere. I'm thankful. I carry Cassie into the house and find a bed that looks cleanish. I place her carefully down and whisper to her that she is safe which has her slipping back into her deep sleep. It surprises me she didn't wake, but also tells me her body is struggling to keep up with all of this. Thankfully, though, it gives me time to quickly open the barn doors, and there in front of me is the brand-new Range Rover, as promised. I transfer our bags into it and only bring inside what we need for tonight.

Setting myself up on a chair and using the dresser in the room as a makeshift table, I set to work on everything I need to get done. Cassie sleeps through the whole time I'm working. It gives me some relief that she trusts me enough to be able to sleep as deep as she is right now. Looking at the time, I see it's just after midnight, and I know it would be stupid of me to miss the chance of a small sleep to recharge, ready for another long day of traveling.

I have one last thing to do before I lie down and snuggle up to Cassie.

Opening Bull's email, the first line is exactly like I expected.

I'm going to fucking kill you, Ghost, you stupid dickhead!

Yep, I'd be disappointed with anything less. What else has he got to say?

Chapter Twelve

GHOST

I didn't tell Bull about Cassie.

Not because I don't trust him. I trust this man with my life, and that means with hers too. But I don't want to drag him into this and put his or his family's lives in danger. These men will stop at nothing to get to her. My life doesn't matter, but his does.

So, if he thinks it's just me going dark, then it's better for all of us. It's one less person to be worried about and have on my conscience.

Continuing to read on, I try not to smirk at the vision I have of his fist slamming on the desk when he opened my email and the poor keyboard being punished as he unleashed his annoyance at me in this reply.

I'm going to fucking kill you, Ghost, you stupid dickhead!

Why the fuck do you think you need to do whatever this is ALONE?! Always the hardhead who won't take help.

For fuck's sake!

You know I called Badger straight away to ask if you were taking a vacation. All he answered was that it was under control. Asshole!

I'm going to punch you both so hard when I see you, and I better see you soon.

I don't know what's going on, but no matter what it is, even though I'm pissed at you, I'm still here. I'll always have your back, ALWAYS!

I wish I had your freakish computer-hacking skills because I would track your ass down, dickhead, and tell you all this myself.

Right, enough yelling at you, and I know you are sitting there laughing at me. Not fucking funny, dumbass. Now keep your head down and eyes open.

Get in touch when you can, and DON'T DO ANYTHING STUPID! OR MORE STUPID! Or it will be me you're running from, when I come to kick your ass.

Love you, Bro,
Bull

He is the closest I have to family, and it hurts to once again be leaving my family behind. The first time, it was actually easier to walk away from my biological family because they didn't care about me anyway. To them I was just there, existing in the chaos of the house. This time I know I'm going to miss Bull. As much as we spend our whole time together giving each other shit, we do it with the underlying love for each other as brothers. We are the type of men that don't talk about that part of our relationship, so Bull telling me he loves me lets me know he's worried and wants to make sure nothing is left unsaid. I get it, and all I can reply is with the same one line.

Love you too, Bro. Signing off.

I can't keep communicating with him at the moment because it runs the risk of us being tracked, no matter that I have covered our tracks and my security on the net is tight. I'm good at what I do but not arrogant enough to know that there aren't people out there who are better. Money talks and people will sell their soul for it. But I want Bull to know I got his message and read it loud and clear.

Shutting down my laptop, I don't bother changing. As I crawl into the bed behind Cassie, she instinctively wriggles her body back into mine. It's like we are made to fit. It's only been just over a month, but our bodies know where they are meant to be. My body belongs wrapped tightly around hers.

Forever.

CASSIE

What is that disgusting smell?

Moving my face a little to the side, I realize it's the pillow my head is on. Where the hell are we?

I don't need to open my eyes to know I'm safe because I can feel Ghost holding me tight. But that smell! I thought the last house was bad, but this is just... I can't even describe the stench.

It's making my stomach start to roll.

Fuck, not again.

I slap my hand over my mouth as I try to jump up quickly. Ghost's arms won't let me go, but I can't open my mouth to yell at him. I do the only thing I can think of. I dig my nails as hard as I can into his arm.

"What the hell, Cassie," he screams, pulling away from me. I don't have time to look at him. Jumping up, I run toward the door. I don't even know where to go.

My hand over my mouth must have given away the problem, as I hear him yelling from behind me, "Go right, second door."

No waiting, I burst through that second door, and the relief I feel at seeing the toilet bowl in front of me, I don't even care how dirty it looks.

The first burst of vomit hits the ceramic bowl, and that's all I care about. The thought of having to clean up my own vomit off the floor has me retching again. While I'm kneeling on the floor, I feel him wrapping my hair in his hand and holding it back out of my face. With his other hand, he rubs my back, trying to soothe me.

Lord, please make it stop. I don't think I even ate enough yesterday for the amount that is coming out. I mean, seriously, nobody should have to do this in front of the hottest guy she has ever met. It's just wrong.

I try to take a deep breath, hold it, and slowly let it out, and I can feel my stomach finally starting to stop rolling over. Grabbing some toilet paper mounted on the wall in front of me, I wipe my mouth. I just want to rinse it out. The aftertaste is feral. Sliding to the side and sitting on my backside, I look up into the concerned eyes of Ghost. I just want to curl up into a ball in embarrassment.

"You okay?" He crouches his big body down in the small space so we're face to face.

I want to say no, but lying to him, I slowly answer him, "Yes, just the stress again." I know he doesn't believe me, but at the moment, it's about all either of us can process.

Taking a look around me so I don't have to feel the intensity of Ghost's stare, I try to work out what's happening.

There is only a toilet in this room, but everything is filthy. The more I take it all in, I start scrambling up off the floor, knocking Ghost backwards into the wall with a heavy thud.

"Whoa, steady there, baby." Springing to his feet like a cat, he's up and ready before I even manage to get my balance.

"This is absolutely disgusting. Where the hell are we?" I look at my hands in horror at what germs are now on them after hanging onto the toilet that I can see has stains all over it. My stomach starts to roll again, and I'm moving from this room before it makes me sick again.

"Beggars can't be choosers, Cassie." His voice isn't soft and caring like it was before when he was holding my hair back.

"Obviously! But this place needs to be condemned, surely." I look around the room I'm guessing is the living room. Not that it has anything in it. "Why do I have the feeling that we're in someone's house who is on the wrong side of the law?" I didn't even realize that Ghost wasn't still in the room with me, that he had left to grab me a bottle of water from my bag.

"Rinse your mouth. Wash your hands with the same water and get in the car." This guy's split personality is really testing my patience.

"Don't speak to—" Before I even get to finish, he's talking.

"Stop! Just do what I said." He holds his hand up in front of me, signaling that he wants me to do as I'm told. In my head I'm telling him to get fucked, but my body obeys his words like they're orders. What is it about his warrior voice and body language that has me almost mesmerized to do what he wants.

Standing frozen and swallowing, the revolting taste snaps me into moving and washing out my mouth. I spit it into a sink in the bathroom next to the toilet. The brown rust stains on it tell me what I suspected. This place isn't lived in. It's just used as a place to hide, but from *what* is the question. I know I should be grateful we could get some rest, because from what Ghost said yesterday, we have another big day of traveling ahead of us. But to be honest, I think I would have rather taken the risk and slept in the car parked off the side of the road somewhere.

Yeah, right, like Ghost would have agreed to that or would have slept one minute. Trying to wash my hands with the water that is left still doesn't make them feel any cleaner. I follow the sound of the door opening, where I'm guessing Ghost has gone with our bag. Not that I remember seeing much of the room I was in because my stomach didn't give me a whole lot of warning from the moment I started to wake.

The back door of the house is open and no screen door on it. I notice it lying on the grass, broken, and part of the frame off the house still attached. The disgust I was feeling before is morphing into fear. I don't feel safe here. Even with Ghost, this place tells me that bad things have happened here, and I don't want to touch anything else. I have enough darkness in my life, I don't want to be caught up in any more.

Looking at Ghost loading the bag and his computer into the back of a brand-new-looking black car in the barn to the side of the house, I'm confused. I know we need to swap cars, but how the hell is there a brand-new Range Rover in this dump? With my head spinning more than the churning still happening in my gut, slowly I make my way toward him.

"Ghost?"

"Don't ask, just get in." He still isn't in the mood to talk obviously, and I'm not feeling great again, so giving in, I just walk to the passenger side and climb in. I almost want to strip off the clothes I'm wearing so I don't dirty the car with whatever was in that house. Part of me is glad I didn't really see the bed I was sleeping on. I push the thought out of my head when the bile rises in my throat again.

Ghost is in now and programming his phone into the Bluetooth. Then he reaches across in front of me, opening the glove compartment.

"Same thing as before. There if you need it. Understood?" He's not yelling at me, but his tone is short and to the point.

Just nodding, I don't want to open my mouth to speak because I'm afraid of what I might say. Or more to the point, what I might scream at him. Maybe I shouldn't be such a hypocrite about his split personality because I feel like I'm having a bit of it myself these last few days.

Driving back out onto the road, silence settles in the car until Ghost pushes a few buttons on the steering wheel and music cuts in to break the mood.

The old saying that music soothes the savage beast might just be true. I feel my shoulders start to drop a little and my body melt back into the seat, the voice of *Fly By Midnight* singing *Tomorrow*. I don't know if it's a random pick in his playlist or if Ghost is trying to tell me something. The song is asking me, if we get through today, will I still be here tomorrow? Maybe it's words he's not sure how to say or just that he is as scared as I am, and if that's the case, then we are in deep, deep trouble.

I'm not sure how long we've been on the road when Ghost pushes the call button on the steering wheel and the phone starts calling someone on speaker. The name on the screen says Badger. I'm guessing he's the person Ghost was talking to yesterday that has been helping him.

"Did you sleep?" a raspy voice breaks through the thick silence that is hovering in the car.

"Enough to get through. Badger, meet Cassie. Cassie, meet Badger. You can trust him with anything, including your life." I don't know what to think of this guy that I'm being introduced to. Ghost obviously trusts him, but trust is something I don't know how to give out that easily.

"Hello." That didn't come out too confidently, but it's the best I've got at the moment.

"Cassie, nice to meet you. Is he treating you right?" I'm picturing the man behind this voice and try to imagine what he's like.

"Most of the time." I can't help myself smirking at Ghost which finally breaks the stone face he has been carrying since I finished being sick.

"Well, we better fix that. Ghost?" Badger starts to laugh, which interrupts the tension in the car.

"Fuck off, asshole, I'm not the one who had us sleeping in that brothel last night."

"Oh my God! Please tell me you are joking." I can't help myself, I yell at both of them. "You better not have had me sleeping in come stains on that bed last night. Ghost! What the hell!" Pulling back my ranting, I hear them both laughing at me.

"What!" I slap him on the arm, but he grabs my hand before I can pull it back.

"Cassie, it was a figure of speech. It might have been filthy but not in that way." He entwines his hand around mine and places it down on his thigh.

"That's on me. Don't blame Ghost for that one. We didn't have much time. Sorry, that's all I had in that area out of sight. We can't afford for you to be seen." My heart drops, and I feel guilty firstly for being ungrateful, and secondly, that I took it out on Ghost.

"Sorry, I'm just not myself at the moment," I say, looking at Ghost but also wanting Badger to hear me too.

"Understandable," Badger says, his voice booming through the car. Ghost just nods at me as he raises my hand to his lips to kiss it.

"No!" I yelp, pulling my hand back like a crazy woman. "It's all dirty, don't kiss it," I continue yelling as Badger's voice is also screaming over top of mine.

"What's happening?" What is it about these badass men and their controlling voices?

"Sorry, Badger, but I don't want him kissing me until I can wash properly with soap somewhere. No offence, but that house was rank! God knows what diseases are breeding in there." Now I sound like some sort of drama queen.

"Buddy, can you find me somewhere clean for Cassie with a shower, and I can grab us a coffee and breakfast? Because I'll be fucked if I'm not allowed to kiss her for much longer." I'm about to laugh, but I can see the seriousness on his face.

"On it. I can see where you are, so just give me five, and I'll message through the coordinates. Any other requirements, Cassie?"

"Nope, just clean would be a start."

"Can do. And by the way, he's one of the best. And I don't say that easily. Later." The phone disconnects with a click through the speaker, and the music drops back into the car.

I don't want the conversation to stop again, so I ask the obvious question. "You seem angry." I try to keep a calmness in my voice that I'm not feeling on the inside.

"I'm fine." Those two words are such a bullshit answer.

"Right. Okay, understood." Looking out the window, I try not to show the hurt at him shutting me out.

"Cassie, just leave it." The strain in those words tells me he can't talk about it, so it's either me or something about me. Either way, it's not great for me.

"Mhmm." I pick up my bottle of water and take another sip, still trying to get the acidic taste out of my mouth.

The chime from the phone takes both our attention as we scan the text message on the screen on the dashboard. Badger has booked a hotel room in a drive-in motel only ten minutes from here. The last line of the text makes me laugh.

Badger: *And they assure me it's spotlessly clean.*

"You even have Badger running scared." He rolls his eyes at me but smiles at the same time.

"I doubt Badger is scared of anyone," I reply, trying to relax a little. I can't keep all this stress on board. I can't imagine life on the run is going to be all peaches and cream. I need to learn to roll with the punches.

"You're spot-on. Now, let's get to this motel and get you showered and fed." There isn't much more to be said as Ghost starts paying attention to the GPS map that is taking us to the address Badger gave us.

"It even smells clean." I sigh with relief as we enter the room. I stayed in the car while Ghost got us checked in. I can just imagine what they will think when we check out again in an hour's time.

"You wash up first. I need to talk to Badger." He is still a bit short with me, but I don't care right now. That shower is calling my name. Stripping down, I want to burn the clothes from last night, and even though I don't have that many, I decide to throw them in the trash in the bathroom. I just don't want them anywhere near the rest of my clothes.

Before I even step into the shower, I grab my toothbrush and toothpaste. I need to get rid of the crap taste in my mouth.

The steaming water is soon streaming down over my body, and it's like the soap is washing away not only my bad mood but my clouded brain along with it. This is four days in a row I have felt sick in the morning and the second I have been vomiting. My greatest fear is now closing in around me. This could be the worst thing to happen. Laying my head on the tiles, I try to think about what I can do. I don't want to add to the stress that Ghost is already carrying because of me, but my gut feeling is that I'm about to dump a whole lot more on top.

The knock on the door tells me it's time to get out and get a plan together.

———

"Feel better?" Ghost is standing at the door as I open it, leaning in to kiss me.

"No kissing until you have showered. And yes, I feel amazing." As I step around him, I hear the groan.

"You're killing me." The grumble echoes in the bathroom as he slams the door.

I grab my shoes, knowing I don't have much time to waste. He will be in and out in a flash. I slip the phone he gave me into my pocket and take cash from my bag. Then I text a message to his phone that I see sitting on the table.

I'm probably about to do the dumbest thing of my life, but I have to know. When we pulled into the motel, I saw a Target across the road. Snatching the key to the room and quickly grabbing Ghost's cap off the table, I push all my wet hair up under the hat and pull it down low over my face. It's not much of a disguise, but it's all I've got in a hurry. I wait for the water to start, and I'm out the door and past the car parked outside. My heart is beating so fast, and I can't stop swiveling my head from side to side. I don't even know what I'm looking for. How would I know if someone is watching me? All I can hope is that I'm in a place where there are a lot of people, so if someone tries to grab me, I'll scream the house down and people will save me.

It sounds good in theory, but of course, if there's a gun involved, people are likely to just run away. Gun, shit, I didn't think of that. They won't be grabbing me, they will just shoot me dead and be gone before anyone sees who it was.

I'm such an idiot!

Hesitating on the median strip in the middle of the road, my brain is going crazy. Should I turn back? An old truck rumbling past me lets out a backfire that has me screaming and jumping forward, almost getting hit by an oncoming car.

They lay on the horn at me for stepping out in front of them. Running as fast as I can to the other side of the road, I figure there's no going back now.

People are looking at me weirdly as I barge through the doors, looking up at all the signs for the department I need. Medical, drugs, and personal care. Yep, that'll be it.

I move quickly down the aisle, looking at both sides. *Come on, come on where are you?* Almost to the end and finally I see it.

My stomach sinks at the reality of what I think is about to happen.

Taking two boxes off the shelf, I run back to the checkout, drawing attention to myself, which is the most dangerous thing I could be doing.

"In a hurry?" The little old lady on the register looks at me with compassion when she sees what I hand her.

"Just a little. Running late," I say, trying to make her believe that my craziness is just because I'm supposed to be somewhere and I'm in a hurry.

"I guess you are, if you're buying pregnancy tests." Fuck, I didn't mean that, but if she must know, yes, I'm fucking late, and the sickness I'm sure is not stress.

"Oh no, they're for a friend." Why did I even say that. I'm a grown-ass woman, and she has no idea who I am. Yet I can't manage to say the words, that these are for me, and I don't know what it will mean.

"Sure they are, dear." She pats my hand as I pick them up off the counter in the bag she put them in. I hand over the cash.

Watching her get the change, I just wish she would hurry the hell up.

"Tell your friend no matter the circumstances she's in, a child is a gift. One she will love until the day she dies." Her words are spinning in my head. I snatch the change from her hand. That day could be sooner than she thinks if I don't hurry up. Purely from the fact that Ghost is going to want to kill me when he finds out I left the room without him and went out where there are people and surveillance cameras.

"Thank you," I yell over my shoulder as I'm off out the doors again, not even looking back to see her face.

Dodging cars, I'm across the street and just about to put the key in the door as it smashes open in front of me, with Ghost holstering his gun under his jacket.

"Stubborn pain in the ass of a woman!" His words are probably the most accurate summation of me right now.

Stopping dead in his tracks, the fire that is in his eyes and steam off his body, I know I'm about get his full wrath.

"Inside now!" His growl scares me, and I don't even blink, just push past him. Hearing the door bang behind me, he's pacing back and forth across the room. I'm not eager to turn around. I can tell he's so mad that he can't even speak.

I need to get away from him for a minute, plus I can't wait a minute longer.

Walking straight into the bathroom, I slide the lock on the door and pull the cap off my head. Seeing myself in the small mirror, I think about my mom for a split second. It gives me a slither of strength right when I need it.

"Cassie!" his voice booms through the door.

"I just need to pee. I'm sorry, just give me a minute and I'll explain." Pulling the test out and sitting down, I take a deep breath and start to wee on to the stick.

Whatever will be will be.

Through the door I can hear him mumbling.

"Sorry, she's fucking sorry. I'll show her fucking sorry. If I have to tie her to the goddamn seat, or me for that matter, I will. Crazy woman, does she want to die? What the hell was she thinking? What could she possibly need so importantly that she needs to risk her life by leaving here unprotected and without me? I bet she is just sitting in there hiding from me and waiting for me to calm down. Well, she'll be waiting a fucking long time!" His voice is still rambling with anger, but I can't hear the words anymore.

Looking down into my hand, I watch the second line start to show up as clear as ever.

My heart stops, and I forget to breathe. The room darkens in front of my eyes.

No, no, no, don't pass out...

I hear my voice, but it sounds distant as I call out. "Ghost..."

The floor comes up to meet me, and then there is nothing for a few moments.

A loud crack stirs me a little, and looking up from the floor into his eyes, I see the door is cracked around the lock and his hands are on my face.

"Talk to me, beautiful." His hands are under me and lifting me up, carrying me out of the bathroom.

My pants are still around my ankles, and my hand is clasped tightly around the test.

Sitting down onto the bed with me on his lap, not even worrying about my pants, his hand is on my cheek.

I stammer, trying to get the words out, but I know I need to.

"I'm pregnant," I whisper as I open my hand, and we both look down at the test, with two bright blue lines across it. "I had to know."

And then the tears start down my face. From pure shock, but as I bury my head in Ghost's shoulder and he wraps his arms around me as tight as he can, I know part of the tears are from happiness. I have a little baby growing inside me, and even though I'm petrified about what that means, I know it is that gift the lady told me a baby would be.

A little soul created from our love.

Maybe something good can come from this mess.

I have to believe that, to get through what is staring up at me in my hand.

Fear starts running through my body. Ghost hasn't said a word.

What if he doesn't want the baby? We don't even know each other. It's not what he signed up for when he said he wanted me.

Why is this even happening to us? My life is spiraling down when I didn't think it was possible it could sink any further.

"Cassie, look at me," he says, but I push my head into the crook of his neck harder. I don't know how to face him.

But he won't let me stay hidden. His strong hand on the back of my head is directing me up to look him in the eye.

"I'm not shocked." The compassion in his eyes says everything.

"What do you mean?"

"Remember, I'm the details man, I take in everything around me. You've been sick, we've been having sex every day, more than once a day for over a month, and you haven't had a period. Then your mood swings are getting bigger, which is not new, but these ones are different." I want to argue about that, but he's right.

All of a sudden, it makes sense.

"That's why you were angry this morning." My heart sinks; he doesn't want the baby. "It's okay, I understand. I can cope on my own."

"No, you don't understand at all. Yes, I was angry, and I still am. But it's not what you think." He runs his hand down my body, and suddenly, we both realize I'm half dressed.

"Shit, Cassie, sorry." He stands me up and pulls up my pants, and I can't help letting out a little giggle.

I sit myself back in his lap and curl into his body again.

"Let's get this straight. I'm angry because this isn't how it should be. Finding out we're having a baby should be the most amazing time in our lives. Yet here we are, in hiding, and you're stressed and panicking. I can see it in your eyes. And all I feel is rage at what they are putting you through." He takes a breath, his hands on my waist and lifting me again so I'm straddling his big, muscled thighs. We're facing each other so neither of us can look away.

"But all of that aside, knowing you are carrying my child…" His hand is now lying on my lower stomach. "Is the most beautiful thing in this world. And it just makes this even more important that I get you away from here. I promise you that I will keep both you and our baby safe. They will never find you."

"You can't promise that, Ghost."

"Watch me!"

The news settling in for both of us, we just look into each other's souls, hoping he's right.

"I hope she has your bright eyes." Ghost kisses me on my forehead.

"Maybe it's a boy," I whisper.

"No matter what our baby is, just know they will be loved." My heart is exploding with his words. "Just as much I love you, Cassie." The three words I have been holding onto for what feels like forever, finally I can say them out loud back to him.

"Oh, Noah, I love you too. So much I didn't know it was possible."

My tears are running down my cheeks again, but not one of them is a sad one.

Our lips join and seal our words.

Finally parting, I try out the words on my lips. "We're having a baby…"

"Yes, beautiful, we are having a baby."

How and where that is going to happen is now the question. I have to trust Ghost to take care of that. My job is just to stay calm for the little one.

Just stay calm…

Chapter Thirteen

GHOST

S hit just got real!

That's a lie, it was already real, but it just got extra crazy. My brain is going in so many directions. How do I hide a pregnant woman who needs care and doctors and all the scans and tests? I pride myself on being calm in any situation, but for once, I feel totally over the edge.

A baby! A tiny little human that I need to keep safe too. I don't know how to do that. I've never even touched a baby, well, not that I can remember anyway. I'm sure I bottle-fed my sisters when I was little, but all those memories are long gone in my brain, wiped when I walked away, to protect me from the pain.

This is so far out of my league that I have avoided it at all costs. I have no one to blame but myself. I never should have slept with her bare. Now I have not only put Cassie in greater danger but also our unborn child.

That's the part that I can't get my head around.

Bull's email jumps back into my head again. *"Don't do anything stupid."* Bit late, buddy, I think I've already ticked that off the bucket list for this job. What would he say if he knew?

His voice in my head has the swarm of bees settling. *"You've got this. You know what to do."*

He would be right. And the one thing that I can't do is panic.

Taking in a deep breath, it's like the oxygen is filtering my calmness back into my brain.

Looking down to the top of Cassie's head where she has dropped her forehead onto my chest, everything slots into place in my head.

Lifting her face up by her chin, she voices the words that are a mirror of what her face is telling me. "I'm petrified," she says with a small quiver, not much more than a whisper.

"I know, beautiful, I know, but I've got this. Trust me to get us through this," I say, taking her face between my hands. No matter what life throws at me, my world will start and stop with this face.

I pull her toward me. I've been waiting all morning for this.

"Just so you know, I don't care if you are covered in mud or have bathed in beautiful perfume, have morning breath or have just eaten garlic. Nothing, and I mean nothing, will stand in the way of me kissing you. Got it?"

I swallow her answer in my mouth, taking her. I didn't realize how much I had pent up inside me, but it's all coming out now, wrestling with her tongue to gain the dominance I need. It pulls out my inner desperation to have complete control of everything, and that includes this moment.

I slide my right hand up into her brown hair that is still wet from her shower and hanging in clumps, my fingers wrapping the strands and straining against her scalp. Her moan sends the fire through me that I know we both need to feel. The kiss doesn't slow, and her hands are now on my back, having slid them up under my jacket and shirt. I need her skin too, but not just in my hands.

Wrapping my arm around her waist to steady her, I push up onto my feet and turn in one motion, not stopping my devouring of her mouth. Laying her down on the bed, my weight on top of her is what she needs to feel to center herself, and I grind my cock into her so she knows what I want, what I think we both want. My desperation is taking over any softness I should be offering her right now.

Releasing her lips for a minute, no words between us are needed. Kneeling above her, I don't waste time. My jacket is off and my holster on the floor next to us. It's never far from me. Scrunching the t-shirt in my hand and pulling it over my head, I watch her eyes fully dilate. I know she is as ravenous as I am to fuck—and fuck hard.

Pulling her top over her head, the roughness of pulling her bra off in a hurry has me up off the bed, kicking off my boots and dropping my cargo pants and boxers. Taking my cock in my hand and slowly with the firmness I need, I stroke myself, trying to hold off the explosive arousal that I have inside me. As much as I want to slam into her, I don't want to hurt her. It's not the baby because I'm not stupid and know it's safe, but it's the woman now naked, stretched out before me, that I never want to hurt in any way.

She deserves more than that. For everything she is suffering and has lived with, love is all she should know, and I intend to be the one to show it to her.

"Noah?" Looking up at me, my name on her lips is like the trigger I need, and she knows it.

"I've got you." And I do. I don't take the time for the foreplay we both love; this is about pure carnal lust and acceptance of our love. My hand on my cock above her sex, I drag it through her wetness, and I know she wants all of me now. Pushing hard and fast into her pussy, her body lifts up off the bed, and the hitch in her breath is enough that I hold my position for a few seconds. On my elbows above her, our faces together, I just want to kiss her until she can't breathe without my air in her lungs. Feeling her body relax slightly and sinking into the bed, it's the signal I've been waiting for.

I pull out and pound back into her over and over again. Her head drops back on the pillow, mouth open, and the filthy words coming out of her spur me on to bury myself so deep that she feels every part of me. My balls tighten, pulling up inside me, and I know I'm not far off. I want her to feel the same ecstasy that is about to race through my body. Judging by the flurry of short breaths from her pink glossy lips that she's now biting on, I know she is just as close.

"Let go, bright eyes, we both need to let go." Dropping my mouth to her rock-hard brown nipple that I have been watching the whole time, I take it between my teeth and bite down firmly.

The pain and the pleasure are all that she can take.

"Noah... fuck!" And there it is, what I was waiting for. Her wet pussy contracts tightly around my cock, and I release every piece of tension that is lying deep down inside me. Her body quivers, her cheeks flushed, and her chest with that layer of sweat makes her olive skin glisten in the light. A more beautiful sight I have never seen.

Her eyes are still open and fixated on me as I jerk through the last releases of come that I am emptying inside her. Marking her again. That feeling of her being mine is what keeps me strong.

My head is clear as a bell now, with all the endorphins and adrenaline pumping through it.

"No matter what happens, I will always love you." Placing my lips softly on hers, I need her to know that. In our world, tomorrow is never guaranteed, so she needs to carry my love with her and know it's unconditional.

"I feel like I've always loved you." Her words hit me hard because she has just described what I couldn't put into words.

Falling to the side of her on the bed and pulling her into my side, I wrap her in my arms as tightly as I can. We lie there, just absorbing it.

Us, our love, and our baby. Nothing else matters.

We will make it through whatever is coming for us.

"You are my safe place, Noah."

"Always," is all I can manage to say.

Cassie, you crush my walls.

We have been traveling now for four days, and we're finally getting close to home.

I knew one day it would become home, but I never in my wildest dreams pictured Cassie and a baby here with me. This was going to be the place I could hide from the world and anyone who wanted to hurt me. That danger I imagined just being physical, but now, it's so much more. The pain of losing my new little family would kill me, without the need for any weapons.

The word *family* was not something I ever contemplated for myself once I chose to leave mine behind, and it was something I had consciously chosen not to have. The young years of my life were enough to ruin any happiness that I thought was associated with the word family. Those shows on the TV and hearing kids at school talk about their perfect lives, I presumed it was all fake because there was no love or joy in my house.

Badger managed to make sure we had somewhere appropriate to sleep along the way, and we decided to stop at a twenty-four-hour medical center in the last big town we went through yesterday, with fake names and a blonde wig for Cassie and a hoodie for me that I picked up in a secondhand shop close by. We knew it was risky, but we needed to check that everything was okay with the baby and get an idea on what she should be doing. No blood tests, though, we didn't want any record of her being there that could be traced.

It's still early in the pregnancy, so they couldn't tell us much, but for Cassie, I could see her relax the moment the doctor told her she was healthy and that if she just keeps up her eating and exercise, tries to stay away from stress, then she should have the dream pregnancy. I can't do all they described, but the food and exercise will be easy where we're going. I'm relying on the fresh mountain air to set the relaxing vibe.

I'm not sure if it's the baby or the strain of the week but Cassie has been asleep for the last three hours, making the most adorable little noise that is almost a snore but not quite. I'm torn as to whether I should wake her up before we arrive but have decided against it. Turning down the overgrown gravel drive, the crunching of the wheels and the swiping of leaves on the car has her stirring from her slumber anyway.

I can tell that no one has been down here in a very long time, which makes me feel assured that we are going to be in the middle of nowhere and that no one will know we're here.

I bring the Range Rover to a slow crawl while I'm trying to avoid the sharp branches sticking out. It would be nice to at least last a week without a scratch on the new vehicle. I'm not one to go crazy about the look of my cars but they just need to have all the safety features and speed that I require.

The back of the car is full of groceries. I can hear them jiggling around as we ride over the rough terrain. Badger organized for me to pick them up from the closest shop which is about forty-five minutes away. Told them we were passing through to one of the camping sites that are two hours down the road. It's a common thing, so they didn't even bat an eyelid at the order.

I don't know what I would do without Badger. He may not be as tech savvy as me, but his contacts are ones that money can't buy.

"Are we here?" Cassie rubs her eyes, starting to sit up a little straighter in her seat and taking a look at the forest around her.

"Almost." I take her hand and kiss her palm before placing it in my favorite place on my thigh. Feeling a connection even when I'm driving just does something for me. It's not a sexual thing, just her touch that has my heart ticking along at a regular and peaceful beat.

"Good, because… I don't want to hear any crap from you, but I need to pee again." Oh, that is the cutest thing I've seen for a while. The tiny blush on her cheeks is something I love seeing on my fire-breathing girl.

I try to hold in any laughter before she lets loose at me with a diatribe of what an ass I am.

"You don't have a very big bladder, do you?" I tease, grinning at her. I don't actually care if she needs to stop every ten minutes. Well, maybe not that often, that could be problematic, but still, whatever she needs, I'll do it.

"Hey." She points her finger at me, with a smile on her face. "I'm blaming your child. Before you planted your little seed, I could go all day, but now maybe not." Both of us start to laugh until she crosses her legs and stops suddenly.

"Oh God, don't make me laugh, that's not helping."

"I can stop here," I suggest, pushing my foot down on the brake pedal to watch her reaction.

"I swear, if you value your life, Ghost, I would keep driving and make it quick. I am not squatting in the trees ever again. Do you understand me? You promised me running water and an indoor toilet. I'm not fussy, and it's not too much to ask. So, I suggest you get me to that toilet, and it better be clean… or clean*ish* if you haven't been here in a while, not that you have even told me yet why or how you have this place. Anyway, I'll take dust over the scratches of leaves on my ass as I squat."

Now that is the Cassie I have grown to love. Never afraid of telling me what she thinks or wants.

"Yes, ma'am!" I say, mock saluting her, which just gets me a groan as she turns to look out the window and distract herself.

I have forgotten how thick the forest is on the property. It's late in the afternoon, but driving down the gravel road, it almost looks like night, with the overhanging of the trees blocking the waning sunlight. Getting to the part in the road that takes a dip down to the right, I'm reminded that I wanted to show her something, but tomorrow will do. I just need to get her settled and the generator up and running to make sure we have power. I always intended to get power to the house from the junction on the property, but it just hasn't been a priority. Until now!

The big reveal I was hoping for is now blown, with her legs bouncing on the floor as we pull up to the cottage. Not wasting time, I jump out with my keys and unlock the extra padlock I had on the door. She's behind me, about to barrel past me, but I told her back with my arm. She'll get used to this, but she will never be able to enter a room first while we're on the run.

"I'll be quick," I tell her, opening the door with my hand on my gun. I'm not expecting anything more than a wild animal, but in this job, you always know to be on alert at all times and expect the unexpected.

The cabin isn't huge but perfect for what we need. I move quickly into the main room that is a large open space, containing the living/dining room and kitchen all in one. Checking the bedroom on the way past and then pushing open the door to the bathroom, I turn to call Cassie that all is clear, but I should have known better.

"Move that hot ass." Pushing past me, the door closes in my face and the sound of running water is all I can hear, with a big sigh of relief. Well, I should be happy there are no screams from the bathroom, meaning that it meets her expectations. Or she was just so desperate that she didn't look.

Smiling to myself, I move from the door to give her some privacy, and I start opening curtains and windows. The night air creeping over the valley is cool but letting out the stale air in here is worth the chill it's bringing in. Doesn't matter what time of the year it is, the nights are always a little chilly up here in the mountains.

I start to carry in the bags from the car, always my guns and computers first, no matter where I am. I feel safe here but never want to be caught off guard, and trust me, that can happen in the first few minutes of arriving somewhere that you thought would be okay. It wouldn't be the first or the last time it happened to me if things turn to shit here. I just have to trust in my gut that it won't.

Leaving Cassie's bag outside the bathroom door for her and letting her know it's there, I tell her to freshen up while I get everything settled. Bringing a load of groceries in, I hear the shower running, which will still be cold, but I'm glad she took me up on the suggestion. That gives me time to strip the sheets off the bed and put fresh ones on, which I keep in a sealed container in the cupboard. Knowing it could be years between my visits, I needed to combat the dust and the creepy crawlies that are natural to have in a log cabin. It's been a long few days, and I want a place Cassie can lie down straight away if she needs to.

This place is far from perfect, but it's home now, and I hope Cassie will take to it like I did when I first arrived here. There is something here that speaks to a part of me I never knew existed. From the moment I drove down what was merely a track back then, I felt I belonged somewhere for the first time in my life. That this was meant to be mine, and I knew that eventually I would end up here. I must admit, though, I kind of thought it would be later in life, but here we are.

Wiping out the fridge, I stack it full of the food that will need to stay cold. I need to go for a walk to start the generator for power, and to turn on the gas for the fridge and hot water, but I don't want Cassie to come out the bathroom and freak out that I'm missing and then go running off into the forest and get herself lost looking for me. One of her traits that we are going to have to push down is to act first and think later. That's not really going to help us with the situation we're in. Even with the best intensions, it could be the thing that puts us in danger, when it could have been avoided by just slowing the fuck down and taking a breath.

With the light getting dimmer as night closes in, I find matches and light a few candles that are scattered around the room before I get the generator on for the lighting. Not that they're much brighter than candles. Last time I was here, I didn't need them and preferred to sit in front of the fire with a few candles. Totally switching off from the world was the only way I could let some things I have lived through go from my head, and my heart at times.

The bathroom door opening has me turning to see Cassie with the flickering light from the candles on her face. I have never seen her look more beautiful fully clothed. I can imagine what she looks like dressed in the stunning evening gowns, fully made up with so much makeup, dripping with expensive jewels and heels that help to show off her amazing legs. I've seen the pictures that Jason used to make sure were in all the papers, creating the image of him and his trophy girlfriend who were so perfectly in love, or so he would have you believe.

But Cassie is standing here in front of me, her long brown hair a little wavy after she has taken it out of her braid from the car. She's wearing a pair of light gray track pants that are hanging loosely on her hips, a white crop top with short sleeves and a scoop neck that is showing off her perfect cleavage. The bare olive skin of her stomach and the cutest little belly button have me already hard and wanting to kiss every inch of her. I push down those thoughts because we have things to do, but damn, I'd rather be christening our bed right now instead.

"Ghost." Her voice is a little unsure, and we can't have that. It's time to let her know what is going on and who I really am. I haven't ever shared the full story with anyone, but it's time. She is the one, and I think deep down I knew that the moment I first laid eyes on her photo in that file. She may have looked sad and scared, but there was something that told me deep down, her strength was what I was looking for. Someone who matches my strong will and determination, even though in her I call it stubbornness, it truly is the same thing. I need her softness, but the fight that she isn't afraid to use with me too.

Walking toward her, I can see her confusion at my lack of words and the way I'm mesmerized by her presence in the room. Taking her hand, I walk backwards and pull her toward the front door. Her eyes are asking me what I'm doing but no words are spoken. Stepping out into the open, I stop and place my hands on her cheeks, my thumb stroking her skin with all the tenderness she deserves. Letting one hand drop to beside my waist, I lean toward her soft lips that look smooth from the balm she has just put on in the bathroom.

Our lips meet, and it's not hot and heavy like we're about to explode if we don't take it further. It's exactly what I want to show her, that this has never just been about the sexual attraction between us that is like a fire that rages hot, day and night. This is so much more than I can say with words. I could use the excuse that I'm a guy and we aren't good with romantic words, but it's not just that.

Growing up, I didn't hear my parents tell each other they loved one another, not once. There was never the snuggle on the couch I would hear others at school saying, about how disgusting it was seeing their parents making out, kissing, or cuddling. The closest to affection I saw was when Mom would slam Dad's dinner down on the table in front of him and it was his favorite meal. He didn't say thank you, but it would mean we would get through a meal without an argument, and that was his way of saying he appreciated the meal. As fucked up as it was, that was all I knew.

When I finally broke free from that toxicity, I quickly understood that there was more to life than that. As much as I dreamed of having more, I pushed every woman away that even came near me and wanted more than sex. I would blame my job or that they just weren't the right one for some obscure reason I could find. It was my job most of the time, but Cassie is the first and only woman I would walk away from my job that has been my whole life. Regardless of our current situation where I had no choice, I had already decided that first time I kissed her that my time in this job was over, because I was never letting her go.

Pouring all that into our kiss, our lips are wet and swollen as I withdraw.

A gasp of my name from her lips is all I need to hear.

I startle her by quickly moving my arms and scooping her off her feet in a bridal carry in front of the door. A small squeal echoes through the forest around us, along with the little giggle now coming out of Cassie's mouth.

"Now to do this the right way that I couldn't do when we arrived," I say, kissing her forehead quickly. "Welcome home, Cassie, and our little bubba. I've been waiting for you both." The emotion takes all the volume from my voice as I get to the last few words. Tears are welling in her eyes, and to be honest, I think in mine too.

"I love you, Noah, and this baby will too. You are our safe place." As she snuggles into me, I walk over the threshold of our log cabin, Cassie in my arms, to start our new life together. But before we do, Cassie needs to know the real me.

Looking down at her, I know that I'm not here to save Cassie. She could have done that on her own, I'm sure, but I'm here to be her protector. Something that is no longer my job but now my life's journey.

Placing her down gently on the couch, I place another gentle kiss, this time on her nose.

"I didn't know I could love until you." I stand and walk to the door, the emotion overwhelming me. I need fresh air.

My mouth is dry, and I'm struggling to talk, but I get out what I need.

"Just turning on the generator. Back in a minute." My feet take me as quickly as they can without running out into the forest to the area where I built a little generator shed. Filling the fuel and priming it, luckily it starts with the first pull of the rope. Locking the shed door again to keep the animals out, I'm back at the side of the cabin, turning on the gas and pushing the pilot light to get it going. Thank goodness everything has stayed in working order and now we have hot water, gas to cook, and the fridge to keep our food fresh. The rest we will work out later. Food, a place to sleep, and apparently according to Cassie, a clean toilet are all we need to live undercover for as long as it takes.

Standing, I take one last look around outside before I head back in, and for the first time in a very long time, I feel happy. And not just the regular everyday happy but that deep-down sense of happiness you feel in your soul. I know how strange that sounds when Cassie's life is in danger, but if her life were any different, I wouldn't have met her, and that is not something I even want to imagine now. A life without Cassie just isn't a life.

"Ghost, is everything okay?" Her voice brings me out of my inner thoughts. I push the lock on the car keys that are in my pocket so we're settled in for the rest of the night.

"Yeah," I call back as I turn and walk back into the cabin, shutting the door behind me.

"No, I don't mean out there. I mean, are you okay?" Cassie is now sitting on the couch, legs crossed and her hands in her lap, looking a little anxious. I have to learn I can't get anything past her; she sees me, all of me.

"Everything is perfect. Let me get you a snack and some water and we can talk." Heading to the bags of food on the counter that we haven't put away yet, I find the cookies that she demanded were on the list we gave Badger, so I'm guessing they're her favorite. This is good to know. It's the little things that we still haven't found out about each other, but we have all the time in the world to learn. I grab two waters that are still cool from the shop, even though the fridge will take a while to get cold properly.

"Oh, yes!" Cassie's excitement all over her face has taken away that worried look from a moment ago. Food trumps it all, it seems.

"If cookies are this exciting now, I can't imagine what it will be like when the pregnancy cravings kick in." Settling on the couch next to her, I look at her mouth, full of the cookie and with crumbs on her lips where she is devouring it.

She gives me a shove in my shoulder, and we both let our bodies sink into the softness of this couch that has been here since I bought the place. When I sat on it and felt like I could fall asleep, I knew it had to stay. The dark green color looks like it belongs in the rustic room.

The first cookie gone and a few big mouthfuls of water swallowed, and Cassie is looking at me with anticipation.

"Spill, Ghost. What do we need to talk about? I feel like you have something that is eating at you, and that freaks the shit out of me."

Our tender moment from minutes ago is long gone and my sassy girl is back. She doesn't beat around the bush when she wants to know something.

"You know I hate secrets." Her eyes are boring into my soul. Even if I tried to deny it, I have a feeling she would get it out of me anyway.

Luckily, I'm ready to tell her everything.

"Relax, bright eyes, it's not bad. It's just, I'm not quite who I appear…"

I know by the stunned look on her face that I need to keep talking before she starts with the million questions which will probably come anyway.

Chapter Fourteen

CASSIE

I don't think Ghost was listening to the doctor when they said no stress. You can't tell a woman, "We need to talk because I'm not who you think," and then not expect me to start freaking out. Even if I didn't have hormones that were sending me extra loopy, I'd still be jumping out of my skin.

Jason isn't who he said he was either. I can't do this again.

"What the—" My words are muffled as he places his finger on my lips, silencing me, which just pisses me off more.

"Cassie, stop talking before you get the wrong idea! I'm not Jason. I can see the fear in your eyes. I'm me, but there is just extra you need to know. Do you think you can hold it until I talk?"

I shake my head back and forth because I know I can't.

Rolling his eyes at me, he slowly lets my lips go when he must realize there is no way humanly possible that I'll sit here quiet. From the moment we met, I've never been able to keep my opinion to myself.

"You can't just drop that sentence and not expect me to fire up at you wondering..." My blood is bubbling with the anxiety.

"Cassie!" Shit, he's brought out the big tough voice. He knows that does funny things to me. "Stop. Talking. Now!" Oh, he means business. As wound up as I feel, that voice is sexy as fuck and has my body tingling when I should still be in fight mode.

How the hell does he do that to me?

Stopping me mid thought, now I've lost what I was going to say. Which is exactly what he was intending to happen. I'm about to open my mouth again to tell him he distracted me when he blurts out one thing I wasn't expecting.

"I'm a billionaire, Cassie." He looks at me, waiting for a reaction, but I've got nothing. I'm not sure I even heard what he said correctly. I rewind his words in my head and replay them over and over again. And every time it sounds the same.

"What?" is all I can manage, sitting up a little straighter and trying to get my head around that.

"Finally, I have rendered you speechless. Miracles do exist," he says, laughing at me, probably still looking stunned, like he has never seen me before.

"Not funny." I'm annoyed at his laughing.

"I know, I'm sorry, but it was the only way to stop you from freaking out so you would let me explain. I had to be blunt and straight to the point. It's not a word I would normally use, and to be honest, I've never said it out loud, but yes, I'm a very wealthy man." He takes both my hands in his and squeezes them to center me.

"Wait, how? Like, where…" My mind is spinning so fast that I can't even string a proper sentence together.

Watching him take a deep breath, I can tell there is a big story behind this, and I'm desperate for him to say it all in fast forward so I can know it all now. Patience has never been my strong point.

"You know about my family and how dysfunctional they are; well, that's not all of my family members. I had a grandfather who we never got to see very often when I was growing up. He was my father's father, and he was appalled at the way he and my mom lived their lives. I didn't know until after he died that when I was born, he tried to get shared custody of me so that he could keep an eye on me. Not that I'm sure I agree with his methods, and I think it's a bit high-handed to try to take someone's child away from them, but I can see he was just trying to care for me when he was worried they wouldn't do a very good job at it."

What an awful dilemma for the old man, I'm sure, but I agree with Ghost, and no matter what, no one will ever take this baby from me. Not while I'm living and breathing.

I don't comment at all, and now understand that I just need to sit here and listen until he gets it all out. I feel bad for the yelling I did in the beginning.

"Obviously, he lost that battle in the courts, and he and my parents had a big falling out after that. He didn't even bother trying again when my sisters were born, as he knew he wouldn't win. We never went to his house that I can remember as a child, and the few times he visited, he looked and dressed just like my father. He was reaching out to them and trying to make amends, but it never worked, and there was shouting after we were sent outside to play or to our rooms. It was hard to imagine he wasn't just the same as our family. Middle class, just trying to get by with the money we got each paycheck.

"Thinking back after he died, over the years there were a few arguments between Mom and Dad that made so much more sense now. I just assumed it was sarcasm when she would scream at him that she was just there for the money or one of them would say something about when this is over, I can't wait to get as far away from you as possible. Again, in the scale of things, it seemed normal in our house. They hated each other, and that was the truth."

I can only assume they stayed together because they thought it may have been needed to inherit the money. The sadness in his eyes is slaying me. He may not love his family anymore, but there is a longing there, wishing in some small way that it would change one day.

"Oh, Ghost, I don't even know what to say. My heart is hurting for you." And it is. I can't imagine growing up like that. I pull his hand with mine to my stomach, holding it and looking into his eyes. "Our child will never grow up in a house with anything else but an abundance of love. That's a promise." His smile tells me my words are a comfort for him.

Adjusting myself now so that I'm facing him on the couch, he moves his leg up onto the couch too, leaving one foot on the ground, and we both lean sideways onto the back of the couch. We're getting comfortable for the long conversation we are entering into. He needs to get out everything he has been holding on the inside all his life, and I need to listen so I know all there is to know about Ghost, my protector, and Noah, the man I love.

"Anyway, not long after I moved away from the family, after I had the disagreement with my sister who was just wanting to use me, I had a call from a law firm. At first my heart dropped, thinking that my parents had done something stupid and they were chasing me for money. Not that I had much at that stage. But instead, it was to tell me that my grandfather, Lionel, had passed away and that they wanted me to come in to collect a letter he had left for me. I was a bit confused about why he would write a letter to me and no one else. I was busy at work and put it off for a week. I was disappointed that I hadn't even heard from my parents to tell me he had passed. But I found out later they didn't even know, he had left instructions that they weren't to be told until I was seen by the lawyer and his assets were sold and everything converted to cash." Stopping to take a moment, Ghost is sorting through his words, and this is so not like him.

I don't want to interrupt, so I just nod at him to keep going. This wasn't easy, I'm sure, and I don't want to cause him any more pain than is needed.

"Imagine my absolute disbelief when they told me that he had made me the sole beneficiary of his estate. His wife had died before I was born, my dad was an only child, and we were his only grandchildren. In his letter to me, he spoke of how devastated he was every day that he had no part in our lives and that to him his son was dead. He had watched me grow up from the sidelines, and he said I was the only one who had followed his footsteps in working hard and making a decent man of myself." I can't fight the tears that are slowly dripping down my face. Ghost's hand softly wipes them away. I'm not sure if I'm crying for him or his grandfather or both.

"Overnight I had become a multi-millionaire, with strict instructions from him not to give any of it to my family unless they turned their lives around and became decent people, his words not mine." His eyes wander toward the candle on the table beside us, flickering around in the slight breeze that is blowing in through one of the windows.

"I was scared, Cassie. I didn't know how my family would react. I was torn if I should just give them some of the money. Christ, I could never spend that amount of money in ten lifetimes, so why shouldn't they have some. I waited for them to be told, and then it was suggested we have a meeting at the lawyer's office. I arrived a little early, like I always do. My parents were waiting outside for me. All my dad said to me was *'It's my fucking money, you thieving little shit. I'm telling them your mother had an affair and you aren't mine. So, then the inheritance has to come to me.'* My mom stood next to him, holding his hand and nodding her agreement. I had never seen them hold hands in all my life, and the first time they agreed on something, it was to disown their son for money."

I can't help myself, gasping at the thought of how that must've made him feel. How could anyone do that to their own child.

His head falls back onto the couch, and he continues speaking toward the ceiling because I don't think he can look at me right now. It's too hard.

"I know what you're thinking, how could they, but money breeds evil, and my family fell into that trap of greed before anything else." Now restless, he stands and starts to pace.

I don't know if I'm even able to ask, but I must. "What did you do next?" I feel my heart beating a little harder, watching him with the anger starting to pulse through him.

"I turned and walked away from them and have never seen them since. I called the lawyer and told him the deal was off and that I would not be sharing one single dollar with them." I can imagine him stomping down the pavement and issuing the instructions with all the hurt he had built up inside of him. "It was around that time I had heard about the jobs at WITSEC, so I changed my name, invested the money offshore under various aliases, and joined WITSEC under my new identity." He stops in his stride across the room and looks straight at me.

"I promise you with all I am, Cassie, I never did anything illegal with that money, and every dollar I have accumulated I did through good investments. When you're all alone in the world there is plenty of time to research companies and also spot the ones where something doesn't seem right. So, I just kept the money safe from anyone taking it and made anonymous donations all over the world to people who really need it. I'm a good person, Cassie, I'm not evil like them."

I jump from the couch and wrap him as tightly as I can in my arms, and his head drops onto my shoulder. The loudest sob escapes him, and it has my tears now pouring out of me too. Standing here, both of us let it all out, all the trauma we have both been holding onto for years. I doubt Ghost has even grieved for his grandfather, a man he was never allowed to know, or the immense pain he is holding at being abandoned by the people who are always supposed to love you, no matter what. My tears are for the little boy who never knew love and who has been holding on, for all his adult life, the thought that maybe deep down he is evil like his parents.

"Shh, shh," I soothe, rubbing his back as the sobs subsids and his breathing slowly settles back into a normal rhythm.

"Noah, you are the most loving, honorable, gentle, but at the same time the strongest man I know. You are loyal to a fault, and although I wish you wouldn't put others' lives before your own, you always do. So, no, Noah, you are not evil. You may share their DNA, but evil's not in your heart."

His head finally raises up off my shoulder. "That's how stupid they were. All I would have to do was take a DNA test and it would've squashed their claim, but they were ready to disown me anyway." Standing up straighter, he lifts the bottom of his shirt, wiping my tears off and then his own.

"They say real men don't cry." His voice is hoarse from the emotion, but he's trying to break the moment.

"Bullshit. They aren't a real man if they can't show emotion, and I don't want a man who is made of stone, Noah. Wait, is that even your real name?" I want to hit myself for saying that. It's not like I'm using my real name, so what does it matter?

He shakes his head back and forth. "My birth name was Boyce, but like you, I don't want anything to do with that life. Noah was my grandfather's middle name, so I took that as my legal name in the real world. But I've never told another person who mattered to me this name... except you. I've had to use the name Noah for legalities with my investments, but never with anyone in my circle of friends. Bull doesn't even know my legal name, and to be honest, you saying it sounds foreign sometimes, because no one ever calls me by that name."

Reaching up on my toes, I whisper in his ear, "The number of times you've made me come and have me screaming your name, I doubt it sounds foreign anymore." The low groan from him sounds like it's coming from deep inside his body. A place of desperate need.

Biting his earlobe a little and dropping back to my feet, I can see the change from moments earlier.

"Keep that up and you'll be screaming it over the back of this couch." Lust is burning red hot in his eyes.

"Really..." I drag my hands slowly down his abs, feeling every rise and fall of his breath. Opening my mouth, I run my tongue around my lips. "Make me then, or are you just all talk?" Stepping to the side of him, I watch over my shoulder as I sway my hips, walking around to the rear of the couch. "Do you mean right here?" I whisper as I pat the couch in front of me.

"Cassie." My name on his lips has me shivering. "I'm wound too tight, I'll hurt you." He's torn between the need to fuck my brains out to take away the pain, and the softness of the emotions he just released.

"Maybe I want you to hurt me, in the best possible way," I say, flicking my shoes to the side and dropping my sweatpants and underwear in one go.

KAREN DEEN

Noah is still standing there frozen with his fists clenched, trying to hold back, but I don't plan on making it easy.

"Get dressed." The deepness of his voice just makes me wetter than I was before he spoke. No deterrent to me at all.

I pull my crop top ever so slowly up over my head, with his eyes glued to my breasts. So, I give him what he wants.

"Did you say undressed, Nooaaahhh?" I taunt, dropping my bra to the floor.

With him still standing in front of me, I use the last trick in my book which is pushing me so far past my comfort zone, I'm not sure how I feel, but I will do it for him. Whatever he needs.

I drop my hand down to my sex and slowly drag my fingers through the wetness. Noah can't hide how turned on he is becoming. He grabs his cock through his pants to try to control himself.

My self-consciousness kicks in at that moment, and as I'm starting to pull my hand away, he finally speaks.

"Don't! You started this, now you are going to give me the show you promised. Keep stroking, you know you want to." He's right, and I can't stop the little moan that drops from my mouth as I swipe over my clit the first time.

"Oh yeah, that's it. Get yourself nice and wet." I watch his shirt come off, and he flicks the button on his pants open now. The more I stroke, the bigger his pupils dilate. I never knew this could be so sensual and feel so beautiful. His pants are now sitting on his hips, open, and his cock is out in his hand. He slowly pumps himself backwards and forwards to gain some relief.

"So sexy." His voice is heightened now. "I want you to make yourself come, Cassie. I want to see you enjoy your own body and for you to know how much you are making me want to fuck you harder than I ever have before." Between his words and the over-powering need to find my release, I can't stop now. My other hand is on my breast and squeezing hard, pulling my nipple just like I love Noah doing to me with his teeth.

"Yeah, baby, you're close. I can see your body starting to quiver." Oh God, I don't know if I can do this, that awful word in my head now.

"I'm not a slut," I whimper as my body is stuck on the edge of a cliff I just can't seem to jump off.

"You are mine, and you are beautiful. Come now for me, Cassie, shout my name!"

His words are enough to have me screaming, "Noah!" like a wild animal, for the whole world to hear who I belong to.

My eyes slam shut at the sheer force of the electricity running through my body.

I'm so sensitive but can't stop, it feels so good. As my body stops shaking, I feel him behind me. He has moved, and I didn't hear over the rush of white noise as I came so loudly.

"I told you I would fuck my name out of you, so now it's my turn." Before I even have a chance to move, he pushes me forward and his cock enters me in one hard thrust. He pulls back, pounding me over and over again. I can't speak it's so intense. I don't know if I'll survive another orgasm, but there's nothing I can do to stop it.

"That was fucking hot watching you. Never forget how sexy you are." His voice is in my ear, speaking his words, when he is caught out by his own need to come.

"Oh fuck... Cassie!" His cock pulsing inside of me has me coming around it as he empties every last drop, claiming me.

Our bodies both drop down as far as we can over the back of the couch, hot and sweaty and totally satisfied, limp with exhaustion from the sheer release of not only the orgasms but the emotions we have shared.

His brain kicking back to life, Ghost is up and pulling me with him, turning me to face him.

"Shit, Cassie, did I hurt you? Are you okay, I didn't hurt your stomach?" Fear is written all over his face, his jaw tight and anguish in his eyes.

"I'm perfect. That was... incredible..." Reaching up and taking the softest kiss from him, I show him how gentle he can be with me too.

"Thank you," he whispers, wrapping me in his arms. It's all he needs to say for me to know how he feels. Standing here for a few minutes not speaking is what we're both craving. Just the skin-to-skin connection to cement in our hearts that we are both going to be okay.

Without warning, his hands are under my ass and he's hoisting me into his arms. My legs wrap around him with force so he doesn't drop me.

"This is becoming a habit, sweeping me off my feet." Secretly I'm loving it. Jason was nothing like this. It was all so stilted and planned. Never any spontaneity. Yet in the most intense time of both our lives, I'm the happiest I've ever been.

"Get used to it. I intend to keep doing it." Carrying me back into the bedroom, he stops at the edge of the bed. "Tonight, I'm going to worship your body, but first, I need to feed you. Stay here and get comfortable." Now on the bed, I'm wriggling my backside backwards so I can lean against the headboard. Feeling a little self-conscious just sitting here naked, I pull the sheet and blanket back and tug it up over my body. Ghost is now out in the kitchen, and I can hear him rummaging through the bags for whatever he is making us for dinner.

This room has a warmth to it. The bed is a dark heavy timber and the blanket is a plain rust color that blends in with the wood. The room needs some color, but at least it has so much more life about it than our first safe house.

There is one thing that they don't tell you when you are agreeing to go into witness protection, and that is that you might be important in a case, but nobody cares about where you are being hidden. Not that we should be treated like royalty, but they could at least keep the house in good condition and styled in this decade at least. It doesn't take much to redecorate a room. A fresh coat of paint, new bed linen, and a couple of cushions. I would love to have done that to the last place.

Ghost thinks I was sketching in my book, pictures, which is true, but not quite like he is imagining. I was redesigning the rooms and how I would decorate them. Well, that's how it was in the beginning, and then I started designing random rooms that popped into my head. I would see something in a movie or read a description in a book, and then before I knew it, I was sketching a new room or creating the one in the book and making it come to life off the page.

The breeze coming in the window is cool and sends a shiver over my shoulders and arms. There are no curtains on the window, and I can see the shapes of the trees outside with the light coming from the couple of candles that are in here. I should feel scared at the darkness and that I have no idea where I am, but instead, my mind is intrigued by the shapes of the shadows in the forest, along with the sounds that are now starting to get louder the darker it gets.

I remember going camping with my parents once when I was younger, and lying in the tent at night, there were so many noises. At first, I was petrified, until my dad told me it was just the chatter of all the forest animals out with their friends, catching up. They had to sleep or do their jobs during the day, so the only time they could meet was at night. I took that explanation and went to sleep and never worried another night we were there. Dad traveled a lot for work, so family trips were always treasured.

The memory puts a smile on my face as Ghost comes back into the room carrying a tray containing plates of food and two glasses of apple juice. No more wine for me for a while.

"What has my chef prepared? You weren't kidding on that first day, were you, when you said you would be my personal cook?" Placing the tray down on the bed, I can see two half-full bowls of soup with crusty bread and fruit to finish off with.

"I wouldn't call this cooking, it's merely reheating with style. But yes, you wait, I will be showing off my culinary skills for you." Pulling his gun out of his pants pocket, he places it on the cupboard next to the bed. It reminds me that we are not off on some romantic holiday in a mountain cabin. This is real, and danger is just on the outside of this property, waiting for us at any moment.

Trying to push that thought straight out of my head so it doesn't ruin the night, I shift from the food to looking back at Ghost who is still standing next to the bed, shirtless, with his cargo pants on.

"Don't you even think about getting in this bed with those clothes on." Taking a large piece of banana off the plate, it's almost the size of half the fruit. I pop it between my lips, holding it and sliding it slowly into my mouth. Then I pull it back out until there is just a small amount in my mouth, biting it and swallowing it down. "Mmmm, otherwise, I'll just have to keep eating more bananas."

His pants drop to the floor, and I can't help noticing that he is semi hard again. Visions of that in my mouth instead of the banana flash through my mind.

"I knew you were going to be trouble from the start, but I didn't imagine that trouble would be this bad." Leaning forward, he bites the other end of the piece of banana that I was about to place back in my mouth. "And your bad is so fucking good."

That voice, it gets me every damn time. And my nipples are aching and rock hard again.

Gulping the banana down and holding the tray so he can slip under the covers with me, I know I'm not getting much sleep tonight.

When I reach to pick up the spoon, he almost growls at me. "No. Let me. I told you I was going to feed you. Soup might not be the most romantic, but it was quick and will give you the energy you are going to need."

With the determination in his words, I'm not about to argue.

The first spoonful of soup in my mouth and my senses are on overload. Not from the soup that is probably out of a can, but it's Ghost. I've never had a man want to care for me so intensely. The pure joy he's getting from feeding me is so sensual. It's almost like he could get off just doing this for me. It's his protective instincts on overload, and I'm all for it.

I've been a kept woman, and I hated every minute of it, because it just didn't feel right and there was certainly no love involved. This is nothing like that. When the words are hard for Ghost, then his actions speak for him. He's showing me how cherished I am. It's a feeling I haven't felt since I lost my parents. I could get used to this, although part of me is already worried how intense he will be as the baby gets bigger. I know how protective I'm feeling of the little one I'm carrying, and that is not part of my personality on a day-to-day basis.

Lord help me, with Ghost, this is going to get crazy, fast.

My body is so limp and relaxed after dinner, I'm just taking the opportunity to rest, with my head on Ghost's chest. I let my fingers roam over his nipples and up and down his pecs. Playing in the smattering of chest hair that is soft and blond.

"You need to tell Badger he did better this time," I say, tilting my head to look up at Ghost for a minute.

"With what?" he asks, his hand pushing my loose hair behind my ear.

"This safe house." The smile on his face tells me there is more to this.

"No way he gets the credit for this one."

"Oh, you found it, did you, clever boy." My voice is patronizing, and his smirk tells me he doesn't care one bit, slowly dropping my head down a little again.

"No. I own it."

My head whips back with a startle. Christ, no more surprises today, please.

"This is mine, Cassie, and the place of our forever home."

"What do you mean?"

"Tomorrow, I'll show you and you'll understand."

"Is there anything else I don't know yet? Because I don't think I can take any more bombshells."

"Not today, beautiful. Now sleep, and tomorrow, all will be revealed."

Sleep?! How the hell does he expect that to happen now!

His hand sliding down and into my sex, my hips rise instinctively off the mattress.

Ooooh, that's how.

My new sleep aid is going to kill me the way he's going.

What a way to die!

Chapter Fifteen

7 MONTHS LATER

CASSIE

S itting on this chair on our balcony, the sun on my face and on my belly, it feels so amazing. If you'd asked me that first morning after we arrived here, when Ghost and I walked up to this clearing to show me the view, if I could be happy here, my smile would have been my answer. And if Ghost had explained this is where he was going to build our home, and it'd be finished before the baby is born, then I also would have laughed. But thinking back to the last few months, I should never doubt my husband of anything he puts his mind to.

The word husband still feels amazing to say. I can't believe that Badger went and got himself ordained so he could marry us over a Zoom call. Ghost was adamant that he wanted us married before our little one came into this world and that I would always be looked after financially if anything ever happened to him.

I hate those talks, but in this life we are living, they're necessary. Our wills are done and lodged with our lawyer who is someone

Badger trusts and now Ghost has been using him for years. He knew bits and pieces before, but now he knows everything. Well, almost everything. He doesn't know who I was before now or the reason I'm here. Ghost refuses to disclose that to anyone. Not even Bull, who I know he is missing terribly. Not that my big tough guy would admit it. He talks about him all the time when we take a moment to just sit under the stars and be still in our own world.

It's hard to get him to take that time off often. I'm learning he has so much energy, that he needs to burn it off one way or another. My favorite method is getting a little more difficult these days, being over eight months pregnant, but we find a way. I don't remember hearing anyone talking about being pregnant and how horny it makes you. It's crazy, I feel like I could jump Ghost multiple times a day. It's just my energy levels holding me back. Luckily, I have a husband who is happy to take the load for me. I'm never left unsatisfied, and he's doing all the work. I giggled with him last week, asking him how he is going to last for six weeks with no sex after the baby is born. All I got was a grunt and his eyes rolling. Oh yeah, this is going to be a challenge for both of us. I'm guessing the house will get completely finished with all that extra energy he will have to use up.

The house in a way has been a savior for Ghost. He is getting anxious about the birth, and I know it worries him that we are going to be doing it on our own. Well, technically on our own. We have a doctor that will be helping Ghost on Zoom, and he has been studying every piece of information he can get a hold of on the way to deliver a baby safely. I'm not sure why, but I feel calm about it. Women have had babies in the middle of nowhere with no medical intervention for millennia. Is it ideal? Absolutely not, but we have no other choice right now. As a last resort we will go to the nearest hospital, which is two hours away, but only if it's an emergency, and at that distance, I'm not sure if it would help us if we got to that point. We just have to keep thinking positive.

The cabin looks like a mini security-operations bunker. Our living room is full of computers and screens, there's a gun safe in our bedroom, and we have totally outgrown the space. One of the first things Ghost did was to build an escape tunnel out of the cabin in case I needed to get away from danger while he distracts intruders. My husband is full-on, and there is no persuading him to change his mind once he decides he is doing it.

Building our dream home has been a challenge, and I've spent many days hiding in the cabin when we have people on site. Ghost has managed to keep the number of people here to an absolute minimum.

We spent that first morning on a rug, watching the sunrise while he told me that he already had a whole house designed and manufactured, ready to go. It was sitting in a warehouse he owns, waiting for when the time came that he wanted to do this. It was made from pre-fab modules that link together. They deliver straight to building site, and it basically gets put together like Lego, and the house structure is up in no time. Ghost had already had the concrete slab poured years ago so it would be ready.

Once that was done, he then did a lot of the inside work himself —well, as much as he could, but for some of the more intricate steps, he wasn't qualified. Mind you, even if he wasn't trained, he would teach himself off the internet. I wanted to help, but of course there was no way my husband would let me, so I became the person who would hand him the tools or pass the food and water up to the man who was working all sorts of stupid hours on the house. He was worried I would be disappointed I didn't get a say in the design of the building, but I was just so excited at being allowed to decorate the inside from scratch. Choosing the colors, furnishings, and finishing touches has been amazing.

Fast forward seven months and now I'm relaxing on our balcony as Ghost is inside touching up the last of the paint work. We have all the furnishings in storage, so when he says the word, Badger is going to organize to have a truck arrive and deliver everything to us. Again, just like when we go into the nearest town, which is not often, we will have our wigs and disguises on for the delivery. I hate being a blonde, or redhead, or a woman with short curly black hair. We have several different ones so we don't become familiar to anyone.

Once my pregnancy really started showing and it couldn't be hidden with clothes, I stopped leaving the property. It would look too suspicious if there was a random pregnant woman who kept turning up with different-colored hair. People would start to talk, and we can't have that, even in a small town up in the mountains. So, the trips have been left to Ghost while I stay in the car, behind the dark glass and my wigs and hats. We don't park in the common areas, and don't ask me how, but he has several license plates from different states that he swaps on the car. Then when he leaves me, he is a quick as possible.

Ghost has gone from clean-shaven to full beard and everything in between, with different wigs, hats, and bandanas tied on his head. He complains how hot it is working in a disguise with other trades-people on site. He's careful never to mix the tradesmen, so each group sees a different-looking Ghost. He also brings new groups on site from farther areas who wouldn't have any chance of knowing each other. Sometimes people that Badger recommends just turn up, do the job, and don't ask any questions. We can't do it any other way.

I don't know if I should be worried or not, but I decided early on to let Ghost do the worrying for me in relation to Jason. Things have gone quiet for months now, but that is not necessarily a good thing. Jason walked away with a clean record from all the charges. As Rocket told us when he turned up at the safe house, Camilla was charged and painted in the media as the scorned lover. They said that she was jealous of my relationship with Jason, so she decided to get back at him and frame him. Before she could even make it to trial, she "accidently" fell down the stairs in her apart-ment and died. Ghost and I don't believe that for a minute. But of course, there was enough evidence presented to the courts that Jason was totally cleared, and his financial backers and followers helped build the media coverage of the poor man who only wants to do good in the world, and he was attacked by such an evil woman.

And apparently, I couldn't take the stress of it all, so I have left him with his blessing to move to a quieter life. That made me almost choke on my water when Ghost read me out that article from *The Washington Post.*

Part of me is sad for Camilla that she died, but I can't help but believe in my gut that she was involved in it as well. And anyone who is condoning the trafficking of women or risking the safety of our country's servicemen and women, then I can't feel too sorry for them. Hearing Camilla's conversation that night in the garden, it was obvious something was going on. I didn't know what at the time and still don't know who that man was, but they were involved, of that I'm certain.

We know there are still several hits ordered on me out there on the dark web, and Ghost tells me they won't go away until they believe I'm dead. Of course, Ghost built the story and evidence that I freaked out when he was trying to get me to safety, and I disappeared without a trace. He had searched for me but to no avail, and he is devastated he failed the department, his client, and himself.

Ghost has done his best to send updates from his work computer while he was supposedly searching for me. Of course, he's sending them through secure networks that they can't track. He even placed a few phone calls via his computer so they couldn't track what cell tower it was bouncing off. The alarm at the safe house alerted him to the agents arriving but still hasn't given us any insight into who the mole is yet. I don't know all the details, and to be honest, I don't need to. That's what Ghost is good at, and I leave him to do what is needed.

Rocket was furious, and I'm not sure he believed him, but in the end, he had no other choice, and the facts in front of him backed up the story.

It was mutually agreed that he would continue to do some work for Rocket, undercover and off the grid, without the knowledge of WITSEC. Ghost has looked hard into Rocket and has settled back into thinking he's on our side, and if he isn't, his plan is to keep the enemy close just to be safe. But the condition for the job was that he would take some time for himself first to get over losing a client and from his broken heart. Well, that is what he told Rocket. If he truly knew Ghost, he would have called bullshit on that, but luckily, he didn't. The rest of the team, including Bull, was told he needed time out after the job went wrong. Nothing was mentioned about the broken heart. The truth was he needed to get our house complete, the baby born, and us all locked up tight in his high-security home before he could concentrate on anything else. It's not that he needs the money to work, and in fact won't be paid, but he has to have something to do. Plus, he will get to keep Bull and his friends safe from a distance, which is all he truly cares about.

They say vitamin D is good for you and the baby. My naked belly on show, I can tell by the amount of kicking under my ribs and what feels like an elbow poking in and out, that my little one is enjoying the rays as much as I am. The baby has been moving a lot the last few days and has dropped down, so there is not as much pressure up on my ribs, but instead, they're now sitting constantly on my bladder, and I feel like I'm walking with a beachball between my legs.

I've been able to move around the property without fear since Ghost set up the best high-tech security system he could find, and of course, he then tweaked it and made it even better. This man could run security for the Pentagon, but he just laughed when I said that. He thinks that would be a waste of his time; he would rather be helping people out in the real world who need him. That the government have all the power and money at their disposal and they just abuse it anyway. Not everyone is like Jason, but I'm afraid he has made Ghost skeptical of all politicians. Then again, who am I to argue? Ghost sees so much hidden evil in this world, more than I ever want to know about. As long as he keeps our little family safe, including himself, that's all I care about.

At first the reason we came here was to hide, but the longer we have been here and the house has taken shape, I don't think I ever want to leave. One day we hope that I will be safe to travel farther than the little town here, but it's no guarantee. That frightened me, and I thought I would feel claustrophobic, but instead, I have never felt so free. There is something about this place that makes me feel at home. Maybe it's where I've always been meant to end up, and with the man who completes me. This baby is just our added bonus.

"How are my two precious people?" His deep voice from behind me makes me jump a little, and that of course sets the baby off with what feels like break dancing inside me.

He reaches over my shoulder with his hand, roughened from all the manual work he has been doing, and he lays it on top of the baby, rubbing my sun-warmed skin as his lips find mine like a magnet.

"Mmm," I murmur, looking up into his eyes. "You taste good, all salty from your sweat." What is it about a sweaty shirtless man that just makes me get all hot and bothered on the inside.

He's chuckling as he walks around and squats next to me.

"And in answer to your question," I said, "your wife is doing great, just relaxing here, but your baby is attending some dance party, and my bladder really wishes they would just chill out for a little while and give me a break from going to the toilet what feels like every five minutes."

"I think we might be in trouble with this one. Our little one might have my energy, and I'll just say I'm sorry in advance." He kisses me and his baby on my stomach, with the all the tenderness he keeps only for us.

"It's okay, Daddy, that just means you will have the job of chasing after this one once they're moving. That is your punishment," I tease, running my hand over the top of his head that is shaven, with just a small amount of stubble regrowth.

"My energy level and your stubbornness, oh man, what are we in for?" Standing beside me, he holds his hands out to take mine and help me up. Both of us laugh at that thought. Laughing is never good when you're this pregnant, I've found that out in the last few weeks. Again, I'm leaking a little as I get to my feet.

I try hard to stop the flow, but shit, I can't, and I actually have no control over the fluid running down my legs. I grip his hands a little tighter as a sharp pain pulls across both my front and lower back.

"Ghost!"

"Cassie, what's wrong?" Looking down at our feet, he sees the puddle on the wood floor.

"Fuck! It's too soon." It's all I can get out as another pain grips me, and I hunch forward to lean on Ghost.

For all my confidence that we will be okay, I'm ready to throw that all out the window.

"We can't do this, we aren't doctors, what were we thinking?!" I'm now screaming into his chest with fear.

His smooth, calm voice rumbles in my ear as he starts taking control. Thank God, because I can't even manage to think straight about what I need to do. It's not supposed to be this intense this quickly, is it?

"I'm taking you to the cabin. We will be fine. It's only a week early. You've got this Cassie, trust me."

"I trust you... but I don't know if I trust me to be able to do this." Tears of fear are now running down my face, my voice quivering. How was I sitting there all calm and dreaming of my little baby's face and now it feels like that same baby is trying to break free by ripping me apart from the inside.

"Keep her safe, Noah?" I whimper, looking into his eyes, begging him to make it all okay.

"It's a girl, huh?" He stands me up a little straighter and smiles down at me.

"I've been dreaming about her." I try to put one foot in front of the other as we head down the stairs.

"Well, we will know soon enough. Let's get you to the truck."

"Not too soon. At least let me make it to a bed!" I scream a little as the next contraction takes hold, rendering me speechless.

GHOST

My plans that I had made in my head are all shuffling like an old-fashioned juke box, flipping through the records before it finds the one that was picked.

Come on, I need to remember what to do for water breaking and intense labor pains from the start. Like the computer in my brain uses my thoughts as its search engine, my memory pulls what I need to the front, and I switch into action.

Trying to get Cassie into my truck is proving difficult. It's just one of the vehicles that I have here now, as well as the Range Rover. We don't get too many steps before she needs to stop again. I'm strong, but I fear if I try to pick her up, she will jerk in pain, and I might drop her. It's a risk I'm not taking.

Finally, I have helped her up into the seat and breathed through a contraction with her, and we are now rumbling down the road to our little sanctuary in the trees.

I've lived through gun fights, I've hidden out and faced days without water and food, taken a bullet and many slashes with all sorts of blades. None of that pain compares to the feeling of my heart being ripped apart listening to Cassie crying out in agony.

"Nearly there, hang on, and I'll get the painkillers." Her hand squeezes mine like she is about to break every bone in it. I don't care, break away, beautiful.

"I don't want… the drugs, I told you… that!" she says between breathing, telling me in no uncertain terms that she is doing this on her own.

"Maybe so, but if I think you need them, then you are taking them!" Just like I said, my wife is so fucking stubborn.

I get her finally settled on our bed and the computer logged in and Zoom call activated. We've tested this many times and have the camera positioned so that neither Cassie's nor my face can be seen. We can hear the doctor, but we're muted, so I can talk to Cassie and not worry about either of us using our actual names. Especially when she is yelling at me, which I'm fully expecting. I'll just unmute the call when I need to.

The labor pains have been so intense, and it's been forty-five minutes since her water broke. The fetal monitor we had shipped here shows the baby is a little distressed. The doctor agrees she is fully dilated, and I can see the top of the baby's head.

Looking into her exhausted eyes, I just want to take the pain away for her, but she won't let me. I hate not being in control of decisions, and the only person who I can't seem to overrule is Cassie. She won't give in and is doing this all on her own. I knew she was strong, but today she has shown me I had no idea truly how deep that strength goes.

"Cassie, it's time to start pushing. Next contraction, I need you to push down hard." Her hair is plastered to her face, lying back on the pillows I have her propped up on.

For all the reading I have done and research videos I have watched, nothing could've prepared me for how scared I feel. I'm no doctor, what was I even thinking?! I have the two most important people in the world relying on me, and if I can't do this right, then I lose them both. That's not an option I can even contemplate.

"Here we go." I see her face changing. Sitting up, she bites down on her lip and grunts loudly. I push her knees up toward her stomach, watching intently as the top of the baby's head starts crowning. "That's it, I see the head, keep going, keep going."

I'm so torn. I want to be holding her and comforting her, but I have to do this part. When we made this decision, at first I thought Cassie was crazy for suggesting it, but she knew deep down that she would manage. Despite her initial fear, there haven't been many words from her. She has just gone into her own zone and has been concentrating on getting through it.

The baby's head has just popped out as Cassie drops back on the bed, looking like she almost has nothing left to give.

"You did it, the head's out. One more push, Cassie, just one more big one." I don't want to hurt her, but she gives a little cry of pain as I push my finger into her to make sure the cord isn't wrapped around the baby's neck. Lifting it up and over, I take a little breath of relief that it's not going to be a problem.

"I don't think I can…" Cassie murmurs as I hear the doctor's voice telling me to get ready, that as soon as one of the shoulders breaks through, the baby will be born instantly, and I have to be ready to catch a slippery little body.

"Yes, you can, you don't have a choice. Your baby needs you!" I'm yelling at her a little louder than I should be, but it does the trick, and as the contraction hits her, with all her ferocity she is up again, pushing and screaming, but this time, it's at me.

"Noooooaaaaaaahhhhh!"

With a towel ready, the doctor was right. The speed the baby is born almost takes me by surprise, along with the amount of fluid that is rushing out at the same time.

It's like time stands still as I look down at the little squished-up face and body covered in blood and muck.

A little girl, a perfect little girl.

The first little cry from our daughter brings me back into the chaos as Cassie is crying and mumbling my name over and over again, lying back on the bed, totally exhausted and starting to shake a little.

Lifting our daughter up onto her mother's naked chest brings Cassie back to life and settles the shivers. She wraps her arms around the little bundle.

"A girl, Noah. A daughter." We're both still and just here in the moment, tears streaming and staring at the miracle that has been gifted to us in the worst possible time of our lives.

Another contraction, much softer, hits Cassie, reminding me that this isn't over yet. The doctor is now talking quietly to me and helping me through birthing the placenta safely and making sure that the bleeding stops. It's like I'm just working on auto pilot, listening to his voice and doing as he instructs. When I get to cutting the cord, I say a prayer to the universe that I am a big enough man to keep both my girls safe in this world. As I make the final cut, my little girl is on her own now, and Cassie's body is no longer her safe space.

Thanking the doctor and disconnecting the video, I'm just standing frozen, looking at the scene before me.

I should be seeing all the blood and the mess on the sheets we layered over a piece of plastic on the bed, ready for when the time came.

But I don't see any of that.

My eyes are drawn to my wife holding my daughter. It's a vision I never believed that I would be blessed with. It's like there is this golden aura around them of pureness and love. Cassie is stroking our little one's cheek, and her happy tears are still sliding down her face. I want to be in the moment with them too.

Not even thinking, I pull off my clothes and climb onto the bed next to Cassie, our skin touching and my arm wrapping around them both. I kiss Cassie on the lips, like she is breathing her beauty and light into my soul. My tears are back falling as I kiss my daughter for the first time.

My mouth is dry and trying to talk is difficult, but it's important.

"I'd never known love until you, and now look what we created." It's a mere whisper out of my mouth, but it's the best I can do.

"She is so beautiful, Noah. I can't believe we did it." Cassie's bright eyes, the ones that pulled me in from the moment I saw her, are now looking up at me from the little pink face in her arms. I'm a goner.

"You did it, my warrior queen. I was just here to watch in awe," I praise, kissing her forehead and trying to get even closer to them both, even though I don't think it's possible without smothering them.

"Thank you." The way Cassie is looking up at me has my heart beating faster. "For keeping us both safe." Fuck, this woman overwhelms my heart with her words.

"Always and forever," is all I can get out.

We lie together a little longer until our little girl starts to cry out the tiniest little squeal. We look at each other, slightly startled about what it means, but by the time the second one follows, Cassie the mother is already kicking in.

"I should try to feed her. She might be hungry." She's trying to look confident, but I know we are both terrified on the inside. We are completely on our own and only have each other—oh, and the internet—to rely on. I've never been so thankful for technology.

While Cassie is trying to latch her, I start cleaning up around them, getting rid of everything that needs throwing away. I use a damp cloth to wipe all of Cassie down and make her feel clean and refreshed. Thankfully the feeding seems to be going okay and there is no crying yet, from either of them. Because I'm sure there will be times that the emotions of being here alone and not sharing such a special time with anyone is going to get the better of Cassie, and I don't blame her one bit.

After helping Cassie to get dressed a little so she doesn't feel so exposed after such an intense time, both of the girls are now lying in the bed. With Cassie's help, I clean up our little girl and wrap her in a blanket. They both look settled, but I'm sure Cassie is going to need sleep, and hopefully they will both nap shortly and I can go ahead and get our daughter's birth registered and sort out all her papers and a passport. I must be ready in case we need to fly at a moment's notice. A lot of what I'm doing is breaking the law, but I don't see it as a bad thing. When I am doing this to keep them both safe, then to me, that's acceptable.

"Is she just as you dreamed?" I ask Cassie, remembering what she said as she went into labor earlier.

"So much more," she replies, not taking her eyes off her.

"What are we going to name our princess?" I sit on the bed, looking down at the two most precious beings.

"I know we had some names picked out, but my heart is telling me who she should be. My mom's name was Beatrice, but I can't call her that because it's too dangerous for her. All my mom's friends called her Bessy, so I would like our little girl to be Bessy too. Do you like that?" The memory of the mother she lost, and who she is missing more than ever right now, is written all over her expression as she looks at her own daughter.

"Bessy," I repeat, trying it on my lips. "It's a perfect name for our princess."

Cassie leans over and kisses Bessy on the cheek, as I follow her on Bessy's other cheek. "Welcome to our family, Bessy," Cassie whispers as a few tears escape from her again.

"Shh, beautiful. Sleep. You need it. Take it while you can. I'll watch over you both."

Her eyes close without any protest. The adrenaline she would have needed to get through the birth is now waning, and her body is totally spent.

"Mhmm, stay." She reaches her hand out to mine and holds tight as she starts drifting off.

I thought I was a tough guy, but today, I have had two epiphanies.

The first is that my wife's inner strength is far greater than mine. And the second is that both of these girls in front of me can bring me to my knees far quicker than anything else in the world.

I will never forget this moment for as long as I live. And I'm determined to make sure I'm living until I'm old and gray.

I know why I'm in this world now, to be a protector, but not just any protector.

Their protector!

Chapter Sixteen

7 YEARS LATER - CURRENT DAY

GHOST

"Cassie, I'll be in my office. Bull's in trouble," I call to her as I'm running past the nursery, where she is feeding Eli, our son. I wish I could stop and just take in the view of the two of them in the rocking chair and Bessy lying on the floor coloring a picture, being guarded by our not-so-fierce dogs Ace and Bandit, but I can't. Time is of the essence, and Cassie understands that.

I lost the vote when I suggested we get some dogs to help with security. I was politely told no, we are getting cute fluffy dogs for Bessy to play with. We all know who won that argument, with the two Cavalier King Charles spaniels curled up sleeping at her feet. They might look cute but looks can be deceiving. They still know to alert me of any movement around the place that isn't normal.

"Bad trouble?" Cassie's voice comes from behind me. She has never met Bull or talked to him, hell, he doesn't even know she exists, but she knows how much he means to me. I've been watching over him for the past seven years from afar, doing my best to keep the dumbass alive.

"Bad enough that I'm bringing him here!" I yell as I enter my secure office, hand on the door before I close it, and all I hear is part of her sentence.

"Oh fu—" I hope she managed to pull herself back and not say what she was thinking in front of Bessy. That kid will have the worst vocabulary before she turns ten, the way she always manages to hear me saying the wrong thing when her little ears are around.

Cassie will know how much danger Bull is in, with me bringing him to our home. Since the home was finished and we moved into it after Bessy was born, no one has ever been here. I have locked things up tight and made sure my family was safe but had the freedom to live happily. It's been a struggle, I'm not going to lie. With Jason getting slowly more active again after Bessy was born, there was no way I was letting anyone near Cassie, Bessy, and now little Eli.

When Cassie suggested having another baby, I didn't know if I could go through another home birth, but she was restless and didn't want Bessy to be an only child like she had been. Especially with us being in the middle of nowhere with no one for Bessy to play with. She has had a strange upbringing being locked up here, but we have tried to make it as normal as we could.

It's been a full day since I've left my office which is more like a security bunker, just keeping an eye on things and doing some background work. I've pulled Bull out of some scrapes before, and I have to admit, the last big one a few years ago that went wrong was his deciding factor, and I was glad he decided to leave WITSEC and go live a normal life back at home with his family. We have stayed in touch but not as much as either of us would have liked, and we haven't seen each other, and to be honest, it's long overdue. I know I'm going to be in big trouble when he gets here and finds out about my family, but part of me is happy it's finally happening. Since Asha has come into his life recently, I think he will understand why I did what I did. But if he doesn't, too bad, I wouldn't change a thing.

Working rapidly, I'm putting everything into place to get him and Asha here safely. Since I started working undercover for Rocket, after Bessy was born, my life has changed. I now run a private security company from here with my partner, Ashton Taylor. It's very high-end and usually undercover. We aren't the company you call to provide five security guards for an event to check people's licenses and do crowd control. We are the people you call when you know you need serious protection and will pay whatever it takes.

Badger is on board when I need him, but he's become a drifter too. He's never asked to come here, and I'm thankful for his respect in that. I know he is like a vault with information; whatever I talk to him about, stays with him. I have learned to confide in him things I normally would have told Bull. That pisses me off, that my life has taken that turn, but I wouldn't change the reason I'm here for anything in this world.

Badger has also built up his network of contacts over the years, so when we need a specific person for a job, he usually knows a guy who knows a guy. I trust him unconditionally, and when we decided to start this business, I asked him if he wanted in. But he said it's just not him, so I decided to make him our silent partner, and Ashton agreed with me. So much so, that it's even silent from Badger, and he has no idea what we do behind the scenes for him. I have been putting money away for him from the profits from the beginning, and when the time comes that he wants to settle somewhere and watch the world go by, he'll be doing it comfortably whether he likes it or not.

I met Ashton through Badger a few years ago. They had worked together doing contract security jobs with a group of guys who are all ex-military, based out of Chicago. Ashton and Badger hit it off straight away, with common backgrounds. Then once all three of us were connected together on a job that I needed some help with, everything clicked between us as a group.

Ashton had just recovered from being injured on deployment, and when I was doing my background check, which is usually much more thorough than any normal agency check, a few things sank into my gut that I have never been able to share with anyone, not even Ashton. I promised myself that I would make sure he was looked after like the rest of my extended family. He doesn't know that and assumes it's just because we're buddies that are perfect for each other. One day, the time will be right, and I will share everything I know, because it doesn't change anything in his life going forward. But now is not the time. For the moment, I have his back and he has mine, and that's all that matters.

In Chicago, Ashton has a close group of friends, people he met once he got home from being in the military. He reconnected with Mason White, an ex-Army pilot buddy from when they served together. From what he has mentioned, he's happy there, and it makes a good place for him to be based.

"Yep." His voice is in my ear as I'm punching away on the keyboard. We don't bother with pleasantries, it's just how we are.

"Like we thought it would, it's all gone to shit with Bull. We need to extract them both now." My voice is calm, even though this job is different, and Ashton knows that. I've been keeping him in the loop since Bull called me not long ago. If there is one thing I learned a very long time ago in this job, it's to trust your gut instinct, and mine was telling me that this was going to end up here.

"On it. I'll get a plane in the air." We're partners, and Ashton knows a lot about me, but we have never met in person, and he doesn't know where my house is either. That's why we click, because he doesn't give a fuck. We both have our roles, and mine is here behind the computer screens, while he's on the ground and all the muscle we need.

"Sending you the coordinates of the airport we'll use, get me an ETA for the plane. I will then line up the airstrip and the vehicles needed. We are time sensitive."

"I'm here with my buddy Mason, and I think I can make this super quick. Hold on." The voices in the background are mumbled, and I know he wouldn't bring him in on the job unless he trusts him.

"Done. Mason has a private plane ready to go." There is no

long chitchat between us, just straight to the point. "We can be on standby in less than thirty minutes."

"Thanks, Ashton." Hanging up, I'm thinking about his name; he still won't let me give him a code name, the bastard. He tells me he's not into spy games. It's funny because in the Army, usually everyone ends up with a nickname, but he's not sharing his and he remains adamant that he is Ashton. Whatever, I don't have time to worry about that shit right now.

I've been busy all afternoon and have everything in place. Plans are set, and Bull is ready to put it into action tonight. Now we sit and wait. The worst part is that I've never been a patient man, and neither is Bull, although we've both had to learn to be, as much as it almost kills us.

Cassie sent me a message a little while ago to let me know she was putting the kids to bed and will get me some dinner. I'm not hungry, but who knows how long it'll be until I leave this room. The smartest thing I did was build a toilet in this office and a couch that is big enough it can double as a bed when I need to nap, which means I don't have to leave when things are crazy. She's used to it and ignores me when I tell her that I don't need any food. But when she arrives with something that usually smells and tastes amazing, my plate is empty before I know it.

The door opening behind me, I can smell the lasagna that she makes to perfection. If there is one thing we've had living up here, it's plenty of spare time. Cassie has become a spectacular cook, and I've had to work twice as hard in the gym to stop myself from getting out of shape.

"I knew you wouldn't be able to resist this." She stands next to me with the plate of food and wearing one of my t-shirts as a nightgown.

"Are you talking about the food or you?"

Cassie giving me the side-eye as she lays the plate down on the clear spot on my desk. "We both know you don't have time for that." She turns to leave so she doesn't distract me.

"Doesn't mean I don't want it. Love you," I say as the door

closes, and I'm already lifting the first mouthful to my lips on the fork.

She is gone as quick as she came in here, and I know how blessed I am to have a wife who understands my work and that some days it's more important than her. And that tastes like acid on my tongue, but it's the truth.

Mmmm, this is like sin on a fork. And just like she does every time, she makes me realize how hungry I actually was.

Using my finger to wipe the last bit of sauce off the plate and suck it into my mouth, my phone goes off again, and the plan is already off to a rocky start. Bull is moving, and I strap myself in for a long night. Ashton is already in transit with transportation and will be in place by the time he is needed.

I push a button on my earpiece to pick up Bull's call.

"I have her." My heart settles a little, but the adrenaline is still coursing through my body because we are long way from this being over, but now that Asha is safe in his arms, then the rest we will manage to pull off.

I can hear myself talking, but my mind is already moving forward and processing what he's saying about the people involved, since things are turning out a little different to what we first expected. That's why you need to stay fluid, because the people you suspect can turn on a dime and others that you think are the issue have surprised you and stepped out from the shadows only to reveal they have been on your side all along.

"For fuck's sake, you never do anything simple, do you, Bull?" I ask him as I get a message on my screen from Ashton. He's in place at the airstrip and ready, waiting for Bull to arrive with his precious cargo. I give Bull his directions to the airfield where he will meet up with Ashton and his pilot friend, Mason. And I finally let him in on his final destination. I can hear the shock in his voice.

"Fuck, am I finally going to see the secret Ghost lair? I was starting to think it didn't even exist and that you lived in some basement in the Bronx or something normal like that." He's trying to bring in some humor to try to break his stress.

"Nothing normal about where I live, Bull." And that's more truth than he realizes.

"Got it, no normal home for a man who doesn't have one normal bone in his body." Bull is about to learn that that's not exactly true. Well, Cassie might agree, but all I let the kids see is as much of a normal father as I can be. But what I will admit is how much I miss Bull's witty mouth and our conversations full of banter.

"No matter what, that smartass part of you is always lurking, isn't it," I grumble at him, because as much as I want to see him, part of me is nervous that I'm about to break the seal on my family's secure bubble here, and that is hard to swallow.

"Keeps me calm. Now let's talk strategy and details while I'm driving," Bull replies, and I can totally relate to the calmness. It's how we work together. Throwing shit at each other until it's go time, and then it gets pushed aside. Although it's never far from the surface, and that's why he's like my brother.

Finally, I flop backwards into the chair as Ashton reports in that they are airborne and on route to me. I have done so many jobs over the years, but this one has my blood pressure up more than normal. It's the middle of the night, and Cassie will be fast asleep. I should just crash here in the office again, on the couch, but I need to be close to her. There is something pulling at me with her the last few weeks. I'm not sure what it is, but my stupid gut has been twitching again. The air is a little thick, and I don't like it that way. Usually, it's telling me there is trouble coming, and I'm praying it's just all about Bull, but I can't seem to fully believe it, and I find myself repeating the words *"Trouble is coming"* like a mantra in my head.

Knowing that it will be hours before Bull and Asha arrive, I shut down my system and switch it to my phone and smart watch for the alerts. I let Ashton know I'm going to catch a little shut-eye and he is my eyes and ears. I have several numbers on my phone that are set to ring and at a high volume every single time they call, no matter if my phone is on do-not-disturb or in sleep mode. Doesn't matter what I'm doing, I need to speak to them.

Stepping out of my boots at the door to our room, I walk as softly as I can to the bathroom. Not quite making it, I stop halfway to the end of our bed. The moonlight is streaming through the windows across the room and onto the bed, illuminating Cassie's olive skin on her back. She's asleep on my side of the bed which is what she always does when I'm not in here with her. I've never asked her why, but I can guess. It'll be the same as when I finally climb in with her tonight and nuzzle my nose into her hair and breathe in her scent. My senses then tell my body I'm home.

Lying on her stomach, the sheet is positioned just covering her backside, and one of her legs is sticking out from under it. Her long wavy brown hair is strewn down her back across her shoulders and then falling off onto the bed. With her face turned to the side of the window and just out of the rays from the moon, the light is just enough to show her features in the shadows. With all the chaos around me, her beauty still captivates me.

I can't help myself from lifting my phone from my pocket and snapping a picture for my secret album, one that Cassie has full access to, but she never bothers to look; I would never disrespect her by doing something behind her back, but she knows this is just for me. Not nudes but sensual beauty, just like this. I don't share, and she knows that. Not now, not ever. I'm sure if people knew we were up here they would think I'm a controlling man who has her trapped here, when she should have left years ago.

They're wrong on two counts. One, they don't know why she's here. And two, she doesn't want to leave.

This is our life, and she is happy here.

Stripping off my clothing in the bathroom and readying myself for some sleep, I switch off the light and open the door. My eyes adjust to the darkness again. They do it quickly, as it's something we get used to in our job. Having good night vision is important.

"Fuck!" A low growl slips out of my mouth at the vision stretched out before me.

Cassie has turned in her sleep while I was gone and is now lying naked on her back. The sheet is scrunched up underneath her, her perky, full breasts standing to attention, with her nipples pebbled and the moon lighting them up like beacons in the night for me to home in on. Her stomach still shows the silver stretch marks from her last pregnancy with Eli and a few lingering ones from Bessy. I love those little lines. They are her war marks from when she has gone into battle twice, like the warrior queen I love. Bringing two children into the world on her own is one hell of an achievement but not one I want to try again. The older we get the more risk we are taking, and to me, now that risk is getting too high.

My eyes can't help but look at her sex, sitting there perfectly for the taking. I can feel my cock now rock hard, and I run my tongue over my lips, getting ready for what I want, and to be honest, I think it's something I need to ground me. Cassie is always my base to center me. And tonight, I feel off center, and she is my remedy.

Walking from my office to the bedroom I discovered how tired I was, but the goddess in front of me has just given me the energy I didn't know I was still holding inside.

Crawling on the bed next to her is enough for her to stir from her sleep. She doesn't open her eyes but her sleepy words remind me how much I love her. Her care for people she has never met is already showing.

"Are they safe, Ghost?" Her voice is barely above a whisper.

"They will be, baby," I reply, kissing her lips ever so softly.

"I know this is hard for you. Are you okay?" She always sees behind the walls, no matter how strong I build them. And here she hasn't even looked at me, with her eyes closed, but she can sense my thoughts.

My honesty comes out, even though I was trying to hold it in. "No," I tell her. She opens her bright eyes slowly, looking straight into my soul. "I need you." I'm telling her just how I feel, no lies and not hiding a thing.

"Then take me. I'm yours, Noah, every inch of me." She slides her hand up behind my neck and pulls my head toward her breasts. I can't say no to her body, and she knows that.

Her words are the green light I need, and I take her body in my arms. Wrapping them underneath her, it arches her back up, and I take her breast in my mouth, devouring her. I bite down on her nipple as I drag it with me, pulling backwards. My lips pop off as she is mewling out my name, and I place her back down onto the mattress.

I need everything from her. Not just sinking inside her.

Slipping down the bed, I pull her legs apart and kneel between them, lifting them up onto my forearms. I can see how wet she is in the moonlight, her pussy glistening just for me. Tasting her is my addiction, and she knows that. Leaning forward and taking the first swipe with my tongue, I can feel tension start to leave my body. I can't hold back any longer, and the moment her hands are on my head, pushing me to take what I want, I get lost in my wife.

Her words don't even make sense as she is trying to move back and forth as I slide my finger in and continue sucking on her with everything I've got. The inside of her thighs tense, and her body is quivering. My girl is about to reach her peak, and there's no way I'm stopping now. It takes all I have some days not to come just from watching her orgasm from my touch. But not tonight. I want it all, sinking inside her wet pussy and feeling every ripple of her muscles as I bury myself as deep as I can get.

Her body comes down slightly from the first high, but I'm not letting her rest. Releasing her legs and lying on top of her, I hold myself up a little on my forearms. But our skin is still touching as I look into her eyes. The sweat on her body shows in the moonlight, giving me a shiver knowing I put that sheen there. My beautiful, sexy wife. How in the hell did I get so lucky?

"Noah, please." Not holding back, I push inside her. I'm not gentle anymore, that's gone, but now I'm being as rough as I feel. If I unleash the nervous energy inside me, then we won't be stopping for hours. My libido is telling me to go for it, but my body is letting me know I need sleep. Danger is hovering around us, and I must be on my A game. Not letting any of those thoughts take hold of me, I just want Cassie. She hooks her feet around my back and settles them on my ass. Her hips are matching my rhythm. It's raw and primal, and I need to own her. Show her that no matter what happens from here on in, she's mine, and I'll be with her, always.

My mouth takes hers, and I tell her through the kiss about the fear inside me that I can't put into words. I don't know what it is that's brewing, but the fear that is hovering in the universe around me is more than just Bull, and deep down I know that.

Cassie pulls away from my mouth, and my name is now being whispered on her lips as she quietly orgasms without shouting to wake the kids. Watching her hold herself together, yet still falling apart for me is enough to push me over the edge.

I'm not as quiet as her, and I need to let loose.

"Cassie." My voice might not be loud, but it's a growl that is sheer desire.

My cock twitches inside her as I empty every last drop of what she does to me.

Lying down on her and then rolling us over so I'm on the bottom, I bury my head into her shoulder, surrounded by her hair. I take the breaths I need.

"It's okay, Ghost, it'll be okay. Sleep, you need it."

Pulling both her hands between us and clasping them over my heart, I do as she says. Holding on tight and keeping her close, my eyes close and my brain slows. It never stops, but for tonight at least, it's resting.

Only having three hours' sleep was enough, and I've been up working since before the sun rose. I know I need to talk to Cassie before Bull and Asha arrive. Bessy has been down to the village a few times but not often. She's not used to having people here, and I need her to understand what having visitors means. I'm afraid that she will bombard them the moment they step onto the property. I don't know how this will go, and I'm relying on Cassie to help me settle her excitement.

Cassie was going to talk to her last night, and I bet it took a long time to get her to sleep after that conversation. The excitement would have been at an all-time high. I also wanted to make sure that Bessy understands that Bull and Asha are people she can trust. I don't want her to know him as Bull but just Kurt and Asha who are friends of Daddy's.

It's still quiet in the house, but I know by the tracker on the car that Bull and Asha aren't far away. I saw on the house monitors that Cassie is up and just finished feeding Eli.

It's time to head out from my office bunker and be ready for their arrival.

"Morning, precious boy," I say, leaning down to kiss Eli on the cheek. He's in a milk-drunk state on Cassie's shoulder in the nursery.

"Morning." Looking into Cassie's big brown eyes warms me up on the inside. I kiss her lips and then her forehead on my way to stand back up after leaning over her on the rocking chair.

"Morning, did you sleep much?" she asks in her sweet voice as she is still rubbing Eli on the back to bring up any wind after his feed.

"Enough," I reply, and she rolls her eyes at me.

"I doubt it, but you'll never change." Trying to stand from the chair, I reach my hands out to pull her toward me. I draw both her and Eli into a hug which is warm and smells all baby, with a twist of her sweet scent I would know anywhere.

"They're only about five minutes away, so I'll meet them outside and then bring them in. Hopefully Bessy might stay asleep a little longer."

"You wish, I'm surprised she isn't already up. Remember, she's your daughter. Nothing gets past her." We walk together toward the kitchen where I can smell that Cassie has already been up and cooking, ready for their arrival. Maybe Bessy isn't the only one that's excited. "I need to change Eli, so I will meet you out here after that. Don't want to overwhelm them as soon as they get out of the car."

As she turns and heads back to the nursery, my phone alerts me of the car coming up to the gate, and pushing the button to open it, my heart takes a little skip of a beat. I have to trust that I haven't just let the outside world in and brought the danger with it.

I should have guessed the dogs would have picked up on the noise of the car coming down the drive. As I open the door, they are out past me and barking as they bound down the stairs to the man I have missed and the woman who has captured his heart. I can see it in his eyes.

"Ace and Bandit, do not lick them to death," I call, trying to get them to heel like they are supposed to with strangers, but I'm guessing they can sense these two aren't any threat.

Our back-and-forth banter is already starting as I reach forward and drag Bull into a hug. I'm not sure who needed it more, me or him, but everything we couldn't say out loud is felt in every second of the embrace.

Since this morning there has been movement in Asha's case, and I need to get Bull up to speed, but there's time for that. Bringing them through the front door, it still makes me smile every time I look out at the view of the valley, through the floor-to-ceiling windows, which I never told Cassie about, but they're bulletproof. The dogs are still trailing Asha and have attached to her already. She has a gentle side, I can already see. That blonde hair is such a contrast to Cassie, but the eyes are the same, warm and loving.

I think feeding them and some caffeine is a good start, while I start explaining about the cabin they will be staying in. After we moved into this house and Cassie and Bessy settled into a routine, we went back and fixed up the cabin, just in case one day we had a need to use it. We'd hoped it would be for visitors, but I should have guessed it would be for someone on the run. I mean, what else is this property for?

Before I get to finish settling them in, I hear her feet and know I finally get to share my news with my best friend. I just hope he can forgive me for keeping them a secret from him all this time. I'm not sure how I would feel if the tables were reversed.

"Daddy?" Her soft little voice is behind me, coming out of the hallway. Turning, I see her little brown ringlets that I adore bouncing as she is running toward me now. Putting my arms out, she climbs me like a tree and is clinging on to both her stuffed bear and me at the same time.

The look from Kurt is pure shock, which I don't think I have ever seen from him before.

"Morning, my precious girl. Did you sleep well?" I pull her in for a snuggle which I'm not sure is to calm her or me.

Introducing her to Kurt and Asha goes well, and I can tell she is not scared one bit at having strangers in the house, chatting away to them.

"Where's Mommy, Bessy?" Because I feel like part of me is missing in the room. Hearing her voice has me watching Kurt again. The poor guy looks like he is either going to pass out or punch me, and he can't decide which it is.

As Cassie introduces herself and Eli to both Asha and Kurt, I almost breathe a sigh of relief, as Kurt is replying to her in our usual banter, but he makes sure he is looking straight at me as he says the last words.

"The big fella here has a lot of explaining to do later." Kurt is shaking Cassie's hand, and the smiles on Cassie and Asha's faces already tell me there is a kindred spirit between them. One that they are about discover and rely on as the days in front of us get more intense.

And they always do. Nothing stays the same.

We just have to ride the wave and hope for a better day ahead.

Chapter Seventeen

CASSIE

I can't even describe the feeling of having another woman here the last few days. And not just any woman. Someone who understands me and my life. I don't have to pretend with her. She gets it.

Seeing Asha and Kurt with the kids has been amazing. It gave me flutters in my stomach and a warm buzz in my heart. I haven't seen Bessy interact with other adults like this, and it brought tears to my eyes just watching the joy on her face every single second. I don't know how I'm going to handle Bessy when they leave, and I just hope they can come back soon. Unfortunately, I know nothing is guaranteed in this life.

Things have turned bad again for Asha and the situation she is running from, so they are preparing to go a lot sooner than we were hoping. But Ghost has promised me that no matter where they are, I can video call Asha as much as I like, and Bessy can talk to her too. He doesn't know how much that means to both of us. I have done my best, but this is a lonely place at times. I didn't realize how much I missed a woman to talk to until she arrived, and I feel like I've known Asha my whole life. It makes sense really, with the boys being so close, that naturally the women they love will get along too.

"Stay safe and give them hell. I can't lose you now," I whisper in her ear as I give her the last hug, knowing they will be gone in the early-morning light. I try to hold the tears in because we can't let Bessy know, she thinks she is just saying good night. Asha is hanging on to me just as tightly as I am to her.

"I'll be back, I promise. They won't beat me, not with Kurt and Ghost on my side." Looking at me one last time before we pull apart, we are then both drawn into our guys' embraces.

I'm getting sick of life's twists and turns. When will we be able to live a normal life? I've almost forgotten what that's like. What even is a normal life?

I turn and walk away, Eli in my arms, holding him just a little tighter now. Bessy is skipping down the hallway in front of me like she doesn't have a care in the world. I wish I felt the same. Feeling another headache coming on, I know the stress is taking a toll on me again. They seem to be getting more intense, but I'm not telling Ghost that, he'll worry, and he doesn't need that on top of everything else right now. Kurt and Asha are his main priority, along with whoever else he is keeping safe at the moment, because there is always someone. More accurately, there are usually numerous others. Hopefully they are all under control so he can be fully invested in this one. Ghost wouldn't survive if something happened to Bull and now Asha too.

I don't know all the details, and because it doesn't involve me, I don't need to. What I do know, though, is that come early morning, they will be gone, and Ghost will be in his bunker until it's over. I wouldn't expect anything less.

Wrapping Eli tightly and placing him carefully down in his crib, I give him his last kiss of the night on his forehead and send the same prayer out to the universe I do every night. That if anything should happen to me that my family will be safe. My biggest hope is that my children live a long, happy, healthy, and safe life. I wouldn't wish this on anyone, and I hope it won't be their whole life either.

Walking out of the nursery, I hear Bessy already reading a story to herself in her own words. She is reading a little, and I have tried hard to teach her, but I'm not a teacher, and to be honest, I don't want to be. My little independent girl is going to need someone else to do that. She is going to have Ghost's brains, and that means as she gets older, she will be ahead of me and what I can do to keep that mind interested. It would be easy to say that's Ghost's job, but that won't work either. His work keeps him busy, and we never know when he is going to disappear into his world and not surface for a few days. And the other reason is that I have a sneaky suspicion that as Bessy gets older, or should I call her mini-Ghost, there are going to be many times that they will be butting heads. Both thinking they're right about something and neither giving an inch. I'm definitely not looking forward to that time of our lives. Thank God that Eli is much more placid, and I hope he stays that way. Not that I can say he takes after me. Ghost will be the first to say that my stubbornness and temper will get in my way at times. Let's be honest, it's more than a few times, but hey, it helped me to get my man and survive the last seven years.

"Hey, princess, what are we reading tonight?" I ask, trying not to laugh at her snuggled into the bed with what looks like twenty different stuffed animals. Ghost spoils her at times.

Mystery packages arrive, and it always seems to be when life is getting to us all up here. It's not all sunshine and roses every day. I don't want to live anywhere else in the world, but being able to leave here for holidays or see friends would help. Or even just to take a day trip and be able to buy clothes in a shop, test out the smell of a new perfume, or see a movie in a theatre along with a hundred other people who are all laughing or crying at the same place in the story. Hell, I haven't even been able to go on a date with Ghost. I know all this is stirring in my head tonight with Asha leaving and feeling like I am going back into my little family bubble that I love and hate at the same time.

"*Frozen*, Mommy. You can be Elsa and I'll be Anna." Kind of ironic she likes this story so much. In a way we are just the same, trapped in our castle and not willing to open the doors to anyone. Letting Bull and Asha in was huge, and I know Ghost is worried about how it will affect Bessy, but still, he didn't hesitate to give his friend a safe place to regroup and take a breath. Deep down, I wonder if Ghost also needed the human contact after all these years. Talking to someone on the phone or via video isn't the same as face to face.

"Oh, so I get to make you a snowman tonight." Giving her a little tickle, I sit down on the bed next to her. Her giggle takes away my sadness just for a short time as we dive into the story and our world of make believe.

Bessy's words slowing down, I know she's getting tired. It's been a huge few days for our princess.

"Sleep time." Taking the book out of her hands, I tuck her in tight.

"I like Asha and Kurt, Mommy." Her words are barely above a whisper.

"Me too, baby," I tell her, kissing her on the forehead and sending the same prayer to the universe as I did for Eli.

Ghost didn't understand at first why I was prepared to go through the risk of another baby up here on our own, until I explained my fears. Yes, Bessy needs a friend, but I need to know that if something happens to me, and God forbid Ghost too, that they have each other. The feeling I had when my parents died was one of total hopelessness. I was alone in this world, and I know as an adult that happens eventually, as we all leave this world when it's our time. But at eighteen, it was too early. I hadn't learned how to pave my way in the world yet. I needed that person behind me to say it will be okay, keep going, take that leap. In a way, Ghost and I are the same. I lost my parents through death, but he lost his a long time before that. I'm not sure he ever totally had them, to be honest.

So, once I explained my fears, he understood at a level most people wouldn't. The kids will have more money than they ever need, and now that I have met Kurt, I know he would love them like his own. Which is the reason we had him listed as their godfather and sole appointed guardian for them in our will. Thankfully, we have now been able to tell him that since he arrived. Asha cried, hugging us both, promising that she will always be there for Bessy and Eli. And for only knowing someone for a few days, it's weird, but as soon as she said it, it gave me some peace of mind.

Walking from Bessy's room, the house is so quiet again, too quiet. A week ago, I wouldn't even be thinking about it, but tonight, it's bugging me. Ghost will be in his office, just checking in on all his jobs and making sure everything is perfectly in place ready for Kurt and Asha's trip tomorrow. I fear for them. Normally I don't know the people Ghost is helping, but I have put a face to the names now, felt their hugs and laughed until we cried together, so it makes it more personal. I also know what it's like when you are in the thick of the danger. It's not nice and takes every piece of strength you can muster to get through it.

I go through my normal routine of cleaning up after the kids, putting the washing on so it's done for the morning, and then making my cup of herbal tea to take to bed with me. I read a lot on the nights Ghost is working. All sorts of books—biographies, home styling, self-help, and of course, fiction. I can't read crime, it's too close to home, but I'm not picky with what I read.

I slapped Ghost in a playful way when I found out that Asha is an author and that he knew. I downloaded all her books straight away, and I can't put them down. She is awesome and has sucked me in with that first chapter of the first book. Ghost's excuse was that he's seen what's on her computer and didn't want me thinking about any other half-naked man, other than him. We all burst out laughing as he said it, knowing that he was joking and couldn't care less about it. He is a man comfortable in his own skin, and he knows how much I love and adore him. That's never been in doubt since the moment we met.

Listening to Asha talk about writing was fascinating. I could tell how proud of her Kurt is. That through all the adversity and fear she has lived through, she's kept her eye on the prize and continued to follow her dream.

I curl up in bed, opening my e-reader and trying to get into the story, but my headache is getting stronger and making my vision blurry, so I abandon my plans. A few sips of my tea later and it's not hitting the spot like it normally does either. I just don't feel right, and I'm sure it's from the impending danger my new friends are heading into, as well as how it will affect Ghost if anything bad happens. I'm restless, and I haven't been that way in a long time. I hate it.

Feeling his weight on the bed making the mattress dip next to me, I'm surprised. I wasn't expecting him to sleep in here tonight. Only being half awake, my body moves on instinct. Curling into Ghost's body, his arms wrap me up tight with my head on his chest. My head still reminds me of my headache, but the warmth of his body and the beat of his heart has me sliding back into my sleep quickly. This is home, right here in his arms.

Waking the next morning, he's gone from our bed, and I know Bull and Asha will be gone from my home too. Looking at the clock, I see it's six in the morning, and I need to get up and start the day. I'm surprised Eli hasn't woken yet; he's probably exhausted just like the rest of us. I don't even feel like getting up, which is not like me. The headache hasn't completely shifted but is now just a dull ache that I'll take some aspirin for. But first, coffee.

I love the days when Ghost is not working too hard, and he's up and moving before me. The smell of the freshly brewed coffee has me salivating before I even make it to the kitchen. This morning I wasn't expecting to smell anything, but I do, and it smells amazing. He must have done it after Kurt and Asha left before he headed into the office. He knew that I would need a nice little pick-me-up this morning, and he is spot-on.

The last few days have been hell. Bessy has been acting up, complaining she is bored now that she doesn't have friends to play with. I knew it would be hard but was hoping she would settle quickly when I told her that they would be back for a visit one day.

To her, time is irrelevant, and if I say one day, she assumes I mean tomorrow.

I got Ghost's message a few hours ago to let me know it was over and everyone was safe. My emotions have been all over the place, so I cried at the message. Yesterday I yelled at Bessy, and that's not like me at all. Scarily, it reminded me of when I was pregnant with Eli. I don't think I can take another baby now. It was in the back of my mind that three kids might be nice, but now with the two, I think we are perfect the way we are.

Trying to think of when my last period was is hard, as they haven't been in a routine yet after Eli. I know that they say if you're breastfeeding you shouldn't get pregnant, but that's not true. I would never rely on that. Ghost, as much as he hates it, has been wearing condoms, just to be safe. So, I'm ninety-nine percent sure it's not a baby on the way, but never say never. I'll give it a few more days and then test. I don't want to scare poor Ghost. I know he was bragging to Bull that he is now a doctor after delivering two babies, but I beg to differ. We have just been extremely lucky that nothing went wrong. We will look back in years to come and realize how insane we were to attempt it.

After another long day, the kids are in bed asleep, and I'm desperate to see my man. I need his touch. The tight hug, the sensual touch of his lips, and all that usually follows that kiss. Skin to skin is what I need. It always calms me, and I'm craving that feeling.

Sliding his blue shirt on over my naked body, I can smell him. I hold the collar up to my nose and breathe him in. Oh, my Noah, how I've missed you. It's time we got reacquainted.

I secure only the two buttons between my breasts, and I know this will have him hard as soon as he sees me. His broad shoulders and solid arms that bulge nicely in his clothes means that the shirt is big enough to look like a short dress on me. The hem just covers my buttocks but is enough to drive him crazy.

I poke my head into both the kids' rooms on my way down the

hallway, making sure they are still asleep, because I don't want them seeing their mother dressed like this. I'm keeping this vision just for their father.

Placing my thumbprint on the security pad, I know he will be expecting me. I've seen the screens in his office, and he'd probably know if I sneeze somewhere in the house, to be honest. I creep in quietly just in case he's on a call that I don't want to interrupt. The speed his work moves sometimes means I never know what I'm walking into. Seeing him pull out his earpiece, I know I'm safe to go to him.

"Hey there, handsome, I think you need a break. And more importantly, some sleep," I murmur, placing my hands on his shoulders and feeling the rock-hard tension that has built in his muscles. I lean down and kiss him, just needing to get my lips on him. I need to get him out of this office and into our bed with me. I let him know the kids are tucked up tight in bed, and that piece of information will make him unable to resist the invitation for a shower together. Instantly, that has everything now moving, including me.

Ghost pulls me onto his lap so I can feel his hard cock underneath me, and the arousal in his eyes tells me we are both on the same page now. His shirt I'm wearing parts slightly to expose my nakedness underneath. The hitch in his breath is like heaven to my ears.

His hand sliding up my bare legs has my arousal already building. Yes... this is what I want. No, it's what I *need!*

His mouth is now all over me, and his whispered words take my mind away to the place where I don't think of anything except our mutual pleasure.

Using his teeth, he rips the few buttons so I'm fully open to him, my breast on show, and he takes his fill of me.

He owns me, and I give myself willingly.

I can't hold it in any longer. I moan his name, his real name. The one I hold deep inside me for when we are totally raw and open to each other.

"Noah."

We need to move from this room. From day one I knew this is a sex-free zone. I get why, but the naughty girl in me keeps trying. One day he will give in and lay me out over this desk in front of him. Spread-eagle and devouring me to the point I can't even speak, and then he will fuck me into submission. I'm sure he knows that's a fantasy of mine, and he always humors me up to a certain point, and then we are moving to anywhere he can find, somewhere to push my body up against and have me screaming his name. Even if it's a silent scream to hide from the kids.

Now is that breaking point. I can hear the change in his voice as soon as he starts to talk again. "Shower, now. Get the soap ready so I can clean you after I make you filthy dirty for the first time tonight, but rest assured, it won't be the last time."

Not wanting the intensity to drop, as I'm walking away, I flip off his shirt and sway my naked ass at him as I head to the shower. The groan behind me tells me it worked.

As soon as I'm clear of the door, I'm running down the hallway to our shower. Lighting a few candles in the bathroom, I know I don't have long. He will be in here, and I want to be wet and waiting. There is something so sensual about a shower where Noah is washing me while worshiping my body at the same time. It's hard to concentrate through the overload of sensations.

The minutes are ticking away, and I'm starting to worry that someone is in trouble and I'll be left here hanging. It wouldn't be the first time it's happened. But he always more than makes up for it when the crisis is over.

I hear his footsteps entering the bathroom and his shadow moves in the candlelight.

"What took you so long? I was going to start…" I begin, trying to hurry him to be in here with me.

"Mommy, we have a visitor." His voice is solid and calm.

My body moving automatically, mother mode kicks my arousal sadly to the side. Peeking my head out the door, I see a bare-chested Noah with Bessy in his arms, looking sad and a little lost.

"Ohhh." I silently thank him for stopping me before I said anything that could have had both of us trying to explain to Miss Inquisitive.

"What's wrong, Bessy?"

After the explanation that she is missing her daddy and that another story will fix the problem, I'm left standing here in the shower on my own. The hot water streaming down over me, the vanilla scent from the candle mixing in the steam around me, and my sex throbbing for my husband. I lost my shyness of masturbating years ago thanks to my husband, but tonight is not about just getting off. I need that connection with Noah, and I'm waiting for his love, no matter how long it takes. He promised to resolve my issue, and I'll be here with anticipation just like he is expecting.

I knew as soon as Bessy was born, she was his princess, and no matter what, he would always bow to her with all the love he has inside him. And I wouldn't have it any other way.

Turning off the shower and toweling off, I take the candles into our room, leaving the lights off and throwing the blanket back. My emotions feel raw, and that's how I want him to find me. Something is not right with me, but I just can't pinpoint what it is. Noah always manages to make everything right.

Tonight, I'm relying on him for that.

I can't believe it's been over a month since Kurt and Asha were here for their second visit. Having them back for that second time was so special and so much less stressful than the first trip.

Life has settled into a pattern again, but now with the added phone calls and video chats between us all. We have even managed to have a few dinners together via Zoom, and it feels so good to have other people to talk to over a meal. I've noticed a change in Ghost too. Having Bull back in his life, he seems a little more relaxed. Even though Bull doesn't want to work with Ghost and Ashton in their business, back in the high-paced world of danger, but I have a feeling down the track there will be times he won't be able to help himself or Ghost will need him and that will have him stepping in without even being asked.

Watching Ghost and Bessy outside on the swing has me smiling.

Eli is in the pouch on Ghost's chest, and there is nothing that makes my heart swoon more than seeing him with his kids.

My hands on the side of the kitchen sink, everything around me becomes a little blurred. Shaking my head trying to clear it, things become worse. Dizziness now overtaking me, I try to get to the ground before I fall there. What the hell is going on? Even if I called to Ghost, he wouldn't hear me.

I'm okay, I just need to breathe a bit deeper. Get more oxygen.

In and out, I tell myself. Big deep breaths, in and slowly out. Things are a little fuzzy still, and in the background, I can hear Bessy giggling. I try to concentrate on her voice so I don't pass out.

I have no idea how much time has passed before my sight is returning and the thumping in my chest is settling back so I can't feel my heart pumping so hard. As things in my head are returning to normal, I realize I can hear running water above me. Shit, I was rinsing some tomatoes before I felt weird. Pushing myself up carefully so I don't fall, I reach my hand out to the tap and turn it off. I'm clutching the counter hard enough my knuckles are white, but I need the stability until I'm sure it won't happen again.

I can see my family in the backyard still, Bessy now on the trampoline, bouncing gently, with Eli sitting on there too. Ghost is holding on tight to him and talking to both of them. Eli has a big smile, and Bessy is being the protective big sister, giving cuddles in between the little bounces she gives him to make him grin.

Feeling more normal, I try to get on with preparing dinner, but I can't help but feel anxious as to what the hell just happened. If I tell Ghost, he will be online to a doctor before I can blink and scouring the internet. He has enough to do with keeping us all safe. He doesn't need to be worrying about me and a little fainting spell. I'll be fine, I probably just let myself get a little dehydrated. Being busy with the kids all day, I'm trying to think how much I actually drank. Or maybe it's a sugar problem, not enough of that today. It doesn't matter. I feel okay now, just a bit rattled, and I can feel the start of another headache coming.

Chopping up the salad vegetables, my headache is increasing, and I'm trying to figure out what I can cook that's less complicated than what I had planned. For once I wish we were somewhere I could just order in some dinner. There wouldn't be many children who haven't even had a kids' meal from one of the fast-food chains. It's not a bad thing, but in a way, Bessy is missing out on a rite of passage.

Hearing them before I see them, I know they're back inside the house and heading my way. Trying to look alert and not have them notice anything wrong, I keep them behind me as I face the sink again. Washing some tomatoes that have already been more than drowned in water when I left the tap going.

"Mommy, Mommy, we bounced Eli really high." Bessy is so excited, coming up behind me.

"I saw. How about you get Daddy to bathe you and Eli while I get dinner ready."

"Yes! Bubble time!" she screams as she runs back toward Ghost who has detoured via the nursery, probably to change Eli.

"Daddy, Mommy said it's bubble bath time with you." He is probably groaning at that but won't say no to her.

"What a great idea, Mommy." Hearing the sarcasm in his voice, I know he will be cursing me. Bubbles and a bath with Bessy and Eli is like being in a pool. You may as well have your swimsuit on, you end up that wet.

It will give me time to get myself together and no one will even know what happened.

Ghost has given me a few side-eye looks tonight at dinner, meaning I don't look right, as much as I'm trying to, but he hasn't said anything with the kids around. Eli is fed and fast asleep in his milk-drunk state, and Bessy is getting the last story for the night with her dad. I can hear his voice getting quieter which means that she is asleep, and he is making sure she is into a deep sleep now. My headache has really increased as the night went on. To be honest, all I want to do is curl up in bed and sleep it off.

The kettle boiling for my cup of herbal tea is the last thing I hear as my body starts with a twitch. Now I'm jerking uncontrollably, and I see the fear on Ghost's face coming toward me as the world is going black, and I'm falling...

Chapter Eighteen

GHOST

"Cassie!" I race to catch her jerking body before it hits the floor, then I lower her onto the floor while she is shaking.

"Answer me." I know it's a stupid thing to be yelling at her. She's having a seizure and won't be able to hear me or answer me. We are both now on the floor, my hands between the floor and her head so at least I can soften the blow as her skull is pounding into my hand. I've done enough first-aid courses over the years to know I can't restrain her, but I just don't want her hurt.

"Fuck, come on, baby, stop shaking." My heart's racing and my brain is freaking out. I should be in total control, that's what I do, but I can't think clearly.

Why?

Why the fuck is this happening?

I knew she wasn't right at dinner. The sparkle in her eyes was missing. Even when she was in the peak of pain in childbirth, she never lost the twinkle. I was on my way out to talk to her and find out what was going on. Never in my wildest dreams was I expecting something like this.

Seizures are serious, and for her to be having one out of the blue, I know we need help.

How we have managed to last as long as we have here, without something like this happening, is purely a miracle.

The force of her head hitting my hands is getting less and her body is slowing. I just want her in my arms, but I need to wait. Think, Ghost, think. What do I do now? He body's finally going limp. I pick her up and I'm running with her to the bedroom. I want her on the bed where it's soft, in case she starts again, which I pray to God she doesn't. I'm also trying to hide her from Bessy in case she wakes. I don't want her to feel as scared as I do right now.

"Just relax. I've got you. You're okay now, I'm here." I hope she can hear me as she starts to come out of the unconscious state that the seizure will have put her in. Her eyes are slowly opening and she looks up at me. I'm not sure she even knows who I am or where she is. I can feel little tremors still in her body where I'm holding on to her. I run my hands up and down her arms so she can feel I'm here and know that she is not alone. I don't know how long it's been but finally her mouth starts to move ever so slowly.

The first word is slurred, and I can see she is trying so hard to get it out.

"It's okay, Cassie, just take your time. Don't push yourself." Her eyes drop shut again, and she is almost asleep when the words she was trying to tell me slip out.

"I'm... okay... Noah..." A little snore follows, telling me her body is in a recovery snooze, trying to get back in rhythm.

My hand on her forehead, I wipe the damp hair that is stuck to her face away. There is a thick layer of sweat all over her body. Sliding my body down onto the bed next to hers, I just need a moment to be with her. To breathe her in and listen to her inhaling and exhaling. I've never felt such fear, and I've been in a lot of dangerous places. I know this isn't over, and it's going to be a long night, but I'm thankful that for now she is peaceful and not fighting her body.

Moving from the bed, I strip her shirt and pants from her, finding fresh ones and replacing them. I don't want her lying in her own sweat for longer than she needs to be. Once she is feeling up to it, I will shower her. But I don't want her doing anything she doesn't feel strong enough to handle, even with my help. Grabbing my phone from my pocket, I'm dialing the first person who can help me.

"Yep." Ashton's deep voice helps me slide back into work mode where I know how to control my world.

"I need a doctor. Cassie just had a seizure." My own voice is flat and no change in tone.

"Fuck, like, you need a doctor to your house?" His question stuns me for a moment. I should be saying yes, but I'm struggling to know what the right thing to do in this situation is. My gut is telling me to throw Cassie and the kids in the Range Rover and hightail it to the nearest hospital now. But my head is telling me to slow down and not do anything crazy. Assess the situation and then make controlled decisions.

"No. She will kill me if I do that," I say, running my hand over her cheek as I look down at her from the side of the bed where I'm still standing. "I need to talk to someone we can trust. Find them and make it quick!" Hanging up, I'm already searching the internet just on my phone to see what can cause seizures, and I don't like what I'm seeing. I want to be in the bunker, so I have full access to everything, but I'm not about to leave Cassie on her own.

Frustrated, I grab Cassie's laptop that is sitting on the cupboard where she must have left it this morning. My fingers are quickly trying to find answers to questions when I don't even know what I should be asking.

My phone vibrating in my pocket has me abandoning the computer and dropping back onto the bed to sit with her. I reach for her hand with the one not holding my phone to my ear.

"I've got a guy who is a close friend of both mine and Mason's on the line. Tate, meet Ghost. Tate McIntyre is a neurosurgeon, and I figured you would want the best, and that's him."

"Fuck yes, I want the best. This is my wife, not just anybody, Ashton!" I growl, finding it hard to control my frustration at being totally out of control.

I can hear Ashton typing on the computer in the background, working while he is staying on the line in case I need him.

"Well, then you have me," Tate says. "Now tell me what happened." I like this guy already. Not ashamed to claim his title as the best, and as long as it's true, we will get along just fine.

I relay what has happened today that I know of. I wish that I could ask her more, but she's still sleeping.

"Has she suffered headaches on a regular basis?" Tate asks, and the more I think about it, they have become more frequent and more intense. Why haven't I realized this until now? Too busy worrying about saving other people when I should have been more attentive in my own home.

"She always said it was from the stress. Our life isn't the normal run-of-the-mill kind." My head drops my chin on my chest. I feel like I have failed her.

"You can trust me, Ghost, Ashton has explained some of it. I'll sign whatever you need me to sign, but I can assure you nothing will leave these lips that will put either of you in danger. I'm on your side. Any friend of Ashton and Mason is a friend of mine. Now, let's see if we can wake her a little so I can get you to check a few vitals for me."

This is something I never thought I would do, but today, I know I have no choice.

"Do you need to video chat so you can see her?" My muscles are straining in my neck, and I want to be in the gym punching into the bag so desperately.

"That's your decision to make, Ghost. I'd prefer it, but I understand if you don't want to. Your call, buddy." Something about this guy's voice tells me that he is one of the good guys. And that is a shock to my system. I have never leaned on a stranger before, and there's a reason I've always been a lone wolf, because I have been let down before.

There are very few people I trust in this world, but I think I've just found one more to add to my list.

Saying a silent pray that I'm not making a huge mistake, I flick the call over to a video chat with him. The first thing I see is guy in blue scrubs and in what looks like an office.

"Hey." His eyes look as kind as his voice. You can tell a lot about a person through their eyes, whether they like it or not.

"Thank you," is all I can get out. My mouth is so dry, it feels like my tongue is stuck to the roof of my mouth.

"I've got your back. We're in my office alone. No one can see this call." He doesn't understand how much I need to hear that right now.

I just nod my gratitude.

"Right, now let's see if we can wake your wife a little so I can talk to her." His confident and calm voice is helping me. "I just want you to very gently shake her on the shoulder and call her name."

Letting go of her hand and taking her shoulder, I start talking to her. "Cassie, baby, wake up for me."

"Mhmm…" she replies the first time.

"Keep trying," Tate's voice comes from my hand where I'm still clutching my phone.

"Cassie, you need to open your eyes. Please, Cassie, the doctor wants to see your bright eyes." *And so do I.* The word doctor is what finally gets them opening, although I can see it's a struggle for her to keep them open.

"No doctor." She's looking at me, and if I didn't know better, I would say she is pissed at me.

"You need one. No argument."

She gives me a loud "Hmph!" My heart starts to settle. I'm right, she is annoyed at me, and I couldn't give a fuck. As long as she's okay, that's all I care about.

"This is Doctor McIntyre, he needs to talk to you." Turning the phone toward her, she is still looking at me with a sense of shock to see him on the video chat.

"Hi, Cassie, your husband tells me you had a seizure, and I need to know a bit more."

Cassie is still looking at me with the question of whether she should trust him written all over her dazed face.

"You can trust him. He's Ashton's friend." A bit of relief washes over her, but she is still so far from being herself.

"Okay." She gives him a little nod of her head.

Tate continues to ask her some questions, and I'm furious to find out she almost fainted earlier. He has me using her phone's flashlight while he's on the video call on my phone and has me flashing it in her eyes so he can see her reactions. If she wasn't so sick, we would be in the middle of an argument right now about keeping secrets from me. We promised to be honest with each other, and I could only keep things from her if it was for her benefit and safety.

So much has been happening in the last six months that I haven't shared with her for those exact reasons. Jason has become more active again and is back doing the same things and some worse. He is now higher up the food chain in the government with an inside into the defense department, which is dangerous for all concerned. I have been monitoring him and compiling data. When I dump him in the FBI's lap this time, there needs to be so much evidence that there is no way he can get out of it, along with the others involved. There seems to be another main person involved that I can't flush out yet, but I will. Nothing is going to stop me from closing this whole operation down for good.

Even worse than all of this is that there have been searches happening on Cassie's old name and the name she was placed in WITSEC with. So, someone knows inside information, just like I thought all along, and they are still after her. To me this is more serious than anything else!

I just wasn't telling Cassie while she's been dealing with a new baby in the house and the shock of having the first visitors in our home. Looking back, I'm so thankful that I didn't share with her. Who knows what the extra stress would have done to her body.

Seeing her close her eyes again and Tate's voice telling her to sleep as long as she feels she needs to, I turn the phone back off video and switch just to a voice call between us. I walk over to the side of the room so she can't hear anything he is saying into the phone, even if she is sleeping.

"She'll be okay for now." I don't like the use of the words "*for now.*"

"What's happening?" I need answers, and I need them now.

"I don't know yet, and you aren't going to like what I'm about to say."

"If you want to keep living, it better not be anything bad!" My voice comes out far sterner than it should. He is trying to help us, but my emotions are all over the place.

"Fuck, I can see why you and Ashton get along. Now, calm the fuck down. She needs you to keep her stable until we get to the bottom of this." I want to rip into him for speaking to me like that, but I probably deserved it.

"Like I said, you won't like it, but I'm concerned about her symptoms, and I need her to have an MRI so I can see what is going on inside her head."

"Shit!" I slam my fist onto the wall beside me where I've been leaning. I'm on the other side of the room so I wasn't disturbing Cassie resting. I hope the bang of my fist won't wake her.

"It's the only way, I'm sorry." I can hear the sorrow in his voice. He knows the torment I'm feeling right now.

"I just can't lose her. Leaving here is a massive risk, but not leaving here for this test is an even bigger risk, isn't it." I hope that he is going to deny what I said, but the slow *yes* he replies tells me that there is no choice.

"How much time do we have to get it done?" It's not like I can just put her in the car and take her to the nearest medical center.

"I can't say, but I wouldn't wait. Ghost?" Tate could hear I was already drifting off, trying to process it all and work out how the fuck I can do this without anyone finding her.

"Ghost!" Ashton's voice booms in my ear.

"What the fuck! Alright, I'm listening. I forgot you were there."

"And that statement tells me everything. You are not solid right now." Ashton never pulls any punches. He is a straight shooter.

"Bullshit!" I can't be vulnerable, I have to be her protector.

"I will send Bull and Asha back on the plane to look after the kids. Then you get back on the same plane with Cassie and we'll bring her to Tate. It's the safest way we have. No one needs to know she's here until we know what you're dealing with."

"Like fuck I'm leaving my kids alone!" Pacing the room now, I can't stand still.

"You don't have a choice, dickhead. Cassie needs this, and the kids are safer in your fortress with Bull than here. Plus, you can concentrate on keeping Cassie safe. If they're here, your loyalties are spread too thin and in too many directions. You always told me you trusted Bull with your life, and I've been living up to this legend since we met. So, prove it! Show me that you trust him with your life which is your family!"

"Asshole! Who the hell do you think you are! Of course, I fucking trust him." As the words are coming out of my mouth, I understand what Ashton has done. He is making me face the reality of the situation, and now I know what I need to do.

Silence hangs between us for a few seconds.

"I'm your buddy who cares, that's who I am. We've got you, Ghost, you just have to trust us to look after you and your family this time. It's time to accept some help, let us be your pack. You don't need to be the lone wolf anymore." For the first time, I understand that I may not have my original family, but I have built a new one around me. I just have to let them in.

Stopping and looking at my beautiful wife who needs me, I say the only thing I can.

"Okay, make it happen." I swallow the bile that is rising in my throat. "And Ashton… thanks." I need him to know how grateful I am, not just for what he is about to do but for the day he came into my life.

Tate comes back on the line. "Ghost, Ashton will send you my number. I want you to call me if you need anything through the night. I don't care what time it is. Or if Cassie is scared and just wants to talk to me. I'll check back in with you in the morning, and I'll send you a list of things to look out for. Let's get Cassie here, and I promise to look after her. I'm married too, and if anyone or anything threatened Bella or my kids, I would end their life. We are wired the same, Ghost, and I won't apologize to anyone for my caveman attitude. They are our everything, it's that simple." Tate's voice is deeper and rougher than his doctor's tone he used with Cassie.

"Yeah, it's that simple. Thank you doesn't seem enough."

"It is. Talk soon." The call ends in my ear, and I know Ashton will already be gone out of the call once I gave him the decision that we are moving Cassie to Chicago. Tate thinks I don't know who he is, but I do background checks on everyone I know and all their friends and associates, no matter how much I trust them. It's just who I am, and as Tate said, I won't make excuses for that. Ashton will be busy now enacting the plan and taking over my workload, knowing that I need to be with my wife tonight.

Tate didn't say what he was looking for in that MRI, but I have a fair idea. I'm not stupid, but I'm not voicing it out loud. No way am I giving it air, because it's not happening. No way no how am I losing Cassie.

Her body is calling me, to be close to each other. She needs to know I'm here and she is safe.

Rolling her onto her side and spooning her from behind, I wrap my arms tightly around her and pull her back into me so there is nothing between us.

"We haven't been through all this for nothing, bright eyes. You are my warrior queen. We can beat anything this world throws at us. I promise to protect you always."

I made that promise to myself the first day I met her, and nothing has changed.

"She's mine, and no matter what, I'm not letting her go," I whisper to the universe so it knows. It can throw anything at us, but no matter what, I'll fight back.

"You can't ask me to leave my kids alone! Not happening! I'll be fine, you're just overreacting. This is why I didn't tell you."

And here we are again, my stubborn wife who is pushing me

because she can. She's the only one who has the guts to stand up and go toe to toe with me. But I'm not backing down this time.

No fucking way.

"Keep your voice down, I don't want the kids awake while you're being irrational." Shit, that probably wasn't the right word. Looking at her, I can see the explosion is coming.

"Irrational, you think I'm irrational. Fuck you, Ghost, fuck you! You have kept me here in this prison for seven years, and now you tell me it's fine, we can just go to a huge city hospital with thousands of people. That I can leave my children behind when they have never had anyone with them except us. Irrational doesn't even cut it. The way I feel right now is angry. No, I'm fucking furious! Once again, my choices in my life are being taken away from me. You promised you wouldn't do that to me… yet here we are!"

Calling our home a prison feels like a dagger into my heart and the biggest kick in the guts. I know she doesn't mean it, but those words will stay with me forever.

One of the things Tate told me to watch for was unusual behavior in Cassie. Part of me thinks this fits that description, but to be truthful, this is how she copes when her life is spiraling, and I'm letting her use me as her verbal punching bag.

I know she's scared, and I am too, not that I'll ever admit that to anyone. We just don't have a choice, this is what we must do. Somehow, I have to make her see that.

"Cassie…" I walk toward her with my arms out, and she puts her hands up in front of herself to stop me.

"Don't you touch me. I'm not finished. You think you can contain my anger, but you can't. The only thing that will make me calm down is when you agree we just ignore yesterday happened. We are staying home, and we will worry about tomorrow when we get there. I don't have a headache today, I'm fine… perfectly… fine."

And we are finally at the point I knew would come. Ignoring her hands that she is trying to use as her wall of defense against her fear that I'm not letting her run from, I step straight into her personal space. Her hands land on my chest, but instead of them pushing me away, she's fisting my shirt like her life depends on it, and the tears that always follow the rage are starting. I'll take the yelling any day over tears. Seeing my love cry, and this time from fear, is the hardest thing to deal with.

Cassie's body collapses into me, and I wrap her as tight as I can while she's sobbing. She's overwhelmed, and there is nothing I can do to change any of this. My body is at war with itself, and I can't share that with anyone. The emotions that are engulfing me are the extremes of anger, down to the lowest depths of devastation I'm feeling at what my poor wife has had to tackle in her life. No one should have to keep standing up after being knocked down the number of times she has. I'd give anything to take her pain away, but knowing her, she wouldn't let me anyway.

The woman who is in my arms, breaking down because she just can't hold it in anymore, will come up swinging and ready to take on the world. That's what she does, and I'm counting on her to do it again this time. Otherwise, I can't fight this battle on my own; she has to be fighting it just as hard as I am. And all the while in the background, every other battle I'm fighting for her that she doesn't need the worry of, because I won't let them win.

"Noah…" Hearing my name in amongst her tears of pure desperation tells me how vulnerable she feels.

"I've got you, baby. I've got you," I whisper, lifting her feet off the ground and walking us backwards to the window seat so we can see the amazing view of the valley. Pulling her into my lap, she curls herself up in a tight ball and tries to make herself as small as possible. I've seen her do it before, it's how she copes. She's retreating into her inner place where she feels like she can hide.

But she can't hide from me. I see past any wall she tries to put up.

The tears are slowly subsiding, and her body is melting even further into mine and feeling less tense. Letting her take a moment to just breathe and collect her thoughts, we both sit staring out to the day that is just dawning. She slept solidly through the night in bed, and I must admit, I think I may have only slept for a few twenty-minute power naps. I was too frightened to let my body fall into a deep sleep in case she needed me. And since she has woken and we have moved to the window, I can feel the exhaustion in my body, but I need to keep pushing it back.

"What if they need me and I'm not here?" Her words are voicing my same fear.

"Then Asha and Bull will cuddle them tight and tell them Daddy is bringing Mommy home to them very soon." Gently placing my finger under her chin, I lift it so she is looking at me.

"But what if I don't come home?" The question in her eyes is one I can't answer but will tell her what I believe every single time she will ask this.

"You will. There's no other option I'll accept, Cassie." I say it with all the confidence I can show her, while on the inside I pray it's true.

We sat for a few more minutes, talking through everything Tate had told me and what the plan is to get her to Chicago and back. I had a message from Bull and Asha during the night that I showed her. They have promised to do everything we need, but most importantly, they both have professed they will lay down their lives to protect our children, something that gave us both inner peace. It just irritates me that they should have to. My family is my responsibility, not theirs.

The noise coming through the monitor alerts us that Eli is awake. Cassie jumps up off me to go to him. Normally I would go and bring him to her, but I can see the yearning in her to have him in her arms. Today is going to be a tough one for both of us. I'm not prepared to wait, and the sooner she has this MRI and we know what we're dealing with, then the quicker I can bring her home to our safe haven. Giving her space with him on her own, I head down the hallway to the bunker and check in on everything else. It helps to calm my brain that is racing. I have the home security cameras up on the big screen so I can keep an eye on her. Watching her talking to Eli while she feeds him, I wonder what she is telling him. The love Cassie shares is endless, and our kids benefit from it every day.

She looks settled, so it's time to call Ashton and get everything underway. I don't care what it costs, I want that plane in the air today and Cassie in Chicago by tonight.

"Everything okay?" Ashton's voice soothes my nerves.

"As much as it can be. Talk to me."

We continue to lock in details while my attention is split between him and watching my wife, now joined by Bessy who is sitting at Cassie's feet, talking away happily with a smile on her face. Which is in turn making her mother smile, which is what we all need at the moment.

To be positive and to find something to smile about, because it's the only thing we have to cling to.

"We're set to go. I'll let you know once they land and are on their way to you."

"Roger that. Later." Disconnecting the call with Ashton, I can see that Cassie is dressing Eli for the day. I push off my chair and head back to her to help. From what Tate said, her energy level will be low today after the seizure, not that he knows my wife. Her determination to do something is next-level. There is no way she will let her body slow her down in front of the kids. Not that Eli understands anything, Bessy's energy level makes up for the two of them and probably another child as well, if the truth be known.

Setting Eli in his rocker in front of the television, Bessy lies next him on her stomach. Elbows on the ground, chin cupped by her hands, and her legs up in the air, ankles crossed. Her favorite spot is next to her brother and chatting to him about what she's watching.

With breakfast out of the way, it's time to break the news to Cassie before Tate calls.

With my backside leaning against the counter farthest from the kids, I reach my hands out for her as she passes me, buzzing around the kitchen trying to distract herself.

Draping my arms over her shoulders, she is trapped and has to look at me.

"We leave at three pm today." It's all I need to say, and her face screws up, trying to hold in the tears. Worrying about what is happening in her brain must be scary enough, but what Cassie is going through, where she knows there are people out there being paid to kill her, I can't even imagine her anxiety level.

Words are too much for her. A slight nod and her forehead dropping to my chest tells me all I need to know.

"Love you," I say, kissing the top of her head. We both stand together, summoning the strength we find in each other.

Walking out that front door this afternoon will be one of the hardest things we will ever do.

But we will do it, and we will do it together. The same way we do everything.

It's the only way we know.

Chapter Nineteen

CASSIE

I *can do this, I can do this, I can do this.*

If I say it enough in my head, maybe I'll believe it.

Trying to explain to Bessy that Daddy and I are leaving for a few days was hard, but as soon as she heard Kurt and Asha were arriving to stay with her, she was screaming with excitement. What a way to deflate the ego, but it helps to see her talking so fast to Kurt, sitting on his lap. Asha is standing, rocking Eli to sleep. She asked if I wanted to do it before I left, but I knew it would be too hard to put him down into the crib. It was difficult handing him over to her, but it's better if I do it quickly. Like ripping off a band-aid. It's going to hurt either way, so I may as well get the pain over with quickly. Not that the ache that is already in my heart will stop until both of them are back in my arms again.

Feeling Ghost's hand on the small of my back makes my heart thump harder.

"Cassie." I don't know if he says anything else to me because just hearing my name, I know what it means. It's time to leave, and I can't show my total heartbreak as we do it.

Walking to Asha, the tears are welling, but I can't let them break free. I repeat it in my head again, over and over, that I can do this.

I lower my lips to Eli's cheek that is closest to me, softly touching his skin with my kiss, breathing in the smell that is my little baby. Pulling ever so slightly back, I whisper in his ear, "Mommy loves you, my little angel." With a last kiss on his forehead, I just nod at Asha, knowing that if she talks to me or tries to hug me then the tears will be falling, and I can't afford that.

"Bessy, come and give me a hug." I call her to me and crouch down as she runs over, while Ghost says his goodbye to his son and gives his last instructions to Kurt.

"Have fun, Mommy. Can you bring me back a present? Uncle Kurt said that moms and dads bring back the best presents when they go on a holiday." She has started calling them Uncle Kurt and Auntie Asha, which is adorable. They are the only ones she will ever have.

Giving her the tightest hug, I'm so grateful to Kurt for lightening the moment. All she is thinking about is what gift she is getting but has no idea what a holiday is or what she is missing out on by not leaving the house.

"We will have to remind Uncle Kurt that every time he visits us for a holiday then, won't we, Bessy," I hear Ghost say behind me, and he places his hand on my shoulder, letting me know it's time.

Kissing Bessy's cheek and forehead too, she beats me to it. "Love you, Mommy."

I can't stop the first tear from falling. "Love you, my princess, forever and ever." Standing and walking straight for the door, I can't stop. She can't know how hard this is.

Behind me, I hear her asking the question. "Is Mommy crying? Did I make her sad?" The confusion in her voice makes me break as I stop to hold onto the open front door.

"No, princess," Ghost tells her, "you make her the happiest person in the world. I think she just got some dirt in her eye."

I clamp my hand over my mouth to hold in the sobs, while hearing her reply gives me relief. "Like when the wind blew that bug in my eye, and it hurt, and I cried." So innocent but just what I needed.

"Exactly. Now be good, Bessy, for Uncle Kurt and Auntie Asha. We will call you later. Love you, Bessy." I can't wait any longer, walking out to the Range Rover that Kurt and Asha arrived in. Our cars are staying here for them to use because they're set up for the kids' seats in case they need to leave in an emergency. Ghost thinks of everything.

Climbing into the passenger seat, seatbelt on, I'm glad the windows are tinted dark so no one can see me. Not that they will bring the kids to the door, but just in case Bessy decides she wants to chase me down. Closing my eyes and dropping my head back on the headrest, I take deep slow breaths, trying to pull myself together again.

The door opens and his scent and the sound of his breathing are already encircling my senses. He gets the car started and moving, and I'm glad he understands I can't speak and just need to put some distance between us and the kids. The vibration of the car tires on the road is a calming constant noise to drown out the deafening silence in the car. I want to talk to Ghost, but every time I open my mouth, nothing comes out. Giving up, I peel my eyes open, and I watch out the window the scenery that I haven't seen in quite a while.

I feel Ghost's hand on my thigh, squeezing and making the connection we need between us. I rest my hand on top of his and entwine our fingers, turning and looking at him as he lifts it up to his lips. The kiss tells me everything he can't say, and the extra tight grip I have on his hand is my unspoken reply. It's enough for now.

I don't know how long we've been driving, but I can feel another headache coming on. I promised I would tell Ghost everything going forward. No point hiding anything now. I know he was hurt to hear all the symptoms I told Doctor McIntyre that I had been experiencing for quite a while. I was the one who made him promise no secrets, yet I'd been keeping some pretty big ones about my health. I know I should have told him, but I think part of it was that I didn't realize until it was too late that things were changing and not for the better.

"Ghost, where did you put the Tylenol? I need some." I don't want it getting bad enough that it triggers another seizure.

His forehead wrinkles with a worried frown. "Do you need me to stop?" The car is already slowing.

"No, I'm okay, I just need the painkillers. I don't want it to get worse."

It's like we don't know how to act around each other. Our words are stilted and so full of stress. I hate it, but I'm not sure how to fix it. We are both dealing with our feelings on our own, which is not like us. Feelings are better shared.

He points to the glove compartment, and I open it to find the packet, and there's an unopened water bottle in my door compartment. Swallowing the tablets, I pray they'll take the pain away.

"We aren't far from the airstrip where Ashton and Mason are waiting for us." I know they have worked with Ghost for years, but meeting new people is terrifying. I have become a hermit, even though it was never by choice. Ghost must have sensed my unease. "I need you to trust me." His voice is deeper now and full of emotion.

"With everything I am." And I mean every word of it.

"Then that's all I need to get you through this. If I tell you to do something, I don't want to be questioned. Do you understand? It could be the difference between life and death." His face is taut and his jaw clenched.

"Finally, we're going to talk about this." My hidden anxiety rises to the surface quickly. Not about my health but everything else around me.

"No. I'm going to talk, and you're going to listen. Very. Carefully." Oh, I haven't seen this Ghost in a long time, and at the worst possible time, there are parts of me that are tingling at the dominant man beside me. I shouldn't be thinking about how hot he is when he gets all protective, but I can't stop my libido.

"Growly Ghost is back, he's been MIA for a while," I say, trying not to laugh at the agitation my comment is giving him. I need to break this stale air between us. I can't deal with it. It's just not us.

"Cassie!" There is no joking.

"Right, got it! Yes, sir, I'm listening." I offer a mock salute, like he is my captain of this two-person army.

"I knew the day I met you that you would push my limits," he grumbles, rolling his eyes, but I can see he is relaxing a little—not much, but it's a smidgin.

"Pushing limits can give so much pleasure." Letting out a little giggle has him groaning, but finally, there is a small smirk on his face.

"For fuck's sake, Cassie, can you be serious?"

"Oh, fucking is serious, for sure, we can both agree on that. Seriously awesome, actually, and my favorite pastime." I reach my hand over his cock that is already semi hard.

"You know what will give me pleasure, Cassie?" he asks, and I shrug, wondering what he'll say, while I can feel him getting firmer under my hand, and that's making me more aroused than I should be right now.

"What?" I ask, fluttering my eyelashes at him.

"Right, that's it. There isn't any maybe now, it's definitely happening. When this is over, I'm going to spank you just like you're asking for, you little minx. Leaving my handprints on your perfect ass while you are begging me to fuck you so hard, to give you the release I've been denying you all night. If you're lucky, I might let you come, but the way you're pushing me, it's a big if."

I have his rock-hard cock in my hand, and I can feel how wet I am for him.

Lifting my hand up and placing it back in my own lap, the cocky Ghost is in the car now, and I love watching the power he has over me. "You win, I'll shut up."

"I usually do, beautiful, I usually do."

More relaxed now, he tries again, saying, "Now are you listening?" but he's looking at me, to get me to understand he means it this time.

"Yes." And I am because I can't do this on my own, but I also don't want to be the person who gets someone else hurt.

Feeling better after Ghost has given me all that he wants me to know, I can tell he has this under control. Not that I ever doubted him, but hearing his words and all the hidden parts in the plan, it just helps me to settle. If I'm brutally honest, the danger that surrounds us, and has since the day I ran from Jason, frightens me more than my health. Because what is going on in my head won't mean a fucking thing if I'm dead from a bullet through the skull. In the nightmares I've always had, that's how it happens. The gun being held to the side of my head and them making Ghost watch as they press the trigger. I can feel my stomach rolling now and the sensation to be sick hanging low. I try to push the feeling back down; I need to think of something else.

"Can you tell me a story?" I ask, taking in the quizzical look on Ghost's face. "I need a distraction. Something you have never told me before, make it up, I don't care. I just need to get out of my head." Leaning back on the headrest of my seat, I close my eyes so I can focus on his voice. The deep timbre he has settles in my heart and slows the beats back down.

"Oh, I have plenty of stupid Bull stories, or even some Badger ones. Hmmm, okay, let me think. Yep, this one will work. When you finally meet Badger, you will take great joy in letting him know that you know this about him."

Pushing the world away and only tuning into my husband's words is soothing my soul.

It reminds me of the times when my dad's voice would be the thing that I would concentrate on to help me sleep. I missed him when he was away working, I'm sure my mom did too. But he always knew what to say and do when I was scared, to make me feel safe. Sometimes it was a story he would read, but then he started to make up stories or would tell me about him traveling with work. I knew the made-up ones because they were always about faraway places, spots we had never been, since none of us had ever left America. But he would talk about the beauty of the Eiffel Tower, sitting at a café drinking coffee and watching the lovers walk the streets. Or being in Germany in winter and the beauty of the snow in the countryside. It was almost like he had a magic carpet, and he was taking me on a ride to a place that took away any fear.

I wonder if Dad sent Ghost to me, to keep me safe now that he can't. I send a prayer up to him for that, because I still miss them every day, but each day is so much easier with Ghost and my kids in it.

Ghost's voice wraps around me like the hug I need now. "We were on this job, the three of us together. Bull had recently joined our crew. Badger, being the grumpy old man of the group, thought he would put Bull to the test. Told him that if he could beat me at poker that he'd get to take over the job as lead agent protecting the guy we had under our guard."

Knowing that Ghost is a card shark, I'm thinking this didn't end well for Bull.

"Being the guy he is, Bull stood up to Badger, trying to impress him, and upped the bet a little higher. That if I lost, Badger would also have to do the end-of-day reports to head office as well. Nobody likes paperwork, so Badger jumped on that straight away." Feeling his hand on mine gives me comfort while he continues.

"Our clients were all in bed asleep, so the cards were placed on the table. This was the first time Badger had worked with Bull, so he didn't know how close we had become, something he learned quickly that night. The cards were dealt, and I won a few games just to be consistent and to keep Badger thinking he was going to win the bet for sure. And then I started to lose a couple, and Bull carried on, all cocky. The tension started to pick up, and I thought Badger was going to kill me when I lost the final round and Bull was declared the winner. But of course, I didn't really lose, but I just let Bull win. He tries to tell me that he beat me fair and square, but he knows the truth. I can count cards, and he never even had a chance. But Badger knew that too, and that's why he took on the bet.

"They have been arguing for years about who really won that

day, and the answer is me. Because I didn't have to put up with the asshole client or do any paperwork. So, for me it was a win/win situation. And watching the young apprentice school the master at his own bag of tricks was just brilliant."

Having a little chuckle to himself is an added benefit of the story. We both needed to break the tension and focus on something different. Even if it was only for a short while. I don't want to, but I can feel sleep trying to claim me, and it's probably what I need.

Ghost notices the change in my breathing and my body sinking into my seat that little bit more, and he just squeezes my thigh and in a low voice reassures me, "Sleep, Cassie, you're safe with me." And I know he means it. I just don't know if he can guarantee it.

My body is too spent to think anymore, and the noise around me is disappearing.

Sleep is claiming me.

"Cassie, you need to wake up. Take your time, beautiful." I can hear the words in the distance, and trying to pull myself out of the groggy sleep is not much fun. "Once we're on the plane you can sleep again." That sounds like a perfect option, but it's coming back to me where we are.

"No. I want to meet Ashton and Mason." I blink my eyes open as I fight the fatigue.

Finally opening them fully, I see Ghost's face so close to me from the side. He has already gotten out of the car and come around to my door, and I didn't hear a thing. That concerns me because I should be on alert.

"There she is. My bright eyes," he says, his thumb running down my cheek. I'll never get over how lucky I am to wake up to this man in front of me. Besides how ridiculously hot he is, it's more the love he has inside him that is protected and saved all for me. That love is explosive in the way he looks at me.

His lips, soft and tender, take mine. What a way to wake up.

"I could have carried you asleep to the plane, but we both

know you hate missing out on anything, that's why I woke you." He thinks he's funny, and I smile at him, giving him the acknowledgment he's after. We need the humor, and one thing you can guarantee is that Ghost always knows what I need and when I need it.

"Says the man who spies on people for a living. Or because he thinks he needs to. Pretty sure you aren't missing out on anything in people's lives either."

"Touché, beautiful, touché. Now, time to walk to the plane. You okay with your balance after the headache?"

To be honest, I have no idea. Taking it slowly, I turn and slide my feet to the ground. My confidence has been shaken since the seizure. I was trying to keep up a strong front with the kids, but now that it's just the two of us, I've dropped my guard. Not sure I have enough energy to keep it up. Ghost doesn't want that anyway. He wants everything on the table, and I'm trying.

His arm slips around my waist as we walk toward the plane. I see the two men standing at the bottom of the stairs. A face I wasn't expecting to see but one I know so well.

"Badger, I didn't know you were coming." I reach out to hug the man who has played such a pivotal role in how my life has turned out.

"Neither did I," I hear Ghost's growl behind me.

"You think I was missing out on a chance to get my arms around this little spitfire?" I can feel Badger's deep laugh rumbling in his chest as he squeezes me tightly.

"If you want to keep those arms, I suggest you remove them from MY wife!" Possessiveness is crystal clear in Ghost's voice.

"Oh, a little touchy, isn't he." Badger kisses me on the cheek as he releases me. "How you feeling, darlin'?"

Ghost pulls me back to his side instantly the moment Badger lets me go. The two of them might be close, but we all know what Ghost is like. Hence why they like to push his buttons.

"I'm fine," I say out of habit, even though I'm far from it.

"I doubt it, but yep, let's go with that." His eyes are full of compassion.

"Am I allowed to hug her? Just checking because I like my hands too!" The man I'm guessing is Ashton steps toward me.

"Once, and then never again. Got it?" Wow, my husband really is laying the ground rules today, isn't he. Secretly I'm loving the caveman vibe. I guess he hasn't ever had to share me with anyone, so this is all new to him. "Cassie, meet Ashton." His voice is almost a growl.

Ignoring my husband, I step out of his arms and into Ashton's. This man is responsible for keeping my man sane while we are trapped up in the mountains, and he's also the one who is in charge of getting me to Chicago and back without a hiccup.

"Hi, Ashton, nice to put a face to the name." Ghost always thought it was better they didn't see me, and I didn't see them either. He thought keeping his two worlds apart was safer. Now his two worlds are colliding, and I can see why it's rocking him to the core.

"Likewise, Cassie." What is it about these men? They're built big and tough, but when they hug me, it's like they're big teddy bears.

"Thank you," I whisper, and he gives me an extra little squeeze, acknowledging what I'm saying. I can't say it out loud, but I want him to know how much I appreciate him having Ghost's back, at a time where he is really struggling. My man who never relies on anyone is having to let his walls down too, and it's hard for him. I can see the strain in his face. Control is his life, and not to have complete control of this is almost killing him.

"Enough." His stern voice from behind me makes me giggle as I pull away.

"Down, boy. See this ring?" I say, pointing to my wedding band on my left hand. "Says I belong with you." The guys are now roaring with laughter, and Ghost gives me that look I normally get right before he chases me through the house to trap me and kiss the hell out of me and stake his claim on me.

"Damn right it does. Remember that, gentlemen." His eyes are telling them more than his words are.

"Okay, well, as much as this is cute and all, we need to get moving. Ghost, take Cassie in, and we'll get your bags while you meet Mason and settle into your seats." Badger slaps him on the back, and the guys are moving to the back of the car to unload our bags. Ghost's hand is now on my lower back as he guides me carefully up the stairs.

"I might be weak, but I'm not made of glass." I'm already feeling frustrated at not being trusted to move on my own.

"Don't care," is all I get in reply, and I just keep moving. Not worth the argument.

Stepping into the cabin, the captain comes out of the cockpit toward us. Damn, to be a part of this group, is it a prerequisite you have to have abs that are ripped like a god, arm muscles that bulge in any shirt, and to be strikingly tall, so they give that instant look of power the moment they stand in front of you? I will never voice any of this to Ghost, but man, wait until I can call Asha. We will be debriefing about these men that she didn't warn me not to drool too much over. It doesn't matter that they are nothing compared to my husband, but it's still okay to appreciate fine specimens. I'm not dead yet.

My brain stops at that sentence. Things that you would say as a joke are no longer funny.

But fuck that! I'm not dead, and I don't intend on being, either.

Holding out my hand for him to shake, before Ghost loses his shit about another man hugging me, I quickly introduce myself to the generous man in front of me who is using his and his wife's private jet to rescue me. I know Ghost is paying him, but Mason told Ashton he would do it for nothing, and that meant a lot to both Ghost and me. I mean, if you own a private jet, it's not like you need the money anyway, so they are doing it because they care.

I didn't understand until now that in a way I'm like Ghost. I'm used to not relying on anyone else. It's just been us for so long, that having all these people around us who are willing to help people they have never met is hard to process.

Leaving Ghost to chat with Mason, I wander into the plane, my brain on overload at the beauty in front of me. I've never flown on a plane like this before. It's been cattle class all the way for me on the few flights I have taken in my life. Even when I was with Jason, he would fly all the time but very rarely took me with him, usually it was Camilla. At the time I didn't think anything of it. I was working and she was his assistant, of course he needed her there. Just turned out she was assisting him in things that were out of her job description. Sadly, that didn't work out the way she expected.

Not wanting to think about them, I move to one of the seats and slowly run my hands over the cream leather that feels so soft. I choose a seat near the window so I can see the ground beneath me as we take off and land. Doctor McIntyre had explained to me that they will be flying the plane at the lowest altitude they can, because we don't know what the change in pressure will do to my head. It's a risk that we all weighed up, and unfortunately, we didn't have much choice. We don't have the time frame for the long drive, and it's also exposing me more to outside danger. The quicker we get in and out of Chicago, the less the risk of being spotted by anyone that will recognize me, or Ghost for that matter. We will wear a disguise at the airport, but in the hospital it's impossible, and I just have to be me. We know there was someone on the inside in WITSEC, so they know what Ghost looks like, and it's more than likely they know I'm with him. He tried his best to cover my disappearance, but I doubt many people believed it.

Watching Ghost from a distance, I have forgotten what a force he can be when he's working. He radiates power without even trying. Sadly, this is what this trip is, work, and hard work at that. It's like a job, where his brain is working overtime and trying to plan for every possible scenario before it even becomes a thing. My health is just making what was already a complex trip that much more of a concern for him. My head feels at times like it is going to explode with pain, but I'm sure his is the same, with so much information in there and trying to keep track of it.

As the other guys come onto the plane, they're all stowing away the luggage, and I watch Ghost take his bag that has all his technology in it, like he's guarding a million dollars. To him that is what keeps me alive. It's his ability to see what is happening around us that others don't even know. Most people couldn't ever comprehend the darkness in this world. That bag is our lifeline in more ways than one. It's also how we keep in communication with our kids, Asha, and Kurt. To me, that is the most important thing in this world.

Everyone gets settled in seats, Ghost next to me with his hand wrapped tightly around mine. I know I have to do this, but feeling the plane start to taxi, ready to take off, my stomach is churning, heart racing, and my head is still pounding like it has been for the last few hours.

We have no idea what is going to happen as we gain altitude, and I know Doctor McIntyre is on standby if Ghost needs him.

The fear in everyone is being projected at me, and it's not helping my anxiety.

All sets of eyes are on me and watching for any change in me as we start climbing into the air.

I turn to look out the window; I can't handle the worry from them.

The ground dropping away at a rapid rate, I feel my heart free falling too.

Will I ever get to come back here and see my kids again?

The tears slowly fall as reality sets in. I have to tell him just in case.

Turning, I look Noah straight in the eyes. "I will love you and them forever. Never forget that." More tears fall and his hand is grasping me so hard.

"I know, and you can tell me that for rest of our lives until we are old and gray. Understood?"

My tears are almost breaking him too, but he has to stay strong —for me, for him, and everyone else who relies on him.

My poor Noah, when will he ever get to feel peace in his life? I pray that one day it will happen.

Chapter Twenty

GHOST

Watch her eyes, no rolling back in her head.
Watch her limbs, no twitching or shaking.
Watch her face for pain.
Listen to her speech for any slurring.
Is her grip on my hand still strong?

I have everything that Tate told me to watch out for memorized. Any change in her that could mean the pressure is too great. I should have taken Tate up on his offer to be on the plane with us. He said he would cancel surgeries he had booked in and be here. As much as I wanted that, I couldn't in good conscience take him away from other people who need him too. I want to say that Cassie is the most important person in the world, and she is to me. But to other people, she isn't.

The others all know what to look for, and I can see they are watching her as intently as I am. Normally, I would be pissed at men for staring at my wife, but today, I need all eyes on her until we land this plane.

I know she's scared, her words just hit me like a brick. She is worrying something can happen any minute, and she's right. I was so torn. This is a risky as hell, but we couldn't wait. Especially once I heard her tell Tate all the symptoms that she has been experiencing for a while. Not sharing that with me hurt, a lot. But I can't take that up with her at the moment. As little stress as possible is what Tate said. Yeah, right, like that's even fucking possible.

Mason's voice comes into the cabin, telling us he has leveled out and we can move around, and it's a welcome relief. So far, so good with Cassie. She is quiet and lying back on the seat slightly, just looking out the window. I think she will be trying to process everything. Her fear of this flight, what will happen when we land, and of course, her heart has already been ripped clean out of her chest today, leaving the kids behind.

"You two want a drink?" Badger is already up and moving.

"No, thanks," Cassie replies and then turns back to the window. I want to pick her up and have her in my lap, but I know that's not what she needs. As much as it kills me to sit here and watch her struggle, she needs space. I'm man enough to know that crowding her now because I need her is not the right thing to do. This has to be about Cassie. What I want and need comes second until we are back home. Then I can be selfish and tell her how much I'm panicking that I might lose her. And not in the way I have had sleepless nights about for the last seven years. I can protect her from what I can see, but I can't protect her from the hidden things that we don't know about.

That is what infuriates me!

Hopelessness.

Finally, I convinced her to go to sleep again, and hopefully, that will keep her body as relaxed as it can be. Not moving far from her, I have the laptop open and working while her eyes are closed. I message with Bull and hear that the kids are perfectly fine. I knew they would be, but it doesn't stop me from worrying that I can't be there to watch over them.

I quickly search what Jason has been up to today and what his plans are for the next few days. We need to keep track of him at all times. Not that he will ever be the person to try to do anything to

Cassie, but he would recognize her the moment he laid eyes on her, and that is what we need to avoid at all costs. The background checks I ran on the staff at the hospital of who will be anywhere near her are coming back clean which is a relief. I know I shouldn't be checking into these people without their permission, but I'm not taking risks. They won't even know it's been done. Again, that doesn't make it right, but I will do whatever it takes to keep Cassie safe, and I don't make excuses for that—ever!

As the sun is setting, the view out the plane window is spectacular. I take a moment just to look and breathe. I don't think I've done that in the last twenty-four hours. Cassie is reclined on the seat next to me, still sleeping, and I can tell how much everything is taking out of her. Her face on its side towards me, the lines on her forehead are still there. She might be resting but her mind isn't. I wish I could take her anguish away, but I can't.

The darker it gets outside, I know the closer to Chicago we are getting. I want to get this over with and get her home, so let's get this plane landed, Cassie into the car, and over to the apartment we have. We aren't staying in a hotel and risking being caught on any security cameras. It will be bad enough at the hospital, but we can't avoid that. I can go in after and erase anything I can find, but once we hit the hospital, then my eyes need to be on Cassie and everyone around her, not on my computer screen.

Ashton has been in talking to Mason, and walking back toward me, he gives me the signal we are starting the descent. I don't want to wake Cassie, so I lean across her and click her seatbelt into place as quietly as I can. I should have known better. Just the movement near her is enough, and she's moving, trying to sit up quickly.

"Cassie, don't move, stay there." The tone in my voice makes it more of an order than asking her. Thank God it works and she stops, looking straight at me, her eyes all startled.

I try to soften my voice. "It's okay, beautiful, we are just getting ready to land. You can stay there, perhaps just start to wake up, okay?" I say, running my hand over her head and smoothing her hair back from her face.

"How long was I out of it?"

"Most of the flight, which is what you needed." My hand resting on her cheek, I lean over to kiss her softly.

"Why can't I stay awake? It scares me." And I can see that in her eyes.

"Don't worry, Tate said it's normal. It's just your body looking after you."

"This is bad, isn't it, Ghost?" Her whisper makes my body shiver.

"I don't know, sweetheart, but we are about to find out." My heart is thumping in my chest and the hair on the back of my neck is standing up. That's never a good sign because my body has always been my best warning system when something is about to go south on a job. I don't like the feeling when it's about Cassie, but I will never tell her that.

"We've got this. Remember, we got this far. We won't let anything stand in our way now."

She just nods at me, and as she raises the seat so she is sitting again, her head drops onto my shoulder, and we just hold each other in silence. We seem to be doing that a lot lately. It's because neither of us know what to say, and we don't want to make promises we may not be able to keep.

As the plane comes to a stop on the private airstrip, I can see the car waiting for us that Ashton has organized. I know I carried on like an asshole initially, but I'm so grateful for the network of friends I have built around us over the years. We couldn't be doing this without them.

Thanking Mason, Ashton heads out after Badger just to make sure all is clear for us to leave the plane's cabin. It's a weird sensation to have others doing that for me. I'm usually the one giving the all-clear signal. Watching from inside the door, Badger gives me the thumbs-up, it's time to get this show underway.

"Ready?" I ask, turning back to Cassie standing behind me.

"No, but let's do it anyway."

"That's my girl." Always brave in the face of danger.

Standing in the living room of the apartment next door to Ashton's, it's nothing like I expected it to be. For all the years I've known him, he seems like a hard-ass. A straight-down-the-line, rough-around-the-edges kind of guy. Yet here we are standing in a place that looks like it's had the touches of a woman in it and has a soft homey feel to it.

"Remind me again why you have a spare apartment next door to yours that you own? A little odd, buddy." I slap him on the back as I walk to look out the windows at the view.

"Says the man who is now thankful for the safe place to stay. Let's just say I seem to keep attracting friends who need somewhere for a short stay, for one reason or another. And don't worry, this place is set up with all the top security. I made sure of that the first time I had someone staying here." I never doubted that. We are both cut from the same cloth in the way we think about security.

I give him a nod of acknowledgment.

"This place is adorable, Ashton." Cassie runs her hand along the back of the couch as she looks around at the decor. "I've forgotten what the sound of traffic is like, though. It's been so long, and I never thought I would say this, but I kind of miss it. The hustle and bustle of the people, the noise, the smells of big cities. I would never swap it for our home, but it would be nice to visit every so often." The longing in her eyes for a life we have both given up worries me. Will she ever get to a point of resentment for our life, or me for that matter?

"Well, you are welcome here whenever you want. One day we will make that happen," Ashton says, moving to the kitchen to open the fridge and retrieve some bottles of water. Passing them to us both, I wish it was a beer, but there is no way I will be drinking until we are all home safe and in an environment I can control.

"I'm starting to give up on that life." Her dejected expression hurts me deep down in a place I didn't know was there. It's a place of panic that Cassie is changing, and by bringing her out of our home, it is making her longing worse.

"Don't," I can't help growling at her.

"Don't what?" she snaps back at me, the tension building between us. Both of us are in our own dark places.

"Don't give up!" There's anger behind my words. I don't know if it's at her for giving up on us or anger at myself, because in all these years, I haven't been able to fix this for her.

"Easy for you to say." There is heated frustration in what she's saying, and I can feel the air in here getting more tense, and this is about to escalate. It's what we do, how we cope when shit gets real, and it can't be any more real than it is today.

"On that note, I'll be next door. You know how to get a hold of me. Badger is around." And sensing the tension in the air, Ashton doesn't wait for an answer from either of us and is out of the apartment with a quiet closing of the door.

"Easy for you to do too! The minute you give up, we are fucked." Rubbing my hands over the top my head, I'm already pacing.

"Why is this all on me? I can't be the only one with strength." Cassie can't sit either; her hands are clenched into fists, and I can see her white knuckles from here.

"Cassie, this is all about you, can't you see that? But the focus is nothing to do with you being the strong one. I just need you to let me be that for you, but I can't do it if you aren't fighting with me. Everything I do, every breath I take, is about you! Fuck, Cassie, I live my life to make sure you still have yours. Let me make this about you!"

"I don't want to spend this night that could… I just don't want it to be fighting with you."

I'm done. Storming across the room to where she is standing, the fight slips from her, and her shoulders are dropping.

"No, you don't get to say that. I know what words were about to slip out of your mouth, and don't you ever voice that. See? You are giving up before we even start the fight. Not happening, baby."

I'm wound so tight nothing is going to be soft and gentle. My lips land on hers as I pull her to me. My hand on the back of her neck guides her mouth exactly where I want it. My other hand secures her on the ass, her body slamming into me with all the force I need.

"Fight, oh yeah, baby, we are going to fight all night long. You will be screaming at me to let you come. To fill you deep until you can't take it anymore. Fight me to give you what you need. Because you might want to give up, but I'm never going to stop fighting you, Cassie. That's right, fighting you is what I do, it's what you need me to do. So, if you are screaming at me, releasing tension, I'm pushing back at you. It's what you want from me. What makes us work."

Her breathing is rapid, and the sheen of sweat on her face and the fire in her eyes is all I need to know we are almost there.

"You want me to control you until you finally submit to me and let it all go. The stress, the worry, and the pain you carry every day. Let go, baby, I can take you to our place, but fuck, I beg you never to stop fighting me."

She's so close that pushing her is all it takes.

"Say it! Say my name!" Demanding it from her in the way she loves is the final push she's craving.

All her weight is on me, and her body is mine as the word falls from her lips that she keeps just for me. It's her way of telling me that she's mine and needs me to prove it.

"Noah..." The way she says it is all the longing from her body for what she is begging for.

"I've got you."

I slide my hand from her ass, around, and grabbing at her sex, put pressure on it to show her what she's in for. We are both supercharged full of emotion, and there is no way I can go slow, and that's not what she wants from me anyway.

"Ooohhhh..." My hand is now rubbing up and down, and I want all those moans just for me. The pleasure, the pain, and the downright begging for the ecstasy that she demands.

My hunger is insatiable.

Our lips seek each other out, but this time, I'm not stopping. The moment we connect, my tongue pushes into her mouth and takes what I want from her. I explore every part of her and give her the preview of what I'm about to do to her with my cock that is screaming to be inside her. The pulsing I can feel is bordering on pain, which only urges me on in our kissing. I want every man who sees her tomorrow to see the rash on her lips and know it's from me, like a mark of being totally owned in a kiss.

I've never felt as territorial as I do tonight. Moving my lips to her neck, I nip my way down on her skin. Every time my teeth make a mark, she cries out a little louder in pleasure. We are both lost in each other, and for the first time since Bessy was born, we don't have to keep those cries silent. The noise of sex has never sounded more perfect.

"Don't move!" She's already in the head space she was craving, and my order just brings the smile I love.

"Mhmm," is all I get, while I turn off the lights and make sure the door is locked.

The curtains are still open, and like any big city, there is always light that streams in the windows. I already know that the windows have the reflective coating on the outside so no one can see in, but Cassie doesn't know that, and I'm not telling her because it will make what I'm about to do all the more sensual and help her find that release she is longing for. I know I should be gentle with her body, but her mind needs this from me, it's the only way she will keep her demons at bay for the night.

"You miss people, you want to feel seen in this world? Then it's time to feel part of that noise and chaos again." My hands are up under her comfortable shirt she'd been wearing to travel in, making my access now a breeze, but even if it wasn't, I would have shredded whatever she was wearing. Her top is up and over her head before she even has time to gasp, and her nipples are poking out through the gaps in the lace bra. When I met her, Cassie didn't feel beautiful and had lost all the freedom to feel sexy. I've made sure over the years to give her everything she needed to feel as sexy as she wants, and in turn, I get the benefit of the vision in front of me right now.

It's too much temptation, and I bite down on a nipple and pull it between my teeth, at the same time pinching her other nipple between my fingers. Her body arches into me, and the scream of pain and pleasure echoes in the darkness. I want to torment her more, but I need her naked, and if I don't get out of these pants, then the pressure I'm feeling on my cock is going to have me coming without control, and that can't happen. She needs to orgasm multiple times before I can let go of my pleasure.

"Noah... fuck, more... *more.*"

Time to let loose with her.

"Naked now!" My growl has her hands moving, and the rest of her clothes drops around us, followed by mine. The whispering of the air on my skin is relief and torture at the same time.

I drag over a single dining room chair with us, taking her other hand. The chair is wooden, with a back made of vertical rungs that you can see through.

Placing it in front of the floor-to-ceiling window, we can see the outside world of people moving about in the city at night.

Lowering Cassie onto the chair, I spread her legs apart and see her glistening sex in the moonlight.

"Fuck..." The vision before me is heaven. My angel waiting for me. Picking up my shirt off the ground, I push her hands behind the chair and tie them together. She needs this, the restraint to make her let it all go, but the shirt is soft enough that it won't mark her or hurt her. I could never do that.

"Don't move," I whisper in her ear as I return to the front of her. "Time for you to feel seen." She knows that with the lights off they can't see us, but she can see them. Being so far inside her own head, that's all she needs.

"Please..." The begging is starting, and it makes me leak that little bit more.

"Oh, baby, you need more words than that." I hold my cock in my fist, tight as I can to hold off coming just at the sight of my wife in front of me.

"Please, Noah... touch."

"Oh, I'm going to do more than touch you. I'm about to own you." Her eyes are dilated and wide with apprehension.

"Yessssss," she moans, trying to close her legs to get some relief.

"Don't." Her feet stop, and the look of submission has my heart racing. She is out of her head now and where she wants to be. Her place of pure pleasure, no thoughts about anything except what I'm doing.

I step between her legs, my cock like a solid rod of steel, the head purple and bulging, waiting for release. Dragging my hand across her lips, it makes her mouth open nice and wide without me even asking.

"Take it!" Not giving her more than a split second to decide, I push past her lips, waiting for her to take the rest.

Hissing, she sucks me to the back of her throat with the ferocity of a woman who is desperate. Like she has never tasted dick before. My wife loves this, and I could take this all night long. Burying her nose in my hair around my cock every time she takes it all, she is branding herself with my smell. I tangle my hands in her hair that is falling down around her face and make sure she can feel me in control. Pulling it as she tries to reach forward creates the moan around my cock that has me aching into my balls.

"Enough," I grit out, knowing if I don't stop now, I'll be coming any minute, right down her tight little throat, and that's not what I've got planned for her.

"Noooo…" Saliva dribbles out her mouth from where my cock has just slipped out.

"I make the decisions. Your pleasure is mine." Dropping to my knees in front of her, it's time for her to reach that first peak.

Leaning into her sex and just taking a deep breath, I can smell everything I crave. The sight of her splayed open for me is like heaven. Pushing her knees apart as wide as I can, I pull her toward me, her ass sliding on the chair until she is just sitting on the edge of it. Her body arches back, breasts in the air, so plump and her dark nipples longing for my mouth. But they will have to wait.

"Oh, if you could see how beautiful you look right now." *All mine* is all I can think.

"I can." The little whisper slips out, and I realize she can see her reflection in the window, making this perfect.

She has been waiting long enough. Not wasting another minute,

I lick up her crease and her sweet taste brings my senses close to overloading. But it's not enough. I'm not holding back on her. She needs to be ravaged. I push my tongue hard on her nub that is so engorged and aroused. My hands running up the inside of her legs quickly, I keep the pressure on her to stay wide for me. Her body is fighting as her moans and screams are intensifying. The moment I push two fingers inside her and suck her clit hard into my mouth and clench my teeth down on it, her whole body is quivering, and her orgasm explodes in my mouth.

The sound of my name is being screamed all around me, a sound I'll never get sick of hearing.

I'm not letting up. With my fingers working over her G-spot, I lift my head slightly, and all I can see is her eyes closed, her head thrown back, and trying not to completely pass out as the next orgasm is building with such intensity.

"You can handle it. Let go and let the power of your body own you, like I own you." I shouldn't be pushing her this hard tonight, but we both need this.

"Can't… too much… Noah, no, can't…" The mumbling in her state of bliss has me dropping my head, ready to feast on her again.

"You don't get to choose. I do, and you will come again for me now." My tongue and fingers work together as the power in her legs is pushing so hard against me, I let her give into it as she orgasms again with such force that her ass is lifting off the seat. She wraps her legs around my head, her sex pulsating into my face, and I can't stop taking everything she'll give me.

"Fuccccccckkkkkkkkkk." Her scream is music to my ears. I stand straight up, with her orgasm still on my face. Her limp body is slumped on the chair, but we aren't done. I get to say when she has had enough, and she knows that. Untying her arms and moving them to the front of her, I then retie them as quickly as I can. Picking her up, I spin her in my arms so her back is to me.

Laying her carefully over the back of the couch, her wet and plump pussy is perfectly bared for me. The height is like it was made to fuck on. Her tied arms stretch out above her head and her face is turned to one side as her cheek is lying on one of the cushions.

"You are mine. And God damn it, like I already told you, you will fucking fight me every single day until we are old and gray." Not waiting, I pound my cock into her and sink as deep as I can. At this angle, she sucks every inch of me until my balls are slapping onto her. Wanting her to understand, I keep pounding into her over and over again. I slap her ass and leave my perfect red handprints on her cheeks, reminding her she is mine until death do us part. And she needs to fight the death part with all she has.

The words and my hand start pushing her over the edge she didn't think she could ever reach.

"Please… need… yes… oh, can't stop… Agggggghhhhhh!" The roar of her coming has my balls pulling up into me, and I explode inside of her with everything that I've been holding from her—my fear of losing the only love that I have ever known. My body jerks, and I can't hold back anymore. The tears are coming too, and the sob I let out is joined by Cassie who is sobbing below me.

Pulling out, I don't even care about cleaning her up. The shirt on her hands is off, and I have her up and in my arms as I cradle her as tightly as I can, walking back around to the couch. Settling with her in my lap, she buries her head in my neck, and she curls up in a tight ball so I can wrap myself around her. Both our sobs fill the empty room and give us the release that our bodies and minds need. No matter how big the orgasms were, they can't fix this. We need to let it out because that is the only way we can face tomorrow.

Letting our bodies recover, we sit together, hanging on tightly. We both needed that, but as she lifts her head to look me in the eyes, I know what else she needs from me tonight.

"No one could actually see in, could they?" Her quiet whisper makes me smile. She trusts me completely.

"I would never share you with anyone, not like that. And I will never put you in danger of being seen unnecessarily. It will always just be us." She lets out a contented sigh, and the love written all over her face is comforting, but she wants more from me.

"Noah, I need you to love me." I feel the completeness at her words of how our life is. We fight for what we can, but in the end, we will always come back to the indescribably deep love we feel for each other.

"All night long and forever and ever, Cassie."

Standing and walking into the bedroom, I get her settled on the bed where my queen should be worshiped, and that's what I intend to do.

The night slips away from us, and in the early hours of the morning, I'm stroking her head as she lies on my chest sleeping and listening to my heart.

She tells me it makes her feel safe.

"I'm your safe place, but you are my home," I whisper as I try to close my eyes to sleep.

Tomorrow I will need every bit of strength I have.

Enough for both of us.

Chapter Twenty-One

CASSIE

W alking into the hospital, my skin is crawling with the nerves of being around so many people. Ghost's body is so stiff, and he isn't talking. I know it's taking all his concentration and restraint to do this. Ashton is walking in front of us, taking us to Doctor McIntyre's office. I'm sure Badger is also around in the shadows somewhere, I just haven't seen him. The guys were talking this morning, but I'm at the point I can't listen to them. I just need to think about one thing. My headache this morning is bad, and I'm scared. That's all I can worry about.

Video-chatting with the kids this morning took all the energy I had to look happy and calm. They're fine, and Bessy was talking a hundred miles an hour telling me all the things she has been doing. I'm sure Asha and Kurt will need to sleep for a week to get over this visit. The moment the call finished, I burst into tears, and Ghost held me, rocking me until I could pull it together again. I'm glad they're okay, but it's harder to see them than I thought it would be. I thought it would calm me, but instead, it just upset me. I don't know what today will bring, but I'm not sure I will have the energy to go through a call like that again tonight.

Stepping into the elevator, an enclosed space with a few strangers, has my breathing starting to race. Ghost places his hand on my back, rubbing it up and down; he can see what's happening. Leaning down to me, his quiet whisper of three words is enough to make me concentrate. "I've got you." He takes my hand closest to him and lets me squeeze it at has hard as I need to in order to get through this. The ding alerting us that we're arriving on our floor, and the door opening, couldn't have happened soon enough. I can breathe again, although I still feel a little off balance. What is wrong with me? I've never had a problem with small spaces before now. I used to ride the elevator to my office on the twenty-third floor every day, and the only thing that used to bother me was the bad body odor or the smell of someone's food they had eaten for lunch that had way too much garlic or spices in it.

I can't tell if it's from having been out of the normal world for so long, or if my head is making me do strange things. Either way, I don't like it.

Ashton stops in front of a door, and my heart's thumping in my chest. This is his office, the man that is going to tell me what is happening in my body. Ghost's words from last night echo in my head now.

I have to fight and fight hard.

No matter what today brings, I can't give up.

The door opens, and I feel like I'm a robot just going through the motions, stepping into a room with Doctor McIntyre that I met online. Damn it, another one of these hot men. What even is this place?

"Cassie, it's good to see you, take a seat." His voice snaps me out of my own little world.

"Thank you, Doctor McIntyre." Ghost shakes his hand too and gives him that chin lift that means what he can't voice. That he is trusting him with something so precious that he better not get this wrong.

"Oh, Cassie, please just call me Tate, like your husband does.

I'm here as a friend as well as your doctor." I nod at him, acknowledging what he's saying, but speaking feels hard.

My whole body is tingling, and I don't know why. Their voices are getting further away as I feel my body being moved, and I hear the words *"Get her on the floor"* being yelled.

Then it goes black again.

Oh, my head hurts, but my body feels too heavy to move.

Where am I?

Why can't I open my eyes? The buzz in my head is making it hurt worse.

Sleep, I just need to keep sleeping.

"Cassie, we need you to wake up."

I don't want to.

"You're okay, you're in the hospital. It's time to open your eyes." That voice isn't my Noah. Who is it?

Where is my Noah?

Then I feel him, his hand touching mine, the feeling back in my fingers. I'd know that touch anywhere, even if I can't see him. It's my Noah. I need to go to him.

"Open up and show me your bright eyes." His words make me push as hard as I can.

A slow blink, and I can see his face. It's blurry, but it's him.

"Hi there, Cassie." The source of the voice to the other side of me is now coming over top of me with a light. Ugh, I want to close my eyes again. "No, keep them open for me, Cassie, I need to check on you."

"Baby, listen to Tate. Stay awake for us." Ghost is squeezing my hand, tight then soft. I try to squeeze it back. "Yes, that's it, keep moving your hand."

Tate… the name is coming back to me. He's the doctor. I'm not at home, I'm here in Chicago.

Oh no, why am I on a bed now?

"What happened?" My words are a little mumbled, but they understand me.

"You had another seizure in my office, Cassie. Do you remember anything from today?" He has a nice voice. I just wish I could answer him. My mind is so confused.

"Sore head, pancakes," is all I can get out.

"Yes, good girl, we had pancakes for breakfast. Ashton tried to say his are the best." Always a competition with men. I don't remember much from before, but I feel like Ghost's words are making me smile. It's a weird feeling of not being completely connected to my body.

"Okay, I'd expect the headache is what brought on the seizure, and her responses aren't perfect, but they are improving. She will want to sleep this off again. I think the best thing is to get her in the MRI machine now and then admitted to the hospital as my patient while I run my tests. That way she can sleep while I work out what's happening."

"That's a lot of words," I complain, because it doesn't all make sense to me just yet.

"Don't you worry about anything. Let me look after you." With that, Tate disappears out my line of sight, and I can hear him on the phone.

"I'm scared," I whisper, gripping Ghost's hand a little harder than before.

"I know, but we will figure this out. You just sleep. I won't leave your side. I promise you." His deep voice always soothes me. Closing my eyes again, the blackness returns, and the noise drifts into the background until I can't hear anything.

GHOST

Standing in the viewing room watching Cassie being slid into the MRI machine is horrendous. There is a wall between us, and I promised I wouldn't leave her. The technician wanted me outside in the corridor, but there was no way that was happening. Tate convinced him there was a valid reason for me to be there and not to question the doctor.

I can't help but worry the loud noise in the machine will trigger another seizure, but Tate tells me that she is fine and in a sleeping state, so with the earphones on, hopefully she will sleep right through it. I have never watched my wife's feet so intently in all my life, waiting for any movement or the slightest twitch. Not that I can do anything from here, but I just want her to get through this scan so we have some answers.

Tate is standing behind the technician as it slowly takes the images for them to look at. To me it just looks like a brain that I have seen on some of the images when I've been researching. This is past anything I can work out. I want to ask them to tell me as soon as they see something, but that would be stupid. I need to step back and let Tate handle this. There is a reason he's the best, and I have to trust him.

After what feels like the longest twenty minutes of my life, Cassie is free of the machine and still snoring, which is a good sign that it didn't cause her any distress.

"Send it to me, thanks, Stewart," Tate says to the tech before guiding me out of the room and toward where the nurse is pushing Cassie's bed out of the scanning chamber. Pulling his phone from his pocket and reading a message, Tate is quickly replying. I keep forgetting that we aren't his only patient in this hospital.

I follow them down the corridors and into the elevator to take Cassie up to the private room upstairs that I made sure we were booked into. I'd pay to have the whole floor if it wouldn't bring attention to us.

"I'll be with you in a minute, I need to check on another patient, something isn't looking right." With that, he disappears down another corridor with haste, and I can tell he's concerned.

I get Cassie settled in the room and make sure the blinds are drawn so the room is only dimly lit until she is fully awake and we know that she's not sensitive to the light anymore.

I hate waiting and not having anything to occupy my mind. It leaves me in a bad place because I start worrying about things. I'm best when I can be solving something.

The silence in here has me deciding on one thing. We can't live like this anymore; it's not healthy for Cassie, the kids—or me, for that matter. Just seeing friends in the flesh instead of over a video call in the last twenty-four hours has been playing on me the whole time. I always thought being on my own was the way to get through this. But now I know, the only way through it is to finish it. Jason needs to be taken down, either through the courts or I'll arrange it myself.

My family deserves a normal life.

But first, I need to get Cassie through this. Jason is the last person I want on my mind.

Tate's minute turned into two hours, but I would never complain. Someone's loved one needed him, and while Cassie is resting, nothing can be done anyway.

The door slowly opening has me looking up from her face, but my hand goes to the small pistol under my jacket. Ashton brought us in through a back access to the hospital, so we weren't detected with our weapons. I don't ask questions with him, because I trust he has everything taken care of.

The look on Tate's face as he walks in tells me all I need to know.

We have a problem.

Now I just need to know how bad this problem is.

"Has she been awake at all?" Tate takes her pulse and listens to her heart.

"Not since we got her settled in here. I've let her rest."

"Good. It's for the best," he says, reading the tablet in his hand.

"Just tell me. No bullshit, no technical terminology, just straight words. Is it a tumor?" I'm not waiting for Cassie to be awake for the answer, and he knows that.

"I'm afraid so, but you knew that was going to be my answer, didn't you."

I nod at him. From the moment I met him online, I could tell that was what he suspected, I saw it written all over his face. I like this guy, he says it how it is, and that's what I need.

"The problem I have, though, is I can't tell from the scan if it's benign or malignant. It isn't always obvious in the MRI. I wish it had been, but it wasn't. I'm going to have to do a biopsy to work it out, but regardless of the results of the biopsy, it has to be removed. It's in a section of the brain that will continue to make the seizures worse if we don't take it out. Luckily, though, it is in a position I can get to easily and get rid of it, but of course, there are risks like with any surgery. I know you don't want to hear this, but you are going to be here for a few days at least while we work all this out."

The noise in my head is rushing. This is the worst scenario. Having Cassie exposed and vulnerable for who knows how long, while my kids are nowhere near me if they need me.

"When can you do it?"

"You don't even want to know the details and risks?" Tate looks at me, perplexed.

"Just being here is as big a risk as what's in her head. I trust you; are you telling me I shouldn't?" I ask, standing up and looking the guy in the eye.

"I told you, I'm the best, and that's a fact. She needs me to sort out her head, but the rest is on you." He doesn't know our story, but he knows enough.

"Deal, now get your part done." I'll guard her while we're here, and if he can just get that tumor out of her head, test it, and give me the results I want, then I'll breathe again.

"I'll get back to you. I assume you're staying here tonight?"

I thought I'd made myself clear from the very beginning that I won't be leaving her alone. "Not leaving her."

"Fair enough. I'll organize a cot for you." I almost told him I'll sleep on the floor, I don't care about a bed, but he doesn't need to hear it. I think he gets the message with my body language.

"I'm looking at my surgery roster, and providing she settles tonight, I'll come in early tomorrow morning and do the biopsy

before I start my day. That way we can send the sample for testing, and by the time I'm out of surgery later in the day, hopefully
we'll have our answers." Yes, this is what I need, a man of action.
"I'll have the consent forms brought in, so when she wakes, have
Cassie sign them and we will be ready to go. You have my
number, but the nurses will also let me know if there's any
change."

The way he's typing away into his tablet, not even looking at me,
I can tell the man has a brain like mine. It's firing in ten different
directions at any one time, and he is managing all of it with ease.
The door opens slowly and another doctor steps quietly into the
room.

It's a woman with her dark hair pulled tightly back in a bun but
with the kindest eyes. I know from my background research that she
is Tate's wife, Arabella.

"Hi there, you must be Earl. I'm Bella, Tate's wife. He's told me
about you and your wife." It sounds funny hearing her use my fake
name we're using while Cassie's in the hospital. Tate smiles at me,
and this is the moment I know I can fully trust him. He has kept the
full story from his wife, and a man does not do that lightly.

As she gets closer, he turns to her and kisses her on the forehead.
The love between them is clear. Even when they are both in their
professional roles, they can't hide it. The first night we met, he told
me he understood my protectiveness, but now I see it oozing
from him.

I trusted him because Ashton told me I could, but now that I'm
here, I know I wouldn't want anyone else looking after Cassie. Tate
is the man.

"How is she doing?" Leaning forward, Bella brushes Cassie's
forehead with such tenderness.

"As we expected. Just couldn't see what I needed to on the scan."
Tate holds the tablet sideways for his wife to see.

"Damn, so when are you doing the biopsy?" I can see the two
doctors are having an unspoken conversation between themselves
about what the scan shows.

"In the morning. Can you sort out the kids? I'll come in early before my first booked-in surgery."

"Of course," she answers, nodding to her husband. "Don't worry, she is in the best hands," she tells me. And I can tell this isn't just the biased words of a wife, they are the words of respect from a fellow doctor who admires his talent. That is comforting.

"Thank you." Tonight's going to be a long one, and I think tomorrow will be even longer.

"Ready to head home?" Tate looks down at Arabella now, and his whole demeanor has changed. No longer the neurosurgeon but just a man who is ready to take the love of his life home for the night.

"Absolutely, it's been a hell of a day. Get some sleep, Earl, and I'll pop in tomorrow if I get a chance to meet Cassie when she's awake. Any friends of Ashton are friends of ours."

"Call me if you need me." And with that, Tate and Arabella are gone, and I'm left watching over Cassie. Just the two of us, the way it always is.

CASSIE

It feels like a lifetime ago that I woke during the night and Ghost told me everything that happened. I haven't slept one minute since. I knew deep down that I had a tumor in my brain, but I prayed for a different answer, we both did. Last night there was shock as I tried getting my head around it, and I even pretended to sleep at one stage so Ghost would get some rest. He is going to need it today. I just needed to be alone with my own thoughts and process everything.

But this morning I'm angry.

Why me?

Surely life has thrown enough at me. First my parents' deaths, then Jason, and although that brought me Ghost and I wouldn't change that for the world, this still sucks. How many stressful things am I expected to handle and keep bouncing back?

This is just the beginning of my story, and I don't even know

how to cope with it. I have two children who depend on me that I
need to be here for. That's been the whole reason I have hidden and
had no life all these years, and now it could have all been for nothing. I can't voice this to Ghost, because I promised him to fight and
that I would tell him everything. I just can't. If I start, I may not
stop, and the way my brain is acting at the moment, I might say
things to him that come out wrong or things I don't mean. Instead,
it's buried down inside, and it can stay there. I'll be damned if I
waste time arguing with him now.

I'm lying here in the hospital gown waiting for them to come
and take me to the operating room. Tate was in early to see me and
tried to reassure me, but no words will take away the fear that I'm
feeling. I'm thankful that Ghost isn't talking either. We are both in
our own worlds of anguish.

The door opening startles us both.

"I love you," I blurt out as Ghost is already moving to me at the
same time.

We wrap our arms around each other and hold on tight.

"Love you more than life itself." His gruffness tells me that he is
barely hanging on too.

Knowing we need to let go, he stands up tall and is still holding
onto my hand. "I'll walk with you as far as I can, and I'll be here
when you wake up," he promises, trying to reassure me that, on top
of the tumor, he has everything under control.

There was an argument between him and Tate this morning
when he was refused the right to be in the operating theatre.
Watching two alpha males take a stand is a sight to see. In the end, I
had to calm Ghost and tell him we don't want to draw attention,
and it's not normal for a patient's husband to be allowed in there.
We need to stay under the radar here, and as much as I want him
there, he can't be.

At times I think maybe we are overreacting. It has been years
since everything happened, and Jason has probably long forgotten
about me and covered up his tracks on whatever he thinks I knew
anyway. What he doesn't know is that I took two copies of all the
information and only gave one to the FBI. That thumb drive has

been in our safe all these years, plus Ghost now has multiple copies stored in secure places in case anything ever happens to the original. There are photos on there of all the papers that were hidden in the hollow book and everything I could find on the computer. They are only parts of a huge puzzle that Ghost has been piecing together, but I'm sure there is enough on there to prove it was him and not Camilla.

I'm hoping I'm right about the overreacting and that all we need to worry about is my health, and then life can go back to our normal.

Looking up at Ghost as we go through the corridor, I see Ashton standing at the door that says only authorized staff past this point. His smirk at me tells me he knows his partner too well. He is here to make sure Ghost doesn't make a scene when they take me through the doors. I mouth *"thank you"* to him, and he replies back, *"I've got him,"* and I know he has.

The tears are slowly rolling down the side of my eyes to the pillow as our hands slip apart, and I hear his voice from behind me.

"See you soon." And I have to believe that will be the case. *It's just a test*, I keep telling myself, but that's not so easy when someone is about to drill into your head and take a piece out of it.

The operating room is a hive of activity, bright lights that are hurting my eyes, and the clanging of metal as things are being placed on trays. I can feel my breathing starting to speed up and the nerves are racing all through me. This whole procedure freaks me out, but with every person around me a stranger, my panic of who they are and if they are a threat is sending me into a spin. I need to get out of here, I can't do this.

"Just breathe, Cassie, I'm here with you." Tate's face appears above me, and he takes my hand, holding it tightly to his chest. I don't know if he does this for all his patients, but I appreciate it so much. "That's it, just slow it down. This will be over before you know it. I'll have you waking up to that ugly guy that is pacing outside the doors."

I can't help but let out a little giggle amongst the tears. Tate knew what I needed, and that is to just focus on my husband and getting back to him before he pulls the hospital apart. Lord help Ashton and Badger having to put up with Ghost when it's time for the actual operation that will take hours, compared to this one.

"Are you ready?" Tate asks, gently placing my hand back on the table.

"Why does everyone keep asking me that?" I joke, trying to make light of the situation.

"Because remember, no matter what, you are always in control. This is your life, you get to choose."

He always seems to know what I need to hear.

"Then I'm ready."

As the anesthetist places the mask over my face from behind and pushes the drugs through my IV, it's the last thing I remember.

GHOST

"You need to try to eat something, Cassie." The raw adrenaline coursing through my body the longer this day goes on is not helping me to stay calm with her.

"I'm not hungry." She may be tired, but the stubbornness hasn't gone away, that's for sure.

"Don't care. Eat!" What she isn't counting on is my stubbornness is just as bad.

She rolls her eyes and crosses her arms over her chest but opens her mouth as I put another mouthful of the tuna bake they brought her for dinner. Why is hospital food always shit? I mean, who eats tuna bake by choice? That was what my mom used to cook for us, and just the smell of it makes me want to gag, but Cassie needs her strength. I need to be doing something, and even though she can feed herself, I'm doing it for her because it gives me something to concentrate on. And for Cassie, it gives her something to complain about.

The last nurse that came in to check on her gave us the message that Tate had been held up in surgery and would be up to see us as soon as he could. That can't come soon enough. We are both going stir crazy in here. I could hack the computer system and find out the results, but for once in my life, I don't want to. The fear of reading the words that will change our lives for the worse, instead has me just pacing the room or trying to watch the television with Cassie. I couldn't even tell you what was on, and I doubt she could either.

"Have you even eaten anything today?" she asks. I can tell the grogginess of the anesthesia is starting to wear off now. She is asking questions she won't like the answers to, so I speak in riddles.

"Yes." It's not a lie, but the single piece of toast I ate this morning, because she insisted on it, is not what she meant. I can go days without food if I need to. It's not ideal, and it's been a long time since I've done it, but I'm not leaving her to find food. Ashton keeps messaging me to arrange some to be delivered, but I refuse. He's smart enough to accept my answer and not push it. The honest answer is that I can't eat, I feel like I'm going to be sick, and this is not how I handle stress. All my life I've been the strong, stoic one, who can handle any situation I'm thrown into. Even when Cassie and I were on the run, nothing rattled me. Because I was creating the narrative. I knew what I was doing and had all the tools I needed to keep her safe.

But this, this is completely different.

It's my wife's life we're talking about, and in a way I can't control, and I fucking hate it!

My phone buzzes in my pocket, and I'm assuming it's Ashton, but I'm sure my heart skips a beat as I see the message that tells me it's time.

Tate: *I'm on my way up.*

Ghost: *Okay.*

Cassie's staring straight ahead, zoned out, and I contemplate not telling her, but that wouldn't be fair. She needs time to prepare.

"Tate is on his way up here. Won't be long and we'll know."

The look of terror on her face is so hard to take.

As I sit on the edge of her bed and pull her up into my arms, I can feel her shivering. I'm worried it's another seizure coming, and she must have sensed my panic.

"I'm sure it's just my nerves. Just keep holding on tight." Oh, baby, I'm holding on so tight to you and everything else. You have no idea.

The door bursting open has me jumping and pushing Cassie as much behind my body as possible, until I see it's Tate. That man has no idea how to enter the room of someone who has a hit out on her. He's lucky he doesn't have a gun in his face, but only my instincts told me not to go that far because Ashton is outside watching, so he would have stopped the stranger before they made it past the door.

"It's benign," he blurts out, which is not how I picture him normally delivering the news. "I'm so sorry it took so long. One of my operations didn't go as planned, it happens. But I got here as soon as I could."

Cassie is back in my arms, and we're both crying. I never show emotion in front of others, but I'm just so overwhelmed with relief I can't contain it. I've cried with Cassie more in the last few days than I have my entire life.

"Not cancer, Ghost, it's not cancer," is all she keeps repeating into my chest. In my head I'm saying the same thing. Tate just stands back and gives us time to pull it together, and I see no judgment from him at my breaking down in front of him. He'd be used to it, I'm sure, but I'm not. Thank goodness neither Bull nor Badger are here to see it. I would never hear the end of this. I'm settling on the bed next to Cassie again as Tate pulls up a chair to sit with us.

"We aren't out of the woods yet, not by a long shot, but this is a good result. Now, let's talk about where we go from here." His voice is now calm and full of authority, nothing like the one he burst into the room with. I have a feeling over the last few days we have gained another friend, and we might mean a little more to him than his average patient. Same goes both ways. This man in front of me will have me watching his back and that of his family, keeping them all safe for as long as we are both living. It's the best way I can repay him. My money would mean nothing to him, but his family's safety is priceless.

Waiting two days for this surgery has been horrendous, but there are people who are in more urgent need for the operation than Cassie is. In a way, that should be comforting, but it's not. I just want it over and to get her home. No amount of money or outside danger to her can change her priority in the surgery schedule, and nor should it.

We have said all we need to say at three am this morning. Neither of us could sleep, and it was time to be raw and say the things that should never be left unsaid. As much as I trust Tate and I know he's the best, this surgery is risky, and anything can happen. We held each other and talked until the sun rose, about our hopes and dreams for both of us and the kids. Cassie wanted me to know that she has written letters and they are at the house, which was hard to hear, but I would have done the same if the situation were reversed. The percentage rate of her not making it home, from the tumor and also due to the outside danger, was so much higher than the average person, and she wanted to be prepared. Especially for the kids. She knows what it's like to lose a parent early in life, and she wanted to tell them everything she might miss out on being able to say.

We cried, we laughed, but most of all, we were together just loving each other.

Since then, the morning has been a constant in-and-out of nurses and doctors to get her prepared for the surgery. Any minute they will be here to take her. All the test results have been done on the sample, and Tate has everything he needs. Even the DNA genetic mapping of the tumor was tested to see if it is something we need to watch with the kids in the future. Tate has sent it all to me to keep for the future. It will also be there if, God forbid, another one forms for Cassie and we aren't anywhere near Chicago and Tate. We don't know what life will bring us in the future, and there is always the chance we could need to run again. The chances are slim but never zero.

The door to her room opens, and we know it's time.

Again, I walk her to the door that feels like such a bigger barrier to me than a few pieces of wood that swing open and closed. The orderly stops to let me say my goodbye, even though I will never say those words.

We don't need many words, we have already said them all.

"I love you." I kiss her on the lips like I'll die without touching her.

Pulling back, she looks at me with her beautiful bright eyes that always get to me. "I love you too, and remember... tomorrow will be a better day."

Barely holding it together, I signal for them to take her before I can't let go.

"Fight," I call to her as she's pushed away, and she raises her hand, with her other hand pointing to her wedding-ring finger. That's all I need to know.

She's fighting for us.

The doors close, and I lean my back into the wall beside them, trying to use the wall to hold myself up. Looking up to the ceiling to whoever is up there listening, I thump my fist so hard on the wall, that the pain is shooting up my arm.

"You can't have her... she's MINE!"

With that, I storm down the corridor to get my laptop from Ashton. I need to end this.

Jason, I'm coming for you!

Chapter Twenty-Two

CASSIE

Floating, no pain, but I can feel his hand in mine. I feel safe.

Remember the story from Paris? You loved that one. A little apartment looking at the Eiffel Tower. I could sit there with my coffee, sweet pastries, and croissants for breakfast. You wanted to know what I had on the croissant, and of course, it was ham and cheese. Like there was any other choice. I brought you that little bottle of French perfume that you loved to spray on yourself and your teddies. I miss those times. I wish things didn't have to change, but they did. Why did you do that?

Confusion surrounds me. Do what? I wasn't there.

But it's okay, I'm here now, I can fix this. I'll fix what's broken. There will be punishment, but you knew that. I need you to wake up first. It will take a while, but I'll wait. You always did like your sleep; I'm guessing it hasn't changed. Don't be afraid, though. I'm here to take care of you. I'll come to you when it's time.

Daddy always looked after me. His stories making me feel better when I was scared. I'm so scared because I can't open my eyes. I can hear him, and I can feel him, but I'm still floating. But it's not his hand I want, it's my Noah. He grounds me and is my home. I want to feel his touch.

Fight, come on, fight. You promised him.

My head is spinning again, but I can hear the beeps of machines. The hospital, I'm alive, the rest is dreaming. Don't be too scared.

The hand is there again, and his soothing voice is in my head, talking to me.

I can see the fear on your face, and it reminds me of when you were little. Noises in the night had you freaking out. So, I would tell you about my adventures. Your mother never believed the stories, but you always did. You trusted me unconditionally. I need you to do that now. We have things to sort out, so when I come for you, I need you to trust me and believe me it's for the best. I don't want to lose you again.

Other voices are talking around me.

"Her pulse and BP are stable, just having trouble waking. She should be well out of the anesthetic by now." A lady, I don't know her voice.

What does she mean I should be awake? I'm trying. I can hear you, I'm here, just hold my eyes open and I'll see you.

No, get Ghost, he knows how. His voice, my body responds to it. Let him see me, I need him.

"It's been longer than it should be. Call Dr. McIntyre and let him know. Tell him she's breathing on her own and the tube is out, but she won't wake properly."

Yes, call Tate, he will fix me. He told me he would take care of me.

I'm trying, I promise! It's hard, my eyes don't open, and everything feels weird.

"He's on his way down. Just talking to the husband." The woman's voice is circling me.

It was gone, but it's back. I can feel his hand again.

I have to go now, my little girl, but I'll be back when it's time.
We will be together once more.
Just you and me.

"No… I don't… want… to go… with… you. Not… yet." Is that my voice out loud or inside my head? I can't tell.

"That's it, Cassie, you're back with us. Keep pushing through the fog. I need you to open those eyes for me." A hand is rubbing up and down each of my arms. I can feel it finally, and it's soft, but enough to register the sensation.

"Cassie, talk to me, let me know you can hear me. I need to send a message to your husband before he storms into this recovery room." Tate's voice is a comfort. He's here. He'll take me to Ghost.

"Have we got a grumpy one out there?" the nurse said.

My eyes finally open, and with all the strength I have, I tell her, "No! …Loves me… protects me! …My… grumpy!" My voice is husky, and my throat is sore from the breathing tube I'm guessing. Just getting that out is all I could do, and I can't keep my eyes open anymore. The feeling of the fuzziness comes back again.

"That's my girl. Welcome back, Cassie." Tate's voice is distant but still there. "Let's get her up to ICU for monitoring and let her husband see her." The noise is drifting off again, but I can feel some sort of movement.

Yes, I can rest if I know I'm with him.

GHOST

Watching them wheel Cassie through the doors of the ICU was the most relief I have ever felt. I was worried when she was in labor at home on her own with just me, but nothing like what the last seven hours have been.

She looks limp and her face is pale, but she's here and she's breathing. The rest will happen in good time. I don't care if her speech is affected, she has a limp, or doesn't have perfect eyesight. None of that will matter to me, as long as I still have her with us.

Tate is following close behind her with his trusty tablet in his hand, and he's on the phone, talking in technical medical terminology that I can't even begin to understand, and I understand a lot.

"Page me if that doesn't work." His phone disappears back into his white jacket pocket, and he's standing between me and the door that I was about to walk through.

"Just give them a minute. They need to hook her up to monitors and don't need you in the road. Another few minutes won't kill you."

"Debatable!" Yeah, I know I sound like an asshole, but he is the person standing in between me and my Cassie.

"Whatever. Now, she is going to be out of it for a while. I'm not sure why but she has had an adverse reaction to the anesthetic, and we had trouble bringing her out of it, but it does happen. The good thing is she's on her way back and talking to me. Opened her eyes and told us you were grumpy, but you're her grumpy." The smirk on his face tells me how happy he was to relay that story.

"Damn straight I am. Now let me in there, otherwise you will see more than grumpy." The chuckle that Tate lets out as he steps to the side just makes me more agitated. I need to pull it back, be gentle with her and nice to him. He still has her life in his hands.

The day I get to take her home, I'll let him know in my best friendly way what an asshole he is.

I'm moving toward her on a mission, but the moment I'm close enough to touch her, all that aggression is gone and the love that I've been hanging onto is pouring through me in waves. I wish she had her eyes open so I could tell she's really okay, but just being able to touch her and leaning down to kiss her lips that are all dry from the tube, is enough to center me again. She smells like a hospital, but still, under all the sterile things they have used on her, I can still detect a hint of that sweetness that is all Cassie. Every day she uses a jasmine-scented body lotion. Even if she misses putting it on, I can always still smell it in her skin. Just like I can now.

Tate's hand on my shoulder pushes me into a chair next to her. He understands how overwhelmed I am. Taking her hand in mine, she takes a big breath, and the machines give a few weird, out-of-rhythm beeps, but then they settle back into normal, and her body seems to relax a little more into the bed.

"She knows you're here, buddy. That was her way of telling you. Talk to her. She can hear you. She'll wake up when she's ready, but in the meantime, keep talking to her to reassure her that it's safe out here. She doesn't need to hide inside there." She squeezes my hand with whatever strength she can muster at hearing Tate's words.

"I know, baby, you're fighting. I believe you," I whisper, raising her hand to my mouth and kissing the back of it. There is no way I'm leaving this seat until those eyes are open and I can't shut her up from talking.

I have things to do but nothing is more important than this.

Once she is out of danger, then the plan will be put into place to finally take Jason down. It didn't take long to work it out, and everyone is on board. We all agree it's time, and we have enough evidence that there is no way he can get out of it this time. Ashton's words to me were, *"What took you so long, dickhead?"* but then he hasn't been here from the start. It's easy for him to say, Cassie isn't his wife. Bull told me if I had tried to do this on my own, he would have come and killed me himself. All this time I thought I was on my own in this world, besides Cassie. But it's not the case. These guys have always been there for me, I'm finally just realizing it.

I'm not a big talker, but I've come prepared, after having so much time on my hands today. Reaching into my backpack that has my laptop and a set of earbuds in there, I also pull out her phone I have been carrying with me. I make sure it's on airplane mode, so it doesn't upset any of the machines that are important in this room. Carefully putting one of the earbuds into each of Cassie's ear, I start the recordings I have loaded up for her.

Our home security has cameras and sound in the kids' bedrooms, so I have taken hours and hours of me reading stories to Bessy or both of the kids together. You can hear Bessy talking and Eli making himself heard at times, with his chatter or a little cry. I don't want her to feel alone. I will be here holding her hand, and she can hear us all around her until she is ready to wake up. She may be ready to murder me by then, sick of hearing the children's stories, but I don't care.

Between every story finishing and the new one starting is my voice telling her, *"I love you, keep fighting for us."*

CASSIE

Ghost's voice.

He's here, just like he promised.

His hand, I can feel it. This time the touch feels like home.

I can rest now. He's got me.

My Bessy, sometimes she just needs to slow down when she is trying to read. Her sweet voice is like a lullaby. The purity in her words. I love this story, but Eli doesn't. He's crying, why is he crying? I need to go to him. Why can't I get to him? Ghost has him, it's okay. He is always there for me. Keep reading, Bessy, I love to hear you.

I remember more of this story than the last. Maybe I can wake up. I want to tell the story, mine is better. Bessy laughs at my animal noises and so does Eli. Ghost isn't any good. They need my *"Moooooo… mooooo…"* No, that chicken is terrible, we need to work on that. Need to wake up, come on, eyes, open!

Where did the farm go? We are back in the ice castle. No, not again, I've read this book a thousand times already.

Enough, enough, no more, enough.

"Enough, no… more… snowman…"

The earbuds are pulled out of my ears and the story is gone. Instead, I hear him, his voice much deeper and tired.

"Cassie, baby, talk to me." I can hear a small laugh in his voice. "I promise no more snowman if you open up your eyes for me. I love you, please, I'm begging you to show me those bright eyes."

The light hurts.

"Too… bright." There is movement around me, and it's darker as I try again, and finally his face comes into view.

"Noah," I mouth with not much voice behind it, not knowing who's here.

"Yeah, baby, I'm here." His voice is like a soft blanket falling over my body. "Fuck, I've missed you." And now his words are heating me through to my core.

It's hard, but I don't want to close my eyes again. Concentrating on looking into his eyes is what is making me hold on. He is stressed, tired, and the longer I search his soul, I can start to see the relief in his face coming.

One lone tear sliding down his face shatters me.

"You scared me." His whisper is like he is giving me a key to his greatest fear. The fear of losing me is something he just can't deal with. He is the strongest man I know, but when it comes to me, I am his greatest weakness, and that frightens him.

Using strength in my body I didn't know was there, I lift my hand to his face above me, cupping his cheek and feeling the weight of his head falling into it. That tells me how hard it was for him.

"I'm here." His lips touch mine in the softest way, like he is worried I might break if he pushes me too hard. But I need to feel him, all the way to my toes. "Kiss me like you mean it," I say, and it's enough to have him cupping my face in both his hands and trying to breathe the life into me that he thinks I need. My body starts to feel a warm tingle all over, and my brain finally feels like everything is going to be okay.

"Give the poor woman a chance to wake up properly." Tate's laughter breaks us apart, and as he pulls back, I can see the first real smile on Ghost since we left home.

"She started it." Ghost winks at me as he stands from the bed.

"How old are you, man?" That has them both laughing, and surprisingly, I feel myself laughing with the faintest giggle.

"Old enough to know that if you hadn't walked in, I'd still be enjoying kissing my wife." Ghost pretends to be offended, but I can hear the respect he has for Tate and sense a friendship developing.

"Whatever. Now, as her super surgeon, I think I trump your kiss with the news that I got all the tumor, and from what I can see, you aren't having any adverse effects yet. It's still early, though, so let's just take it easy, Cassie. Don't let this guy push you too fast." It's his way of warning Ghost that he is still in charge until I leave his hospital, no matter what Ghost thinks.

There aren't many men I can imagine my husband backing down to, but I think Tate could be one of them.

"That's a relief," I voice quietly, but on the inside, I feel like screaming with joy. They both look at me now, finishing their standoff as to who is in control of this room.

"Yes, I agree. Thank you from both of us." Ghost's hand is out to shake Tate's. "Now, when can I take her home?"

Tate just rolls his eyes at him, replying with an answer that I doubt Ghost is impressed with. "When I say you can. Understand?" There is force behind the words.

"Roger that." Ghost takes it better than I thought, although I'm sure on the inside he is not happy.

Everything happening around me is exhausting, and I'm not sure I can stay awake for much longer. My eyes are getting heavy again.

"Sleep, Cassie, it's okay." Ghost kisses me on the forehead, and I feel myself drifting off into the darkness again. This time I'm not as scared because I know it's just tiredness and not that I won't wake up. Between the two men in this room, I know they won't let that happen.

GHOST

"Let's step outside for a minute." Tate tilts his head to the side so I know he means just outside the room, which is about as far as I'm willing to be away from her.

I follow him, wanting to ask more questions that I don't want Cassie worrying about.

"I expect her to sleep on and off for a few days. Brain surgery is not for the weak. Plus, she has struggled more than most with the anesthetic. So, I don't want any pressure on her at the moment. We need the brain to heal and her body to regain strength. Then, when she's stronger, we can look at moving her out of the hospital back to the apartment for a few days before you put her on a plane back home. We can't risk any brain bleeds by her flying too soon. It will already be sooner than I would like, but I know I'm not going to get much say about that, am I?"

There is no point giving him a bullshit answer.

"No. As soon as I can, I'm taking her home where I know she is safe. We are too exposed here, and I don't like it."

His nod tells me he gets it. "Understood. Now, I'm heading home to my wife and boys. It's been a long day, and it's not finished yet. Father duties await me at home." I don't know how he does it. This job must be draining, and I know firsthand how tiring little ones can be too. Although I'm sure he wouldn't have it any other way.

Really looking at him now, I figure my questions can wait; he looks exhausted. Let the man sleep, and then I can get my answers tomorrow. Most of them are just me being the person I am and wanting to know everything.

"Thanks again, Tate, I mean it."

"I know." With that, he pulls his vibrating phone from his pocket, and his look tells me he needs to take it.

"Go." I signal and walk back in to Cassie as I hear him talking on his way toward the elevator.

Talking to the kids without Cassie is a challenge. Obviously, Eli has no idea, he just smiles and drools, but Bessy wants to talk to Mommy, and the reasons as to why she can't are running out fast. But finally, it has been a few days, and Cassie has her bandages off her head and just a small band-aid that we can cover with her hair. Luckily the patch they had to shave off isn't too big and not directly at the front of her head which makes it easier to hide. Getting her dressed into her own clothes rather than a hospital gown will hide where we are, and with the app's ability to change the background, we're in business.

I jump on first and tell Bessy it will be a quick call, as Mommy and I have to go out. She's a little confused, but I tell her to fill me in on everything she has been doing first, so by the time we get Cassie on, she won't need to talk for long. It will wear her out just trying to be so upbeat for Bessy.

After talking for a few minutes, Cassie waves to Bessy. "I have to go now, princess, but Mommy misses you." I can see Cassie is struggling not to cry saying goodbye.

"Daddy, I had a bad dream last night, can you tell me a story?" Bessy says and throws us both. Taking the tablet out of Cassie's hands straight away, I can see her bottom lip quivering. She will be upset she wasn't there for Bessy when she needed her.

"Sure, princess," I tell her, moving across the room so Cassie can't be heard sniffling.

"Uncle Kurt told me a funny story, but it just wasn't as good as yours." That made me happy and sad at the same time. Glad I'm not being replaced by Bull but frustrated I wasn't there to chase the demons away.

We chatted for a few more minutes, and then she was happily giggling and ready to go off with Uncle Kurt for a walk to the cabin where they were going to do some drawings for Mommy. He had been using the cabin as a distraction for Bessy and a change of scenery for her too. I need to get off the call too, so I can comfort Cassie, and I tell Bull I will call him later.

Walking back over to Cassie, I sit on the bed and pull her tightly into my embrace, and she just settles there like it's made for her.

"They're fine. We will be back with them in a few days." I haven't yet told her that I will then be leaving her with Bull to make sure my plan for Jason succeeds. That will have her screaming at me, and in a place where we can't afford other people to hear us.

"I know, it's just hard. I know what it was like when my dad went away…" She trails off then pulls away from me, sitting up straight, and I can tell she's thinking hard about something.

"He came to me when I was unconscious. He was talking to me to calm me. Holding my hand like when I was little. I remember now. It felt so real." The longing in her eyes tells me how much she misses her parents.

"I'm sure they are both watching over you." My hand is now resting on her thigh.

"I can hear his voice, the words he was saying. They didn't always make sense, though. Something about going with him when the time was right."

My stomach drops at the thought of when she was unconscious, there was a chance she was going to be taken away from us. I'm glad her dad decided it wasn't time yet.

"Let's remind him that no time before the age of one hundred for you will be the right time for him to take you away. He'd better be listening." My words put a smile on her face.

"You'll be sick of me well before then," she says as she lays her head back down onto the pillow.

"Never!" I kiss her again to make sure she understands how much I mean it.

"Tate said we can probably take you to the apartment tomorrow, thank goodness. This roll-out bed is shit, and you know how I hate sleeping apart from you when I don't have to. I need to be touching you all the time." It's not healthy for a man to sleep apart from his wife. There are nights I've had to when I'm working, and I absolutely hate it. And it's never for more than one night. It may not be for the whole night, but a few hours of holding her tight is all I need to recharge and recenter.

"I'm surprised you haven't asked Tate how long until we can have sex again." The sound of her laughing after her tears will never get old.

"Oh, my poor deluded wife, of course I have. One to two weeks depending on you. So, we are getting close. Why, are you feeling a little lost without me inside you?" Raising my eyebrows at her brings more laughter. "What, it's not funny. I'm fucking aching over here, woman." I'm not used to abstaining from sex for so long. If there is one good thing about being tucked away in the mountains, it's all the free time I have to please my lady whenever she's ready. And that is all the time. Her sexual appetite has no problem keeping up with mine.

For that my cock is very grateful.

"You need to stop, otherwise I'll keep thinking about it, and we aren't allowed yet."

"Who said I have to listen to Tate?" I tease, running my hand up the inside of her leg under her long t-shirt we dressed her in for the call.

"Me, because I'm not doing anything to risk having to stay here a moment longer. I want to go home to my kids!" The longing for me is now replaced with the torment of being away from her children so long.

"I get it, but when you're ready, look out, beautiful, because it will be a wild ride, I can promise you that." I take my hand back before I'm tempted to do more.

"It always is, Ghost, it always is."

"Especially when you're the one riding!" Now I'm standing and walking to the window. I can't look at her for a minute. My cock needs to stop thinking about the vision of her on top of me naked, tits bouncing as she rides me hard. Head back, mouth open, moaning, her beautiful glistening skin with the sheen of sweat all over it that I put there and her pussy squeezing me so tight as she orgasms hard from the pleasure I'm giving her.

"Fuck, shouldn't have said that," I groan, pacing back and forth in the room.

"You can always go into the bathroom and use your hand. I remember once upon a time, you excelled at going solo in a shower." Her laughing is now low and sexy, tormenting me even more, but at least I know it's doing the same to her. I watch her pushing her thighs together. Oh yeah, she feels it too. It won't be long, and she will be back in my arms where she belongs.

"Not fucking funny! And for your information, that was the last time I needed my hand. Because I have this woman in my life now who is insatiable, and it takes all I've got to keep up with her."

"In your dreams, big boy. You are just as bad, and I love it!" Her voice a little hoarse with sexual frustration like mine.

Thank God Ashton chose now to knock and poke his head in the room.

"Hey, Cassie, can I borrow Ghost for a minute?" I don't like the look on his face.

"Sure, he could use a few rounds of boxing to take away a certain bit of pent-up frustration." Her giggle gives us away, and I'm sure the rock-hard cock that is pushing at the front of my pants will confirm his thoughts. Although the non-reaction from him has it deflating quickly.

"Okay." His blunt reply is all I need to know something isn't right. Normally he would have been all over giving me shit about a hard-on over my wife in a hospital room.

Walking back to her and kissing her like I'm about to fuck her hard, I leave her panting as I head to the door.

"Won't be long, and I'll be just outside the door." I close it with a smile on my face, watching her still squashing her thighs together, but as soon as the door is shut, everything changes.

"What's wrong?" My voice is brash and straight to the point.

"We have a problem." Ashton is in full work mode, I can tell by his body language.

"No shit, spit it out." I don't have any patience for details, just straight facts.

"Susan, who we have working intelligence while you're with Cassie, has found a cut in the security tape from the recovery room. Someone else was on that feed and looped a few minutes over again, while the current feed was hidden."

"What the fuck!" My teeth are grinding. We were watching it live! How could we miss this? Well, we thought we were, but there must have been a few seconds of a delay.

"They're good, Ghost. There were two cuts in the transmission, but she's managed to retrieve them."

"They know she's here." I can hardly speak. The hair on the back of my neck is up, and I can feel the instinct of wanting to hurt anyone who gets near her sitting just below the surface.

"It's worse than that. You need to see this." Ashton shoves a tablet into my hand, shielding the screen to keep it private, but I'm afraid to press play. As my finger hovers over the button, I realize it's go time for what we have planned. I need Jason taken down, now.

No more waiting!

"Fuck," is all I can say as it plays out in front of me.

Chapter Twenty-Three

GHOST

"Are you sure it's him?" I ask again, keeping my voice low as I replay the video for the fourth time. The image isn't perfect, and with the surgical scrubs on, the mask and the hat, you can't see a lot of his face.

"Susan has done the facial recognition. Even with all the gear on, with what we can see of his face, his eyes are a perfect match." Ashton is looking at me with pity, and I hate that.

"How the fuck did he find her? Or get the fuck near her?"

I want answers, and I want them now.

I knew I should have been the one on the computers, but I can't be everywhere. Reading my mind, Ashton replies to my questions.

"I'm on it. We always knew something like this was a risk. It would have been more of a surprise if we got away with it. Be honest with yourself. You can't do everything, Ghost. Keeping her hidden for this long was a fucking miracle."

"But I should have known this. Why the fuck didn't I see this information on him on the dark web?" I'm questioning myself, that every single thing I've done over the last seven years has been for nothing.

"Maybe because he's old-school, and he doesn't exist on there. Like I said, they're good, but we're better. Trust yourself, don't let any bullshit doubt creep in now. We need you now more than ever. Let's nail these bastards and get Cassie her life back."

I stand frozen, looking down at his image on the tablet in my hand.

Ashton's words are echoing in my head. Get Cassie her life back.

"We're moving her now?" Ashton asks. I can see his mind already in motion.

"No, we are going to draw him out. He wants to play with me, then game on, asshole, but he better understand one thing," I say, looking at the eyes that I never expected to see.

"I. Never. Lose!" I hiss, grinding my teeth in anger.

"We're going to do what?" Ashton's shock doesn't deter me. "Are you sure it wasn't you that had part of your brain taken out?"

"Nope. Better to catch him with the element of surprise. Bring him into our domain. He thinks we don't know he's here. Well, surprise. Come at me, prick."

I straighten my shoulders, and I can see Ashton doing the same.

"Listen up. This is what's happening!" This whole time we have been standing here our talking has been at the lowest level possible so no one can hear us. I want to shout, but it's surprising how mad you can still sound while whispering.

I get through my quick instructions, that are of course somewhat in a code that Ashton understands so we aren't giving anything away. No more words are needed. Ashton gives me the lift of his chin and turns away as he heads down the corridor to put everything in place. We are going to need Tate's help, and that's not something I ask lightly. I didn't want anyone else involved, but I can't do it without them.

I'm guessing while we are watching the security feeds in the hospital, so are they, which is why Ashton held the tablet cover over the top of the screen at an angle, so only I could see under the cover what was being played. We need them to think they are still pulling it over on us, and Ashton is right. Deep down I knew they were coming for her. The feeling in my body has been on high alert for a few weeks, even before we arrived in Chicago. Badger had even been in contact to check in, which told me the man with the weird senses knew something was coming even before we found out Cassie was sick. Stupidly I wrote it off as that, but I should have been more thorough. I let my fear of Cassie's operation cloud my concentration.

I've never had trouble multitasking before, but this time I did, and it cost me. The thought of losing her on that operating table was all I could think of, but she is fighting danger from two sides, and I should have been too. I let them sneak under my radar, and if something happens because of that, I will never forgive myself.

Taking a deep breath, I let my shoulders fall down again and release the tense look, so Cassie won't suspect something is wrong. Counting to ten, it's time to go back in and face my wife. I will need to tell her but not just yet. We need her to stay calm, and hopefully it will all be over quickly. She already knows I have a small camera in the room, so my team always have the visual feed of her and can keep her safe. It's a tiny camera and no one would know it's there, but it's my secret weapon in this attack. I will be able to see him and know when to move.

Not that I want to let him that close to her again, but it's the best way of ending this. Now, to work out how to explain all this to Cassie when the time is right.

Pushing the door open to her room, the vision of my wife in front of me tells me why I'm doing this. I don't care what happens to me, but my kids need their mom. She is listening to Bessy reading a story on speaker phone, while my wife's head is lying back on her pillow with her eyes closed. I'm sure she is picturing her in her bedroom and following the words in the book with her finger, concentrating so hard to read the big words, and I can hear Asha helping her with them. This is my world, my family, and I'll give everything to keep them safe. Even if it's giving my life to make sure they can live theirs.

Deliberately clearing my throat to make a noise, I see her eyes slowly open, and she mouths the words to me, so not to interrupt Bessy. "Everything okay?"

I just nod to her with the best smile I can paint on my face. Her look is skeptical, but she lets it slide for the moment. When Bessy stops to turn a page, Cassie uses the opportunity to announce my arrival.

"Daddy is here too."

"Daddy!" Bessy's scream tells me she is excited to hear I'm here.

"Hi, princess, your reading is getting better." Sitting down on the bed and taking Cassie's hand, I draw it to my lips and kiss it just so I can taste her skin, needing to be close to her.

"I've been practicing with Uncle Kurt and Auntie Asha. They like to hear me reading." Her words convey how proud she is of herself.

"I bet they do, princess. It's time for Mommy and me to do some more holiday things now. We will call you later, okay?" She is used to this now. I can't thank our friends enough for keeping her so busy that she hasn't missed us too much.

"Okay, we are going to make some cookies now. I'll save you some. Unless Uncle Kurt eats them all." Hearing Asha laughing in the background, I know I have no chance of any cookies being left by the time I get home.

"Thanks, Bessy. Love you, princess." I squeeze Cassie's hand as she also tells our daughter she loves her and that we will be home soon. I don't want to promise Bessy a specific day, because with everything about to go down, the last thing I want to do is lead them to our home and kids. If we need to, we will be bunkering down here or somewhere else until it's over. I know my kids are safe where they are.

The call disconnects, and Cassie lets out a big yawn.

"You're tired, why don't you have another sleep?" I suggest, running my free hand through her hair and pushing the wispy bits off her face. We could have come here in disguise, but it would have been too difficult. Cassie wouldn't be able to wear the wig in the operation, which she was lucky they only had to shave a small patch so it can be easily covered when needed. There is one thing that

Cassie has guarded since running from her life with Jason and that is her long brown hair. I didn't understand at first, but one night as we sat out on the deck when Bessy was first born, her little baby hands were wrapped in Cassie's hair, and I asked her if it would be easier to just cut it short. After she bit my head off with her response, then came the explanation that her memory of her mother is with the same long brown hair. I could see the love in her eyes that she was missing, and then it all made sense. That was a little way she could keep the memory of her mother alive. The way she tells stories to the kids also holds the memory of her father close.

"No, I'm not resting. I'm sick of sleeping, Ghost. I just want to go home to my babies. They are going to forget what I look like." The pout on her face would be cute if things weren't so crazy here. If we were just on a holiday and she was missing her kids, I'd either distract her so she wasn't thinking about them or would pack her up on the first plane and take her home. But things aren't quite that easy, and this is far from some relaxing holiday at an island resort.

"Okay, your body, your choice." I learned a long time ago not to push Cassie when it's not needed. Pick your battles, as the saying goes.

"Exactly! Now tell me what Ashton's visit was about, and don't you dare tell me it was nothing. I saw it in his eyes when he opened the door, and you might think you can hide things from me, Ghost, but I can see straight through you. Your eyes aren't soft anymore, they are in 'battle mode.' Your body is tense, and the adrenaline is oozing out of your pores in your skin, I can smell it. You are ready to go to war with someone, and I can feel it in my bones, that person you are fighting for is me."

How can this woman nail my emotions every time? I can hide from the world, but it seems I can't hide from my wife. I can't sit here. Up and walking the room, I'm trying to untangle the words in my head. I wasn't going to tell her yet, but she is going to see straight through me if I try to lie to her now. Then we'll just end up fighting, which isn't good for her recovery. But the shock of this is equally as bad, and I can't do what I would normally do to calm her down after we fight. Make-up sex with Cassie is like dynamite exploding, and then the bliss of the post-orgasm glow. That's off the table too, so once she starts getting wound up, there will be no pulling her back from that. There are times I love her stubbornness, but now is not one of them.

"Ghost, I'm waiting." Her voice is soft but not gentle. There is determination behind it. She wants an answer, even if it's not the one she wishes.

"You are supposed to be recovering and relaxing. Can you just let me deal with this for a bit, and I'll tell you more when it's time?" The look on her face tells me it's not going to wash with her, but I had to try.

"Ghost." Her voice is sterner this time, and she pats the bed for me to sit. She's asking a lot when my body is humming with energy and adrenaline. My skin is prickly, and my legs need to move. But as per usual, I can't say no to Cassie.

Sitting on the bed, I need to be touching her so it helps to still my body. "You have to promise me that you won't freak out and trust me that we have this under control."

The fight is in her eyes already. "Ghost, for fuck's sake, just tell me," she says, sitting up a straighter in the bed now.

"Umm, that's not staying calm."

"Ghost!" The pressure valve is about to pop. I think I have pushed my luck far enough.

"We have found evidence that they know we're here."

Her eyes turn black with fear. This is the first time I've seen them so dark.

"Who?"

"Whoever is connected with Jason and his syndicate." I can't tell her that the man has touched her and that we have no idea how he is connected to this whole mess. That part I'm keeping from her until I work it out. And I will work it out, if it's the last thing I do. She needs to know the truth about her life.

"How? I know it was a risk, but after all these years… we were so careful." All the fight in her voice is waning, and I can see tears just under the surface, but she isn't letting them fall. She's trying to stay strong.

Looking at her, it occurs to me that I'm attacking this all wrong.

Cassie is my weakness, but it's only because I don't allow her to be my strength. Keeping her in the dark on this could be the biggest mistake I make. Not knowing what is coming at her makes her vulnerable, and that in turn puts her in greater danger. If I tell her everything, then I can clear more space in my head to concentrate as this unfolds. We need to be a team. We started that way, and it's time to finish it the same way. I just wish she was healthier, but we didn't get to pick the timing of this.

"I don't know the answer to that, but I'll tell you what I do know, and we can figure the rest out. I just want you to understand that the whole team is working on this, and they have our backs. And especially Bull. The kids are safe in our home, we know that, and the next best thing to us being there is having Bull protecting them. And I mean that with everything I have."

Just nodding her head at me, I continue and get ready to pick up the pieces when I get to the end of this.

"We discovered a breach into the recovery ward in the hospital. Not sure how yet, but we're working on that. They manipulated the video feed that we were seeing, and we have only just discovered it now. There was a man who stood next to you and took your hand. He was talking to you while you were unconscious. Don't worry, he didn't touch you anywhere else, but that was enough. He should never have gotten that close to you." I can feel my heart racing at the mere thought of another man touching my woman when she is unable to defend herself. I don't give a fuck who he is.

Her hands are now over her mouth as she gasps. The shock of someone being that close to her is hitting hard.

"But he... why? He could have killed me then... I'm confused."

I want to tell her she's about to be a lot more confused, but I think the easiest way to explain it is to show her.

Reaching for my tablet on the side table, I log into the message that Ashton forwarded to me.

"You need to watch this, and remember, I'm here for you, always." Her face drops, afraid of what I'm about to show her. But that way, she will feel better knowing what happened to her in that room. I can see the stress lines on her forehead, and I'm sure her mind is racing right now, wondering how bad the interaction was. The thoughts she will conjure up will be worse than what actually happened, but the image of the person is going to shake her to the core.

I turn so I'm sitting with my body beside her on the bed, one arm around her shoulders, and I press play with the other hand. There's no sound, but the image starts as we see him enter the room. His head is down until he reaches her bed, waiting for the opportune moment when no other nurse is hovering over her. He is decked out in full hospital scrubs and can be mistaken for either a nurse or a doctor. The room is a busy place, and you need your security pass to access it, therefore no one questions anyone extra in the room.

Her breathing hitches as he reaches out and takes her hand, leaning down to talk quietly to her. He's just talking and then another nurse walks past. He straightens a little, and that is when his face comes into full view of the camera. She sees it straight away. Her body goes stiff, and her breathing is quickening to a concerning speed.

She hits pause on the screen while she just stares.

"Breathe, baby, breathe for me. Slow it down… in and hold… out slowly… in and hold … breathe out slowly."

"It can't—" Her hand is hovering over the stilled picture.

"I think it is," I reply, pulling her tighter into my side. As much as I want to say it's not, she knew the instant his eyes were in the shot. Normally this would be one of the happiest days of her life, but instead, it's the continuation of a nightmare.

"Dad… I wasn't dreaming." She chokes on her own words. She has no idea how to process what is happening.

"I wish you were." I didn't mean to say it, but the truth falls from my lips.

Her head spins to look at me. "But he's alive…" She can't seem to finish any sentence she starts, which I'm hoping is just from shock and not her brain struggling. "There must be a reason… maybe he's hiding like me?" She is hoping for a miracle answer.

"Yes, perhaps, but why now and why in secret? It doesn't add up, Cassie. He can't be here for any good reason. Surely you understand that." And finally, the tears escape as reality sinks in for her. We have so much ground to cover, but letting it out will help her to digest the shock of learning that her father is alive, and he has come back to hurt her. If it was my family, it would have been so much easier to cope with, because I would have expected it. But from all the stories she's told me, they were the perfect loving family, her mom staying home to care for Cassie and her dad traveling across the country visiting hospitals and doctors with new products in his work as a rep for a pharmaceutical company. When you are a child, you don't always ask too many questions. My guess is whatever he was doing was not anything legal like her mom would have thought her husband was doing. It's just not fair how much Cassie has had to go through in this life. For all the things she has suffered through and the strength she has used to push through the pain of loss and fear. But nothing will compare to the betrayal she is struggling with now.

"I need proof. He's my dad, he wouldn't hurt me…" Listening to the pain in her voice is so hard.

I hate to do this, but it's the only way she will understand. Pressing the play button for the video to continue, we see him reach into his pocket and pull out a needle with fluid in it, holding her hand with the catheter in his other hand. From the angle of the camera, we can't see what happens next, before he gets interrupted by the other nurses coming over to Cassie's bed and talking. They are checking on her and looking concerned, trying to wake her. He slips the needle back in his pocket and leaves the room. I don't know what was in the needle, but part of me is wondering if it somehow has anything to do with her having trouble waking up. Did he manage to get to inject something into her IV? I'm going crazy just thinking about this, but I need to keep my focus on Cassie right now. She needs me.

Looking up at me, the devastation is all over her face. Every memory she has of her father has just been dirtied by the video.

"But they found parts of his body."

"I don't know what happened, but my guess is that what they

found wasn't him. It was a staged disappearance, and sadly, I'm guessing your mother was murdered. I hope I'm wrong, but I rarely am. I don't think the explosion was an accident." I can't be anything but honest with her now. Her life is on the line, and we need to work together to keep her safe.

"But why? My mom… she didn't deserve…"

"No, baby, she didn't. I never met her, but if she was anything like you, then I know she was amazing," I say, running my hand over the back of her head, still so gently in case it's tender.

"I promise I will get to the bottom of this, Cassie. For you and for your mom. If he did this, he'll pay for it."

I honestly didn't know what to expect from Cassie, if there would be screaming or tears. I'm sure the anger will come later.

"How did you know it was him?" Cassie's mind is racing.

"The eyes, it was like seeing your eyes in front of me, just older, but you get your eyes from him. We still can't be a hundred percent sure, but your reaction just confirmed what I suspected. I know it's hard, but I need you to think back to what he said when you thought it was a dream. It's all we've got right now."

The lines across her forehead deepen, and I know she is digging back into her subconscious and trying her hardest to pull the memory forward. Her telling me about the dream was the other thing that told me that the man at her bedside was her father. It's just too coincidental.

Thoughts of my two children are in my head.

How could you ever do anything to hurt someone that you brought into this world?

I never contemplated children before I had Bessy, but my life changed in an instant when she entered the world. The love you have for them is like no other, and I would lay down my life for them, not want to end theirs instead.

How can someone be that evil?

CASSIE

There has to be a mistake. My dad would never do this. He loved my mom and me. Our lives were perfect. Nothing bad ever happened, and it was always calm. Nothing like Ghost's family. We laughed together, spent so much time doing fun things when Dad wasn't away. Now I can't even remember how long his trips were. What was he doing when he was gone? Did my mom know where he was? What did he tell her?

The pain in my head is getting intense now, and I know it's not from the tumor this time. It's the emotion of finding out that my whole life has been some kind of lie. I thought it hurt finding out about Jason, but it was nothing compared to this.

What is wrong with me? Why do I have people all around me who kept their true lives hidden from me.

"I have so many questions." I know Ghost doesn't have the answers, but I need them. I'm going to find them out. My dad doesn't get to play with my life and not tell me why. My anger is rising, and I can cope with that. The shock and disillusionment aren't helpful to me now. I can deal with this later, but right now, I need to be strong. Stronger than I have ever been before. I don't know where I'll pull that strength from, but I'm digging deep and it will come, I don't have any other choice.

"Me too. Let's start with what you remember." Ghost is being patient with me, but I can tell he needs to get as much from me as he can quickly, so they know what they're dealing with.

"It seemed so real at the time; at least I know I wasn't imagining it. I thought he was an angel and that I was dying. Because he told me I needed not to ask questions, to trust him when he comes for me. Shit, he said he'll be back so we can be together for the last time. He's going to try to kill me, isn't he?" I feel the blood draining from my body.

"Not happening. As long as I'm still breathing, I will protect you!" From the force in his voice, I know he's angry. I understand why but hate that once again something in my life is putting him in danger. It's like I'm a magnet for darkness that Ghost is always trying to clean up while protecting me. I don't know what the mess is this time, but I'm grateful I have my husband here by my side. The truth is, he's never by my side, he is always in front of me, using his body as my shield. It's something I'll never be able to change about him.

But that's what love is, accepting the person as they are and loving them that way.

Looking into Ghost's eyes, I place my hand on his cheek. "You have a plan, don't you." It's not a question, it's a statement, because I know that before he told me any of this, he would be working out his action plan.

"Yes. But I need your help, and it's going to involve being the strongest you have ever been in your life. I wouldn't ask this of you if I thought there was a better way." This is tearing him up on the inside. I can see straight through him when he's trying to protect me. He can do it with no emotion for so many other people, but when it's me, it is so much more difficult for him to put the walls up on his feelings. If I'm his greatest weakness, then I also need to be his greatest strength.

"I can do that for you," I say, trying to sound more confident than I am.

"I know you can. I believe in you." Ghost is struggling. We need to get past the emotion and onto the plan going forward. The rest of the emotional baggage from my father, his reappearance and what actually happened to my mother, we will deal with once we're home, where he can rest and know that we're safe.

"Start talking, Ghost, I'm guessing we are running out of time."

"Hey, who's the boss here?" He tenderly taps me on the end of the nose with his finger. That's what we need, humor to take away the fear. That's the way we have always gotten through this in the past.

"Always you," I say, rolling my eyes at him.

"When it comes to your safety, damn straight I am. The rest is debatable." I don't have it in me to laugh out loud but smile at him to let him know he is spot-on.

Taking a deep breath, he starts outlining his plan, and my

stomach sinks when he tells me he wants to lure my father into my room so he can take him on his own and work out how this all relates to Jason.

That's the biggest mind fuck that I can't get my head around. My father being connected to Jason and everything he's mixed up in. The man who has done vile things in his life. Is that what my father is connected to as well? I swallow thickly, pushing the nausea down. I feel dirty all over. Do I carry the genes of man who has sold his soul to the devil? My worst nightmare is to be connected to this in some way. It was bad enough that I was so naive and loved a man who sold out his country, and now my own father has more than likely done the same things.

"Are you okay with this, Cassie? Because if you say no, then I will find another way. There's always another way."

I thought I saw fear in Ghost's eyes before my operation, but watching him now as he's waiting for my answer, this time it's fear mixed with anger and determination. I need to take the fear away, he doesn't have time to be battling that too.

Be his strength.

"He needs to pay, and for my mother, I'm going to make it happen."

The relief on his face is all I'm focusing on, trying to keep at bay the thoughts that keep creeping in. *But what if my dad is innocent?*

The only way I will ever know is to see him and risk my life. But it will be worth it to know the truth. I can't live with this hole in my heart that he has now created.

Come to me, Dad, like you promised, but I'm not your little girl anymore. I'm a wife and mother with a whole world to fight for.

You said you will be back for our final time together, and I'm sure Ghost will guarantee it's our last reunion.

You have no idea who you are taking on, Dad!

Chapter Twenty-Four

CASSIE

It feels like a lifetime ago that each day was a simple one. What I wouldn't give to be back in that life and not here surrounded by danger at every turn.

Trying to calm my mind, I picture waking up to Eli with the cutest little smile. He's never impatient for his bottle and loves to snuggle after he's fed. I remember the smell of him, my nose twitching at the thought of it. It's just the innocence of a baby that the world's evil hasn't touched yet. He would then sit happily in his rocker while I get Bessy, my little whirlwind, up and ready for the day. Bessy and I would eat, play, read, learn, and share love in the hours they are both awake. Then enjoying a meal with Ghost, talking, appreciating the view both outside and inside the house. On a warm night, him with no shirt and a pair of shorts sitting low on his waist, or the cool nights with the gray sweatpants he knows I love. Both make me long to touch him. The night finishes with all the love that Ghost and I have bottled up during the day and couldn't let escape in front of the kids. That is our beautiful simple life.

But instead, I'm watching Ghost across from me, locked in total concentration on two computers. He's set up on the small hospital rolling table, standing from nervous energy, and his fingers are moving like crazy. His headset is on and he's talking to Ashton and his team.

We spent the last two hours talking about everything I could think of that might be important about my dad. Tate was in to check on me and talk to both of us. He's on board to help but voiced his concerns to Ghost about the stress on my body. I'm not letting him put all that responsibility on Ghost, like he is the one putting me in danger. I make my own decisions in this life. Standing up out of my bed, much to the dismay of both of them, with my hands on my hips, I made sure they both understood that I'm in control of my life. They just need to do their jobs and leave me to do mine.

All the words they both came out with about why I need to take it easy fell on my closed-off ears. Once they finished, I stared them both down, and I saw the one time Ghost had smiled since he told me about my father. He said the words I have heard before, but they still make me smile. "I knew you would be trouble the moment I saw you."

My reply let him know what he needs to remember. "Ah yes, but I'm your trouble."

Not caring Tate was in the room, Ghost wrapped me in his arms and kissed the hell out of me.

The darkness outside the window tells me it's later than Ghost realizes. I roll onto my side to get comfortable watching him.

"You need some sleep," he says, his voice floating across the room at me. He senses my exhaustion before I do. Pulling his headset off, he looks at me and waits.

"Bossy much?" I retort, even though I know he's right. My mind is strong, but my body is letting me down.

"And you love it." His words have a hint of naughtiness behind them, but I can't go there at the moment. As much as I want to, and boy do I want to, I just can't.

"I love you." My eyelids feel heavy, and I know to get through tomorrow I need rest.

Moving toward me, Ghost places a tender kiss on my lips. My eyes fall shut, and the long slow kiss on my forehead as he repeats that he loves me too is all I need to let sleep claim me.

GHOST

"We are go for movement of laundry cargo." Ashton's voice booms into my ear through my earpiece. "And Diamond is still solo." When I needed a code name for Cassie, Diamond seemed the perfect one —the strongest jewel in the world. Put her under pressure and she sparkles with brilliance.

My breathing is fast, and the heat in this laundry basket is extreme, but it was the only way we could make the switch, creating the illusion that I have left Cassie on her own.

Tate marked in the patient records computer system that Cassie is scheduled to leave the hospital later today, which I think will trigger her father to try one last time to get to her, before she disappears again. But we needed to give him the opportunity to think she was on her own. I left the room, and Susan, who is working my normal role on the computers, is keeping eyes on Cassie through the camera, reporting to Ashton while we do the switch, and Badger takes me back into the room in a laundry cart undetected. He wheels the cart into the bathroom so I can get out and stay in there undetected, then he returns to Cassie in the room. He will stay for a short time and then leave again, leaving me safely tucked into the bathroom in her room, with eyes on Cassie via my laptop.

I don't think it will take long for Frank to strike.

We have multiple eyes on all cameras in the hospital, waiting to pick Frank up when he is on the move. Badger and Ashton are close, so as soon as he enters the room, they will move in on my signal. We have bugged the room, and Cassie insisted we give her time to try to get the truth out of him about what the hell he is doing and the background of how he got here. I told her she has five minutes tops to get him started with anything useful, but if at any time I'm

318

concerned, I'll be in that room with my pistol, with the silencer attached, and he will be dead before he can touch her. No questions asked. She needs to know I will kill him, even if she hates me for the rest of her life. Because at least she will still have a life, and that's all I care about.

Setting myself up with the laptop and my earpiece, I can hear Badger and Cassie talking in her room, which lets me know the audio is working. Even if Cassie's dad, Frank, and the team he has put together with Jason, has hacked the hospital feed, they don't know our private feeds exist inside this room, so they can't interrupt the video and audio I'm getting. They may be good, but I'm fucking better.

Sitting listening to Badger and my girl is giving me an insight into a man that has always been a mystery to all of us.

"You can still say no to this, Cassie. You say the word and I don't leave this room!" The rasp in his voice tells me that I'm not the only one that has become attached to Cassie. "Don't do it for Ghost."

I want to storm out there and tell him that I never pressured her to do anything, but Cassie is answering before I can move. Plus, I can't risk leaving this bathroom, otherwise all the strategic planning will be a waste and our opportunity gone.

"Badger, you have known me long enough to know I don't do anything I don't want to. And I would hope you know Ghost well enough to know that he would never force me to do anything." Once again, she is putting one of my team in their place with her words.

"I had to ask. I care. You, my girl, have gotten under this tough skin." It's the first time I have heard this kind of emotion from Badger, and it makes me nervous. He is normally stone cold in these operations, and I need that today. I'm relying on it.

"Oh, Badger, I love you like a big brother, especially in your cute hospital uniform. I just wish you would let more people under that tough skin. You deserve happiness, and when this is all over, we are talking. Don't roll your eyes at me. You can't avoid me, I don't give up easily."

Ain't that the truth. I'm trying not to laugh at my wife. Poor

Badger. If she sets her sights on him, he has no chance. I'm guessing Bull is thinking the same when his voice in my ear adds, "God help the poor man when Cassie and Asha join forces." Asha is now looking after the kids, and Bull is in my bunker watching and listening, as well as keeping an eye on my kids on the house surveillance feed. He couldn't stand not being involved and seeing for himself that we're safe.

"We'll see about that," Badger tells her with a little chuckle, telling me that he is shutting down this conversation, knowing we're all listening. "Now it's time to leave you. You okay?" he asks, one last check before she's on her own.

"Don't think that I'll drop this conversation, Badger." I know Cassie is using this to distract herself from the fear she must be feeling. "But yes, get out of here, I'm fine. I could do with some time without all the testosterone in the room. You boys are always so intense." On my laptop, I see her smile up at Badger as he leans down and kisses her on the cheek.

I'm thankful for the friends I have when I hear his faint whisper, "You're safe, we've got you both." With that, Badger stands and pushes his laundry trolley out of the room, looking like it has dirty sheets hanging out from the top of it.

"Game on," I tell my team now that Badger has left the room, and there is no turning back. I desperately want this man. I've spent all last night backtracking on the dark web, to the time before Frank's supposed death. There I found what I suspect may be evidence that he has been a double agent with overseas organizations, trading government secrets. For all the hatred I have toward Jason, it has doubled overnight for Frank. I think Jason is a pawn in the whole scheme that Frank is one of the heads of. Which could have been the reason that led to him faking his own death at the time, then going underground, for whatever reason. And Beatrice was just collateral damage. Who does that to the woman they love?

My skin is burning, and I know that means he's close. I used to hate this sixth sense I have, but today, I'm reveling in the warning system that tells me we are getting nearer to ending this.

Cassie is moving her hands constantly with nervous energy. I know she thinks she has this under control, but the moment her father steps into this room, it will be a different story. No matter how thick a wall you put up to protect your heart, when the man you have loved all your life and who you thought was dead is standing in front of you alive, nothing is going to stop the feeling of shock. That has to be a brain explosion for anyone, no matter how tough you are.

"I'm scared on my own," she whispers, knowing I can hear her.

Oh, baby, I know, and I can't say anything to her, but just tapping lightly on the wall is enough.

"Thank you." I can see the water in her eyes, but she knows I'm as close as I can be, only a thin wall between us.

"Storm moving, in stairwell three." Ashton's signal tells us Frank is here and heading for Cassie. My heart is beating at an unhealthy rate. I knew he would come. He was right when he told Cassie in recovery that this would be the final time he would see her, because I will make sure of that. Either by putting him behind bars until his dying days or a bullet in his head, and I don't care which one it is.

I promised Cassie I would warn her before he stepped into the room. I tap the code we decided on, three taps on the wall that mean I love you. Hearing it, I see her whole body go rock solid with fear and tension.

"Eyes on him, entering the corridor." Badger's roughness brings me the reassurance I need. They have him, and no matter what happens in here to me, Cassie is not on her own. They will keep her safe.

Watching the feed, I see him standing at her door, listening and looking around him. When he feels confident, he slowly opens it and sees what looks like a sleeping Cassie. Smart move, beautiful, bring him right into the room before there is any interaction between you. Give yourself time to adjust to him being near you.

Looking around the room, he gets his bearings after he locks the door. We knew he would do that, and the team got the key from Tate, which means nothing will stop them from following him in when I give them the word. Pulling his hospital mask and hat off, I see his full face for the first time, and it's the final puzzle piece we needed. The man standing next to Cassie is her father, Frank Templeton. Of course, if that is even his real name, but it's the one we know him as, and as my stomach rolls, I realize this man is actually my father-in-law.

Watching him moving toward the bathroom door to check that it's empty, panic is racing inside me. But I should trust my wife, she knows what she's doing, distracting him before he reaches me.

Making a noise, she stretches and opens her eyes, looking at him. It stops him in his tracks as they both freeze, looking at each other.

"Daddy?" The pain in her voice is that of a little girl who lost the man she ran to when she needed to feel safe. I watch her grieving for a man she thought she knew, only to find out it was all a lie.

Tears are running down her face, and I knew she would be overwhelmed, because how could she not be? My gun is in my hand hanging by my side; I'm ready to end this pain for her.

"Leah." What I wasn't expecting is the emotion in his voice hearing him say her real name. As someone who did what he has done to his family and who is here to end his daughter's life, he doesn't get the right to feel anything.

Hearing him use her birth name is enough to pull it back for Cassie. That name brings her nothing but hurt now. Seeing her body language change, I know she is pushing her feelings aside and bringing out her inner warrior.

"I don't understand. You were dead." Her voice is flat, and her tears stop. Her father is still just standing in the one spot, trying to regain his own balance being so close to her when she is actually awake and seeing him for the first time.

"It was an accident," he finally manages to get out.

"What was the accident, you not dying but mom being killed? Or an accident that you didn't tell me for all these years that you were alive. What the fuck is going on, Dad?" There's my girl. The spitfire's back and she is after blood.

"Don't you swear at your father," he says sternly, starting to step toward her, but Cassie's hand is up and stopping him.

"Don't you dare touch me. You gave up that right the minute you disappeared and shattered my world. You don't get to show up now and expect me to run into your arms." Cassie's voice is getting louder, yelling at him as her anger starts to build. Her fists are clenched, and the look on Frank's face is also changing. His tenderness for the daughter he lost so many years ago is fading and the cold-hearted killer is coming back.

My finger is rubbing back and forth on the trigger of my gun. I can hear the small amount of chatter from my team in my ear. Ashton and Badger are outside the room, the key is already in the door, and with Cassie now yelling, it gave them a chance to unlock the door without Frank hearing the click. They are ready to move once I give them the signal.

"You don't understand, Leah." Frank's words are stern, like I would expect from a father scolding a child.

"Then start explaining. Like about how you killed my mother like she meant nothing, while you slide into your filthy underworld of crime and espionage. Selling government secrets to the highest bidder, while selling your soul to the devil. Yes, please, feel free to tell me how I don't understand." She sits upright in her bed and stares him down. I hate that she is in a vulnerable position in that bed, but she is safer there. All the rushing adrenaline could make her brain overload and her body give out on her, and we can't risk that.

"Oh, your little boyfriend has finally worked it out, has he. It took him long enough to discover all the things I have done in my life." Instead of killing him, I want to go in there and punch the hell out of him right now. "You always were so gullible. Do you believe everything from the man who has kidnapped you and hid you away from the world for seven years? If he was any kind of agent, he would have worked it out in the beginning. But maybe he did and just hid it all from you, so he could have you as his slave. Maybe I should have given him more credit than I have been." I see the moment of doubt on her face, but it's gone in a split second.

"Don't you dare speak about him. This is about you and me,

Dad, and your world of lies. Are you even really my father or was that a lie too?"

I can see her strength getting to Frank. He wasn't expecting the pushback, which tells me he never really knew his daughter at all, because she is all about the pushback when she wants.

"Of course I'm your father. It was one of the only good things I did in this life," he growls at her insult of questioning him. "How do you think I found you? I have had a tracking computer program alert on your DNA showing up in any medical system since you disappeared. The same DNA as mine, because you belong to me! I knew eventually you would have to show up somewhere. Your man thought he was smart, but I had the secret weapon, my blood. No change of name or location was going to keep you from me."

Everything that I'm thinking in my head, Cassie is answering for me.

"I don't belong to anyone, unless I choose to. And I don't choose you. There is one man in my life I give my heart to, and he doesn't need to demand it. Just because your blood pumps through my veins, that doesn't give you any hold over me." Hearing her take a breath, she delivers the final blow.

"His love is all I need, but what about you? Something I question now, did I ever have that love from you, or was that a lie too?"

Having her anger directed at him is getting him agitated, and he can't stand still now. Starting to pace the room is not a good sign. The more people get charged up, the greater the risk of them doing something irrational.

"You're just like your mother—a drama queen. If she had just done as she was told, then she might still be alive, living in the suburbs like she wanted. Instead, she overheard something she shouldn't have, and she just didn't let it go. The story I told her should have been enough, but no, she had to start digging, and I couldn't let that happen. I took her out on that boat to convince her that if she just shut her mouth, you both would be safe. Life could just go on as normal. She yelled and screamed and carried on like the world was going to end. Lashing out at me was her biggest mistake. When I pushed her away from me, she slipped and hit her head on the side of the boat. So, you see, I didn't kill her, she did it to herself, and you might have lost your mother, but I lost my wife." There's a hitch in his voice, and the way he closes his eyes for a brief second tells me he did love his wife, but just not like I love mine. He might think that was love, but it's not even close.

Cassie gulps, struggling to hear about her mother's death, but she fights on.

"No, you killed her! You don't get to have a clear conscience. If it weren't for your criminal activity, she wouldn't have been out on that boat! I'm sure she was worried about finding out her husband was selling secrets that was leading to the deaths of innocent people. Maybe putting American servicemen and women at risk. Who even are you? You may be here in the body of my dad, but the father I thought I grew up with, he will forever be dead to me. You are no longer my father, now get out!" She has had enough, but I know she is also trying to provoke him to say why he's here.

"Not so fast, Leah. You think you have this all worked out, but I tried to keep your mother safe and to get her to come with me, taking you with us. Why do you think I'm here now? I can take you into another life with me, I can show you the world like all the stories I told you. You would work for me, but we would be happy, I can assure you."

"You are delusional if you think I would willingly leave this room with you, like a *good* daughter. All I see in front of me is pure evil. I can't even imagine how you could think I would consider such a crazy idea." There is a look of confusion on her face.

"You want to tell me what an evil man I am, Leah, well, let me reassure you how right you are. I didn't just come here to have some long-lost sappy reunion. You will be leaving this room with me, either unconscious so I can take you away without a fuss… or sleeping so soundly you will never wake up. It's your fault I'm here. Just like your mother, you couldn't keep things to yourself. Why didn't you just talk to Jason instead of running to the FBI, you stupid little bitch."

I can see the shock of him admitting he is here to either abduct her or kill her has her rattled, but it is the use of the word bitch from her father in reference to her that is the last nail in his coffin. Cassie looks like she is about to get up and punch him herself.

"How do you know about Jason?" That's it, baby, reel him in.

"Oh, I thought you were smarter than this, or at least your pathetic WITSEC agent would have been. I was the one who made sure you ended up as his girlfriend. The respectable Senator Jason Condell to look after my innocent little girl. I may have disappeared, but I always knew where you were. It was the perfect way to keep you close and Jason doing what I needed. He was getting all the information that I needed through his security access to the defense department, and it proved to be very lucrative for me. But you wrecked that, didn't you. Why couldn't you just be the little compliant future wife of a senator? I could have kept you safe."

And that is the word that triggers my wife's explosion.

"Safe! I don't think I was safe with you from the day I was born. And fucking Jason! He was selling women and children. As a man with a daughter you supposedly loved, how could you let that happen? What part of being safe was making sure I was living with a sex trafficker? You really are the devil."

"Standby," I say into the mic, putting my team on notice. We have enough information now to finish all of them, and I'm not leaving Cassie in danger for a moment longer than I need to. And that includes from being so upset that her body will be pushed over the edge. A brain bleed is still a possibility at this stage.

"That was all Jason's money-making business idea. As long as he got me the information I needed, I gave him the contacts he required to trade his women. Powerful men need compliant women, Leah. That's why you never would have been enough for Jason. You expect choices in your life that you aren't entitled to. You are just a woman."

That's it. I'm done waiting. Nobody speaks to my wife like that.

I push open the door, gun raised. My team knows I'm in the room, and any moment when I say the word, they will be in here too. But first, I need a moment just me and him.

"That's where you're wrong. A woman is someone a man should treasure. And before I put a bullet in your head, know that this woman in front of you, my wife, is the strongest and most precious woman of all." His hands twitch ever so slightly, telling me he's going for a weapon. I can't look at Cassie. I need to keep my laser focus.

"Don't even think about reaching behind you. Keep your hands in front. Because I can assure you, I never miss. Your hands won't even make it to your weapon before you are bleeding out on the floor."

"Oh, the big tough boyfriend is here. You think you can protect her forever. I found you once, I'll do it again." Frank's cold look tells me he could easily kill Cassie without feeling a thing.

"I'm her husband," I grit between my teeth. "And not if you're dead. You won't be alive to look for anything."

"You won't kill me. That would hurt her too much. I'm the daddy she loved all her life. She might be angry now, but if you kill me, then it will always be something that will sit between you and niggle away at her. You won't pull the trigger…"

The door slams open and hits the wall with force, and Cassie screams in fright, but I can't turn, keeping my eyes on Frank the whole time, trusting my team that they're watching her.

"He won't have to, because I will, and I'll be smiling while I do it, asshole!" Badger growls at him, gun raised, and the red laser dot of his gun scope sits right between Frank's eyes. Ashton moves behind Frank, grabbing the pistol that was hidden under his scrubs. Not believing it's his only gun, Ashton then whips out a pair of cuffs from his pants pocket and secures Frank's hands behind his back, before he even has time to respond.

"This is a big mistake. You just put a bigger bullseye on you wife. You think I'm the only one here?" This is where he has messed up. Trying to use his words against me is never going to work.

"You wish you had eyes on you in this hospital, backup ready to respond and help you, and there may be someone on a computer, but they aren't here with you. See, the biggest mistake you made was thinking you could do this on your own. Being a lone wolf isn't smart. Every wolf needs a pack, and you are looking at mine, including my wife who is the strongest one." Finally feeling like I can lower my gun now that he's contained, I move to Cassie and pull her tightly into my side while I stand next to her bed.

Through my earpiece, I hear the best piece of news, and my grin widens. "So, surprise, Frank, you actually aren't here alone. The FBI are on their way upstairs now, and the person you had on the computer feed is already in custody. Because as smart as you thought you were…" I look around the room and straight at the camera that is feeding everything to my team who aren't here, and I feel the swell of pride for the friends I have surrounding me and my family. "We as a team… we are smarter."

"Abso-fucking-lutely!" Bull yells in my ear.

I shake my head at Frank. "You think seven years didn't give me time to collect what I needed? You were just the last piece of the puzzle, and stupidly you put yourself in this position to finish my picture for me."

The whole time I'm speaking, I can hear Susan feeding me what she's seeing on the computer images from all over the country.

"As we stand here saying goodbye *for the final time*, as you put it, there are raids happening in several homes, places of businesses, and government offices across the country. Yes, including Jason's, who is currently squealing like a pig about his innocence, dumping you right in the thick of it. I'm sure tomorrow's papers will be telling an interesting story, featuring both you and Jason as the stars. So, say goodbye to your daughter who won't be visiting you while you rot in jail. You will be wishing you did die that day on the boat. We all know what the inmates think of men who hurt children." I can see he still thinks he is getting out of this, but that won't be happening. I'll make sure of it, even if I need to make sure that there is an "accident" behind bars to finish it once and for all.

"Rocket is on his way up with Agent Lester and his officers," Ashton tells me, as he was the only one who has the feed from the FBI in his ear. We need to keep focused and didn't need any unnecessary chatter distracting us. It took a while, but I learned that Rocket was on our side, and I could trust him. So, when it was time to set all this in motion, I knew I wanted him as part of my team, to bring closure to something that has haunted us all these years, not being able to nail Jason.

"Did you ever love me?" The desperate question comes from Cassie, and the coldness in her father softens for a moment. Her tears aren't loud sobs but a pain that she can't contain.

"You won't believe me, but still to this day, I love both you and your mother. That will never change." And as much as I don't think he understands what true love is, in his own way he thinks he loved them. Feeling her body sag further into mine, I know it's enough for her to take to her grave, that although it won't be a love she wants, that she wasn't living a complete lie from the day she was born.

"Is this where the party is?" Rocket's voice coming through the door brings me a sense of relief. Because behind him are so many men in bulletproof vests and armed enough to take out every person in this hospital. Nothing like being inconspicuous.

"Yeah, but it's time to shut it down. I think the room occupants would like some quiet time." Badger is always the father of our team. He knows what we need before we do.

There was a lot of congestion, and after reading Frank his rights and starting to lead him away, the real pain that Cassie has been holding in is finally released.

Her hands are clawing at my skin like she can't breathe, and the noises coming from her are like she has a wound that is more painful than anything she has ever felt in her life. Not caring what is happening around me, I push her down onto the bed and climb onto it with her. Wrapping her as tightly as I can into my body, I whisper to her over and over again, "I love you and you're safe." It's all I can think at the moment, while I finally allow myself to let everything that has happened sink in too.

The room is quiet around us, and I hear Susan's voice in my ear telling me that the audio and video from this room's feed are now off. We are alone except for one other person.

The only voice I hear above Cassie's crying is Tate.

"I'm sedating her, she needs to rest. It's the kindest thing we can do for her now."

"Okay," I reply.

Slowly the crying stops, the room goes deadly silent, and my wife falls asleep in my arms.

Tomorrow we will deal with this, but for now, we just finally need to breathe.

Chapter Twenty-Five

CASSIE

I t's been a few days since everything went down at the hospital. Not that I was awake for the twenty-four hours afterwards. The sedation took a while to work its way out of my system. In a way, it was a blessing, because the emotional pain in my body was bad enough with the drugs; without them, it would have been horrendous.

Before I woke from the initial sedation, Ghost and Tate had me moved to another room that looked different and faced another direction, so what I was seeing out the window was all new. They didn't want me in the room where I last saw my father. The memories of all the words that were said is hard enough.

Today, we are finally leaving the hospital and spending a few days back at Ashton's spare apartment. I want to go home to my kids, but Tate and Ghost are both being bossy, insisting that with everything that has happened, the extra stress on my body, I must stay close by for just a little longer. I know it's the right thing, but I want to be in my own bed, with Bessy and Eli curled up between Ghost and me, Ace and Bandit on the end of the bed, with the rest of the world shut out until I'm ready to see it again. Which might not be for a while.

All the reports that were leaked to the media, from Ghost and the FBI, listed that Leah Templeton died from a brain tumor in the hospital after her father had been arrested trying to murder her. They found another syringe in his pants pocket that had enough drugs in it to kill an elephant. Thank God he never got the chance to get anywhere near me with it. Tate signed the fake death certificate, and it's been filed with all the government agencies. Because if Leah is dead, then she can't testify in any court cases, so only the written testimonies of everything I knew will be admitted to the trial. Ghost is also watching the dark web for any alerts on the hits ordered to kill me that are still out there floating around. Once he is happy things have disappeared, life might be able to move forward like we always dreamed. I'm in no rush.

It's a funny feeling reading about your own death, although to me, Leah died seven years ago, and I don't want any part of that life again. The only good part of my past, I keep in my heart, the memories of my mother. And every time I say Bessy's name, I will always smile thinking of her. There are so many stories I can't wait to share with the kids as they grow up, about a grandma that they will never get to meet, but I'll make sure they know her.

"You ready?" Ghost slips his hand into mine. I've been sitting in the recliner chair in the room the last few days getting used to being out of bed and moving around. I'm regaining my balance and confidence in walking and just being a normal human being.

"More than ready. Break me out of this place," I say, standing and kissing him on the cheek.

"You better not be thinking of leaving without saying goodbye to the best surgeon in the world." Tate walks in with the biggest smile on his face.

Ghost drops my hand and turns to greet him. "You really do need an ego check, don't you." Ghost laughs as he takes Tate in a bro hug. Something wordless is being said between them that I can't hear, and Tate just gives him a chin lift as they pull back from each other.

"Does the patient get a hug too or is this just a bromance moment?" I tease, standing and waiting for them to look at me.

"That's why I'm here." Tate opens his arms out for me.

"Do all your patients get this sort of personal treatment? Or do they get the super-professional Doctor McIntyre, if he even exists?" I ask as I walk into his arms like a long-lost friend.

"Oh, he exists, just ask my interns. They will confirm I can be a grumpy asshole like the best of them. And yes, you are right, most of the time I try to keep my distance from my patients. It just gets too hard, because sadly, sometimes I can't save them. But you, little lady, are such a fighter, someone special." I hear his heart beating strongly in his chest, and I know he has a soft side that he doesn't let out very often.

"You are one of the strongest women I know, Cassie. I'm always here if you ever need me."

I'm trying not to cry on his doctor's coat, even though they would be happy tears this time. "Don't take this the wrong way, but I don't want to be your patient ever again." Laughter breaks out from all of us as he releases me, and my overly protective, alpha husband pulls me closer to him. Not that Tate is any threat, you only have to see the way he looks at his wife. That man is totally off the market. Bella has him wrapped up nicely in their little love bubble. She has popped in a few times over the last few days just to sit and chat. It's been nice to have another woman to talk to, besides Asha.

"But I would still love to be your friend, both of us would," I say. We could use some friends to help us transition back into the real world once it's time.

"Like you even have to ask. Wait until you meet the rest of our crazy *framily*, you might regret that request."

"Your what?" Ghost asks, looking confused at the word, like Tate has mispronounced it.

"Oh, that's a story for another time. I'll let Daisy explain it when you meet her. It's how the brain of a seven-year-old works. By the sounds of what you have told me about Bessy, the two of them will be perfect together." Tate steps away to give us the space to finally leave this room.

Imagining Bessy with little friends to play with is something I didn't ever let my mind wander to, but hopefully, that time is getting closer now.

"I'll talk to you tomorrow. Now get out of here, we need this bed," Tate says, waving us out of the room.

Ghost picks up his backpack with everything he needs in it, especially if the world is about to end. Putting it on his back and then picking up my bag, he takes my hand in his free one. Kissing me on the lips, we start for the doorway like we are heading into a whole new world, and in a way, we are.

———

Settled back in Ashton's apartment, it feels like a home away from home. There is just a special vibe in this place.

"I often wonder what their story is," I say, lying on Ghost's lap on the couch.

"Whose story?" he asks, his fingers running through my hair softly and caressing my scalp. It feels so divine. Tate took out the stitches before I left, as everything was healing well.

"Badger and Ashton, who did you think I meant?" I look up at his stupid grin.

"Oh, I knew who you meant, I just wanted to check. You aren't going to let this go, are you?" His laughter makes my head bounce a little with the movement of his body.

"But don't you ever wonder why Badger is on his own after all these years? He's a big softie and has a lot of love to give under that hard-ass exterior. And Ashton, there is some story with him. Why doesn't he have a code name like the rest of you? How is such a good-looking man still single?"

"Okay, hold up, good-looking man? You been checking out my partner?" The softness in his body has changed, and I can feel the jealous tension stiffening his muscles.

"Steady there, big boy. You can't deny that all the men surrounding you are hot." The lines on his forehead are getting tighter and his lips pulling into a straight line. "They just aren't as hot as you. You make me sizzle." I try to hold it in, but I can't. I laugh at how annoyed he looks at the thought of me thinking about his team.

"You think it's funny to be telling me that? Seriously, Cassie, do you even understand me?"

Better than you think, Ghost. I know I need to calm the savage beast in the best way possible, reassure him that the only man in my life is the one right here with me. The one who has been here the whole time, and I know that no matter what happens, he'll never leave. The man who rocks my world in a way that no other man has.

"I understand you perfectly." Rolling onto my side, I face him and push up onto my hand so my head is level with his. "In the way that if I push you enough, I know that growly protective caveman might just take me to bed and throw caution to the wind with me." I can see the strain on him, trying to hold back.

"Cassie, you know my rules," he growls at me. His head might be telling him what he thinks is the right thing to do, but his body is totally on board with my plans. Looking down into his lap, I can see his cock pushing against his zipper, and his breathing is getting heavier.

I look back up into his eyes that are on fire.

"Don't look at me like that." The huskiness in his voice tells me he is holding on by a thread.

"Like what?" I stare into his soul, and with my look, I'm letting him see what I want—no, what I *need*.

"Like you want me to fuck you all the way through to tomorrow." I lick up his neck until my mouth is at his ear. "Cassie," he lets out on a strangled moan. "We should wait." He grabs the back of my head, my hair tangled in his fingers, and the slight pain is like heaven to my body.

"I'm done waiting. I need you," I purr, kissing just below his ear in that spot that always makes me shiver, hoping it's giving him the same sensation. "To make me feel, to show me I'm alive."

Pulling my head back fast, his lips slam into mine. Our tongues enter into a war for dominance with each other. He drags me up the couch with his strong arms and into his lap as we continue feasting on each other. Noah has me exactly where he wants me.

He angles my head so he can show me who's in charge—something I'm happy to do, giving up any control.

I don't want to be strong tonight, I just want to be loved!

Pulling back slightly, I need him to know it's okay. "Tate said we could." My heavy breathing is all I can hear. As soon as he touches me, I'm not sure I will be able to last.

"I don't need permission from another man to make love to my wife!" In my head I'm laughing, but the possessiveness has me squeezing my thighs tightly together. I don't know why but his dominance over me when we're like this is like liquid lust being pumped through my veins.

"Then what's holding you back?" I push my ass down a little harder on his cock that I can feel getting stiffer the more I move.

"Because I need to be gentle with you, and I'm not sure I'm capable of that right now!" He's at the end of his restraint, I can tell.

"I don't want gentle, Noah. I want your cock buried so fucking hard and deep inside me until there is nothing between us. Don't treat me like I'm fragile." I take a breath as I tell him my greatest fear that I have held onto for so long.

"I'm not weak like they all think I am." It comes out on a whisper, with a sob behind it. I didn't even realize it was something that had been weighing on my subconscious. All the men in my life before Noah thought I was someone who didn't deserve a life of choice.

Not saying a word, we're moving. Noah stands with me in his arms, not even struggling to carry me to the bedroom. I don't think he knows he is mumbling words to himself. His inner thoughts are catching him off guard and being voiced, rather than kept inside his head. He is normally so in control, but the last week has pushed us both out of our comfort zones, making us do things that are out of character.

"Weak, not a fucking weak bone in your body... kill those assholes with my bare hands... hurting my woman..." It becomes more a mumble as he lays me out on the bed. Then silence fills the room as Noah just stands there, staring at me.

"Noah..." Looking up at him, I try to tell him I'm okay. It's the moment I realize how scared he was of losing me. He is still in fight mode—against the tumor, against Jason and my father, against everything he was trying to protect me from. He doesn't know how to let go. I need to show him.

Sitting myself up on the bed, I wrap my hands in the hem of my shirt and slowly slide it up my body. I don't have any sexy lace underwear on, but it doesn't matter. Noah appreciates the show. He sees past any decoration and just wants my body the way it is, flaws and all. I know that, because I feel it every time he touches me.

Dropping my bra to the floor, he still isn't moving and is transfixed by the slow unveiling of my body. Lowering back onto the mattress, I start pushing down on the sweatpants and panties I changed into when we got home. I just wanted to be comfortable. But being naked is the ultimate freedom for your body. The wisp of cool air rushing over my body has my nipples standing up, hard, and just inviting Noah to take them.

My man is stuck in his own world of fear. It's time to bring him home, to the place we both let go of all the emotions that are weighing us down. There is no place to hide in such a passionate moment.

Sitting again, I pull my legs underneath me and then crawl forward on the bed to where he is standing at the end of it.

"Noah..." I take his hand and cup my left breast with it, and the intensity in him groaning my name tells me to keep going.

"Cassie..."

I start to strip him of his clothes, flicking the button on his pants and pushing his zipper down. Not slowly. I want him naked now, and I want to feel him skin to skin, shoving his briefs down to release him. "Fuck!" he exclaims as I wrap my hand around his cock, and the first drops are leaking from him.

It's like my touch is the go button for him.

He wraps his hand tightly around my wrist, stopping me from moving.

"Stop!" he growls, and my heart melts. This is what I want and what I know he needs too. "Lie back down, now!" I look at his long, bulging cock that is now standing tall, the tip purple with all the blood pumping through it. No matter what he thought before, Noah is past stopping now—unless I tell him to; he would never do anything I wasn't asking for.

He brings his hands under my armpits and helps lift me backwards so my head is all the way back on the pillow at the head of the bed, instead of where I just dropped down on the spot at his command. Then he steps out of his pants and strips off the shirt he was still wearing. I hadn't made it very far with undressing him once my hand was wrapped around his cock.

"Tell me to stop if it's too much." I can't even answer him, it's like seeing him naked again is taking all my ability to speak. Just nodding isn't enough for him, though.

"Cassie!"

I know he wants an answer, so I struggle to kick my brain into gear. "Promise." One word is enough as I lie there admiring the view. Noah crawls over top of me. He takes my breast in his mouth, sucking hard and making my body rise, following his mouth as he pulls off me. I don't want to lose the connection.

His elbows are on the bed, and he brings his arms up under mine to grasp my shoulders.

"Take me," I beg him. I need him. I don't need any foreplay, as being so desperate for him has us both more than ready. Feeling his cock push inside me, it's like all the planets are aligning again. "…Hard."

And my husband now delivers my plea.

"Strong." Noah unleashes everything we have both been holding back as we fought through the last week as a team. It's how we do it. We express the explosive love we contain when we are together as one. "You. Are. So. Fucking. Strong."

"Oh, Noah… this is love." I need him to hear me, so he knows that his anger is now being squashed with all the love he has.

And this most intense feeling of love will carry us forward in our life together. Nothing will ever break us!

He's pushing into me, hard and passionately, like we are both craving, and I know neither of us are going to hold on much longer. My body is rippling around him, and I let go of every piece of stress that has been weighing me down as I scream his name. My body takes over, and the orgasm has me twitching and my nerves firing like fireworks. Noah driving into me still has me riding the wave of ecstasy, until finally he gives in and lets the relief wash over him. His own orgasm takes away the agony he's been carrying through this whole thing. I know the lack of control he felt while he's been watching me in pain almost killed him.

Pulling my body with him so we're both on our sides, my euphoria is mixed with tears rolling down my cheeks. Sad tears, angry tears, and definitely happy tears that this is almost over. Noah slips out from inside me but neither of us move. Clinging to him, I just want to stay here, wrapped tightly with his body.

Overwhelmed with all I'm feeling.

Loved, safe, and home.

"Ghost, I think we need to buy a plane like this one," I say. "If we're going to be visiting Chicago, then it makes sense that we have the appropriate transportation." I see Mason trying to hold in his laughter as he watches us stand up to leave the plane, while Ghost nearly chokes on my comments.

"I might have money, baby, but what the fuck am I going to do with a plane I can't fly?"

"Hire a pilot, silly." Walking to Ashton, I stand on my toes to kiss him on the cheek and pull him into a hug. Hearing Ghost groan behind me, I know he is about to lose his mind with me today. My newfound energy and clear mind have meant that I haven't stopped talking the whole flight home.

"Just like that, hire a fucking pilot. Mason, want a job?"

"Pretty sure my wife might have an issue with me taking another job, but good luck with that argument. I mean, I agree a private jet really is the only way to travel."

"Ugh, not helping, buddy." Ghost rolls his eyes at Mason, I watch them sharing a bro hug as I start to let go of Ashton.

"I don't know how to thank you." Surely, I don't have any tears left, but I can feel them coming to the surface again, looking at Ashton, the man who pushed my husband forward when he needed it the most and I had no energy left to give him.

"Just don't let him be a stranger, and I want to meet the kids on the next visit too. That will be thanks enough." I can see the emotion in both Ashton and Ghost as they look at each other. For the first time they have completed a job together in the flesh, instead of Ghost behind his computers. And this job will go down as the most important one they've done, because it was personal.

Being big tough men, they don't know how to say what they're feeling, but watching the hug they are both pouring their emotions into, it's the best way they can share. And for both of them, it's enough. Unspoken words sometimes are the strongest way to convey emotions.

"Alright, enough of this emotional crap. We need to get out of here," Ghost says, breaking away, and I agree with him.

I'm desperate to see Bessy and Eli, and we are so close now, it's hard to contain my excitement. Ashton had a friend go shopping for us and buy lots of presents for the kids just as we promised, but I also placed an order from the bookstore and had Ashton pick it up. I will never get tired of listening to my children read to me. They were my lifeline at a time I felt lost in the darkness.

Ashton is back into work mode now, after dropping his walls just for a moment with Ghost.

"Tell Bull and Asha that we'll be back in a few days to collect them. I'll message the details. But after that, you are on your own. I think Paige would like both her husband and plane back, and I might have used up a lifetime of friend privileges with her." Ashton signals us out the door of the cabin. He has already been out with Ghost, checking the car and loading our luggage into it. We still need to be cautious for a while, but hopefully, one day I'll be able to move around without the area being searched before I get there.

Actually, who am I kidding, Ghost will never stop being Ghost, and I'm over the moon at that thought.

GHOST

"Oh my God, woman, don't tell me you need to stop to pee. You know what happened last time." The way she is moving around in her seat, she reminds me of Bessy when she's too busy watching something on the television and leaves it to the last minute to run to the bathroom. Dancing back and forth to put it off so she doesn't miss something.

"Ha-ha, very funny. No, I don't need to go to the bathroom, but thanks for being a gentleman and checking." The playful slap on my thigh tells me that comment was full of sarcasm. "I'm just full of nervous excitement, and I can't sit still. I've missed my babies, and we're almost home. Can you drive faster?"

I know she doesn't mean it, but I humor her anyway.

"Yep, just pushed another mile higher on the speedometer for you. Should get us there at least one second earlier."

"Ghost!"

"What? Do you truly believe I would put your life in danger by speeding to get home quicker? Not happening, sweetheart!" That's a big no from me. We have not been to hell and back to put her in danger in the last ten minutes of the trip.

"Yeah, yeah, I get it. I just want to squish them so tight and hear their voices. I won't even complain when Eli's crying. I want it all."

Seeing the happiness practically oozing from Cassie makes me feel more relaxed than I have since that first night when she collapsed on the floor in front of me. The events that followed I couldn't have predicted, and it would probably make a great movie if it weren't for the fact that it will always be hidden from the rest of the world. Everything that relates to Cassie's old life is sealed up in her supposed death, and anything that is left over, I'll be erasing from existence as soon as we're home and I can spend time in my office.

"Ugh." I'm not able to contain my groan as an awful thought runs through my head.

"What's wrong?" Cassie looks at me, concerned that I'm about to drop some bombshell that will stop her from seeing the kids.

"I can't imagine what state my computers are in after I let Bull use my bunker. You know how anal I am with them. If he has screwed up anything, I'll kill him with my bare hands." And I'm serious. That room is the lifeline for not only my team and friends, but every client that I help to keep safe too.

"Ghost. You can't tell me you don't have backups upon backups of every single file since the dawn of time. How could Bull have possibly wrecked anything?" Cassie's laughing at me.

"Because it's Bull, he won't be able to help himself, trying to find something he can use against me as ammunition with the team. That man has never beaten me at anything, but he's never given up trying." As much as I'm worried about my high-tech system—which Cassie is spot-on about, of course everything is safe from being lost or destroyed—it's a warm feeling, one which I haven't felt in a very long time, to be close to Bull again, and our usual banter is back, better than ever.

God, I've missed my friend! More than I realized over the years.

———

The squealing, crying, and talking when we arrived home was deafening, but I wouldn't want it any other way. Suggesting that Bull and Asha stay on for a few days with us has been the best medicine for Cassie, giving her time to just be with the kids but having help with meals and the house so she isn't overdoing it. I could have done it on my own, but I must admit, I'm really coming around to this idea of letting friends help.

We haven't been in the space we could let it happen before now, but I'll be making damn sure that we never go back to hiding from them again. No matter what life throws at us, we will be calling in our backup.

The kids are asleep for the night, and after a few beers on the balcony, Bull and Asha have headed down to the cabin to sleep for their last night here. To relive some memories, I'm sure, but I'm not sure how much of it will involve sleep. Although they have just spent over a week with the kids, maybe that's all they are capable of doing, catching up on sleep.

Cassie and I both ended up in tears tonight as we tried to express to them our gratitude for what they did for us. There is no way I could have trusted anyone else to be here and know that my family was safe. Crying in front of a buddy is not my style, but the love for my little family and their safety breaks down my walls. Bull shed a few tears too as we dealt with a lot of the emotions of what we have both been through in our lives since we've been apart after I went into hiding. Almost losing the love of our lives tends to change a man.

Tonight felt like the line drawn in the sand. We've pushed all our trauma behind us and are facing a new beginning full of good times, together.

Lying in bed, Cassie is in her favorite spot, her head on my chest right above my heart. Hearing her little snore that she still insists she doesn't do puts a smile on my face. This is what I've been longing for. Just peace and quiet. Life has been way too noisy for the last few months, and I must be getting old, because I don't crave the adrenaline high like I used to.

I'm not ready to give it up just yet, but maybe it's time I started to share the load. Pull back in from being the person everyone leans on, because if I'm being honest with myself, I don't need it anymore.

I thought if I could just save one more person, find one more piece of the puzzle, send one more bad guy to jail, then my life would be worthwhile and that maybe, just maybe my family would be proud of me.

We bury our hurt in the sneakiest of places in our hearts, and it creeps up on us at the strangest times. But with it rising this time, I feel like it's finally the right opportunity to bury the rejection I have never dealt with. And there is one big reason I feel I'm strong enough to do that now—the woman that is using me as her pillow.

She has my back no matter what, and I can rely on her to be the one to protect my heart, which I've never had before her.

The strength of two hearts is always going to be stronger than being on your own.

She calls me her safe place, but she will never understand how she is the only home I've known.

The love I have found in my own family is all I will ever need. From now until the day I die, I will be here to protect them and make sure that every day is a better day than the one before.

The silence is broken by the words I will never say no to.

"Noah." A soft whisper comes from her lips, not much more than a mumble. "Show me how much you love me."

"Something I promise to do for the rest of our lives, bright eyes."

This is the way every day should end, full of love.

Epilogue

12 MONTHS LATER

GHOST

"I'm sure you've forgotten something. It'll probably be some major detail of the day, but don't worry, I'll pick up your slack. It's not like you're a man who fixates over fine details or anything. Of course you're bound to miss something." Kurt is pushing our friendship to the limit right now.

"Fuck off, Kurt. Otherwise, I'll send you to supervise Bessy and Eli." My mind is going in so many directions, trying to make sure I have everything covered. I mean, I've been over my plan so many times it's imprinted on my brain, but still, I'm so desperate to make sure everything is perfect for her.

"Really? You say that like it's a punishment. My godchildren are angels for me." We're looking at each other now, knowing that the words out of his mouth were utter bullshit. My kids have Kurt wrapped so tightly around their fingers that they can get away with anything. The laughter that bursts out of both of us is what I needed.

I'm nervous, and that is completely ridiculous, totally irrational, and something that is just not me.

What has this woman done to me!?

Kurt puts his hand on my shoulder and looks straight through my panic. "Noah." I'm still adjusting to him calling me that. Now that we're living out in the open, we're trying to keep our code names for work and real names for our normal life. What a normal life is, I'm still trying to decipher.

"She loves you, and she will love all of this," he says, waving his hand around at the arch, chairs, and so many damned flowers that we have decorated the back yard of Kurt's house with.

I had this vision the first time we came to visit Kurt and Asha, at his beach house, but it took me a while to get everything in place. As beautiful as our home is, I knew it needed to be somewhere completely different, a fresh start. Asha and Kurt's little girl being born gave me the perfect reason to fly Cassie and the kids back out here. Of course she was desperate to see the baby, and Bessy was beside herself with excitement to be getting a little cousin. She has no idea there is no blood relationship, but that doesn't matter in our world. Love is family. Having Mason then fly all our old and new friends from Chicago out here to be with us is going to make it perfect. I mean, Tate would have made a song and dance if he wasn't invited. He will forever hold over me that he saved her life. Pfft! Minor detail, buddy.

"What if she says no?" The words just blurt out of my mouth.

"Because it's not like you've already married her once, dick-head," Badger says as he's walking past, hearing me freaking out. He gives me a slap on the shoulder, bringing me back into reality.

"Can I be the backup groom if she says no? I'm a better option anyway, better-looking, that's for sure," Ashton calls out from far enough away he knows I can't punch him. My death stare is all he needs for him to put his hands in the air and back away with a stupid grin on his face.

Kurt shakes his head at both of us. "Just get in there and get that suit on, because the girls are due back shortly with your bride, and we want her to get the full surprise. Plus, you're right. I wouldn't marry you looking like that either." He walks away to make sure everything is ready to go with the music.

"What's wrong with black cargo pants and t-shirt?" I yell at him as he's walking away.

"You look like you're on an undercover op," Badger yells at me from across the yard where he's grabbing himself a beer out of the cooler. "Pretty sure she has seen enough of you looking like that. Try to act like a normal human being, just this once."

I scowl at him. "Drinking already? Don't think the party has started yet."

"Well, I'm starting it now, thanks, buddy," he says, lifting his beer up to me with the biggest smirk on his face.

"Asshole."

"Every day of the week," Badger replies, and I don't know what it is about that man, but I never want to know what our lives would be like without him in it. He's the father I never had, although he's not quite old enough to be my actual father, but it's great to say that to him. Age means nothing; he is the wise soul we all need, whether we ask for it or not.

I can hear Kurt's mom behind me, pushing everyone to get inside and get dressed. It's been her job overseeing the kids, looking after her baby granddaughter, Bessy, and Eli while the girls went out for a pamper session. Kurt's sister Jodie has become part of the girl tribe too, and Cassie's in heaven, the more the merrier. Having friends to share all these experiences with, that she's been missing out on for so long, has made her happy in a way I never could. Women need other women in their lives, it's just how it is. Cassie never complained, but I know it must have been hard for her all these years.

We're still cautious and not too adventurous about leaving the house, but coming here to Kurt's house, we know that there are so many eyes on us, worrying about keeping us safe. I feel she is more protected now than if we were still in WITSEC.

Standing in the guest room, looking in the mirror, I can't

remember the last time I wore a suit. Can't say I've missed it, but I want Cassie to have the wedding she missed out on. I would never change our first one, but I'm sure every little girl dreams of getting married in a white dress, surrounded by loved ones. It's time to make that dream a reality.

"Daddy, look, I'm a princess!" Bessy squeals, coming slowly into the room, holding Eli's hand as he toddles next to her, dressed in his little black pants, vest, and bow tie to match me. Bessy is in a pretty white dress, a gold ribbon tied around her waist and a tulle skirt that when she lets go of Eli's hand and twirls around, it flares out, making her smile so brightly. The older she gets, the more she looks like her mother, which is both adorable and frightening. I'm not sure how I will cope when she starts dating. Maybe keeping them all locked up in our mountain home has more merit than I was first thinking.

As I look at the dress I ordered for Cassie hanging on the cupboard door waiting for her arrival, a warm feeling sinks into my bones. This is how it should be. The chance to show her how much I love her and make her feel as special as she is to all of us.

Kurt sticks his head into the room, in his matching suit. There are a few men out there who I would be honored to have standing up front with me, Badger, Ashton, and surprisingly even Tate, but Kurt was always going to be my best man.

"They're five minutes out. You ready?"

"Absolutely." He leaves, closing the door behind him, and I take a moment to look at the two little lives that our love has created. Nobody is perfect, but these two adorable humans smiling up at me are pretty damn close, if you ask me.

"Are you ready to surprise Mommy, my gorgeous little princess and my handsome prince?"

"Yes!" Bessy jumps up and down, clapping.

"Mommy!" Eli joins his big sister with the clapping and jumping; he has no idea what is going on but loves to clap. He takes more after me, with fine blond hair, and some days, the seriousness in his eyes lets me know he'll be a quiet thinker. He idolizes Bessy, and most days, she is so patient with him. But let's see if that continues when she becomes a teenager. Little brothers I'm sure aren't so cool then. I hope that no matter what happens in their lives, though, that they will always be there for each other. You raise them with all the values you think are important and just pray that when the time comes, they will know what the right thing is to do.

Hearing her voice coming down the hallway, complaining that she can't see, makes me put my hand over my mouth, trying not give too much away from laughing out loud. Being led through the house with a blindfold on will not be sitting well with my wife who likes to be in control—well, most of the time anyway, but that is just something we share between the two of us behind closed doors.

This was a risk because Cassie hates surprises, and I get the reason why. She's certainly had her fair share in life. But hopefully after today, she'll see that sometimes they can bring something beautiful.

I place my finger on my lips to shush the kids as the door is opening, and Asha leads a blindfolded Cassie into the room. Not saying a word, Asha just steps back out of the room, closing the door.

She might still be dressed in a skirt and shirt that I see her in on a regular basis, but she still takes my breath away.

I need to speak because I don't want her freaking out, even though I could stand here all day just taking in her beauty.

"Cassie, take off your blindfold." The moment I start to speak, I can hear the emotion in my own voice.

"Noah?" she says in confusion as she slides the black cloth off her face. Her eyes open wide like saucers as she takes in the three of us before her. Her hand rushes to cover her gaping mouth, and she gulps at the air as I drop down onto one knee.

"Cassie, looking back, people will say they are sorry you went through what you did. But not me. I will never regret our life and where we have been. I never want to see you hurt again, but I hope you agree that it was not all in vain." I can see the tears already falling down her cheeks. "The moment I looked into your bright eyes, you had me, heart and soul. I love your strength and softness, the sassy stubbornness and immense kindness, but most of all, I love the way you see me, every part of me, even the parts I try to hide. I love you more than any of the words I can think to tell you. Please marry me, again, and let me place this diamond on your finger that will show the world what I already know. That you are our strength, our home, the love of my life, and the beautifully adored mother of our children. How about we do it in style this time?"

I hold the ring box out toward her, but Eli is already trying to climb onto my knee, as his patience is gone. Bessy is bouncing on her toes next to me, waiting for Cassie to speak, although I give her five seconds before Bessy will be talking for her. She hasn't said anything, but my nerves are finally settled and all but gone, so I'm not worried.

Just being near her, I know her answer.

Our love binds us together in a bond that will never be broken.

"Oh, Noah, yes, it will always be yes." Her voice is wobbly with the emotion she can't contain, tears falling faster now as she holds out her hand to me. I slip off the old plain white-gold wedding band and replace it with the two-carat solitaire diamond ring set low into the white-gold band so it doesn't sit too high for her.

"I'm keeping this wedding band, and you can have it back once you say I do out there, in front of all our friends." I slip it into my pocket as I stand, Eli on my hip and Bessy hugging both of us, and I place my hand on Cassie's cheek and kiss her like it's the first time all over again.

"What have you done?" she asks me as we pull apart from the kiss that has reconfirmed our love.

"Just a little celebration for the most beautiful lady in a white wedding dress." Stepping aside, I point to the dress that is hanging on the closet door.

"Oh, Noah…" The words leave her as she steps to it and runs her hands over the lace.

"It's so pretty, Mommy. You can look like a princess just like me. Just like Daddy looks like Eli." I love how in Bessy's world we look like our kids, not the other way around. Life is so simple at their age, and I hope that it always stays that way, but living in my world, you know that it won't.

"I'm going to leave you now to get dressed. Asha will be in to help you once she's dressed too. We will meet you outside at the altar, but please don't take too long. I don't know how long I can keep this one clean." Eli looks up at me with the most innocent look. "Yeah, I'm talking about you, buddy." Kissing him on the cheek, I bend to kiss Bessy, and lastly, kissing Cassie softly on the forehead. Taking Bessy's hand, we're walking out of the room when I turn one last time to see my wife standing staring at me.

"You are the reason I was put on this earth, bright eyes. To love and protect you all until the day I die." Starting to choke on my own words, I keep walking, knowing that no more needs to be said.

Cassie will never know a life without love again. It's my job to make sure of that.

CASSIE

Standing watching Bessy and Eli playing with all the other kids is like a dream come true.

I didn't know if we would ever be able to give them a normal life. And I'm hoping that Bessy is young enough that those memories of being on her own for so long will drift away as she starts filling up her bucket with so many more fun and exciting memories.

"Happy?" Noah says in my ear in his deep voice as he comes up behind me, wrapping his arms around my waist.

"More than I can describe." His cologne that he has started wearing tingles my senses. I bought it for him the first time I went shopping with Asha and Jodie. It sounds so silly, but it was the first thing I wanted to do. Pick a present for him, in person, in a shop like a normal person. Every time I smell it, the feeling of freedom thrums in my chest.

"Don't worry about words, I'm just looking forward to you showing me later." The sexy chuckle vibrates through his chest that is pressed firmly against my back.

I swat his arm around my waist, playfully.

"What? You don't understand how hard it is to stand here and be sociable when all I want to do is take you over there into our honeymoon house farther down the beach, away from all these people, and rip it off you." The whisper in my ear, in his deep sex voice that he knows melts me, has me now thinking the same thought. A shiver running through my body, he knows exactly what he is doing to me.

Noah thought of everything. We will stay up in the house near Kurt and Asha's that is out on the sandy point on its own, away from the other houses in this little coastal town. It will give us a few nights on our own but still be close to the kids who will stay with Asha and Kurt. I feel bad, with Asha having a new baby in the house, but she insisted. She has plenty of help around her, and I made her promise that if it all gets too much, she'll call me and we will come and get the kids. Somehow, I doubt we will be getting a call.

"Dance with me?" Noah asks, stepping to the side of me. I nod because I would love nothing more. Pulling me to the makeshift dance floor the boys made on the back deck, suddenly everyone is parting to give us space, and the music stops.

"Our first dance as man and wife," Noah proudly announces to our guests, and all the girls are sighing, and I can see Kurt lifting Noah's phone to film us. A year ago, I would have had a breakdown at the thought of being videoed by anyone, but I know every person in this back yard would never post it on any social media platform, and it will be purely for us as a memento.

The music starts, and I hear the crooning voices of NSYNC through the speakers singing *This I Promise You*. Who doesn't love a boy band? And every word they're singing resonates with us both, talking about being my strength and my hope. My heart swells as we sway together, and everyone else seems to disappear from my vision. I only see him. My Noah, my Ghost, my husband. It's like tonight, finally all the chains on my heart have broken free. There is nothing holding us back from living the life that we choose it to be.

If that means living in the mountains and only leaving a few times a year, then that is our choice. Or buying that plane and traveling the world, seeking out adventures and showing our children how beautiful life can be. We can choose our own destiny, and that is the greatest gift we have now.

I watch Noah's eyes roaming over my face, then down to the top of my swelling breasts that are sitting up nicely the tighter he pulls me to him. My dress is just perfect and something I would have picked myself.

White silk with lace overlay. Strapless, with a sweetheart neckline that scoops down to show my cleavage off nicely, one my husband is appreciating right now. It then swoops around a little lower on my back. It's fitted perfectly, like it was made for me, and follows my curves all the way to just above my knees, where it fans out into soft tulle that has lace motifs on it. Bessy loves that we both have a skirt, and when we were dancing a little earlier, we twirled together. My hair is out and softly curled so it falls on my shoulders. I know how much Noah loves my hair and wrapping it in his fingers, or just a soothing stroke over the top of my head. Plus, it made me feel like my mom was here with me in her own way.

Dancing this close has set off my deepest emotions again, and now, I agree with Noah. We need to leave. It's time to be alone.

Just us, no kids, no friends, and nothing else to think about.

For so long, I could only see the darkness in my life, but now, thanks to this man, all I see is the brightness of love.

Standing on my toes, I place my lips next to his ear. "I need you to show me love."

Those simple words are all it takes.

We say goodbye to the kids and everyone as Noah is practically dragging me to the car out front.

Desperate to be alone and get our hands on each other, Noah lifts me up into the front seat of the Range Rover, growling in my ear so no one else can hear, "Get ready for the ride of your life, sweetheart, because I'm about to fuck you so hard, for the next three days straight, that you'll be lucky to come up for air."

Striding around the car with speed and purpose, he is in the driver's seat and already starting to drive forward out of the driveway.

Wearing the smile of mischief I can already feel on my face, I decide it's time to push the man beside me. He loves it when I'm as strong as he is, and the fight for control just fuels our passion.

"That better be a promise you intend to keep. I don't want to have to take matters into my own hands," I say, pushing my legs together on the seat as he looks at me with fire in his eyes.

"Not happening! Have I ever let you down?" His hand takes mine and places it on his thigh, knowing we need to be connected.

"Never!" I say, sliding my hand up his leg and squeezing his cock that is already hard, and he gives me the groan I was longing to hear. "Now drive faster, I don't want to lose a minute of our time alone."

"Fuck, Cassie," he growls the more I rub my hand over him.

And there he is.

My strong Ghost.

My passionate Noah.

My eternal safe place where I'm loved unconditionally.

TWO DAYS LATER

I'm lying on the day bed under the shade of the tree in the back yard of the house we're staying in. The sound of the ocean, the soft breeze blowing over my skin, and Noah wrapped around me where he has been since we arrived here from the wedding.

A vision just flashed back into my memory.

I sit up, startled, and look down at him on the bed.

"Hey, I just remembered something. When we were leaving the wedding, did you see Badger and Jodie walking down the stairs onto the sand and darkness together?"

Noah just looks up at me and smiles.

Bastard, he knows something, I'm sure from that look.

"Shit, what did I miss? Spill the beans!" I need to find out pronto.

"I promise I don't know anything, but good luck finding out.

This is Badger we're talking about. The king of secret lives." Noah laughs, pulling me back down onto his chest.

"Have you met me? I never give up!"

"And I'm grateful for that every single day, beautiful."

THE END

Please read on for a sneak peek of *Gorgeous Gyno* from *The Chicago Boys* series.

Also by Karen Deen

Love's Wall

Love's Dance

Love's Hiding

Love's Fun

Love's Hot

Time for Love Box Set (All *Love's* books in one set)

Gorgeous Gyno

Private Pilot

Naughty Neuro

Lovable Lawyer

The Chicago Boys Box Set (above 4 books in one set)

The Chicago Boys - NYE in New York City (Novella)

That Day

Defining Us

GORGEOUS
Gyno

KAREN DEEN

Chapter One

MATILDA

Today has disaster written all over it.

Five fifty-seven am and already I have three emails that have the potential to derail tonight's function. Why do people insist on being so disorganized? Truly, it's not that hard.

Have a diary, use your phone, write it down, order the stock – whatever it takes. Either way, don't fuck my order up! I shouldn't have to use my grown-up words before six am on a weekday. Seriously!

I'm standing in the shower with hot water streaming down my body. I feel like I'm about to draw blood with how hard I'm scrubbing my scalp, while I'm thinking about solutions for my problems. It's what I'm good at. Not the hair-pulling but the problem-solving in a crisis. A professional event planner has many sneaky tricks up her sleeve. I just happen to have them up my sleeve, in my pockets, and hiding in my shoes. As a last resort, I pull them out of my ass.

I need to get into the office to find a new supplier that can have nine hundred mint-green cloth serviettes delivered to the hotel by lunchtime today. You would think this is trivial in the world. However, if tonight's event is not perfect, it could be the difference between my dream penthouse apartment or the shoebox I'm living in now. I'll be damned if mint napkins are the deciding factor. Why can't Lucia just settle for white? Oh, that's right, because she is about as easy to please as a child waiting for food. No matter what you say, they complain until they get what they want. Lucia is a nice lady, I'm sure, when she's not being my client from hell.

Standing in the bathroom, foot on the side of the bath, stretching my stockings on, I sneak a glance in the mirror. I hate looking at myself. Who wants to look at their fat rolls and butt dimples. Not me! I should get rid of the mirror and then I wouldn't have to cringe every time I see it. Maybe in that penthouse I'm seeing in my future, there will be a personal trainer and chef included.

Yes! Let's put that in the picture. Need to add that to my vision board. I already have the personal driver posted up on my board—of course, he's sizzling hot. The trains and taxis got old about seven years ago. Well, maybe six years and eleven months. The first month I moved to Chicago I loved it. The hustle and bustle, such a change from the country town I grew up in. Trains running on raised platforms instead of the ground, the amount of taxis that seemed to be in the thousands compared to three that were run by the McKinnon family. Now all the extra time you lose in traffic every day is so frustrating, it's hard to make up in a busy schedule.

I slip my pencil skirt up over my hips, zip up and turn side to side. Happy with my outfit, I slide my suit jacket on, and then I do the last thing, putting on lipstick. Time to take on the world for another day. As stressful as it is and how often I will complain about things going wrong, I love my life. With a passion. Working with my best friend in our own business is the best leap of faith we took together. Leaving our childhood hometown of Williamsport, we were seeking adventure. The new beginning we both needed. It didn't quite start how I thought. Those first few months were tough. I really struggled, but I just didn't feel like I could go home anymore because the feeling of being happy there had changed thanks to my ex-boyfriend. Lucky I had Fleur to get me through that time.

Fleur and I met in preschool. She was busy setting up her toy kitchen in the classroom when I walked in. I say hers, because one of the boys tried to tell her how to arrange it and her look stopped him in his tracks. I remember thinking, he has no idea. I would set it up just how she did. It made perfect sense. I knew we were right. Well, that was what we agreed on and bonded over our PB&J sandwich. That and our OCD behavior, of being painfully pedantic. Sometimes it meant we butted heads being so similar, but not often. We have been inseparable ever since that first day.

We used to lay in the hammock in my parents' backyard while growing up. Dreaming of the adventures we were going to have together. We may as well have been sisters. Our moms always said we were joined at the hip. Which was fine until boys came into the picture. They didn't understand us wanting to spend so much time together. Of course, that changed when our hormones kicked in. Boys became important in our lives, but we never lost our closeness. We have each other's backs no matter what. Still today, she is that one person I will trust with my life is my partner in crime, my bestie.

Leaning my head on the back wall of the elevator as it descends, my mind is already running through my checklist of things I need to tackle the moment I walk into the office. That pre-event anxiety is starting to surface. It's not bad anxiety. It's the kick of adrenaline I use to get me moving. It focuses me and blocks out the rest of the world. The only thing that exists is the job I'm working on. From the moment we started up our business of planning high-end events, we have been working so hard, day and night. It feels like we haven't had time to breathe yet. The point we have been aiming for is so close we can feel it. Being shortlisted for a major contract is such a huge achievement and acknowledgement of our business. Tapping my head, I say to myself, "touch wood". So far, we've never had any disaster functions that we haven't been able to turn around to a success on the day. I put it down to the way Fleur and I work together. We have this mental connection. Not even having to talk, we know what the other is thinking and do it before the other person asks. It's just a perfect combination.

Let's hope that connection is working today.

Walking through the foyer, phone in hand, it chimes. I was in the middle of checking how close my Uber is, but the words in front of my eyes stop me dead in my tracks.

Fleur: *Tonight's guest speaker woke up vomiting – CANCELLED!!!*

"Fuck!" There is no other word needed.

I hear from behind me, "Pardon me, young lady." Shit, it's Mrs. Johnson. My old-fashioned conscience. I have no idea how she seems to pop up at the most random times. I don't even need to turn around and look at her. What confuses me is why she is in the foyer at six forty-five in the morning. When I'm eighty-two years of age, there is no way I'll be up this early.

"Sorry, Mrs. Johnson. I will drop in my dollar for the swear jar tomorrow," I mumble as I'm madly typing back to Fleur.

"See that you do, missy. Otherwise I will chase you down, and you know I'm not joking." I hear her laughing as she shuffles on her way towards the front doors. I'm sure everyone in this building is paying for her nursing home when they finally get her to move there. I don't swear that often—well, I tell myself that in my head, anyway. It just seems Mrs. Johnson manages to be around, every time I curse.

"Got to run, Mrs. Johnson. I will pop in tomorrow," I call out, heading out the front doors. Part of me feels for her. I think the swear jar is more about getting people to call in to visit her apartment. Her husband passed away six months after I moved in. He was a beautiful old man. She misses him terribly and gets quite lonely. She's been adopted by everyone in the building as our stand-in Nana whether we like it or not. Although she is still stuck in the previous century, she has a big heart and just wants to feel like she has a reason to get up every day and live her life.

My ride into work allows me to get a few emails sorted, at the same time I'm thinking on how I'm going to solve the guest speaker problem. Fleur is on the food organization for this one, and I am on everything else. It's the way we work it. Whoever is on food is rostered on for the actual event. If I can get through today, then tonight I get to relax. As much as you can relax when you are a control freak and you aren't there. We need to split the work this way, otherwise we'd never get a day or night off.

The event is for the 'End of the Cycle' program. It's a great organization that helps stop the cycle of poverty and poor education in families. Trying to help the parents learn to budget and get the kids in school and learning. A joint effort to give the next generation a fighting chance of living the life they dream about.

Maybe if I call the CEO, they'll have someone who has been through the program or somehow associated with the mentoring that can give a firsthand account of what it means to the families. Next email on my list. Another skill I have learned: Delegation makes things happen. I can't do it all, and even with Fleur, we need to coordinate with others to make things proceed quickly.

As usual, Thursday morning traffic is slow even at this time of the day. We are crawling at a snail's pace. I could get out and walk faster than this. I contemplate it, but with the summer heat, I know even at this time of the morning, I'd end up a sweaty mess. That is not the look I need when I'm trying to present like the woman in charge. Even if you have no idea what you're doing, you need people to believe you do. Smoke and mirrors, the illusion is part of the performance.

My phone is pinging constantly as I approach the front of the office building. We chose the location in the beginning because it was central to all the big function spaces in the city. Being new to the city, we didn't factor in how busy it is here. Yet the convenience of being so close far outweighs the traffic hassles.

Hustling down the hall, I push open the door of our office.

'FLEURTILLY'.

It still gives me goosebumps seeing our dream name on the door. The one we thought of all those years ago in that hammock. Even more exciting is that it's all ours. No answering to anyone else. We have worked hard, and this is our reward.

The noise in the office tells me Fleur already has everything turned on and is yelling down the phone at someone. Surely, we can't have another disaster even before my first morning coffee.

"What the hell, Scott. I warned you not to go out and party too hard yesterday. Have you even been to bed yet? What the hell are you thinking, or have the drugs just stopped that peanut brain from even working?! You were already on your last warning. Find someone who will put up with your crap. Your job here is terminated, effective immediately." Fleur's office phone bangs down on her desk loud enough I can hear her from across the hall.

"Well, you told him, didn't you? Now who the hell is going to run the waiters tonight?" I ask, walking in to find her sitting at her desk, leaning back in her chair, eyes closed and hands behind her head.

"I know, I know. I should have made him get his sorry ass in and work tonight and then fired him. My bad. I'll fix it, don't worry. Maybe it's time to promote TJ. He's been doing a great job, and I'm sure he's been pretty much doing Scott's job for him anyway."

To be honest, I think she's right. We've suspected for a while that Scott, one of our managers, has been partying harder than just a few drinks with friends. He's become unreliable which is unlike him. Even when he's at work, he's not himself. I tried to talk to him about it and was shut down. Unfortunately, our reputation is too important to risk him screwing up a job because he's high. He's had enough warnings. His loss.

"You fix that, and I'll find a new speaker. Oh, and 900 stupid mint-green napkins. Seriously. Let's hope the morning improves." I turn to walk out of her office and call over my shoulder, "By the way, good morning. Let today be awesome." I smile, waiting for her response.

"As awesome as we are. I see your Good Morning and I raise you a peaceful day and a drama-free evening. Your turn for coffee, woman." And so, our average workday swings into action.

By eleven-thirty, our day is still sliding towards the shit end of the scale. We have had two staff call in sick with the stupid vomiting bug. Lucia has called me a total of thirty-seven times with stupid questions. While I talk through my teeth trying to be polite, I wonder why she's hired event planners when she wants to micromanage everything.

My phone pressed to my ear, Fleur comes in and puts her hand up to high-five me. Thank god, that means she has solved her issues and we are staffed ready to go tonight. It's just my speaker problem, and then we will have jumped the shit pile and be back on our way to the flowers and sunshine.

"Fleurtilly, you are speaking with Matilda." I pause momentarily. "Hello, Mr. Drummond, how are you this morning?" I have my sweet business voice on, looking at Fleur holding her breath for my answer.

"That's great, yes, I'm having a good day too." I roll my eyes at my partner standing in front of me making stupid faces. "Thank you for calling me back. I was just wondering how you went with finding another speaker for this evening's event." I pause while he responds. I try not to show any reaction to keep Fleur guessing what he's saying. "Okay, thank you for looking into it for me. I hope you enjoy tonight. Goodbye." Slowly I put the phone down.

"Tilly, for god's sake, tell me!" She is yelling at me as I slowly stand up and then start the happy dance and high-five her back.

"We have ourselves a pilot who mentors the boys and girls in the program. He was happy to step in last-minute. Mr. Drummond is going to confirm with him now that he has let us know." We both reach out for a hug, still carrying on when Deven interrupts with his normal gusto.

"Is he single, how old, height, and which team is he batting for?" He stands leaning against the doorway, waiting for us to settle down and pay him any attention.

"I already called dibs, Dev. If he is hot, single, and in his thirties then back off, pretty boy. Even if he bats for your team, I bet I can persuade him to change sides." Fleur walks towards him and wraps him in a hug. "Morning, sunshine. How was last night?"

"Let's just say there won't be a second date. He turned up late, kept looking at his phone the whole time, and doesn't drink. Like, not at all. No alcohol. Who even does that? That's a no from me!" We're all laughing now while I start shutting down my computer and pack my briefcase, ready to head over to the function at McCormick Place.

"While I'd love to stay and chat with you girls," I say, making Deven roll his eyes at me, "I have to get moving. Things to do, a function to get finished, so I can go home and put my feet up." I pick up my phone and bag, giving them both a peck on the cheek. "See you both over there later. On my phone if needed." I start hurrying down the corridor to the elevator. I debated calling a car but figured a taxi will be quicker at this time of the day. Just before the lunchtime rush, the doorman should be able to flag one down for me.

Rushing out of the elevator, I see a taxi pulled up to the curb letting someone off. I want to grab it before it takes off again. Cecil the doorman sees me in full high-heeled jog and opens the door knowing what I'm trying to do. He's calling out to the taxi to wait as I come past him, focused on the open door the previous passenger is closing.

"Wait, please…" I call as I run straight into a solid wall of chest. Arms grab me as I'm stumbling sideways. Shit. Please don't let this hurt.

Just as my world is tilting sideways, I'm coming back upright to a white tank top, tight and wet with sweat. So close to my face I can smell the male pheromones and feel the heat on my cheeks radiating from his body.

"Christ, I'm so sorry. Are you okay, gorgeous?" That voice, low, breathy, and a little startled. I'm not game to look up and see the face of this wall of solid abs. "You just came out that door like there's someone chasing you. I couldn't stop in time." His hands start to push me backwards a little so he can see more of me.

"Talk to me, please. Are you okay? I'm so sorry I frightened you. Luckily I stopped you from hitting the deck."

Taking a big breath to pull myself back in control, I slowly follow up his sweaty chest to look at the man the voice is coming from. The sun is behind him so I can't make his face out from the glare. I want to step back to take a better look when I hear the taxi driver yelling at me.

"Are you getting in, lady, or not?" he barks out of the driver's seat.

Damn, I need to get moving.

"Thank you. I'm sorry I ran in front of you. Sorry, I have to go." I start to turn to move to the taxi, yet he hasn't let me go.

"I'm the one who's sorry. Just glad you're okay. Have a good day, gorgeous." He guides me to the back seat of the taxi and closes the door for me after I slide in, then taps the roof to let the driver know he's good to go. As we pull away from the curb, I see his smile of beautiful white teeth as he turns and keeps jogging down the sidewalk. My heart is still pounding, my head is still trying to process what the hell just happened. Can today get any crazier?

GRAYSON

'I'm just a hunk, a hunk of burning love
Just a hunk, a hunk of burning love'
Crap!
What the hell!
I reach out to grab her before I bowl her over and smash her to the ground. Stopping my feet dead in the middle of running takes all the strength I have in my legs. We sway slightly, but I manage to pull her back towards me to stand her back up. Where did this woman come from? Looking down at the top of her head, I can't tell if she's okay or not.

She's not moving or saying anything. It's like she's frozen still. I think I've scared her so much she's in shock.

She's not answering me, so I try to pull her out a little more so I can see her face.

Well, hello my little gorgeous one.

The sun is shining brightly on her face that lights her up with a glow. She's squinting, having trouble seeing me. She opens her mouth to finally talk. I'm ready for her to rip into me for running into her. Yet all I get is sorry and she's trying to escape my grasp. The taxi driver gives her the hurry along. I'd love to make sure she's really okay, but I seem to be holding her up. I help her to the taxi and within seconds she's pulling away from me, turning and watching me from the back window of the cab.

Well, that gave today a new interesting twist.

One gorgeous woman almost falling at my feet. Before I could even settle my breathing from running, I blink, and she's gone. Almost like a little figment of my imagination.

One part I certainly didn't imagine is how freaking beautiful she looked.

I take off running towards Dunbar Park and the basketball court where the guys are waiting for me. Elvis is pumping out more rock in my earbuds and my feet pound the pavement in time with his hip thrusts. I'm a huge Elvis fan, my music tastes stuck in the sixties. There is nothing like the smooth melodic tones of the King. My mom listened to him on her old vinyl records, and we would dance around the kitchen while Dad was at work. I think she was brainwashing me. It totally worked. Although I love all sorts of music, Elvis will always be at the top of my playlist.

"Oh, here's Doctor Dreamy. What, some damsel in distress you couldn't walk away from?" The basketball lands with a thud in the center of my chest from Tate.

"Like you can talk, oh godly one. The surgeon that every nurse in the hospital is either dreaming about fucking, or how she can stab needles in you after she's been fucked over by you." Smacking him on the back as I join the boys on the court, Lex and Mason burst out laughing.

"Welcome to the game, doctors. Sucks you're on the same team today, doesn't it? Less bitching and more bouncing. Let's get this game started. I'm due in court at three and the judge already hates me, so being late won't go well," Lex yelled as he started backing down the court ready to mark and stop us scoring a basket.

"Let me guess, she hates you because you slept with her," I yell back.

"Nope, but I may have spent a night with her daughter, who I had no idea lives with her mother the judge."

"Holy shit, that's the funniest thing I've heard today." Mason throws his head back, laughing out loud. "That story is status-worthy."

"You put one word of that on social media and I won't be the one in court trying to get you out on bail, I'll be there defending why I beat you to a pulp, gossip boy. Now get over here and help me whip the asses off these glamour boys." Lex glares at Mason.

"Like they even have a chance. Bring it, boys." He waves at me to come at him.

Game on, gentlemen.

My watch starts buzzing to tell us time's up in the game. We're all on such tight work schedules that we squeeze in this basketball game together once a week. These guys are my family, well, the kind of family you love one minute and want to kill the next. We've been friends since meeting at Brother Rice High School for Boys, where we all ended up in the same class on the first day. Not sure what the teachers were thinking after the first week when we had bonded and were already making pains of ourselves. Not sure how many times our parents were requested for a 'talk' with the headmaster, but it was more often than is normal, I'm sure. It didn't matter we all went to separate universities or worked in different professions. We had already formed that lifelong friendship that won't ever break.

Sweat dripping off all of us, I'm gulping down water from the water fountain. Not too much, otherwise I'll end up with a muscle cramp by the time I run back to the hospital.

"Right, who's free tonight?" Mason is reading his phone with a blank look on his face.

"I'm up for a drink, I'm off-shift tonight," Tate pipes up as I grin and second him that I'm off too. It doesn't happen often that we all have a night off together. The joys of being a doctor in a hospital.

"I can't, I'm attending a charity dinner. It's for that charity you mentor for, Mason," Lex replies.

"Well, that's perfect. Gray, you are my plus one, and Tate, your date is Lex. I'm now the guest speaker for the night. So, you can all come and listen to the best talk you have witnessed all year. Prepare to be amazed." He brushes each of his shoulders with his hands, trying to show us how impressive he is.

We all moan simultaneously at him.

"Thanks for the support, cock suckers. My memory is long." He huffs a little as he types away a reply on his phone.

Mason is a pilot who spent four years in the military, before he was discharged, struggling with the things he saw. He started to work in the commercial sector but then was picked up by a private charter company. He's perfect for that sort of role. He has the smoothness, wit, and intelligence to mingle with anyone, no matter who they are. He's had great stories of different passengers over the years and places he's flown.

"Why in god's name would anyone think you were interesting enough to talk for more than five minutes. You can't even make that time limit for sex," I say, waiting for the reaction.

"Oh, you are all so fucking funny, aren't you. I'm talking about my role in mentoring kids to reach for their dream jobs no matter how big that dream is." The look on his face tells me he takes this seriously.

"Jokes aside, man, that's a great thing you do. If you can dream it, you can reach it. If you make a difference in one kid's life, then it's worth it." We all stop with the ribbing and start to work out tonight's details. We agree to meet at a bar first for a drink and head to the dinner together. My second alarm on my watch starts up. We all know what that means.

Parting ways, Mason yells over his shoulder to us all, "By the way, it's black tie."

I inwardly groan as I pick up my pace into a steady jog again. I hate wearing a tie. It reminds me of high school wearing one every day. If I can avoid it now, I do. Unfortunately, most of these charity dinners you need to dress to impress. You also need to have your wallet full to hand over a donation. I'm lucky, I've never lived without the luxury of money, so I'm happy to help others where I can.

Running down Michigan Avenue, I can see Mercy Hospital in the distance standing tall and proud. It's my home away from home. This is the place I spend the majority of my waking hours, working, along with some of my sleeping hours too. My heart beats happily in this place. Looking after people and saving lives is the highest rush you can experience in life. With that comes rough days, but you just hope the good outweighs the bad most of the time.

That's why I run and try not to miss the workouts with the boys.

You need to clear the head to stay focused. The patients need the best of us every single time. Tate works with me at Mercy which makes for fun days and nights when we're on shift together. He didn't run with me today as he's in his consult rooms and not on shift at the hospital.

I love summer in Chicago, except, just not this heat in the middle of the day when I'm running and sweating my ass off. It also means the hospital struggles with all the extra caseload we get. Heat stroke in the elderly is an issue, especially if they can't afford the cool air at home. The hospital is the best thing they have for relief. My smart watch tells me it's eighty-six degrees Fahrenheit, but it feels hotter with the humidity.

I don't get the extra caseload, since I don't work in emergency. That's Tate's problem. He's a neurosurgeon who takes on the emergency cases as they arrive in the ER. Super intense, high-pressure work. Not my idea of fun. I had my years of that role, and I'm happy where I am now.

Coming through the front doors of the hospital, I feel the cool air hit me, while the eyes of the nursing staff at the check-in desk follow me to the elevator. The single ones are ready to pounce as soon as you give them any indication you might be interested. Tate takes full advantage of that. Me, not so much. When you're an intern, it seems like a candy shop of all these women who want to claim the fresh meat. The men are just as bad with the new female nurses.

We work in a high-pressure environment, working long hours and not seeing much daylight at times. You need to find a release. That's how I justified it, when I was the intern. I remember walking into a storeroom in my first year as an intern, finding my boss at the time, Leanne, and she was naked from the waist down being fucked against the wall by one of the male nurses. Now I am a qualified doctor who should hold an upstanding position in society, so I rarely get involved in the hospital dating scene anymore.

Fuck, who am I kidding? That's not the reason. It's the fact I got burnt a few years ago by a clinger who tried to get me fired when I tried to move on. Not going down that path again. Don't mix work and play, they say—well, I say. Tate hasn't quite learned that lesson yet. Especially the new batch of interns he gets on rotation every six months. He is a regular man-whore.

Am I a little jealous? Maybe just a tad. Both me and my little friend, who's firming up just thinking about getting ready for some action. It's been a bit of a dry spell. I think it's time to fix that.

Pity my date for tonight, Mason, is not even close to what I'm thinking about.

My cock totally loses interest now in the conversation again.

Can't say I blame him.

Just then the enchanting woman from today comes to mind and my cock is back in the game. I wish I knew who she was.

Now this afternoon's rounds could be interesting if my scrubs are tenting with a hard-on.

The joys of being a large man, if you get my drift.

There's no place to hide him.

Acknowledgments

To my readers,

Thank you for all the support I have received from you, especially my Deen's Diamond Reader Group members. It has given me the strength to keep going and push through to get BETTER DAY finished and in your hot little hands. On the hard days where I doubt myself, you are the ones who tell me to keep writing. I have the best readers in the world, and I am so grateful for all of you.

But as you know, I just write the words, and there is an army of people behind me that get these words to you, looking all perfect and pretty.

Thank you, Contagious Edits, who I would literally be lost without. I am blessed to have the best editor working with me, helping me to make my books the best they can possibly be. Otherwise, you would be reading one long sentence with no commas or full stops.

Sarah Paige, thank you once again for the amazing cover. Nothing is ever too much trouble for you, which I am always so appreciate of.

To Linda and the team at Foreword PR and Marketing, thank you for always looking after me and continuing to push me in the right direction.

What can I say about Lee Reyden, my amazing PA? How do I even manage this author world without you picking up my slack and the trail of mess behind me? You make my life so much easier and never complain when I throw new things at you, usually needing them in a hurry. But hey, that's what this life is, and I did warn you about the crazy! Thank you from the bottom of my heart for taking a chance on me. I'd be totally lost now without you. We make a great team!!

My family are always my strength and there to humor my crazy ideas. Supporting my leaps of faith—and there have been a few big ones lately. Grateful every day for all of you.

Until my next book, happy reading, and I'll meet you between the pages.

Karen xx

Printed in Great Britain
by Amazon

34814900R00219